Shoot
if you
Must

Pam Clark

Pam Clark

Black Rose Writing | Texas

ISBN: 978-1-68433-395-0
PUBLISHED BY BLACK ROSE WRITING
www.blackrosewriting.com

Printed in the United States of America
Suggested Retail Price (SRP) $20.95

Shoot If You Must is printed in Calluna
Cover design courtesy of Lisa Sheirer

*The final word count for this book may not match your standard expectation versus the final page count. In an effort to reduce paper usage and energy costs, Black Rose Writing, as a planet-friendly publisher, does its best to eliminate unnecessary waste without lessening your reading experience.

2020

Acknowledgements

Many people have guided me on this path, but none more so than Joan E. Disburg. She's the one who wanted to write a series of mystery novels but didn't want to go to the workshop by herself. This one's for you, Joan.

The path might have ended there but for the outstanding guidance and efforts of my agent, Jane von Mehren, as well as Reagan Rothe's faith in a fledgling writer and willingness to publish this novel through Black Rose Writing.

And many thanks to the wonderful faculty and staff at the Taos Summer Writers' Conference. Here's a special shout-out to my instructors— Jonis Agee, Laura Brodie, and Summer Wood—and my writing compatriots in those classes. And none of that magic could have happened without the founding director, Sharon Oard Warner and her right hand, Eva Lipton-Ormand.

No author can thrive—or even survive—without beta readers, and mine are simply boffo! A hearty thank you to: Anne, Betty, Debbie, Janet, Jenny, Mary, Pat, Sarah, Suzanne, and Tisha.

This page grows long; however, I must thank my friends and family for their love and support, especially my wonderful husband, Max, and his semi-service dog, Kirby. And a very special thank you to Lisa Sheirer, artist extraordinaire.

I couldn't have done any of this without all of you.

Shoot
if you
Must

"Did someone get photos of this nightmare before the EMTs took the victim away?" the detective asked the uniformed officer who'd been first on scene.

"Yes sir, Lieutenant," Sturgis replied, holding out the camera.

The detective swiped through the photos, studying the girl's crumpled body. She'd fallen on her right side, one arm beneath her the other outstretched toward the middle of the room. Judging by the books tumbled about on the floor, she might've been cradling them in that arm before the attack. Her face was veiled by wisps of blonde hair, the ends darkening where they lay on the bloody floor.

A few hours earlier she'd been an attractive young co-ed sitting in her English class, taking notes, beginning to taste her potential.

He closed his eyes for a moment then looked down at the bloodstain on the scarred oak floor of the old-fashioned museum. Bending forward, he examined the blood-free area where her cheek must have lain, noted how her head and arm's placement had directed the flow of the blood, and was reminded of the spatter-paint leaf prints he'd made with his daughter. Of placing a single fern leaf on a piece of white paper, loading a toothbrush with printer's ink and helping her draw the popsicle stick across it again and again, speckling the paper. Carefully lifting up the leaf, they marveled at the negative-space image. And tossed away the ink-speckled fern.

Watch those boundaries, he thought to himself and turned his attention back to the photos. The victim wore jeans, a pale green sweatshirt, and running shoes—typical casual attire.

Lieutenant Stephen T. Raleigh handed the camera back to the uniform. "Okay, Sturgis," he said, "let's hear your report."

"The call went out at 17:48 reporting a break-in and assault at the Barbara Fritichie Museum. I was on foot patrol nearby and responded within three minutes. The victim—identified as Heather Hillcrest, female, about nineteen—had sustained multiple blows to the head. She was still breathing but unresponsive at that time, so I called for a bus, which pulled up..." He paused to check his notebook. "Seven minutes later. The attack had been called in by a Susan Taylor, a high school student walking home with a friend. Taylor never entered the premises. However, when I went inside, I found her friend, a young, female civilian..."

The officer paused, looking uncertain about how to proceed.

Raleigh let him off the hook. "You mean my daughter."

"Yes sir." His face relaxed. "Lindsay Raleigh—a fifteen-year-old high school student—was sitting by the victim's side. I got her up and sat her over there." He indicated an antique kitchen table and chairs in front of the double-hung window. "She seemed to be in shock and had some blood and what appeared to be brain tissue on her hands and clothes. While the EMTs worked on the victim, I stood in front of the juvenile to block her view of the proceedings."

"Thank you. That was very kind."

"Before I could begin to interview her, Detective Maroni arrived and directed me to set up the crime scene tape, which I did. Since then, I have aided in securing the perimeter."

"Did anyone find a weapon?"

"Not so far, sir."

He nodded. "Thank you, officer. You can get back to riding herd on curious bystanders."

Alone, Raleigh ran a practiced eye over the crime scene. At first glance, there was no sign of a struggle, indicating that she knew or at least hadn't been afraid of her assailant. Or that she was ambushed. Maybe she was so surprised, and it'd happened so fast that she hadn't suffered. But he'd done this kind of work too long to be that hopeful.

Chapter 1

Even with everything else on her mind, Heather couldn't help but be drawn in by the fluorescent-green poster thumbtacked on the overcrowded bulletin board in the hallway. She was headed toward her English professor's office in Tuscarora Community College's main classroom and faculty-office building when the poster sidetracked her. Especially since the bold-faced font screamed out a question: "Firearms Sanctioned at TCC?"

Tugging a lock of her blonde hair from under her backpack's strap, she stopped and read on:

Firearms Sanctioned at TCC?

Gun Violence on College Campuses:
Would arming our security staff make you more safe, or less so?

Come join the discussion in Everett Auditorium
on November 5th at 8:00 p.m.
For more info contact: Professor Meghan Adams
Hamilton Hall room 248, ext. 5255

Huh. Maybe she should go. She'd never given much thought to the issue. But Professor Adams obviously had, because when she reached the office, the notice was also taped on the door. *It figured.* Besides being a great teacher, she was always in the middle of things on campus. Like bringing in kickass speakers and organizing the local #MeToo survivors' march.

Heather admired her teacher's intelligence, her ability to analyze a situation and then take decisive action. That's what had brought her to campus this late in the day. She really needed to talk about the craziness that had been dogging her—the weird texts and the late night drive-bys. Things that had happened ever since she'd found the antique letter amidst the clutter in her great-aunt's attic. She really needed to figure out what to do next.

A few other students walked by—happy, peppy, carefree girls—chatting as they passed the faculty offices on their way to the classrooms beyond. Heather dropped her eyes and hitched the backpack higher on her shoulder, trying to be invisible. A lifelong habit she intended to outgrow.

Once the girls were out of sight, she knocked on the office door. It was shut, and no one was visible through the skinny window. But the lights were on, and the glowing computer screen indicated that the occupant would return soon, even though the professor's office hours were long over. Since the woman spent way more time in her office than most faculty, Heather had dropped by hoping her mentor would be available

She decided to wait a little longer because she needed advice, big time. Although she had confided in Professor Adams about the letter, she hadn't spilled the beans about the texts she was getting that referred to it. She didn't know who was sending them, or even how they'd gotten her phone number. But that last message was sort of the answer to her prayers.

To her, the sender was her unknown benefactor, like Abel Magwitch had been to Pip in *Great Expectations*, even though he'd thought it was Miss Havisham. A fact which underscored the foolishness of making assumptions. About spinning dreams around a letter which had fallen into her lap. Because something about those texts didn't feel quite right.

And then there were those drive-bys at her house the last couple of nights. Always in the wee hours. This whole letter thing was working on her nerves, keeping her up or waking her out of unsettling dreams. Then she'd catch sight of some car crawling down the alley. But the pine tree out back blocked her view of the vehicle. Only its lights were visible. Was it her creepy ex stalking her again? Or something to do with her Unknown Benefactor and those texts? Either way, it was freaking her out. She'd thought about saying something to Lindsay's dad, a detective, but he and her ex had already butted heads. He'd probably want to *do* something, and she wasn't sure how that would turn out. It might end up limiting her options.

Maybe it would be better to tell Professor Adams about all of it. She wouldn't rush into action like guys tended to do. The two of them could brainstorm about possible actions, have a strategy session. *Yeah, that would work.*

"Heather?"

She turned quickly when someone walked up behind her. "Huh?"

Her heart stopped racing when she recognized the woman with the wild curly hair and kind brown eyes. "Oh, hi Professor Adams."

"Sorry I startled you. Were you looking for me?"

"Yeah, I need to talk to you..." She hesitated, uncertain of how to begin.

"About the letter?" Meg said as she slipped into her office, ducked behind the desk and powered off her computer. "I'm sorry, I can't talk right now. You've caught me at a bad time. My car died, and I'm having to bum a ride to my, um...next appointment," she added as she turned toward the door.

Heather's heart sank. Her disappointment must have shown on her face because the woman stopped in the act of turning off the office light and put her hand on Heather's shoulder instead.

"Is something wrong?"

"No, not really. I mean, not so much," she said, soft-pedaling her anxiety. It wasn't an emergency, and the professor needed to go. "It's no big deal. I'll catch up with you tomorrow."

Meg angled her head to one side and gave Heather a searching look. "You're sure? If it's important, I'll cancel my appointment."

Heather pasted on a reassuring smile. "I'm sure. You go ahead. We'll connect later."

Meg snapped off the light and shut the door. Then she laid a hand on Heather's arm. "Whatever it is, we'll sort it out."

"Okay," Heather said as the woman turned and hurried away, leaving Heather to wonder what was up with her professor. She seemed nervous. *That's so weird.*

Shrugging her backpack into place, Heather checked her cell phone for the time. *5:23? Crap. She was cutting it close.* Had to get going and pick up Lindsay if they were going to get to the restaurant on time.

Although things hadn't turned out how she'd hoped, even that brief conversation made her feel calmer. She'd reached out for help. Professor Adams was so knowledgeable...so level-headed that she'd have some insight about what Heather's next steps should be.

• • • • •

"How did I get to be such a hot mess?" Meg Adams muttered as she contemplated ways to extricate herself from her current predicament...dinner with Bad Date Brad.

It would've been far better if she'd stayed at school and talked to Heather about whatever was bothering her. Meeting with *any* student would be better than this fiasco, and Heather was such a gem. Smart, a little shy, but also big-hearted and kind. Meg saw a bright future for the girl. Her own immediate future, not so much.

Sighing, she snuck out her cell phone and hit speed dial. It went straight to voicemail: "Sorry to disappoint you, but Professor Joan Glotfelty is unavailable at the moment. You'll just have to wait until I call you back. Leave a message. Make it interesting. Ciao." Then came the little beep.

"How's this for interesting, Joan? My eHappiness date has the words 'serial rapist' written all over him. I'm stranded at the Barbara Fritchie Restaurant on old Route 40. My truck died...again. It's sitting in the parking lot at school. When I called to tell him we'd have to reschedule, he offered to pick me up and like an idiot I accepted. So I'm stuck out here with him, and Fiesta Cab can't get here for over an hour. I need help *now*." Click.

Meg stood outside the ladies' room as it was being cleaned. She turned and directed a half-hearted wave to the already seated Brad. But before she felt compelled to rejoin him, her cell phone vibrated. "Joan," she answered, "thank god."

"You'd best be thanking *me*, girlfriend. I'm the one returning your call. And tell me, where are you again? With whom?"

"You heard me the first time."

"And I simply chose not to believe you. I know it's been over a year since the divorce, but I just don't understand why you don't put on some smoking-hot makeup, decent clothes, practice your 'come hither' look and go to a swanky bar?"

"That would work for you, but I don't look like an exotic Ethiopian model."

"Yes, well...so few people do. That doesn't mean you shouldn't try."

Whatever. Meg felt confident in her own looks. She had a decent body— short, but curvy and well proportioned. Her eyes were her best feature, a warm brown, very expressive. Her ex-husband, back when he was wooing her, had once said they reminded him of a crayon color—Burnt Umber. Shortly thereafter he'd sealed the deal with a platinum wedding ring, an outrageous mortgage and a fistful of his and hers matching credit cards. But before long he couldn't hide his penchant for bootylicious mistresses. That crayon metaphor was the most original thing he'd ever said to her. And as it turned out, one of the few honest ones.

Meg puffed out a breath. "Are you coming or not, Joan?"

"Don't get all huffy, missy. I'm coming. It might take a while seeing as how I'll have to program the GPS to find this place," she fussed as she hung up.

Meg jammed the phone in the pocket of her hip length, jade green sweater. Just what she needed, wise-assery from her best friend. Post-divorce dating was depressing enough without that.

Designated as "Currently Unclaimeds" in the eHappiness database, she and Brad had hit it off in the intimate vacuum of cyberspace. Since she was an English professor at the local community college, he'd suggested meeting at someplace with literary connections. Her little corner of Maryland boasted many literary luminaries, both living and dead, including Anne Tyler's stomping grounds and F. Scott Fitzgerald's final resting place. But his actual suggestion surprised her.

"I thought we'd go to the Barbara Fritchie Restaurant."

It was a mighty odd choice for a first date. The restaurant had a long history in Frederick, but not as a venue to bill and coo and rendezvous. It was cole slaw, mashed potato and pot roast kind of place. A well-loved, bustling relic with cracks in the vinyl seats of the low-backed booths. The only drinks they served were soft. Could she even hazard a first date without wine?

What she'd taken for Brad's quirky sense of adventure should have been her first clue. His online dating profile photo—mid-thirties, slim bodied, dimpled smile, blue eyes, close-cropped hair—had hidden a genuine creep in sheep's clothing.

As she grudgingly joined him, he lifted his eyebrows at her, laid one denim-clad arm along the back of the booth, parted his lips slightly, and ran the tip of his tongue from the middle of his upper lip to one corner.

Perched on the edge of the opposite bench seat, Meg kept one hand in the pocket of her sweater, fingers curled around the cell, willing it to vibrate.

Brad leaned toward her. "Since your profile said that French fries were your lifeline, I ordered us some as an appetizer." He selected one from the steaming heap in front of him, dipped it in ketchup, bit the fry in half and offered her the remainder.

On a first date? No way. That's hepatitis waiting to happen.

When she didn't take it, he swirled it through the ketchup again and popped it into his mouth.

Eww...an icky double-dipper.

He picked up another fry and waved it around to encompass the room. "I used to eat at swankier places than this. I make good money managing my Sports Authority."

As she recalled, his dating profile said he was an executive with Reebok. She squeezed her cell phone, praying for good vibrations.

"But the old ball-and-chain's alimony is eating me alive."

Since escape wasn't yet possible, she'd at least try to break into the conversation. "Yes, I know from experience how lopsided divorce decrees can be. In fact—"

"Yeah, but I bet your ex didn't try to prejudice the judge against you by doing a character assassination on your ass."

"Well, no. However—"

"Brittany dressed up all prim and proper and then showed the judge a bunch of snapshots she'd had made from the videos of our light bondage sessions..."

Meg's eyes flew wide. *Light* bondage! The kind with fewer calories?

"...making sure she showed him the ones where she was the bottom. Not ones where she was whaling away on my bare butt. I mean, who shares that kind of info with strangers?"

"Excuse me," Meg mumbled as she stood suddenly. "Upset stomach."

She hurried away but toward the exit this time. Swearing under her breath, she shoved all her weight into the door, dashing out of the restaurant and running hands-first into the unyielding midsection of an entering patron. She bounced off of him, and he had to catch her by the elbows to keep her on her feet.

"Oh, crap," she cried as she righted herself. "I'm so very sorry."

"Not to worry, ma'am," he said, his slight Southern accent lengthening the last word. "Are you alright?"

Startled and still agitated, Meg stared at him. She simmered down when he seemed somehow familiar: clean-shaven, tall, athletic build, good suit, dark hair, smoky gray eyes. "I think so," she said, looking back over her shoulder. "But only if I get away from here."

Before either of them could say more, Bad Date came oozing out the door after her. "Hey, where're ya goin'? We haven't ordered yet." The door eased shut behind him.

Meg blinked several times, thoughts muddled.

Still holding her elbows, the tall man surveyed the situation. "Do you need help here?" he said, his voice quiet.

"Please," she whispered. "He's a creepy, creepy first date."

He glanced at the man and back to her. "Then follow my lead. Okay?"

Meg nodded vigorously, feeling like a bobble-headed doll on the dashboard of a taxi. And while her rescuer's voice was familiar, she still couldn't place him.

Repositioning one hand to her upper arm, he guided her into place beside him and placed his free hand in the air in front of Bad Date's chest. "I'm sorry, sir. I have to intervene here."

"Why?" Brad bounced a little on the balls of his feet. "She's my date, not yours."

"My date? No. She's my parolee." Keeping his hold on Meg, he dropped his other hand and pulled back his unbuttoned jacket to reveal the badge clipped to his belt, allowing his gun to become visible in the process. "I'm Lieutenant Raleigh with the Frederick City Police. And she's in violation. I hate to break up your date but she needs to come with me."

"Her...seriously? She's a college professor."

Registering the gun and badge, Meg finally placed him...one of the officers from the civilian police academy that her colleague David had dragooned her into attending. She recalled her rescuer standing in front of a whiteboard littered with scrawled names in that bland, airless police academy classroom. Waiting out his introduction, he had remained alert and composed, more like a civilian than not. His hands—blunt, large and capable—were clasped in front of him in a loosely configured V. Now one of those hands claimed her arm at the place where a blood pressure cuff would ride...and right now it would register a spike. Just nerves, she told herself.

The lieutenant glanced sideways at Meg. "A college professor. Is that what you told him?" He turned back to Brad. "Not hardly. What name is she using this time?"

"Meghan Adams," he said warily. "We were supposed to meet here, but she called and said her car had died. Asked if I could pick her up in the college parking lot."

The officer scowled at Meg. "What are you up to now, *Charmaine?* You know you aren't allowed more than a mile away from home." He nodded toward the hem of her black jeans. "Your ankle bracelet tipped us off. What are you playing at? Were you thinking about moving up to big-time crime, like maybe jacking this gentleman's car?"

Cottoning on, she narrowed her eyes and tried to jerk away from Raleigh's grip. "Hands off," she snarled. "I'm no carjacker."

Brad sidled up to the officer. "Wow. What's on her rap sheet? Possession? Dealing?" He blinked, then grinned. "Ooooh, pros-ti-*tu*-tion."

Meg started to kick him, aiming for the groin, but Raleigh tugged her back.

"I'm not at liberty to reveal that, sir. It would be in violation of her right to privacy. Perhaps it would be best if you stepped back inside."

"Yeah, sure," he said, leering at her. "No problem. Got French fries in there getting cold." He opened the door and disappeared inside, his absence replaced by the aroma of sauerkraut and gravy on someone's turkey dinner.

Meg turned to the officer. "Thanks. I was so weirded out." When he let go of her arm, she felt more touch poor than she had in over a year. And that was odd. Cops rattled her, what with those expressionless faces and hefty utility belts hung with things more dangerous than hammers.

"No problem, ma'am. I am sworn to protect and serve."

For a moment she thought that was it. Mission accomplished.

Then he smiled. "And you looked like you could use a little of both."

Meg's reply caught in her throat when he grabbed her by the shoulders and stepped them both away from a red Prius that nearly clipped him as it zipped noiselessly into the parking lot.

Chapter 2

The car came to an abrupt stop in a parking space, and a very tall, slender, fashionably dressed African American woman in her forties exited the car in a huff. She stormed up and glared at the man. "Unhand her, you scuz ball!"

Raleigh already had, but before he could say anything, Meg turned toward her friend and stammered, "N-no, no. Wait!"

The newcomer planted her feet on the faded blacktop, plunked her hands on her hips and continued her tirade. "Now walk away, you low life, or you'll be answering to me."

He didn't respond, but he didn't take his eyes off the woman berating him, either. "Joan!" Meg cried. "You've got it all wrong! He's not the one."

But Joan, far from winding down, gave a curt toss of her head and continued her verbal assault. "And answering to me is a fate no man wants to contemplate."

Meg caught Raleigh's questioning look, but she focused on her friend.

"JOAN!" Meg balled her fists in frustration. "He's a police officer, not my scary date."

She finally looked at Meg. "Oh." Then she nonchalantly rearranged her elegantly broad shoulders inside her cream-colored jacket and smoothed away an imaginary irregularity in the crease of her matching trousers. "Well, you might have spoken up sooner and saved this fine gentleman a lot of concern about his immediate safety."

No longer on alert status, Raleigh cracked a smile. "I was only a little worried."

The two of them took stock of each other, ending with a mutual nod of accord. Nerves still thrumming, Meg merely watched.

Another vehicle—an older model Outback in a muted green—entered the parking lot and drove slowly by the trio. The lieutenant raised a hand to greet the passing driver while he addressed the women. "Sorry, but I've gotta go. I'm meeting some people." He looked at Joan. "Now that you're here, may I trust you to keep your friend safe and out of trouble?"

"I can but try." Joan sighed theatrically. "However, you see what a big job it is."

"At the moment I don't have enough evidence to corroborate that statement, ma'am. I'll have to take your word for it." Addressing Meg once more, his gray eyes lit with amusement, like a little boy hiding a toad behind his back. "But I wouldn't want to rush to judgment."

Meg was about to respond when Joan spoke up. "Get a move on, girlfriend." She nodded toward the Outback's driver, a blue-jeaned and cotton-sweatered man in his mid-20s, who was walking their way. "These men are busy, and you caught me in the middle of my own life, you know. What if someone sees me here?" She struck a runway pose, air-running a hand down her own trim frame. "Everyone knows that this fine, fine vessel does not ingest sausage gravy or dumplings." Turning toward her car, she gave Meg's defender a jaunty two-fingered salute, singsong-ing, "Thank you, Officer Krupke."

Blushing, Meg stared as her friend sauntered away, then turned toward her bemused rescuer. "I'm so sorry about that. She's really only teasing, which actually means she likes you."

"You needn't apologize for her. No offense taken."

Meg thought he was working to hide his laughter at her distress, but not very hard. "Um...well, I really do appreciate all your help."

"You're entirely welcome. I'm glad I was here to lend a hand." As the other man joined him, he added, "And we didn't even have to call on Detective Maroni for backup."

"Oh. Okay," Meg said, a little flustered, trying to figure out if he was razzing her.

Chuckling, he reprised Joan's salute. "I imagine I'll see you in class tomorrow night."

She blushed again and darted to the Prius, surprised that he'd remembered her. Spilling into the car, she started in on Joan. "I can't believe you just insulted that man. *Officer Krupke*...really? What were you thinking? He's one of the presenters at that civilian police academy I've been going to on Tuesdays."

"Did he look insulted? No. He was enjoying my snappy patter."

"Snappy patter? You vacillated between verbal abuse and flirtation. And you don't even like men."

"I like them well enough to hold discourse with them."

Joan started the engine, and the two women sat glaring at each other, the ghostly quiet Prius taking no sides. It was an oft-repeated squabble: Meg mired in self-doubt; Joan encouraging her friend to move forward.

"And there you were, dumb as a stump," Joan scolded. "You're the one who should've been chatting him up."

"Nope. I'm done dating for the foreseeable future."

"Pish-tosh! That won't even last a week."

Meg ignored her friend and stared in the passenger side mirror, studying the tableau behind her.

The two detectives in the parking lot had moved to lean against a white, high-end SUV parked beneath one of the autumn-leafed trees at the edge of the restaurant. Both were facing the parking lot, talking. Nothing much happening.

Meg felt her friend's attention shift to the rearview mirror, eyeing the two men.

"You know him, right?" Joan said. "An attractive man who appears to drive a Mercedes SUV. Manly, chiseled features. A full head of hair that is decently styled, not some ubiquitous buzz cut. Somewhere between your age and mine, upper 30s, maybe." She canted an eyebrow. "And you're not looking to sail off into the sunset with all that?"

Meg's sigh was neither *yes* nor *no*, so she wasn't surprised when Joan pressed on.

"A man able to trade tit for tat in the witty repartee department." She paused before adding, "And I didn't see a ring, not that *I* have a need to know."

Meg exhaled slowly. "I don't *know* know him. I've just seen him a few times at the Civilian Police Academy. Besides, he's in law enforcement."

"You just ditched some online dating lowlife, and now you get picky? Humph! If you ask me—and you should—that officer isn't some dumb jock of a cop. The kind who lives to ride a fast cruiser and cock his pistol every chance he gets."

"You're right. I'm pretty sure he's not just a regular old cop. Some kind of plainclothes officer or a detective or something like that."

"Stop splitting hairs. He's employed." Her face turned thoughtful. "But he might be on the take if he can afford that ride. Still, he's a fine, fine specimen—if you like men."

"I do," Meg sighed. But she knew that's when things went sour...after the "I do's." The promise to have and hold. From that day forward. As long as they both should live. What a load of crap. "But he's way too handsome for the likes of me."

"Meghan G. Adams, you stop that defeatist rhetoric right now! For someone descended from Abigail Adams, one of our founding feminists, nobody is too good for you, girlfriend. It's always worth a shot." Joan gave her friend a devilish look. "Back in my experimental youth, I'd've had to try him on to see how he fit."

Meg eyes flew wide open as she burst into laughter. "What would your sweet, devoted Chloe say if she heard you talking like that?"

"Fiddle-dee-dee. She was foolish enough to marry one of them before she came to her senses." Batting her eyes, she added, "And into my well-toned arms."

"Ever the modest one, aren't we."

"Humph. You could do worse than him. Oh, excuse me. You already have. Al is a scrawny, scrofulous, weevil-infested bean pole next to Officer Tall, Dark, and Handcuffs."

Meg looked in her mirror again, noticed that the officer had taken off his jacket, and gave him an appraising once-over. "He probably works out. But he's not one of those gym rats whose shoulders are so bulky that it looks like there's an orange tucked into each armpit."

"He looks like he could give a woman a real workout. And you're not interested in that?"

"I'm not interested in men who work with guns. Or have the authority to kill people."

"Not any good people, seeing as how they continue to let him carry a weapon."

"Yeah, well..."

"Please, wouldn't you enjoy whipping out a sidearm and scaring the bejesus out of a student or two if the law were on your side?" She started the car again. "Perhaps Jon Sellers, that smarmy, disrespectful, know-it-all?"

"Okay, you're right. Sellers would be a candidate." She imagined snapping the handcuffs on him, marching him to the back seat of a Crown Vic with those blue and red lights whirling on top, and making sure he didn't crack his skull on the door frame as she slid him in. Okay, she wouldn't try too hard to avoid the skull cracking.

"That's more like it." Joan backed out of her parking space. "Where's Rocinante? What's wrong with your truck this time?"

"He's back at TCC with a bum starter. Rocinante may not be mechanically reliable, but sometimes he's prescient. I should've taken it as a warning and called the whole thing off."

Joan checked the traffic before she pulled out and away, then shot Meg a coy look. "But then Officer Krupke couldn't have come to your aid, could he now?"

·   ·   ·   ·   ·

Raleigh watched Meg walk toward the Prius, reluctant to take his eyes off her. And that was unsettling. He hadn't felt that kind of pull in a long time. Hadn't wanted to.

"Um...Lieutenant," the other officer said. "How come you're still going to those lame-ass classes for the civilians? This is like...week three or four already. You only had to show up at the first one, right?"

Raleigh's shrug didn't satisfy his partner.

"So why're you still goin'?"

Without shifting his focus, the lieutenant answered. "My daughter has play practice at Frederick High on Tuesdays. And there's nothing to see on TV."

"I think you like what you're seeing right now."

"Excuse me?" He snapped his head around to look at his colleague, poker-faced.

Maroni pointed his chin toward Joan's car. "Those black jeans getting into the red Prius."

"I'm just makin' sure she gets into the car without incident." Damn, was he that transparent? Granted, he was out of practice, but there was something about that woman.

"Sure. Okay. It's just that in all the time I've known you, I've never seen you take such an interest in a woman's...'incident' before."

Maroni was green, but he didn't miss much. That's why he'd snagged the rookie away from foot patrol—what was it? two years ago—and taken him under his wing in Criminal Investigations.

"Just 'cause you got promoted to detective last month doesn't mean you get to practice on me." He snuck a glance across the parking lot toward the red car as it backed up to leave.

Maroni didn't speak until after the car pulled away. "You've been widowed for what? Five years now? Isn't it time for you to be making a move?"

The lieutenant's posture stiffened. "I think it's time for you to make good on that bet and buy us dinner." He didn't want any advice. And he damn sure didn't want to talk about his past.

With an abrupt turn, Raleigh strode toward the entrance, stopping to let two cars drive into the parking lot. He recognized the old VW Beetle, nodded at the passenger—his daughter, Lindsay—and watched as her friend parked. When the two young women exited, he was struck, as he often was, by their contrast. Heather, a blonde, with long legs tan beneath a bright blue dress. Lindsay, somewhat shorter and petite, with black, spikey hair. Today her getup was almost normal: red Chuck Taylors, black leggings and an untucked white shirt under one of his old pinstriped vests.

Glancing back at Maroni, he cringed at the stunned hurt on the young man's face. *Damn it.* Sometimes people were just too much trouble. But it'd been that compassion that had him take a chance on the lad. He treated everyone with respect, didn't go all hair trigger on suspects.

He cuffed Maroni on the shoulder. "Hey, I'll split the tab seeing as how it'll include Lindsay and her friend." The younger man's nod indicated no hard feelings. But something else tugged at Raleigh's attention—the car that had entered the lot right behind the Beetle. A late model silver sedan. It had been following closely, close enough to catch his notice.

"Hey, Dad," the red-sneakered girl called out to Raleigh as she walked up. When he merely nodded at her absently, she knocked her shoe into his. "Off duty, remember?"

He dipped his head in apology and reached out to mess with her hair, but she leaned away, laughing. However, when Lindsay turned to address her girlfriend, he continued to track the sedan in his peripheral vision, noted that it backed into a space on the far side of the pock-marked parking lot. And wondered what was tugging at his cop sense.

"Hi, Mr. Maroni," said Lindsay. "You haven't met my friend, Heather." She gestured to her more conventional companion. "Heather, meet Matteo Maroni. He's Sicilian, but not Mafia."

He grinned at Lindsay then turned his smile on her friend. "Nice to meetcha, Heather. Lindsay's mentioned you now and again."

"Me?" Heather asked, puzzled. "Like, when? About what?"

"Yeah, you." Lindsay pushed her friend on the shoulder. "When I babysit for Mr. & Mrs. Maroni, y'know? About what an amazing scholar and poet you are. He's been in training with Dad for two whole years and just made detective. And now they're partners. Cool, huh?"

"Way cool." She looked at Lindsay's father and added, "Hi, Mr. Raleigh."

Sliding his gaze away from the silver sedan, he joined the conversation. "Hi, yourself. How're things going at TCC?"

At first, he'd been a little puzzled at the friendship between the two girls. Five years ago, when he and Lindsay had relocated here from Baltimore, she was almost eleven and Heather was fifteen. But they were both smart and creative, plus Heather lived just four doors down. That was his father's explanation, but he put it in shrink terms, of course. Propinquity, proximity.

Raleigh had soon figured that Heather was drawn to him, too. Not anything inappropriate, thank god. She just needed a dad after hers had taken off for greener pastures, abandoning both his wife and daughter. Heather—pretty, sweet-tempered and smart—deserved better. Any father should be proud of her. He was.

Heather didn't answer him right away. She fiddled with some strands of her long hair, as fine as corn silk. "Goin' good, I guess. Nothing to complain about."

"Not that you would, even if you should," Lindsay said. "You're way too nice sometimes. You oughta toughen up."

Raleigh shook his head at his daughter's advice and bossy tone. Brash, like her mother. There'd been no changing either one of them. "Play nice, Lindsay," he chided. "I was sorta hoping that some of Heather's congeniality would eventually rub off on you."

Lindsay mock glared at him. "Keep on hoping, Stephen."

He didn't react when she used his first name. Best just to go with the flow.

"Hey, Dad. Why are we here at this weird old restaurant? I didn't even know there was anything open for business this far out in the sticks."

Heather turned toward her friend, surprise growing on her face. "Weird? I love this place. It's part of the Barbara Fritchie folklore, something that puts Frederick on the map, Civil War wise. It's been serving meals for more than a hundred years. That says something, doesn't it?"

Raleigh nodded at her but spoke to his daughter. "We're here because Matteo lost the bet. He's paying for dinner, so he gets to pick the spot."

"You lost again." Lindsay sent Maroni a sympathetic look. "What was the bet this time?"

"The color of the next F-150 to pull into the parking lot. We were doing boring surveillance all morning. I bet it'd be a red truck. Your dad bet white."

Lindsay tossed her head and rolled her eyes. "You should've bet on four-door sedans and called it first. Silver. It's, like, the most common color for cars."

"She's right, Maroni," her father chuckled. "That's why I never bet against her."

Lindsay caught Heather by the arm and pulled her forward. "Let's grub up."

Holding the door for the others, Raleigh regarded the parked silver sedan. The engine and air conditioner were both running. The driver within, wearing sunglasses and a gray sweatshirt with the hood pulled up—nondescript, unidentifiable—was lowering a cell phone.

The detective hesitated then followed the others inside.

Chapter 3

The driver of the silver four-door sedan in the parking lot sits patiently, humming a tune from childhood. The air conditioner runs; the car idles. Keeping one hand on the steering wheel, the other frames the shot and presses the shutter on the upraised cell phone camera. Once, twice, three times. The driver pauses between each shot, then lowers the phone. Waiting. Watching.

"Go inside, go inside. You can leave, but you can't hide."

After the door shuts behind the foursome, the driver lowers the sunglasses partway, raises the cell phone again and brings up the three most recent photos. The first is a full-length shot of the two young women, laughing and animated.

"Such playful little puppies."

The second one features heads and torsos. Images larger, more detail. A hand tucking blonde hair behind an ear. Dark hair gelled into barbs. Relaxed and unhurried, the Watcher sighs.

"Ah, yessss. It's so good to see you again. So happy, so unaware."

The third shows only one face, youthful, unblemished. Full of promise and potential, free from worry.

"You have something I want, little one. I mean to take it from you. Soon."

The light-hearted humming continues as the Watcher blanks the screen, tosses the phone on the passenger seat and shifts the car out of park. Foot still on the brake, the Watcher takes a final look at the restaurant door concealing the prize within and slides the sunglasses back in place.

Slowly, the car pulls out of its parking space, traverses the lot, signals its intention to turn, and stops before ultimately merging into the early evening, home-going traffic on Route 40.

Chapter 4

Lindsay plopped down on her bed and rubbed her belly, stuffed from all the downhome food at the Fritchie restaurant. She'd have preferred a vegetarian place, but there'd been plenty of sides to enjoy—especially the green beans and cheesy cauliflower. And the pies! They'd each ordered a different one and shared bites. The lemon meringue was to die for.

Burrrp. Lindsay grimaced at her unladylike belch. Nothing but salads for her tomorrow.

Before crawling between the sheets, she ran her hand over the curve of the sleigh bed's footboard. An antique, hand-rubbed yellow pine. When they'd moved to Frederick, her dad had ordered himself a new bed, just a king sized mattress and box spring. No headboard, only a frame, very practical. Typical Dad. He'd invited her to pick out a new bed for their new house.

She hadn't asked him why he'd given up the sleigh bed. She'd only been ten then; still, something told her not to bring it up. But she loved that bed. She had good memories of banishing scary dreams by climbing up into it and snuggling between her parents. So now the bed was hers.

As she got under the covers her cell phone chimed from the nightstand. A text. Heather's ringtone.

"Really need you with me tomorrow at the museum. Please!"

Lindsay frowned while she composed her reply. They'd already butted heads over this, but Heather insisted that she knew what she was doing. Had called Lindsay paranoid. Still, Lindsay would try one more time to make her friend see reason.

"Still think this is a mistake. Like sneaking off to see Johnny-boy. That didn't end well."

"This is different. Business, not pleasure. People will want in on it. Need to keep it on the DL. You gonna help or what?"

Lindsay slumped back on her pillow. The whole deal sounded bizarre, so somebody had to have Heather's back. "Okay, I'm in. But the timing sucks. Gotta ditch play practice."

Lindsay heard footsteps outside her door and then a gentle knock. "Gotta go. Bed check. TTFN."

She slipped her phone under the covers and called out, "Enter."

Her dad opened the door partway and stuck his head in. "Lindsay, it's a little past ten. Time to close out technology, okay?"

"I already signed off with Heather. Now I'm gonna journal for a little while."

"As long as it's paper, not electronic." He gave her *the look*. "And the phone is...?"

She hopped out of bed, handed over her cell, and got back in. "Satisfied?"

He nodded gravely, but his eyes were playful. "Delighted. Okay, then. See you in the morning. Love you," he said, pulling the door closed behind him.

"Love you," she whispered. And she did. But it didn't pay to let him know that, did it?

From the nightstand, she pulled over her journal. It was an ordinary composition book, black marbled, wide-ruled. Her mom had given her one just like it to get her ready for kindergarten, back when she was learning to print. Since then she'd filled a dozen or more.

Monday: October 27th

Typical boring day at school. Not even a cafeteria fight or a drug-sniffing dog to liven things up.

Heather's all buzzed over that old-timey letter she found. Dunno if it's as valuable as she thinks, but that's not what she wants to hear. She keeps bugging me to go with her tomorrow to meet up with some expert who can help her evaluate it or something. Sounds sketchy to me.

But I'm gonna to try and make it.

Chapter 5

Meg was working hard to alter the mood in the room. A grumpy pall had settled over her Tuesday afternoon American lit class like the stink of a wet, stray dog. The students had just suffered through four figurative language PowerPoint presentations from their peers. The first one had been from an art student and was very informative and flashy. It had gone downhill from there, with the last one being dreadful.

It was typical of Nate's work, a student she'd privately nicknamed after a Scooby-Doo character: Shaggy, the thinly veiled stoner. As might be expected, his presentation was rife with misspellings, omissions, misinformation, and herky-jerky cartoonish illustrations. A slapdash, git-r-done effort, executed with the hope she'd be merciful. Ha. That wasn't her rep. She was known as funny, yes; fair, for sure; but also firm.

"Okay, let's move on to the next item on the syllabus: Edgar Allan Poe."

But the tap-tap-tap of high heels in the corridor caused some to turn and look out the open door. Obliquely, Meg sneaked a peek and saw Dean Plunkard, her personal cross to bear. The old shrew must be spying on faculty again. Good thing she hadn't gotten shirty with Nate. The dean was accompanied by the public relations director, Maria Routzhan, and a seriously overdressed woman who was talking Plunkard's ear off. Hmm...that would bear watching.

Maybe if she paid them no mind, the trio would go away. But then came the rapping on the doorframe. Plunkard, damn it. Impossible to ignore.

"Professor Adams," the dean said. "May I interrupt you for a moment? Your students will enjoy this. It isn't every day that a nationally acclaimed scholar visits our campus or their class." She paused. "Or you either, Meghan," the dean added, her tone sweeter than any sugar substitute.

The guest, a striking, fifty-something blonde wearing Louis Vuitton—or so Meg thought, whereas Joan would know—gave a toss of her head, walked in and shook Meg's hand briskly. "I'm Dr. Charlotte Slattery, here to give a presentation on Civil War poetry."

"Of course. The conference that Dr. Brunner is chairing. Welcome to TCC." Okay, the small talk was over. Time to move along before she lost her students' attention altogether.

Slattery turned to the class. "What are you studying?"

No answer. Meg hadn't expected one. That type of predictable question posed by an intruder deserved to be met with silence.

Neither the dean nor the scholar reacted, but Routzhan looked apoplectic, like the class was exhibiting the sort of coarse rudeness that might reflect badly on her. Her blue eyes bulged as if responding to a sudden upswing in blood pressure.

One of the students relented. "We're just starting on Poe."

"Ah, 'The Raven,' published in 1845. A bit earlier than my area of expertise. Now if you were up to 1863, we could talk about 'Barbara Frietchie,' my specialty."

Meg rustled up a look of regret. "If only this were next week I'd invite you to speak to the class. But we're not quite ready for the Civil War poets."

"Well, that would have been splendid. Unfortunately, my schedule won't allow it." She turned her back on the class and joined the other two women.

"Thanks for dropping by," Meg called out. Then she closed the green metal door against the fading footsteps. But before she could get the class back on track, Nate stole the stage.

"Dude, that was bizarre. It felt like I was back in elementary school. But that scholar lady was seriously decked out. I mean, no teacher here has the coin for that kind of wardrobe." He paused. "Except for that speech professor, Glotfelty. She's classy."

Meg raised an eyebrow. "I'll be sure to tell her. Now, let's get back to..."

"And how about that other lady? The one with the Bette Davis eyes." He giggled. "I bet she got teased a lot in middle school."

"Nate," she snapped. "That's uncalled for."

"No, that's human nature," said Jon Sellers, slouching in his chair. One restless hand traced circles on the Formica desktop while the other arm hung idly at his side. His hair was black, longish, and unkempt. Behind round, steel-rimmed glasses, his eyes narrowed to slits.

The class switched their attention to him before Meg was able to draw them back.

"Humans have always acted out against those who don't meet the norm or won't be an asset to the gene pool," he announced. "That's why bullying is so commonplace. Even in modern-day Kenya, babies born with both sets of genitalia are put to death. No intersex kids in that culture. They whack them on the head with a sweet potato."

"That's horrible!" one of the girls cried.

"And that's more than enough, Jon," Meg said, her eyes flashing. "What you say may be true, but it's still indefensible. We humans have the capacity to evolve beyond superstitions and base reactions, as evidenced by the eradication of the once prevalent practice of slavery."

Satisfied by Jon's disgruntled look, she turned to the whiteboard and wrote: Edgar Allan Poe. "We're moving on. In our next class, we begin our study of Poe. You might not know that he had a connection to Frederick County because John Greenleaf Whittier casts such a large shadow here. It's common knowledge that Whittier wrote a poem about a Civil War resident of Frederick, the legendary Barbara Fritchie. But it is much less well known that there are relatives of Poe's buried in nearby Walkersville. Does anyone know how or where Poe died?"

She paused. "How about you, Mr. Sellers?" Wanna play hardball, big boy? Bring it on.

Jon glared back, no longer bored, his lanky frame tense.

"No?" said Meg innocently. "Anyone else?"

"Baltimore. He died in Baltimore," Heather said, brushing back her feathery bangs.

Meg was impressed. The young woman didn't volunteer often, so she was a bit of an unknown to her peers. Personality-wise, anyhow. Her male classmates seemed acutely aware of her well-toned, sun-tanned legs, tousled mane of blonde hair, and shy hazel eyes.

Heather had been in one of Meg's EN 101 classes last spring as an Open Campus high school student, an almost silent one, and had taken creative writing with her during the summer session. Her poetry was amazing. And this semester she'd worked up the nerve to drop by Meg's office and talk about the class readings and assignments, always staying a step ahead. Meg decided to draw her out of her comfort zone. "What else can you tell us?"

"Well, my mom's a social worker in Baltimore, and some of her clients live in Poe's old neighborhood, but it's, um...sort of rundown nowadays."

"What's your mother got to do with this?" snarled Jon.

Meg turned her attention from Heather to Jon, wondering why he was being so nasty.

Ignoring her questioner, Heather went on. "She took me there one day last fall. To Poe's house and then shopping at the Inner Harbor. But didn't Poe die in a kinda strange way, too?"

Meg sidestepped the oblique invitation, kept the focus on Heather. "Care to elaborate?"

The young woman looked a little uncomfortable but then continued. "He wasn't living in Baltimore at the time, just there on business. Something about its being Election Day and him being found, sick and unconscious, at a tavern that was used as a polling place. So somebody took him to a hospital where he died a few days later. He was buried in Baltimore, and lots of noteworthy people attended his funeral—even Walt Whitman. But Poe was really poor, so at first, his coffin went into a grave with a cheap headstone."

Students were zoning in instead of out and swiveling their heads to look over at Heather.

"Years later, some lady started a movement to build a memorial. Even school kids got involved, collecting pennies to build it. Eventually, leaving pennies became a tradition. The day I went there, I saw coins on the base of the monument left by visitors to honor Poe and the kids who didn't want to see a famous writer fade into oblivion. The monument wasn't finished until ten or so years af...ter..."

Noticing that her classmates were goggling at her, Heather stopped talking.

Meg was impressed at how much more confidence the young woman had gained in two semesters. "Well done, Heather. Your insights have provided a lot of background."

"Thanks," she murmured.

Meg nodded, trying not to make too big a deal of the young woman's riff and escalate her discomfort. "With your interest in connecting writers and places, I think you will particularly enjoy this next project." Actually, Heather had asked for the assignment a week ago and was already working on it. But Meg didn't want to give the others anything to razz her about.

She eyed her audience, judged them ready to continue. "Although he was only forty when he died, Poe is a major figure in American literature. Can anyone name some of his works?"

"I'm sure Heather can," sniped Sellers.

"Doubtless." Meg waited a beat. "However, I'm sure you are also up to the task."

He slit his eyes, but stayed silent. As Meg continued to look at him and the seconds ticked away, he caved.

"'The Tell-Tale Heart,' 'Annabelle Lee,' 'The Raven,' 'Fall of the House of Usher.' A load of crap suitable for high school students, summed up by SparkNotes and Shmoop."

Face reddening, Heather turned around to glare at him. "Just because literature is accessible doesn't make it simplistic."

"Are you sure?" Jon reared back, bringing one sneakered foot to the frayed rip in the knee of his jeans, settling in for a debate.

"I am," Meg said firmly. "And so are countless scholars. While he is popularly known as an author of the macabre, he was a skilled poet, editor, and literary critic. His essay, 'The Philosophy of Composition,' is one by which short stories are still judged today. He's considered the principal architect of the modern short story and father of the detective fiction genre. Sir Arthur Conan Doyle freely admitted that his Sherlock Holmes character was greatly influenced by Poe's C. Auguste Dupin, protagonist of 'The Murders in the Rue Morgue.'"

Dropping his foot to the floor, Sellers leaned forward and let 'er rip. "Poe was the original slacker. He only spent one year at the University of Virginia before he dropped out. When some fool got him an appointment to West Point, he even bailed on that, getting himself court-martialed for disobedience and gross neglect of duty. Plus he was a drunk, a drug abuser, and married his 13-year-old first cousin. That guy was a moral cesspool."

Realizing they'd scented first blood, the class shifted their attention to the front of the class, assessing, wondering if their professor would be the victor or the vanquished.

"An authority on morality, are you Mr. Sellers?" Meg asked, politely.

A softly spoken "Ha!" had the class looking among their ranks for the speaker. From Meg's vantage point, it was clear. But she willed herself not to look at Heather.

"Your insights are only partially correct, Jon, however strongly you hold them. They reflect a lot of half-truths that have grown up around Poe. Let's take the allegations one at a time. First, was Poe a college dropout? Yes. However, let's put that in context. Last year only about 60% of students graduated from their 4-year colleges. I hope all of you will be successful in your goals. But if not, it's not necessarily because you just gave up. Why else might you not finish?"

"Money," Nate blurted.

"Right." She smiled at her Shaggy. "Money was Poe's issue, not a lack of character."

Although she didn't look at Jon, she noted that several students sneaked a peek. "On to Poe's army career. Yes, he was court-martialed for gross neglect of duty. His 'crime'? Refusal to attend classes, formation, or church. Hardly Leavenworth infractions."

At that, some of the students chuckled. Since information was flowing again, the class's blood lust was cooling.

"But Poe did indeed marry his 13-year-old first cousin, and while that's an uncomfortable fact, is it enough for us to dismiss his intellectual gifts? If so, are you also ready to similarly dismiss H.G. Wells, Charles Darwin, and Queen Victoria, all of whom married their first cousins? Or Elvis because he first started dating Priscilla when she was 14?"

Nate's "wowser" summed up the class's reaction. But Jon's reptilian stare didn't unsettle Meg's hard-won equanimity.

"It isn't fair to expect famous people to be better than the rest of us...to expect them to be paragons of probity." Meg paused and looked over the class. "Any questions?"

Nate raised a hand. "What does 'a paragon of probate' mean?"

"Christ," Jon snarled. "It means 'the epitome of integrity,' you moron. You are so—"

"Enough, Mr. Sellers." Meg's stern tone shut down any further insults as she took a stack of assignment sheets from the lectern and began handing them down the rows. "You will be doing both secondary and on-site research on an author from this list: Poe, John Greenleaf Whittier, Thoreau, Francis Scott Key, Frederick Douglass, or Walt Whitman. They all have a Maryland connection. Then you'll focus on one of his works to study in depth."

Mutterings scurried around the room: "Another project so soon?" "When's this one due?" "Doesn't she ever let up?"

Meg waited a moment for the chatter to die down. "If you remember, I previewed this assignment on the first day of class when I went over the syllabus."

Anticipating the groans of "gotta work" and "rising gas prices," she added, "None of the locations is more than an hour away. No farther than Baltimore or Washington D.C." Since she'd outflanked them once again, they settled for merely sighing and cutting looks at their friends.

Meg wrote, "before Thanksgiving break" on the board and underlined the first word. "This is your due date...the last class before break. And if you can think of other authors with a local connection you'd rather research, feel free to discuss your ideas with me."

It was almost 3:15. Sensing an imminent end to the class, the students began to gather their belongings.

"The literary lions are easiest to research...Whitman or Thoreau. But don't dismiss Francis Scott Key. You can't sling a dead cat in Frederick County without coming across that name, as those of you who frequent

Frederick's FSK mall may know. Not to mention our local farm team for the Baltimore Orioles is saddled with the name the Frederick Keys, even though nobody in the stadium can sing Key's national anthem in the key in which it was written."

"Ouch," said one young woman, the habitual responder. "What's with the Key/key thing? Another one of your bad puns, Professor Adams?"

"The *professor* is just showing off," Jon sniped as he uncurled out of his chair and turned toward his classmate. "And *you* couldn't tell a pun from a double entendre."

Before Meg could respond to Jon, Heather stood to face him. "Like you'd know, either." She hitched her backpack on her shoulder and strode toward the door. Just this side of the threshold, she shot back a sarcastic, "Asshole!"

Chapter 6

Class over, Meg dashed to her office before heading to the faculty meeting. Tossing her books and papers inside, she turned around after hearing Joan's silky voice behind her.

"So, have you called Officer Hottie yet?"

"Drop it, 'Mom,'" she snapped. "It's not like I've been celibate since the divorce. I've been known to rustle up some action."

"So you say. However, yesterday, you were all but stampeding away."

"Enough, okay?"

"It's been over a year, sweetie. And nobody's put a smile on your face in all that time."

"Alright, okay. If he's at the Civilian Police Academy again tonight, I'll talk to him." But it would be easier if he weren't in law enforcement. She wasn't comfortable around cops, what with their stiff bodies and stern faces. Still, when he'd taken her elbows to keep her from falling and she'd looked into those gray eyes...

"I bet you'll have a date by the weekend," Joan said with a Cheshire Cat smile.

Meg rolled her eyes. "Right now we have a date with a contentious faculty meeting. Let's get going. I can't wait to start discussing the prospect of arming campus security." Her mouth turned down into a frown. "Just tell me, in what universe would it make sense to empower that idiot Elmer Simpson to carry a gun?"

Joan made no remark. And that in itself got Meg started.

"You know what a putz he is. He's a glorified mall cop with too little training and less sense. He refers to the students from Myanmar as Orientals. I mean, really."

"You're not all that wrong about Elmer. However, you are a little... sensitive about guns on college campuses."

And with good reason. But she didn't want to rehash that with Joan right now.

"It's not like I'm looking to repeal the Second Amendment, or anything," Meg said in an injured tone. "But some sort of limited gun control would avoid a lot of senseless deaths and injuries. I don't want to be one of the three hundred or so Americans who get shot every day."

Meg shut her office door and they joined other faculty members headed the same way.

When Joan didn't respond, Meg gave her a hard stare. "Tell me you're not concerned about having armed security patrolling the grounds and trooping past your classroom?"

"Of course I am. But we may not even have much of a discussion today. The grapevine is buzzing with news about some switch in the agenda."

"Typical. The administration just wants to sweep the issue under the rug."

"Rumor has it Robert is hijacking the meeting. Going on about that Civil War conference the College is hosting and how we're supposed to make nice with the visiting scholars."

Professor Robert Brunner was the current chair of the faculty association and a polarizing figure. But nobody else had wanted the thankless position.

Meg groaned. "Him and his almighty conference. And that PR toady, Maria, probably suggested the switch to avoid starting the debate while we have guests on campus."

"I don't think it's totally off the agenda," Joan said as she sashayed into the meeting room.

They nodded to Brunner, busy at the lectern, as they threaded their way through the rows of plushy chairs in Everett Hall—the new, technology-laden science lecture room. They settled into seats five rows back. Close enough to be engaged, but far enough away to talk quietly.

Meg caught her friend studying Brunner and wondered what comment was coming.

Joan quirked an eyebrow and crooked a finger. Meg leaned closer and got the scoop about a third-shift janitor catching Robert in the darkroom unbuttoning the blouse of the newly hired, red-headed photography adjunct.

"Ick!" Meg whispered.

The room was rapidly filling, boding a high turnout and spirited debate. She noticed David come through the door to join Brunner and another man who had his back to the audience.

David Calloway had been Meg's mentor when she'd first come to the community college, and she was still inordinately fond of him. He was a comfortable-looking man who was coming up fast on fifty, tending toward chubby, with hair that was both graying and thinning. But his bottle green eyes sparkled...if he liked you. Prior to joining the faculty at TCC, he'd been a parole officer, a role which made him a natural for the criminal justice program he administered.

David surveyed the audience, his face relaxing into a warm smile as he sat next to Meg.

"Joan. Meghan. Thank god you're here. The collective I.Q. of any assembly jumps by twenty points every time you two show up."

"Oh, David. Thanks." Meg smiled. "You always say the right thing."

She depended on him for that, but everyone loved him. He'd spent more years on the street than in the classroom, but he'd earned the respect of his current colleagues. She wondered if she could attract someone like David. Younger, though. Seventeen years was a big gap.

His expression turned troubled. "I wish I could say the right thing in this meeting. But I don't have tenure yet, so I can't spearhead anything. You'll have to take the lead. You've got fire in your belly, especially when Dean Plunkard's needling you or eroding our faculty rights."

"Somebody has to stand up to her, that self-righteous harpy," Meg said.

"And we're grateful to you." He patted her on the arm. "You're our champion."

"Thanks for the compliment. I could use it just now. It's been a tough day."

Meg recounted her confrontation with Sellers.

"Ah, him," David nodded. "He's in my night CJ class, the Honors section, hanging on by a thread. Thinks well of himself, doesn't he?"

"He needs to, nobody else does. Especially not Heather Hillcrest. She really skewered him in class. If looks could kill..."

"Yeah, well. He's lucky that girl stopped at hard looks. One of my old compadres at Parole and Probation is friends with Heather's cousin Mackenzie. According to her, Heather and Jon were quite an item at the beginning of the semester. Then Heather found out that lover-boy had posted photos of her on his Facebook page. It got nasty."

"Attention, attention," Brunner called out. "May I have your attention, please?"

"I'd rather have a margarita," David grumbled under his breath.

Brunner waited for total silence before he continued. "It's heartening to have such a robust turnout today, a day devoted to weighty College concerns like the discussion about the possibility of arming campus security."

Meg huffed out a breath and scooched around in her chair until Joan stared her down.

"We'll begin that discussion in a moment, and afterward we have a special treat."

She'd like to treat him to a bout of intestinal flu, the self-important git. But they'd gotten off on the wrong foot from the get-go. He'd been on the hiring committee when she'd applied for the job. She still wasn't sure what she'd done to irk him, but he'd made it clear she was not a suitable choice. Things had not changed.

A few latecomers slunk in, earning themselves a cold look and a rebuke from their leader. "So glad you could join us. Now that we're all assembled, I'll continue."

His audience sat in patient indifference, mirroring the classes that frustrated them.

"As per our agenda, we will begin our discussion on the possibility of arming our campus security guards. To frame the conversation, I thought it would be constructive to invite someone from the Frederick City Police."

Meg glanced down at her agenda and re-read the first item: "The Advisability of Arming Campus Security: Opening Remarks by the FCP." Huh. She hadn't bothered to decode the acronym.

"The police department's Public Information Officer was unable the join us this afternoon and is being replaced by a member of the Criminal Investigation Division."

Typical, Meg thought. The old bait and switch.

"So may I present our guest speaker..."

Looking up, she saw Brunner gesture toward the man David had been speaking to earlier.

"...Lieutenant Stephen T. Raleigh."

She felt a little thrill run through her, but she couldn't tell if it was excitement or dread.

"Let's give him a round of applause, shall we."

Joan elbowed Meg before she brought her hands up to clap enthusiastically.

As Raleigh took the lectern, Meg leaned a little to one side to hide behind the tall, bulky guy from the math department. She'd stay quiet for a while to see what the detective had to say. It paid to understand the opponent's point of view. To be better prepared for the rebuttal.

The lieutenant placed a folder on the lectern and smiled out over the audience. "Thank you for inviting the department to add its voice to this discussion."

The tenor of the room quieted down. Meg wished she could say the same for herself.

"Ever since Columbine, the nation's been stunned by school violence. But it really hit home for colleges with the shootings at Virginia Tech, leaving thirty-two dead. In the wake of that, many colleges and universities have considered arming their campus security. In fact..." He drew a paper out of the folder before him. "By 2013, 76% of university police departments had armed their officers, up from 67% in 2006. And—"

A sweater-vested man in the front row interrupted. "What is the source of your information? I know for a fact that Princeton and Johns Hopkins do not arm their security."

Meg smiled to herself. Ramon was in rare form this afternoon. He was so anti-gun that he made her views look tame. And it was clear he wasn't done yet.

"I trust it's not from some populist source like *USA Today*."

Meg felt a little sorry for the detective. A room full of educators was a tough audience.

"Maybe I should restart the conversation," Raleigh said. "Historically, security guys helped folks get into the cars they'd accidentally locked themselves out of. They were the people who walked around at night, checking to see that everything was locked up. But that's not the job anymore."

Meg tuned out as he talked about the need to provide a safe and secure setting where learning could occur. He knew how to use language to his advantage, she'd give him that. His pitch sounded so reasonable, even reassuring. Until you remembered that people like Elmer would be among the first responders.

The detective stopped talking and studied his audience. "Times have changed significantly. So much so that it's time to consider another change. One that might feel uncomfortable to some."

Then it was more yadda-yadda about how nobody should be armed without extensive training. About how training would help them accurately assess a situation and come up with a suitable response. Yeah, right. She'd like to meet the instructor who could impact Elmer's kneejerk mindset.

"For example," the lieutenant said a little loudly, pulling Meg out of her reverie. She glanced his way to see if she'd been caught woolgathering, caught a flash of humor on his lips.

"A person who is confused, unsteady on his feet and having trouble speaking may be on drugs. But he might also be a diabetic suffering from low blood sugar. And that's a world of difference."

Meg furrowed her brow, unable to find fault with that. She was waiting to see where he was going when one of her colleagues spoke out.

"Statistically, it's unlikely that the College will fall victim to a mass shooting like Virginia Tech."

He nodded. "True. But there are more commonplace dangers. Look at where your students are coming from. All county high schools, as well as selected middle schools, have uniformed school resource officers on site, don't they? Their presence may be primarily symbolic, but not entirely. There are drugs in those schools, as well as gangs, and kids get expelled for bringing in weapons. And those high schools feed into TCC. So it's reasonable to expect that there are guns on your campus on any given day."

Meg shuddered. She'd never considered that possibility.

Raleigh looked around. "How many faculty are in this room? Fifty or so? I'll wager that at least one of you had a student in class today who was carrying a concealed weapon."

Who might it have been in her last class? she wondered. Wasn't it often the kind of student who flew under the radar? Unremarkable and unnoticed. Like little Shaggy.

"That's your real danger. The question is, what do you want to do about it?"

His audience sat in uncomfortable silence, one that Meg decided to turn to her advantage.

"I agree that training is key," she said, aware that all eyes were now on her. "And I think it's a good idea for us to review our protocols and see if our security staff is up to speed. But we can't overlook the potential for catastrophic harm if the College allows its security force to carry guns. What about Braverford University, where one of their armed security officers stopped a student for a simple traffic violation. A busted taillight. The student became mouthy and non-compliant. When he zoomed off, the security guy shot and killed him. True, it came out later that the student was driving on a suspended license and had some pot in his car. But that's nothing to die over, is it?"

Everyone faced forward again, transferring their attention to Raleigh.

"I hear what you're saying. Yes, those circumstances were tragic. And as I recall, when it came to trial, the defense attorney presented evidence that his client had some mental illness issues that were not picked up during his job screening. He should never have been hired to begin with. Perhaps Braverford's hiring protocol for their campus security is the smoking gun in this case. In fact, I think the university is currently being sued over that very issue."

Meg slumped back in her chair, knowing she'd lost that round. She was relieved when Raleigh called on someone who'd raised a hand.

"So far all we've talked about are universities," said another professor.

Joan and Meg looked at each other, faces pained. Joan leaned over and whispered, "Great. Now we get to hear from Hard-Ass Hannah."

"My niece teaches at Quahog Community College up in Massachusetts. The college put together a special committee to explore arming their campus police. Lots of other colleges around them..."

Hannah was always beating the Quahog drum, but Meg waited until she wore down. "Excuse me, Hannah," she said, her voice full of civility. "How many students attend Quahog?"

She narrowed her eyes and was silent for several beats. "About 13,000."

"Well, that tops our 8,000. You surely don't suggest we compare apples and oranges?"

The two women didn't break eye contact, and the tension in the room intensified.

"That's a fair point," Raleigh said, drawing attention back to himself. "You have to look at the size and location of your school in making these decisions. And your campus is so far on the outskirts of Frederick that it's almost in farm country."

Meg glanced over at Raleigh. Had she heard right? Was he agreeing with her?

Brunner surprised everyone by standing up and walking to the lectern. "I think that's all the time we have for this topic today. It was an instructive beginning to what will likely be a lengthy and lively discussion. Thank you for coming, Lieutenant."

"Thank you for having me," he said as he shook hands with the professor and turned toward the exit.

Brunner took the podium again. "Now, I am pleased to introduce another guest."

Meg's eyes followed Raleigh as he left. That whole exchange was puzzling. She was more interested in why he'd supported her point than she was about Robert's next act.

"We are honored to have this nationally acclaimed scholar speaking at the College's fast approaching conference on Frederick's role in the Civil War. May I present the distinguished historian..."

"What?" Meg hissed as Joan poked her in the ribs again.

"...and the author of the definitive work on John Greenleaf Whittier's role as an abolitionist, most notably in his Civil War poem, 'Barbara Frietchie'..."

Joan inclined her head toward the door where Jon Sellers was ushering in the elegantly made-up and over-dressed guest.

"...Dr. Christine Slattery."

Chapter 7

Once again clad in sunglasses and a gray, hooded sweatsuit, the Watcher travels the deserted jogging path beside Carroll Creek, reviewing cell phone pictures of the two girls from the restaurant. Smiles at the last photo.

"Hello, my pretty. I'm on my way."

The path skirts a secluded, ramshackle parking lot located at the back of an aged Cape Cod style brick home: the Barbara Fritchie Museum. But not a formal one, at present privately owned and infrequently open. And by crossing the parking lot, producing a key and unlocking the door, the Watcher's destination.

The perfect place for what's to come...and you were so eager to meet me here.

Grackles roost in bare Bradford pear trees beside the creek. Ever vigilant, the birds turn sleek, black heads toward the approaching figure. One caws. Several others startle away as the wooden door groans open after its swollen planks yield to a thwacking palm.

Soon I'll take what you have to give.

Inside, the Watcher edges past bric-a-brac hanging on pegs affixed to the wall and slinks behind the open door. Avoids the antique, wavy-glassed window overlooking the path which runs beside both pear trees and creek. Closing the door a little, the figure stares outside. Two blocks away, the bells of the carillon in Baker Park chime the half hour.

Come on. It's 5:30, already. Let's get this party started.

The gray shadow doesn't move. Breathing changes—a bit faster, more shallow. Hands clench and loosen. Ears strain to hear.

I explicitly texted, 'Be punctual.' I've planned and planned for this.

Some inner spring tightens. Jaw muscles clench. But no pacing, no fidgeting. Instead, the Watcher's right hand strokes a slight bulge low in the hoodie's pouch.

Gotta keep steady now. I'm closing in on what I want, what I need, and then I'll do what must be done.

Attentive eyes survey the room, settle on the faded cross-stitch sampler, note its age stains and broken stitches, the occasional frayed thread. Staying back from windows, the Watcher steps forward, leans against the archway to the front room, takes inventory: ladder back chair, oil lamp, unbleached muslin curtains. A large, chestnut desk.

Drawn to that, one latex-gloved hand caresses the burnished wood. Here, General Reno wrote his last letter home. Days later he died in combat en route to Antietam. The bloodiest single-day battle of the Civil War.

After one last pass over the polished surface, impatient fingers draw out a cell phone and tap out a message: "Are you coming? I'm on a tight schedule."

In the park the carillon chimes the three-quarter hour.

One hand rubs the hoodie's pouch.

She'll show. I've baited the trap with care. And she's absolutely guileless.

A pedestrian—young, blonde, and leggy—crosses the street toward the museum. Inside, a cell phone pings. The Watcher opens the incoming text: "Almost there. Can't wait to show you my amazing find."

I'll bet. Then I'll show you mine.

The Watcher slides a hand inside the hoodie's long pocket. Tracks the girl's progress across the front of the museum and down the jogging path along its side. Sees her walk through the shabby yard to the back door. The hooded figure—tightly wound clockwork ready to spring—retraces its steps and hides behind the half-open door, its fingers restless in the distended pouch.

Flustered and breathless, the girl dashes up the three steps. Books nestle in the crook of her arm. Crossing the wooden threshold, she steps into the middle of the room, slips a blonde lock behind her ear and looks around. "Hello?"

The door swings shut and the Watcher stands revealed. As the girl turns, a timorous smile flits across her lips.

The hand inside the pouch grips the wooden haft of a ball-peen hammer.

She blinks, steps back. One foot, then the other. Her lips now part as if to speak.

There's no turning back. Not now.

"Hello, Heather. Have you brought the item we discussed?"

The girl's hand flutters down atop the books. Glancing at them, her fingers curl possessively over the edge of an antique envelope peeking out of a leather-bound book.

Just as she looks up, down comes the hammer.

Focus on the follow-through. That's where the power is.

With that single blow, the young woman drops to her knees, pole-axed, then slumps sideways on the floor. Books tumble and scatter. The cell phone clatters to the floor. Outside, the roosting birds protest loudly and skitter aloft.

Forgive me. There is no other way.

Observing the girl struggling weakly on the floor and hearing her groans, the Watcher—breath coming in catches—bends closer. In the failing daylight, the hammer rises again.

History demands this sacrifice.

And yet again.

The carillon chimes out six slow notes.

No mere watcher now, the lean figure closes both eyes and shudders, then returns the reddened hammer to its pouch and pulls in long, calming breaths.

She'll become part of the legend, immortal. My gift to her.

The hooded figure's attention slides past the inert body and focuses on the prize: the letter tucked inside the book now lying on the floor. Both treasures are secreted in a mangled grocery store bag pulled from the sweatpants' pocket.

Cautious eyes scan the room, making sure no clues remain. No errant fibers. No footprints in the glossy blood puddling beneath her head.

Anything else? Ah, blood spatter on my clothes.

Donning the full-length cape hanging beside the door, the murderer returns to the silver sedan and drives carefully away.

Noisy grackles return to roost. The door remains ajar.

Chapter 8

Exiting her dirty and dinged pickup, Meg trudged toward the Civilian Police Academy's beige cinderblock building, unenthusiastic about enduring yet another work-related obligation.

All faculty members did more than teach. They were busy conducting original research, publishing books or articles, honing their artistic skills, participating in juried events as well as presenting at and attending conferences. All with the goal of keeping current in their fields and bringing that knowledge back to their students.

"I should be home grading essays," she grumbled, kicking a stray stone across the blacktop. She'd be at it now if Joan hadn't made clucking noises when she'd played the grading card to avoid going to the Academy. She was all at sixes and sevens about that detective. His rhetoric had favored arming campus security. But at the end, he'd kind of taken her side. *Weird.* And why would she want to date a cop, anyway? Gun-toting control freaks whose hours were way worse than hers, doing a job that could get them killed. *Too much drama for this mama.*

She paused at the concrete apron of the Academy building and considered going home. Her grading was piling up, and maybe she'd already messed up her chances with him by being so outspoken in the faculty meeting. Better to go home and lie to Joan tomorrow, tell her she'd been so disappointed when he never showed up. Easy peasy.

"It's good to see that I'm not the only late arrival," said a man's voice.

Meg turned to see one of her classmates standing behind her. The guy who was running for city council and wanted to score some law enforcement votes.

"No. Not the only latecomer," she began, "but I was just about—"

"To go in. Great." He opened the door for her, whispering, "After you."

As they entered, a few people turned to look. One of them was Lieutenant Raleigh, his gray eyes watchful. Then he returned his attention to the speaker, Sergeant Groves.

"Tonight we have a real treat for you, a demonstration by one of our K-9 teams."

Meg slipped into a chair in the last row, well behind the detective who hadn't looked all that glad to see her. She'd given up a night of much-needed grading to be ignored by some hot guy and then have to pretend to care about a dog doing tricks? Damn that David.

Last spring Calloway had badgered her into teaching a section of English 101 to the cadets from the local Police Academy, a night section at that. But this fall, two weeks into the actual class, he'd wheedled her into enrolling in this venue—the Civilian Police Academy—explaining that she'd have more cachet with the cadets if she dabbled in their world.

"We use German shepherds, mostly," Groves continued. "And we often get our drug dogs from Eastern Europe...Rumania, Ukraine, Yugoslavia. Animals bred there don't have a lot of the physical ailments that plague dogs from American puppy mills."

Meg sent black thoughts David's way. He said she'd be roleplaying traffic stops, drug busts, and domestic violence disputes. Instead? She was stuck in a chair staring at a damn dog.

Officer Groves gestured to the back corner of the room. "Here's Jelka." At his command, a midnight-black German shepherd loped up the middle aisle and paced back and forth in front of the whiteboard. "She's from Rumania, so her commands are in that language. Watch this."

He worked to make eye contact with her. "Jelka." The dog kept pacing, eyeing the class.

"Jelka!" Her ears pricked forward and she looked up at him.

"Good girl. Now, *plotz*."

And Jelka sat.

"The advantage of giving commands in a foreign language is that perps and bystanders can't shout counter commands that might confuse the animal." Jelka butted her big head into the officer's thigh. "Good girl," he said, thumping her shoulder. "Now let's go outside and watch her work."

While they'd been in class, another officer had hidden a kilo of marijuana in a volunteer's car. Once the class filed outside, the dog walked around the cars, straining at her leash. After a couple of minutes, she put her front paws on the left-rear quarter panel of a tan Hyundai, signaling her decision. Groves opened the back door, groped around under the seat and pulled out the plastic-wrapped package.

"Good girl, Jelka. Good girl." Her trainer pulled out a ratty tube sock and played tug of war with her. "We always play after she makes a hit. For her, this is a game, not work. We don't want her to lose interest." He tugged the sock away from Jelka, and she spun in circles, yelping.

Someone in the back yelled, "Give her some Ritalin." Another wag called out, "Or just let her inhale."

Groves joined the class's laughter. "Let's go back inside for a break and some refreshments. While we're busy doing that, Officer Keefer will don the fat suit, and you'll see how Jelka takes down a bad guy."

Folks straggled back into the room, and Meg stood in line, eyeing the cheese cubes and fresh fruit on the snack table. No chocolate kisses, unlike last week. She looked for the lieutenant and saw him mingle with the civilians. Damn, he was fine looking. Yeah, but a fine-looking cop.

He glanced over and started walking toward her, but another participant snagged him.

Paper plate in hand, Meg nudged her grapes aside, situated a Swiss cheese cube atop a cracker and nonchalantly checked out the lieutenant, paying close attention to his hands. *Um, um, umm.* Flirting may begin with the eyes, but she enjoyed checking out a man's hands, imagining them as they skimmed over—

"No chocolate?"

She half-choked on the cracker, embarrassed to find the lieutenant chuckling at her.

"I'm sorry. I didn't mean to alarm you. It's just that you usually go for the chocolate."

"You're right," she said after a quick swallow. He'd noticed her snack choices last week? Really? "It's my one vice."

"Everybody's allowed one. And as my daughter likes to say about her Mountain Dew habit, 'It's not cocaine.'"

"Persuasive girl. How old is she?"

"Fifteen going on thirty-five." He laughed ruefully. "And she'd deliver the line with heavy sarcasm and lots of eye rolling."

She smiled at him. Too bad about the daughter, though. Ring or no ring, men with daughters typically had wives.

"I've taught them at that age. Lots of them don't think they have anything left to learn."

"Oh, so you haven't always taught at Possum U? Our Harvard on the Pike."

She'd hoped for better repartee. Not the same old jokes about the college's Opossumtown Pike address.

"During grad school, I did some substitute teaching in high schools to earn extra money. And I've also taught at Harvard." Then she fessed up. "Just for a summer semester, as a teaching assistant." While pretentious asshole Al finished up his master's degree in economics.

She didn't wait for a response. "But a lot of those kids had attitudes that were too rich for my blood. The Ivy Leagues are prestigious, but community colleges can make a bigger difference for more people."

"Why of course, ma'am. I can tell that you're a woman of the people." His gray eyes grew mischievous. "The state of your pickup truck attests to that."

She was surprised he knew what she drove. But what about that 'ma'am'? A genteel Southern boy. Virginia? No, farther south. And those eyes...late summer, Atlantic-surf gray. She could spend some time swimming in them.

Meg was planning to defend her truck when his expression changed.

"Pardon me a moment." He pulled out his cell phone and answered a call.

Meg bit into a grape, hoping he was divorced.

When he turned back to her, his body language had altered—his posture more crisp, his movements sharper.

"Excuse me. Duty calls. We'll talk later, Professor Adams."

"It's Meg, please."

He nodded, turned, and left.

Maybe this night wasn't such a waste after all. First, Jelka, the Whirling Dervish Wonder Dog and then Officer Tall, Dark, and Handcuffs. But right now she had to find the restroom.

She headed down the hall in that direction but stopped beside a partially opened door to a smaller parking lot where the officers parked their cars. Through the gap, she heard conversation, the voices tense. She peeked out the door to see Raleigh and some other officer standing on the concrete pad outside the door. Feeling the tiniest bit guilty she listened in.

"Homicide?" Raleigh said, surprised.

"Yeah, blunt force trauma...three blows to the head."

Meg shuddered.

"She was still alive when she was found but died on the way to Frederick Memorial."

She'd only ever read about murders in the paper or heard about them on TV. Somehow, the poor victim seemed deader this way.

"You said the attack happened *inside* the Barbara Fritchie House?" Raleigh paused. "Just down from Headquarters? Next to Doc McClellan's veterinary practice, right?"

She knew that part of Frederick. Her therapist was right down the street. Eww.

"Yeah. And lieutenant...your daughter found the body."

"Lindsay?" His words came out in a rush. "Good God! Is she okay? Where is she?"

Meg's hand flew to her mouth. Poor man, how awful. He must be frantic.

"No, no. She's fine. Just scared and upset. She's down at headquarters, in your office. But that's not all. The victim. It's her friend, Heather...Heather Hillcrest."

Meg rushed out the door. "Heather? My student, Heather, dead? That can't be."

The uniformed officer stared at her, expressionless.

She swayed slightly as it hit her. Heather was dead.

"Meg, sit down, please, before you fall down." Raleigh guided her to the stoop. "You're talking a mile a minute, shivering, and none too steady on your feet."

She couldn't quite take it all in. It seemed like a movie.

"Meg, just stay here a minute." He stepped away and took out his cell phone.

Keeping an eye on her, he spoke quietly into the phone. "Lindsay, when you get this message, call me. I just heard about Heather. I'm so sorry, honey. Stay in my office. I'll get to you just as soon as I can. Love you."

He nodded to the officers gathered around a cruiser. Walking back to Meg, he raised her chin to look in her eyes. "Are your ears ringing? Do you feel like you're going to faint?"

"No, no...not going to faint. But I'm so cold."

He tugged off his windbreaker and swung it around her shoulders. "Here, put this on."

She slid her arms in the sleeves. "Okay, thanks."

"I want you to take some deep breaths for me, okay?"

As she did her shivering abated. She met his gaze. "That's helping. The breathing. And the jacket. Thanks."

He took a long look at her. "Tell me about Heather. She was your student, right?"

She nodded. "I've had her in class for two semesters. Well three, if you count summer. Really quiet the first time, but this semester she's dropped by my office fairly often. She's book smart, but a little naïve. We met for coffee at the Campus Grille a couple of times. She wanted to 'friend' me on Facebook." *The girl has a Facebook page. How can she be dead?*

He continued to look at her, waiting for more.

"She was really psyched about this project for class, the one where they do site research."

Raleigh half turned to listen to the radio chatter coming from the cruiser, something about securing the crime scene at the museum.

Meg's head snapped up. "Oh my god." Her face drained of color. "The Barbara Fritchie Museum...Heather was researching it for her big class project."

"And you think that's why she was there?"

Meg nodded, started shivering again.

Raleigh's face clouded with concern, but he pressed on. "When did you last see Heather? Did you have her in class today?"

She closed her eyes to concentrate. "Yes, she was in my 2 o'clock. She talked to me before class, made an appointment for tomorrow." Her teeth began to chatter. "She se-se-seemed excited, agitated about something. I'll ask about it when I see her tomorr..."

Her bottom lip started to tremble, and her eyes filled with tears. "I won't see her tomorrow, will I?"

"No," he said quietly. "You won't,"

Meg glanced away, started rocking back and forth on the step. She looked at the lieutenant again. "Are you interrogating me? Am I a suspect?"

Raleigh knelt down, put a hand on her shoulder and looked into her face. "Well, if I pull this case I'll need to ask you some more questions. But no, you're not a suspect. The girl was attacked between 5:30 and 6:00. I can verify that you've been here since a little after five."

"Oh...yeah, right."

Another burst of static-y chatter had him look away briefly. "But you need to take things easy. You're in shock. We need to get you home."

"But class isn't over yet. Jelka has to take down the guy in the fat suit."

"Class is over for you." He squeezed her shoulder gently.

Meg looked into his eyes, felt their warmth. "How can you be so nice and still want a lot of guns on campus?" *Oops, had she said that out loud?* She must've because he looked surprised.

He smiled. "Maybe we should have coffee sometime and discuss my views on that. But right now I don't want you driving. Do you have someone who can pick you up?"

Meg ran a hand through her messy curls as she considered her options. "My friend David lives over in Clover Hill. He teaches criminal justice, so he won't be freaked out."

"Is this CJ professor the David Calloway formerly with Parole and Probation?"

"Yes."

"He's a good man." Raleigh stood and pulled out his phone. "I'll call him for you."

Knowing that David was coming she relaxed. Good ol' dependable David.

"Hey, Calloway," he said. "Yeah, long time no talk. Bottom line, I need a favor. I need you to come out here to the Police Academy to pick up a colleague of yours..."

Meg tuned out and let her mind float, glad to let someone else be in charge for a change.

Once the lieutenant ended his call, he turned to her and helped her stand. "Whoever's in charge of the case will need to talk to you tomorrow. When's a good time?"

"Tomorrow? That's...uh, Wednesday. Right? Ah..." It was hard to think straight. But she didn't want to come off like a Victorian heroine flinging the back of her hand across her eyes and lowering herself onto a fainting chaise. Steeling herself, she made her words come out clear and firm. "My office hours tomorrow are from 9:30 to 10:30, and I'm done for the day at 2:00."

"Earlier is probably better. Someone will drop by in the morning to get your statement."

"Good, I'm eager to cooperate," she said, starting to take off his windbreaker.

"No, keep the jacket. I'll get it some other time."

"Oh, okay."

Raleigh looked anxious to leave. "When you get home, make sure you hydrate. Okay?"

"Yes. And thank you." She paused. "Again."

He backed away as he spoke. "Always glad to help. Goodnight, Meg."

•   •   •   •   •

Once she was in David's car, Meg leaned back in the seat and closed her eyes.

"You cold? Want some heat?" he asked.

"No, I'm good," she replied mid-yawn.

"I'm not buying that. You've had a hell of a night." He took his eyes off the road a moment to study her. "Bet the adrenaline's wearing off by now."

Meg nodded slowly, trying not to encourage the headache that was blossoming. She didn't want to look directly at David, fearing she might actually fall apart. Poor Heather...and the lieutenant's daughter, finding her friend like that.

"Want to tell me about it?"

She hesitated. "Sort of yes, sort of no."

"You don't have to go over the graphic details," he added hastily. "Raleigh's already filled me in. I'm worried about you, how you're feeling."

"I don't want to say," she finally admitted. "It sounds selfish."

"Come on. Out with it. Confession's good for the soul."

When she spoke, her voice was thick, the words fighting with the tears that wanted to flow. "I'm so glad that it didn't happen to someone I love. What if it were you or Joan?"

"But it wasn't. We're safe." He put his hand on her arm. "Feel that? I'm still here." He squeezed gently. "Joan and I are alive and well. And you're safe, too."

"Yes, safe in the car with you." She yawned.

Twenty minutes later he pulled into her driveway, a half-mile, rutted farm lane. The house sat in the bottom left-hand corner of a fifty-acre farm that was surrounded by much larger farms. Ten miles to the north, the Catoctin Mountains rose, unseen in the dark—old mountains that barely reached 2000 feet. The easternmost ridge of the Appalachians. A few points of light—weekend homes of the D.C. wealthy—shimmered on the mountainside.

Meg barely took in the familiar fields and the lone pond, its surface reflected by the dusk-to-dawn light pole near the barn. Empty now for years.

"Here's something you'll be glad to know," David said as he opened the door for her. "Raleigh allowed as how you were a real trooper. Understandably upset but not hysterical. And he's hard to impress. Seen too much."

But she didn't feel glad. She didn't feel much of anything.

Once she'd unlocked the front door, he stepped inside and flipped the switch for the hall light. Nothing happened. "Meg, you said the landlord was going to fix this faulty wiring." He felt for the table lamp just inside the door, turned it on, and stood back to let her enter.

"He is. I'm sure he'll get to it really soon."

"Right. Just like he's gonna replace that water heater and fix the thermostat. Why do you even live in this godforsaken place?"

"Because the price is right."

Meg sighed, knowing that he was going to launch into his usual rant.

"This place is all but condemned. And knowing that the Beelzebubs used to deal drugs out of here, no one else'll touch it."

"Which is why Sioux lets me stay here rent free," she said, defending her choice for the umpteenth time. "All I have to do is cover the electric bill. How else can I pay off my debt? Undo the damage Al did to my credit?"

Face stern, he continued to scold. "Financial security is not a smart swap for physical safety."

"Don't lecture me, David. It's been a rotten night."

He looked sheepish. "You're right. I'm sorry. Here, let me give you a hug."

Meg went to him, glad for his sudden warmth. Sad to be let go. "Now stop being nice to me or I'll cry. Get out of here. I'm fine."

She stood in the doorway while he walked to his car. But he didn't get in right away.

"Oh, about your truck. When I was out at the Academy, I talked to Groves. He and Keefer will come by later and drop it off." He put an arm on the roof of his car and gave her a serious look. "You should consider staying home tomorrow."

"No can do. Got big tests coming up and the students are nowhere near ready."

He scowled. "Instead of worrying about them, you oughta put yourself first." He rapped his knuckles on the car roof. "It wouldn't hurt this once, would it?"

"Maybe not, but someone from the FPD is coming by the office to ask more questions."

"Okay." He eased behind the wheel. "Be sure to lock up." Before shutting his door, he leaned back out. "And take some aspirin."

Meg locked the door behind him and tossed the windbreaker over the back of the couch. She drew a glass of water and rummaged around for aspirin. Gave Joan call, but when it went to voicemail she hung up.

Tired but too wound up to sleep, she put the jacket on again—his jacket—and opted for a stroll in the back garden, the one she'd reclaimed from the Beelzebubs's personal marijuana patch.

Gravel walkways framed the space into four plots, with rose bushes along the back. A few weeks ago she'd dug up the annuals—geraniums, petunias, zinnias—and pruned back the herb beds. Only the mums and asters were still blooming this late in October. She didn't have the heart to cut them back while they were still had color.

Sitting down in one of the pale blue Adirondack chairs, she let her right arm dangle, hand lightly brushing the tops of some lavender, scenting the air. At an owl's distant hoot, she looked up, observed the velvet-skinned night, experienced its vastness. She could almost hear its slow, slow heartbeat, imagined its breath...an inhale, then eons before the exhale.

No stars tonight, she noted. Like the night Al left.

She dandled the lavender and sighed. Someone always fell out of love first. One person had a foot out the door before the other was even aware. She'd had to work her butt off to make full professor in six years. That had meant a lot of committee work at the College, racking up lots of publications in academic journals and finding a publisher for her first book of poetry. Through it all, Al had been very supportive, encouraging her to work hard, never complaining about the hours she spent. Yeah, right. All that time had freed him up to work on *his* extra-curricular activities. Online betting. Bar hopping. Bedding co-workers, buying them gifts and taking them on business trips instead of her. And then there was Julie—that skanky slut. She sure hadn't seen that coming.

The night after he left, she'd gone out into their garden. Sat in this same chair, looked up, expecting what? Comfort? A sense of connection to a great chain of being?

What happened then was happening again. Acknowledgement of life's impermanence. The grip of fear. The cold miasma of the unknown. Then, as now, she sobbed.

Neither time did she know how long it lasted. But afterward, both times—left feeling worn out and all but transparent—she looked up again at the sky. No solace, no answers, but no lies, either. Just the breathing, restive, velvet-skinned night.

Chapter 9

Safely away from inquisitive eyes, the Watcher parks in a secluded spot, opens the door to activate the dome light, takes the book from the plastic bag, and carefully slides the letter out.

Trembling fingers lift the flap of the antique envelope and slide inside the brittle paper rectangle to pull out a single sheet. Not as old as the envelope and thinner, whiter. Unfolded, its secrets are laid bare.

"What!"

The page is wadded up and thrown against the windshield, then bounces to the dashboard and tumbles to the passenger seat.

"It's only a fucking xerox copy."

Hands balled, breath ragged, and blood pounding, the Watcher struggles for control.

"That little blonde bitch played me."

Slowly calm returns. The Watcher retrieves the letter, smooths it out and reads.

"What a crock of shit. It's only the first page."

Reads it once again.

"She specifically told me that Fritchie named names in the letter. What did the little whore think she was going to accomplish with this? Bait me into giving her some money now with a promise of the authentic letter, a page at a time, so I'd shelled out more money...and more, and more."

For several minutes the Watcher stares into the starless night while moths flit across the headlights' beam and small animals rustle in the bushes.

"It doesn't end here. It can't."

Chapter 10

Lieutenant Raleigh pulled into the city parking deck behind the complex that housed both the police department and the courthouse. Very convenient when he had to testify, but right now he was planning how he'd get himself assigned to this case. He owed the dispatch officer for giving him a heads-up, and for letting him know that the commander hadn't left for the day. He needed to get inside and make his pitch.

Since Frederick had only a couple of murders a year, they didn't have a homicide department. Instead, those cases were assigned to detectives in the Criminal Investigation Division, and every one of them wanted to pull that duty. It was a career builder. He could care less about that, but he cared a lot about catching Heather's killer.

Driving a little too fast, he swung abruptly into one of the spaces reserved for CID, thinking how to best approach his commander. Hoping one of the other detectives hadn't beaten him to the punch.

Inside headquarters, he strode to the commander's office. His secretary had gone home for the day, but the door was ajar. He heard two voices within and snatches of their exchange.

"...Billings is next on the rota, logically—"

"He doesn't have much experience."

Taking a deep breath, Raleigh knocked and was rewarded with the familiar bellow.

"Enter."

He wasn't overly surprised to see his captain there. But the man looked harried, and that didn't happen very often. Shawn Hannon was a very composed, very ordinary looking man. Brown hair, brown eyes, a medium build with a medium skin tone. His posture was unremarkable, and the quality of his voice carried no discernable point of origin. He was perfect for undercover work, and he'd excelled at it. Because intellectually he was anything but ordinary.

Assigning a detective to this case should be his call unless the commander wanted to weigh in. And he always did. Noting that the captain looked tense and that the commander was reared back in his chair, his face splotchy red, Ty figured it wasn't going well.

Michael João, a big man of Portuguese descent, filled his chair like he filled his job—as if he didn't intend to move anytime soon.

"Raleigh," João boomed, "you here about that homicide? Thinking to grab some glory?"

He had expected exactly this from his superior. João was a competent administrator and from all accounts had been a good cop. And yet the two of them rubbed each other wrong.

He thought maybe it was because he'd come to Frederick from the State Police. Or maybe because he didn't actually need the job. When he applied, he'd just inherited a pile of money. But he wanted to be useful, to make a meaningful contribution. Always had.

"Sir. I'm interested in investigating the Hillcrest case."

"Of course you are. Billings is next in line, but Hannon allows as how he's just a sergeant, only worked a few homicides."

"Four," Hannon supplied. "And three of those were drug-related executions."

João shrugged. "I don't like playing favorites."

From his vantage point, Raleigh could see his captain grimace. Fortunately, the commander couldn't.

"Plus, your kid found the body."

At least João hadn't figured out that he knew the victim.

"Come on, João," Hannon said. "She's not a suspect or anything. Lindsay and the Taylor girl were walking home from school. Each alibis the other. Besides, Raleigh's our most qualified cop, murder-wise. You know that. He's had years more experience in that area than anyone else on the force, including me."

And João, the lieutenant thought to himself. Letting his captain sell the idea was good strategy, but it was time to show his cards. "I've already located and talked to the person who may've been the last one to see the girl alive."

The Commander raised an eyebrow. "Ambulance chasing, are we?"

"No sir. I just happened to be at the right place at the right time." He went on to relay what'd transpired at the police academy, leaving out the parts about smoothing out Meg's rough edges.

When he was done João nodded to Hannon then glared at Raleigh.

"Okay, hotshot, you're up. Let's hope your 'vast experience'" he air quoted, "with the State Police Homicide Division gets this solved *tout suite*. Don't screw this up."

Raleigh drew a long breath, trying not to take the "vast experience" bait. *Why did his background stick in the Commander's craw? Out of competition, maybe? Envy?* He'd never quite figured out why and it sure as shit didn't matter right now. He'd caught the case, but he'd've worked it on his own time. He was dead set on nailing this bastard, to be the one to get justice for that poor child. And payback for traumatizing his daughter.

"Thank you, sir. I'll give you my best work."

"See that you do. Dismissed."

•   •   •   •   •

Mission accomplished. He called his partner and told him they'd meet at the crime scene but that he'd be a while getting there. First, he needed to check on his daughter.

Walking to his second-floor office, he passed Officer Louise Satler.

"Howdy, Lieutenant. Rough night, huh?"

Raleigh nodded. "It'll likely get rougher. How's Lindsay?"

"Well, she's usually such a tough little cookie, but when I saw her, she was pretty upset. Not all cocky like she usually is. Kinda quiet, actually. I took her statement and one from the other girl, Susan."

He frowned. "Susan?"

"Susan Taylor. The girl who called it in. She and Lindsay were walking from the high school over to the coffee shop on Shab Row. When Lindsay saw that the back door to the museum was open, she went to check it out and told the her friend to call 911. Fortunately, the other girl never got inside the building. After she gave her statement, I called the mother to come get her, take her home. I stashed Lindsay in your office."

"Thanks, Louise."

Continuing down the hall, he strategized how to proceed. As a dad, he wanted to scoop Lindsay up and soothe away the horror of what she'd seen. But she was a material witness. And a friend of the deceased. She likely had information he needed. That would take some finessing. He turned his chin from one shoulder to the other and grimaced at the cracking noise.

Without announcing himself, he slowly opened his office door. Only the green-shaded banker's lamp was on, not the overheads. Lindsay was sitting diagonally in his high-back desk chair, feet tucked up under her with one hand hanging over the chair's arm and the other curled under her chin. A Goldilocks in a too big chair, eyes closed and hair rumpled. She wasn't wearing her usual out-there attire, just some oversized, dark blue FCPD sweatsuit that Louise must have rustled up. The sight of her tugged at his heart.

"Lindsay," he called softly.

When she didn't answer, he stood there, gazing at her for a long minute. She looked about twelve. A sleeping twelve-year-old. He was reluctant to wake her, but then he saw that she was wearing her iPod earbuds. Her head began to bob as she silently mouthed the words to a song.

He eased over beside her, raised his hand to stroke her cheek but drew it back and drank her in. Then he sat on the corner of the desk, leaned over and gently tugged on the cord to one earbud. "Lindsay."

In a flash she unfolded herself and sat up, bright blue eyes wide and startled. "Get away from me!" she cried, batting at his hand and pulling out the earbuds.

Leaning back, he called her name again, keeping his voice even and calm. "Lindsay. It's me. It's Dad."

She went very still, her eyes remaining wild and scared. Suddenly she stood and almost fell forward into his hug. "Oh, Dad, it was awful."

"I know, baby. I know," he soothed, rocking her from side to side.

He dreaded telling her the rest.

The trembling girl tightened her arms around him and whispered into his chest. "She didn't make it, did she?"

He laid his cheek atop her head. "I'm sorry, darlin'. No. She didn't." Feeling her limbs go slack, he tightened his hug.

Lindsay sniffled. "I tried to help, but I didn't move her or anything." She pulled back and straightened to look into her father's face, study his expression. "I know you're not supposed to move injured people because you can hurt them more. I only checked to see if she could breathe, to see if she was still..."

"You're amazing," he said, voice warm with respect. "So clear-headed."

Her features relaxed.

"I talked to her. Put my hand on her shoulder." The teen's eyes glimmered with forming tears. "Told her I was there and help was on the way. But she never talked back." Lindsay snaked her hands deep inside the sleeves of the baggy sweatshirt until she grasped her elbows. Her voice got quieter and smaller. "At first she just moaned a little."

He laid his hands on her shoulders and squeezed gently, wishing he didn't feel so helpless. Felt bad that he was all she had, was afraid he wasn't enough. She needed her mom.

"Then Heather sort of twitched and whimpered, and all I could think of was that nest of baby rabbits I accidentally ran over with the lawnmower that one time. How they squealed and flopped around..." She stopped talking, looking past her father toward the empty doorway.

He remained quiet, caught between speaking and listening. She needed to talk it out, but he wished she didn't. Why did she have to be caught up in this? She was only a child.

Lindsay pulled her hands free and observed them for a moment. Then she refocused on her father's face, tears streaming silently down her cheeks. "When I first saw her lying there, I yelled to Susan to call 911. I told her to stay outside 'cause she didn't need to see all that. Then the only thing I could do was sit there and wait for the ambulance." She paused. "I wanted to hold her hand, but it was all slippery red...and she was lying on the other one."

She tugged at her sweatshirt cuff and used the material to wipe her eyes

"Lindsay, you comforted her." He brushed at his own eyes. "She knew she wasn't alone. That's huge." His voice was deep and tender. "I'm so sad for you. But also very, very proud."

He stood and cupped her face in his hands, his eyes dark with emotion. She held his gaze for a long moment, then began sniffling again. When the tears came, he pulled her in and held her while she sobbed.

He hugged her tightly and let her cry, said soothing, nonsensical things for a long time. As her sobs became more intermittent and her breathing quieted, he lightly bumped his chin atop her head—once, twice, three times—then drew back and blew gentle breaths through her hair.

In a small voice, she murmured against his chest. "That's nice." Her breath caught a couple of times, then became more regular. "You used to do that to me when I was little if I was sick or hurt. Remember?"

"Of course, I remember. You're my Linny-Linn."

She nodded her head against his cheek. "You haven't called me that in forever."

"You haven't seemed like you'd want me to...in forever."

She pulled back to look at him and half smiled. "I know. I'm such a brat."

He looked into her striking blue eyes, so unlike his own. "Yup. But you're my brat." He pulled her in tightly for another hug and felt his inner turmoil lessen when she let him. Then he ruffled her hair and settled her back in the chair. "You need anything? Want something to drink? Some dinner?"

"No thanks. Louise asked me the same things. I told her I couldn't face any food, but a Mountain Dew would be nice. She said the caffeine wouldn't be good for my system right now." The teen rolled her eyes before continuing. "She made me some crap herbal tea instead." Lindsay faked a shudder. "I put a ji-normous amount of sugar in it, but it was still crap."

"Sounds like Louise. She means well."

They sat in silence for several minutes: Lindsay slumped in the chair; he leaning against his desk. He was reluctant to break the spell.

"I had to fight for it, but I'm on the case." He watched her body tense. "So I'll need to talk to you about what happened this evening."

She picked up her earbuds and slapped the wires against her thigh. "Figures."

"But it doesn't have to be now." Silence. "It can wait until tomorrow."

The girl slapped the wires harder. Refused to make eye contact.

Raleigh took a deep breath. "Lindsay..."

She looked up with narrowed eyes. "I gave Louise that stupid statement. Isn't that enough?"

"Look, I know this is hard, but—"

"Hard! This is way beyond hard."

"Lindsay, I'm—"

She smacked her hands on the arms of the chair. "I'm not even wearing my own clothes. Know why?" Glaring at him, she propelled herself upright. "Because mine are covered in Heather's blood..."

"Lindsay—"

"...and bits of her brain. But you know all about bloody brains. You're a cop."

Raleigh stood, and his face tightened, but he didn't speak.

"I'm only fifteen." She hurled the words at her father. "I shouldn't have to know."

A variety of emotions played across his face, but they coalesced into sadness. "No, you shouldn't." He paused and looked away, remembering the house in Baltimore, her nightmares. "You've seen too much already."

He looked back into his daughter's eyes, blazing hot blue with anger. "And I'm very sorry about that. But you do know. And to catch whoever did this, I need you to talk about it."

Her eyes didn't soften. "And you think you'll catch her killer, Stephen? Really? How can you sound so sure? Even after five years, nobody's caught Mom's."

They stood face to face in the small office, tension mounting, eyes locked. Both of them breathing hard. Lindsay began to tear up again, and her shoulders started to shake. Her father moved toward her, but she stepped away and clasped her elbows.

He leaned against the desk again, head lowered, chest tight. "So, it's not 'Dad' anymore; we're back to 'Stephen.'"

"You're the one who changed things. You and your cop talk."

Raleigh's body recoiled slightly, slapped by her words. Lindsay seemed surprised by the impact of what she'd just said.

Neither of them spoke. He glanced up at the ceiling, started to say something, stopped, then dropped his head again.

Lindsay's next words were hushed. "Murder sucks."

He sighed. "You must be exhausted. We'll talk about this tomorrow." Walking around to the side of the desk, he paused and put his hands in his pockets. "But I'm not going straight home, so we need to get you situated. I'm not leaving you alone tonight." Seeing Lindsay's look turn mutinous, he added, "Even though you are fifteen," and was relieved to see her back down.

Looking out the window, he considered his options. "You want me to call your Aunt Caroline to come up and stay for a few days?" Lindsay might need a woman to talk to, process her feelings with. "She could get up here in about an hour."

Lindsay hesitated, searching her father's face. "No, she's still in Cancun. Besides, it might make me sad. She looks so much like Mom."

He nodded slowly as he turned more toward the window. "Yes. She does." He tilted his head back some and rolled it between his shoulders a few times. "But she's nowhere near as nice," he muttered under his breath.

"I heard that, Stephen," she chided.

When he turned back to face her, he felt tired. And old. "About this 'Stephen' business. That's what people call me at work. If you can't bring yourself to call me 'Dad,' how about my middle name? Tyler. I save that for friends."

She looked down, but she did respond. "Mom used to call you 'Ty.'"

He inhaled a shivery breath and exhaled a quiet, "That'll do."

She hugged herself and shrugged her shoulders. "I'll see." She rocked back and forth several times, then looked up. "But I've figured out where I can go. The Maroni's. When I babysit there, and it's really late, they let me spend the night. How 'bout I just go there?"

"Good plan. You want to go by cab or cruiser?"

"Cab, please. Those cruisers smell like vomit."

"Okay, have Louise arrange for a cab while you phone Mrs. Maroni. I have a coupla things to attend to, then I'll meet you by the elevator and walk you out to the cab. Deal?"

"Deal," she said, gathering her things and walking out the door.

He took out his cell and made the call. It rang many times, but finally, someone answered.

"Betty? This is Ty Raleigh, Lindsay's dad. I know the hospital's been in touch with you. I'm so sorry for your loss." He leaned back, closed his eyes, and listened.

Chapter 11

Lindsay had checked in with Louise and made plans with Mrs. Maroni. Not finding her dad at the elevator, she headed back to his office. Peeking inside, she saw him at his desk, head lowered, one hand holding the phone to his ear, fingers of the other hand lightly drumming on the base of the desk lamp. She leaned against the doorframe and eavesdropped.

"No. No, it's too early to have any leads yet. But there's something I want to do for you. It's customary in these cases to have a family member make a positive identification. But there's no need for you to see your daughter this way. I knew Heather, so I can take care of all that official business for you...no, it's not an imposition, not at all...you're welcome, Betty. And I hate to intrude, but if possible, I'd like to come over tonight and ask you a few questions." He moved his phone from one ear to the other. "Thank you for your cooperation. I know it's a difficult time." He set the phone down, folded his arms atop the desk, and laid his forehead on them.

From the doorway, Lindsay watched him for a time, then said softly, "That was a really nice thing to do...Ty."

"Thanks," he mumbled. But he didn't move right away, just savored the small victory she'd handed him. Putting aside his guilty relief that she was safe and whole, he sat up and met his daughter's solemn eyes.

"And I'm sorry I was bitchy before. I really do want to help you put this fucker away."

Ordinarily, he'd challenge her on the profanity, trying to mold her into the young woman her mother would have expected. "I know you do." He raised an eyebrow. "Now?"

She plopped into his visitor's chair. "Yup. Now."

"Okay, we'll skip over finding Heather." He noticed her features lose some of their tension. He didn't want her to dwell on that right now, or she'd never get to sleep tonight. "What I really need to know is why she was there. And why it would lead to that kind of attack."

"Um, I'm not really sure." Her foot began to jiggle. "But it's probably about the letter she found in that old leather-bound book when she was cleaning out Auntie Ed's attic."

He took out a notepad and pen. "What letter?"

"The one that might have been written by Barbara Fritchie."

Used to the way teens grudgingly relayed information, he lifted his eyebrows and waited.

"She was some old lady here in Frederick back in the day who yelled at the Confederate soldiers as they marched through on their way to some biggity, biggity Civil War battle. Then some poet guy, John...something-something...Whittier wrote a famous poem about it while the war was still going on, and it got people all charged up for the Union side." Lindsay paused, a slight frown wrinkling her brow. "Only she might not have done the yelling at all. They think it might've been some other lady."

He dutifully took notes from her disjointed account but knew he'd need to follow up with someone more knowledgeable about the poem. And he thought of Meg Adams.

"Okay, Lindsay. This's really helpful. Now, tell me why Heather was in the museum."

She hesitated. "Well, I think it was because she was supposed to meet someone who could tell her about the letter. Maybe see if it was genuine, or give her some advice or something. Maybe even buy it? I dunno."

He tried to give her as much latitude as he'd give a typical witness, but she knew more. Why she was stonewalling? This was going to take time, and time was an enemy.

"Let me see if I have this straight. Heather had arranged to meet with someone in the Barbara Fritchie Museum about an antique letter. And you're not sure why?"

"Not really." She fidgeted a little in the chair.

"Did she have the letter with her?"

"Maybe." Shrugging, she added, "I don't know."

He pinned her with his disbelieving-dad stare, hoping she'd crack.

"Okay," she sighed. "I mean, she was excited about finding it and everything. Auntie Ed, she's really Heather's great-aunt, she thought it might be valuable, and people might want to steal it or something. So she made Heather promise to be careful, not flaunt it around, you know. That's why she wouldn't tell me much. I don't know if she had the letter today or not." Lindsay paused. "She said something about maybe wanting to put it in a safe place."

"A safe place. Do you know where?"

"No."

"Did she tell you who this 'someone' was? The guy she was meeting?"

"She didn't know, so she called him her Unknown Benefactor. He only ever contacted her through text messages."

So it was someone who knew Heather's phone number. Or had access to it. And Lindsay was holding something back, alright. Maybe several somethings, but he hadn't pushed her about why she was there. Secrecy was every teen's default mode. It was too much coincidence that she just happened to be walking behind the museum and just happened to notice the open door. But he knew better than to press that point right now, knowing all he'd get was some cock and bull story about serendipity, or about how stranger things have happened. He'd work back around to that later.

"I think that's enough for now, Lindsay. Thanks. I'll get this Auntie Ed's contact information from Mrs. Hillcrest."

Her face fell. "You're gonna go over there tonight? That'll suck."

"Yeah." He leaned back in his chair and scrubbed his face with his hands. Blinking away his fatigue, he held her gaze, cementing their recent intimacy. "Yeah, it'll suck big time."

"But that's the job, right?" With sad blue eyes, she returned his comforting look.

"Yup. It is." He stood and rummaged in his closet for another jacket to conceal his weapon. Putting it on, he turned back to Lindsay. "Your cab is surely here by now, its meter ticking away. Let's get you on your way."

•　　•　　•　　•　　•

Once Lindsay was in the cab, Raleigh walked the long block to the Barbara Fritchie Museum, now awash in lights. It was actually a house that had been turned into a museum. And Fritchie hadn't really lived in it. The current house was a replica of hers, rebuilt after the original had washed away in a flood. Four rooms downstairs and two above. Odd place for a murder.

Tonight, yellow tape defined the little house as a crime scene. He veered off the jogging path behind the museum and into its scraggly backyard. The forensics people were assembling. He scanned their faces, looking for his partner.

Maroni came out the back door, running a hand over his short brown hair. "We're well underway here, sir."

"Sorry to be so long. I was up talking with Lindsay." Knowing that Maroni would ask, he said that she was doing as well as could be expected.

"But you can see for yourself later. Lindsay's spending the night at your house."

"Best place for her."

He frowned. "I don't think she's even had any dinner."

"Jenna will have her play with the kids, stuff her full of leftovers, or break out the Ben & Jerry's. Then tuck her in and send her off to dreamland."

"Well, I'm grateful. And it was her idea, not mine."

"No worries, Lieutenant."

"She did give me some additional information." He brought Maroni up to speed, then asked, "Did you find a letter on scene? Encased in an old envelope. Maybe sticking out of a leather-bound book. An antique letter?"

"No sir."

"We need to locate that letter. Need to figure out whether it's missing or stolen. We might be looking at a robbery gone bad. That's ugly enough. If not, it's likely murder to gain possession of the letter. Since it actually belongs to the deceased's great-aunt, go interview her and see what light she can shed on things. But she's elderly, so wait until tomorrow. I'll get you the address after I interview the mother tonight."

Maroni nodded.

"Do me a favor and ask the first-on-scene to come inside and give me his initial impressions. And then check around and see if the murder weapon has turned up."

"Will do."

Ty entered the museum and took his first look at the murder scene. Engrossed in forming his first impressions, he looked up when a uniformed officer walked toward him.

"Sturgis, did someone get photos of this nightmare before the EMTs took the victim away?"

"Yes sir, Lieutenant," he replied, holding out the camera.

After looking at the photos and listening to the uniform's report, Raleigh was impressed with its thoroughness and the man's respect for both the victim and the witness. He'd note that in his own report. Good work shouldn't have to be its own reward.

Dismissing the uniform, he surveyed the room again. Spotlights on tall tripods glared down on the scene. The door was intact, but Raleigh noted that it moved stiffly on its hinges and was difficult to shut. No sign of a security system, either.

He leaned over and looked at the lock. Wouldn't be hard to pop, but there wasn't any sign of forced entry, either.

"According to the owner, it's always locked," Maroni said as he came back in. "Except for tours on summer weekends and for special events. And then only with a docent present."

When Raleigh didn't comment, his partner continued.

"Owner's a local businessman. Upstanding citizen. Had an alibi for the time in question. I verified. Mostly, he was upset that his museum's a murder scene. He also gave me the names of everyone else who has a set of keys. I'll run that down."

"Good." Then he walked through the rest of the rooms, upstairs and down. His sharp gray eyes made note of the ordinary and searched for the out of place, but it seemed that all the action had been confined to the one area. He returned to the small, bloodstained room.

"Tell me what you see, Maroni. What jumps out?"

"Other than a big-ass pool of blood from a kid too young to be dead? Well, there's a cell phone on the floor. And some books. They don't look like they belong to the museum. Bindings are modern. It looks like she might have been carrying them when she was attacked."

"Good eye. We'll get back to the cell phone. What else?"

The young man looked around, anxious not to have missed anything. "I'm coming up empty, sir."

Moving to the wall beside the door, Raleigh pointed to a row of pegs. "Check this out."

Every peg but one had something hanging from it: apron, bonnet, dried herbs. Maybe something was missing. And if there was, what was it?

"Ask the owner to come in, take a look around. Something might have disappeared. Or is out of place."

The lieutenant turned his back to the door and imagined Heather coming into the room. It was clear to him how it'd gone down, but he wanted Maroni's read. See if the lad could sort it out for himself. "Give me your take. What happened here?"

Maroni took several moments to reply. "From the wounds I saw in the photos, she and her assailant must have been face to face. Blows to the left side of the head from a right-handed attacker. And there were no defensive wounds. Like she knew her attacker."

"Or?"

"Maybe he was behind the door and called out, surprised her. Maybe it all happened so quickly she didn't have time to react. Either way, the poor kid didn't stand a chance."

Clearly, the girl had fallen with her head toward the middle of the room, feet near the door. Ty leaned over to study the bloodstain, less glossy now than it had been in the photos. Some faint smearing indicated that she must have squirmed a bit after she fell. Imagining Lindsay coming in and seeing that, he shoved his hands in his pockets, hard.

"This fucker's going down," he growled.

His partner didn't answer. In fact, Maroni was acting a little off. Ty knew that Matteo had never worked a homicide. Plus he was the father of two young children. It was bound to be getting to him.

The younger man bent over and hunted for something in the field kit he'd set on the floor.

Pulling on the latex gloves Maroni handed him, Ty picked up the cell phone. It was sheathed in a purple OtterBox with the initials HH displayed in rhinestones. Keying it on, he thumbed up the last text message: "Almost there. Can't wait to show you my amazing find." The recipient was listed as Unknown Benefactor, but there were no previous texts in that thread. She must've deleted them. He pushed the little phone icon and waited for the call to go through.

The men looked at each other when they heard a ringtone nearby. Following the sound, they walked out the door and headed toward the jogging path. They stopped beside a wood-sided trash barrel. Raleigh reached in and drew out the ringing phone just as it quit.

Maroni snorted. "Looks like a burner phone. The murderer ditched it as he left."

"It's never easy, is it?" They walked back to the museum and Raleigh slipped both phones into evidence bags and handed them to this partner.

"Take care of those. Get them dusted for prints."

"Will do."

"I'll talk to the mother, then head to the hospital."

"Okay, lieutenant." He paused. "Can't you postpone that morgue thing until morning?"

Ty put a hand on the young man's shoulder. "She won't be any less dead tomorrow." After a quick squeeze, he turned to leave. "Don't stay up all night. Just put in a couple more hours. And say 'hi' to my daughter for me if she's still up."

"Sure thing," he said, walking away. A few steps later, he called back over his shoulder, "And I'll drop Lindsay off in the morning."

"Thanks," Ty said. "And be sure you spend time with Jenna, too. Decompress a little."

•　　•　　•　　•　　•

Raleigh pulled into Frederick Memorial Hospital's parking lot and cut the motor. He wanted to examine the body before they sent it off to Baltimore for autopsy. And he needed to say goodbye to his daughter's best friend. Goodbye and godspeed.

Walking into the hospital, he went over what he'd learned from Heather's mom. Not much. He did get the contact information for Auntie Ed. But as for the Unknown Benefactor and the whereabouts of the letter, the mother had no clue. Seemed that Heather could be just as secretive as Lindsay. The only concrete piece of information was that Heather had shared news of her find with a couple of her professors at TCC. Her history professor, Dr. Brunner. And her English professor, Dr. Adams. Hmm...that Meg Adams just kept turning up.

Badging his way through Security, Raleigh walked into the morgue and the night attendant pulled open a small, square steel door. "Thanks, Andre. I'll let myself out."

He waited until the man left before pulling out the tray, unwilling to trust his emotions. As he lifted the sheet, wispy strands of blonde hair peeked out, the color of buttercups.

"I'm so, so sorry, Heather." He drew in a long breath. "You didn't deserve this."

The preliminary report had noted three forceful blows to the left side of the skull, but that didn't begin to describe the damage. "Jesus...your poor mother sure doesn't need to see this."

But his grief didn't help anybody. Not Heather. Not her mother. Not even Lindsay.

He looked closely at the wounds, searching for a clue to the type of weapon used. He used his cell phone to record some impressions. Three indentations. About an inch in diameter, maybe a little more. Individual depressions. So nothing long, not a pipe or a bar of any kind. No splinters, so not wood. Metal, likely. Maybe some sort of hammer.

With nothing left to see but violence and destruction, he pulled up the sheet, ready to slide the steel bed back into its receptacle. Then he noticed her hand. Her right hand. It was outside the sheet, lying palm up, unsupported by the tray. It looked so uncomfortable hanging there. He tucked her hand under the sheet, wanting to do her some small courtesy, set something to rights.

He slid the tray back and closed the little door. Flipping the light off, he walked toward the parking garage and into the chilly fall night.

Chapter 12

Lindsay turned off the lamp on the nightstand and burrowed under the covers of the spare bed in the Maroni's house. The soft sheets were pale blue, not like the superhero and fire engine ones in the little boys' room down the hall. She drew a long breath to try and settle the shivers that wanted to come, concentrated on the scent of Mrs. Maroni's fabric softener.

Since sleep was playing hide and seek, she lifted her journal off the nightstand and keyed on her cell phone's flashlight. She didn't want to turn on the light and worry the adults. Settling the book on her tummy, it fell open to the place where she'd left her pen. She began to write:

Tuesday: October 28th
Heather died today. At the Barbara Fritchie Museum. She was murdered. I found her, was supposed to meet her there, and I...

"And I don't want to think about it," she whispered.

She returned everything to the nightstand. Turning on her side, she looked out the window and wished she was home with her dad. When she couldn't sleep, he'd make popcorn, put it on the couch between them and channel surf until he found her a chic flick.

The next morning she'd wake up in her own bed. All tucked in, safe and cozy.

Chapter 13

It was still dark when Meg awoke, dry mouthed and disoriented, to find herself on top of the covers and wearing her clothes from the day before—same pale pink blouse, same tan chinos. Then she remembered why. Heather.

Sadness stole back in, scattering the peace of sleep. The blue-glowing numbers of the alarm clock told her it was 4:49 a.m. She worked on going back to sleep, but her brooding thoughts dogged her. Did Heather suffer? Had she been scared?

Meg grabbed the spare pillow—a self-comforting response, something to hug. But the hugging sent her thoughts toward a soft-spoken man with a teasing manner and kind eyes who'd made sure she was warm and steadied her when she stumbled. And who routinely carried a gun.

Unsettled by her complicated and conflicting feelings, she gave up all hope of sleep and eased out of bed. A shower might help. If the hot water held out.

Half an hour later she was downstairs dressed in black gabardine slacks, ankle boots, and a ribbed, red cotton sweater. She was tired and jittery but determined to get herself together. While the coffee brewed and scented the room, she glanced out the window beside the front door to confirm that her truck had made it back in the night. It had. Kudos to Keefer and Groves, those dependable boys in blue from the last evening's academy.

She wrestled two sets of papers out of her book bag, sat at the kitchen table and started reading students' journal responses to poems by Brian Turner, an Iraq war veteran.

An hour or so later, they were finished. She'd polished off the coffee along with some instant oatmeal and was eyeing the next stack of papers. Essays. Longer, harder to grade. Not gonna happen. Whatever concentration she'd had was gone.

Putting the dishes in the sink, she shoved her school things back in the book bag then opened the fridge to slice off a hunk of pumpkin pie and put it in a container. Pie was David's favorite, and he deserved a treat. Maybe she'd even get a couple of Starbucks cards for Groves and Keefer. Eventually.

She went to grab her favorite extra-long cardigan from the coat rack but instead lifted down the borrowed windbreaker. Tugging it on, she sniffed the collar. No cologne. Just him.

Shaking her head to clear it, she gathered her stuff, locked the door, and got in her pickup. When she turned the key, there was no spark of life, only a weak groan. "Come on, sweetie," she coaxed. "It's early, I know." But David would be in his office soon. He'd be up for a visit. Probably expected it.

On the next try, the engine caught. "Yay, Rocinante. Let's go see our buddy." Joan, too. She needed to hear about last night's events. Both the good and the sad.

As the sun brightened, Meg turned on the radio to WFRE and caught the middle of Don McLean's *American Pie*. Usually, she was struck by the song's uncanny timelessness, but today its chorus made her shiver. She turned it off.

A half-hour later as she was exiting Opossumtown Pike and turning onto campus, she forced herself to concentrate on her surroundings, grounding herself in the here and now, taking in the poplar trees that lined the main entrance road and the rose-colored brick buildings. It wasn't a huge campus. Only eleven buildings to serve the 5000 full-time students as well as a plethora of part-timers and continuing ed students. The College offered traditional degree programs like English, math, and history along with career programs like nursing and police science. And because Frederick was home to the state-wide school for the deaf, TCC offered a degree in sign language. But it had kept up with the times, too, adding classes like the graphic design ones that her friend Lavale taught, as well as cybersecurity and emergency management. Meg had had other job offerings, but she loved it here. Loved that in its 50-year history it had grown from 76 students in a small, downtown location to over 8,000 students in all of its offerings, both on-campus and online.

Meg cruised into a space in the only gated faculty-parking area, the one outside Hamilton Hall. It was one of the newest buildings, and as such was a joint-use space that housed classrooms, faculty offices, and student recreational spaces as well as the bookstore, cafeteria, and security.

Her office was on the second floor, but David's was in the Bergan building, across the quad, and through the commemorative garden. Minutes later, she was tapping on his office door. "Hey, I brought you a little something. A thank you for last night's rescue."

"You didn't have to do that." He waved her in, took the pie from her and grinned. "But I'm mighty glad you did." His expression turned serious. "How're y'doin'?"

"Okay, I guess." She plopped into one of his comfy, mismatched visitor chairs. The office was furnished with homey cast offs. It usually relaxed her. "Slept deeply but not long enough." She couldn't unwind, even here. "I woke up thinking about Heather."

"That's understandable."

"I'll have to go over it again when some random detective comes by with questions."

"Oh, I guess you don't know. Well, how could you? Raleigh called me late last night to say he was assigned to Heather's case."

Meg sat straighter, uneasy and excited at the same time.

"That's really good," David continued. "He's very experienced in solving murders."

When she didn't respond, he gave her a searching look. "You aren't feeling like any of this is your fault, are you?"

"No, I'm good," she said, adopting a light tone. But not a particularly believable one. "I mean, it's just coincidence, isn't it? I'm not the one who coshed her over the head."

"Meg-han..."

"Not now, David. I'm trying to keep it together. It's a full morning. Interrogation at 9:30 and class at 11:00."

"You're not a suspect. My boy Ty's not going to grill you," David said gently. "You're just providing background information that could help explain why the girl was at the scene. It's all because of some old letter, right? The one Brunner's been goin' on about."

"Yeah, the one supposedly written by Barbara Fritichie."

He shrugged. "Just tell Raleigh what you know and anything that keeps niggling at you. He'll put it all together. He's a sharp guy. Certainly Frederick's finest."

"Thanks. That helps." She hesitated, her stomach churning a little at her next thought. "You've known him for a while, haven't you?"

"Yeah, we've worked together on a number of task forces over the years." He sipped his coffee. "When he wanted to relocate to Frederick four, five years ago, I hooked him up with a realtor friend who sold him the house over by Hood College."

"Here's the thing." Her discomfort intensified, but she continued. "He and I got to talking last night during break, and it was going really well."

Seeing David raise an eyebrow, her stomach lurched a bit. "But all that happened before either of us knew about Heather, I swear."

He sat back and considered her. "You're not a pair of monsters if that's what you're worried I'm thinking. Life has its own timing. Can't be anticipated or controlled."

"Thanks." Her cheeks puffed out as she sighed. "I'm so mixed up right now. Sad and anxious and stirred up." She'd tried to talk herself out of asking, but she couldn't. "What can you tell me about him?"

His eyes were kind, but his answer stung.

"Nothing."

"Nothing?"

"No, Meghan. It's your job to find out."

"I already know he has a daughter, but I need to know if he's single."

"He's not currently married if that helps." When she started to say more, he shook his head. "I'm sorry, Meg. Really." Then he leaned forward to briefly touch her arm. "But his life story is his to tell."

"Oh. Okay." Did that make it a good or a bad story? Probably a sad one, like hers.

David tapped one hand lightly on the desk blotter. "If memory serves, that's what dating is about, a tennis game of finding things out, back and forth. Seeing what you have in common. Sharing your stories...the funny ones and the ones that define you. And in time, revealing your soft underbelly. That's a lot of what makes it so exciting, isn't it? A jigsaw puzzle of the not-knowing being filled in by the finding-out."

"I hate it when you're right. But I really sort of like this guy, and that's totally unprecedented because he's a cop." She looked away, her anxiety inching up by the minute. "And I'm still hurting from the whole Al thing. My confidence is really, really low."

David pulled at his bottom lip. "Y'know...from time to time I think about giving Al some grief." His serious eyes began to twinkle. "In my days as a parole officer, I knew guys who would break knee caps for a carton of cigarettes. You want I should look up one of them?"

She laughed. "It's tempting, but no." Then her features and voice grew harsh. "However, how about something nastier for his concubine?"

"Meghan..."

"Okay, okay. But I'm still bitter."

"Gotta get over that, my friend."

"Not sure when. But I'm trying to move on, aren't I?"

"Yes, you are. And Raleigh's a cut above your recent dating lineup." He chuckled, and his dark green eyes took on a playful gleam. "Better than the one who was dragged away from the restaurant table by a deputy with a bench warrant. Got arrested for evading child support, didn't he."

"It might be funny now. Back then, it was humiliating."

"Putting aside the whole cop thing, there's no harm in getting to know my boy Raleigh. You have my word."

"And your word is your bond. I know."

He stood and pulled her out of the chair, then put his hand on her shoulder. "Meg, want some advice?"

"Absolutely."

"Go slow. He's been pretty busted up, too. And that daughter's *real* important to him."

"She should be. He's her father. I admire a man who takes his commitments seriously."

"Sorta like me, huh?" he joked. "And my most pressing commitment is to this next class. I'm giving an exam. I can't be late, or they'll freak. Gotta run. Sorry."

•　　•　　•　　•　　•

Opening her office door, Meg sat at the desk and checked her messages. The first one was from the lieutenant, saying he'd be in around 9:30 or so. She glanced around her office and groaned. Stuff in folders that hadn't been refiled and piles of books in the guest chair. Messy stacks of ungraded papers on the desk and a variety of shoes strewn about the floor.

She tidied quickly and haphazardly, stuffing most of it in file drawers. Sitting down, she organized the papers on her desk. Once finished, she realized she'd accumulated something from every one of her students. She blew out a frazzled breath. "I liked it better when I didn't know how bad things were."

"That is so like you, you silly girl," Joan teased.

Meg looked up to see her friend leaning in the doorway.

"Reality has never suited you." She smoothed the hem of her burgundy suit jacket. "It's hard to maintain that pie-in-the-sky optimism if you pay attention to the facts."

Meg sagged for a moment, wondering how to start. "Joan, it's so good to see you."

"Of course. I should imagine it always is."

Unable to say more, Meg sighed, and her eyes moistened.

Joan looked around the orderly office in disbelief. "What's this all about?" When no reply came, she studied her friend's face. "Are those tears?"

"Where were you last night?" Her voice quivered.

"At TJ middle school. Chloe's daughter was singing in their chorale. Then we went out for ice cream." Joan stepped into the office, closer to Meg. "What's wrong, baby-girl?"

"Something terrible."

Joan soared in and drew up a chair close beside her friend. "What? What's terrible?"

"One of my students, Heather, was murdered last night." She straightened in her chair as her spirits sank. "And I think it was my fault."

"Heather Hillcrest? I heard something about that on the radio this morning. She was your student? I'm so sorry, honey. But how could you possibly be responsible?"

Meg fought not to cry. "She was murdered in the Barbara Fritchie Museum, and she must have been there because of my assignment. The one where they have to do on-site research."

"Child, you've handed out that assignment dozens of times, and nobody's ever come to harm before." She touched Meg's elbow. "You're jumping to conclusions."

"Maybe. I don't know. But I have to talk to a police officer about it in a little bit."

"Then let's work on getting you calmed down." She looked around. "And I imagine this impending inquisition explains the unnatural state of your office, too."

"Sort of." Meg took a deep breath and started in. "Because you kept nagging me, I went to that Police Academy last night. And yes, Officer Krupke was there...and yes, he wanted to talk. But that's when things got weird."

Joan's expression was a mix of amusement and confusion. "Go on."

At that invitation, even Katie herself couldn't have barred the door. Meg was breathless by the time she finished her rambling account.

Joan brought up her hand. "Whoa, girl, whoa! This is going to take a lot of processing, and I have class in a few minutes." She frowned, considering. "I can't cancel it because the students are giving their demonstration speeches."

"I don't need you to cancel class. I just needed to unload. I'm okay."

"Meggie, when you babble like this, you are never 'okay.' Nervous, yes. Embarrassed, yes. Stressed, absolutely. But okay? Never."

"No, really. What I needed was to see you, talk to you. Because you're my Valium. I'll be fine now. Or will be in the long run, especially after I talk to the lieutenant about Heather." She stood. "But I will take a hug."

As they broke apart after the embrace, Joan held Meg's hands.

"Sorting this out will take more than a piddly ol' hug, girlfriend. There is too much going on." She squeezed her friend's hands before letting go. "We'll talk more when I get back from class."

At the door, Joan turned back. "Take some time to get back into your skin. Try some diaphragmatic breathing."

"Deep breaths. Seriously? That's it. Where's the Glotfelty wit?"

A smirk built on her face. "You could put on some nice, soothing, white-people music."

They laughed at each other, and Joan sauntered off.

From the hall, she called back. "Try some Beethoven. It'll help you wait and calm you down. Until Lieutenant Handcuffs arrives."

Chapter 14

Unable to find a vacant spot in TCC's main parking lot, Ty pulled his SUV into one of seven spaces clearly marked "For Board Members Only." He encountered few people as he walked into Hamilton Hall where a quick stop at the Security Office provided him with an exemption for his vehicle, directions to the office of TCC's president, and Meg's office number.

A courtesy call to the College administration was SOP. But he'd already been summoned. Before he'd gotten a chance to place the call himself, the duty officer at headquarters phoned him indicating that his presence was requested at President Collins's office at the earliest possible moment. Well, here he was.

Walking into the executive office suite, he showed his credentials and introduced himself to the crisply dressed woman at the front desk.

"Of course, Lieutenant," she said in a discreet voice. She pressed a button on her desk phone. "She's expecting you. Go right in."

Entering the plush-carpeted office, the first thing that struck him was the view of the hump-backed mountains, a vista suitable to a president's status. He imagined that was everybody's reaction. Probably planned that way. The spacious room featured both an executive desk and a sitting area.

Delores Collins rose from one of the green velvet, wingback chairs and offered her hand. "Thank you for coming, Lieutenant Raleigh. This is a terrible shock to us all, but the mayor assures me that you are the right man for the job and will get things taken care of in short order."

Raleigh returned her greeting, taking note of her sensible beige suit and short cap of gray hair. African American, medium skin tone. Light brown eyes, designer eyeglasses. Long, heart-shaped face. 5' 6". Trim build. Mid-60s, probably. A no-nonsense type of woman.

He shifted his attention to the other occupant of the room. A well-groomed, fit, dark-haired woman in a plain, dark blue pantsuit. Early 40s, 5' 9" with an average build and an attractive face. Or it would have been except that her faded blue eyes were sort of bulgy. Probably a thyroid thing.

She nodded her head and gripped his hand with determination. "And I'm Maria Routzhan, Director of Public Relations and also spokesperson for the College. I called your office this morning as soon as I heard the news."

Raleigh studied her. So she was the one. Was she pushy, or proactive?

President Collins took back center stage. "Maria is very efficient, lieutenant. Always on top of things and anticipating problems. She's my right-hand woman, and I've assigned her to be the liaison with you in this matter."

He smiled at Routzhan but got only another curt nod in return.

"As I've just informed President Collins," she began, "the College must do everything it can to contain this situation. It could be very damaging to the school's reputation."

"Yes, of course. I understand the need for discretion." But not why they hadn't mentioned their dead student.

"You'll need to keep me fully informed."

"I'll be sure to give you any necessary information as soon as it's available." If and when he decided to share.

"For my part, I will provide you with all the information you'll need from this end."

"I don't expect that I'll need that much from you, Ms. Routzhan," he drawled. "The police department uses its own PR people for things like this."

"I've already fielded quite a few calls about last evening's incident without having anything to tell them. My top priority is to help resolve this unpleasantness as soon as possible. It couldn't have happened at a more inopportune time."

The PR flack was like so many others he'd encountered over the years, concerned about their own agendas and seemingly oblivious to the rest of the world. He had to concentrate as she went on about how much she had on her plate, how the college didn't need any kind of negative publicity ahead of this week's Civil War conference.

"President Collins was hosting a reception for one of the visiting scholars last evening, and I was so busy setting up for that that I almost didn't have time to get my dog to Doc McClellan's."

"You went to the vet's yesterday evening?" He cut into her litany, realizing the vet details might be of interest. "When, exactly?"

"They close at 5:00 p.m., but I called to say I was running late, and the vet tech waited for me. They needed to keep my Priscilla overnight. I got her there a few minutes after five, the tech got her settled in, then he and I walked out together."

"So you left around 5:15 or so. Did you see anyone as you left? Notice anyone hanging around or hear anything odd?"

"No. I don't think so. Why?"

"The murder occurred next door sometime between 5:30 and 6:00."

"No, really? That's scary. I mean, I was right there. Am I in any danger?"

"I very much doubt it. You say that you didn't see anything, but I'd like the name of the vet tech."

"Alvin. Alvin Lescalleet." She paused, her puzzled look turning brighter. "Oh, I get it. You're going to find out if he saw anything."

"Yes, ma'am. A lot of police work is spent double-checking facts." Maybe he'd get lucky with this Lescalleet character. He'd set Maroni on that little detail.

"This whole business was already very upsetting, but now it's hitting home."

With a sympathetic glance at Maria, President Collins spoke again. "All of us here at the College are deeply disturbed by the death of one of our students. I'll be contacting the girl's mother later this morning to offer my condolences. But it's Maria's job to handle these sorts of incidents. We'll cooperate fully, of course. I'm just relieved it isn't worse. Given the location of the murder, I'm sure your investigation will take place off campus."

He dropped his bombshell as tactfully as he could. "No, not exactly. The College is more involved than you believe. The site of the murder might have been chosen because of an assignment Miss Hillcrest was working on for her English class."

Both women stared at him. The president's expression remained composed, but it was easy to see the wheels turning. He imagined that she was already planning what she'd say in her call to the College's lawyers. Routzhan couldn't hide her agitation.

Collins recovered herself first. "Whose English class?"

Before he could speak, Maria cut in. "I'll bet it was that Meg Adams and her site research project. I've warned her that it's dangerous to encourage students to go to some of those places. The Poe house is located in the projects of Baltimore. Someone could get hurt. But faculty always think they know best," she said with some asperity.

Hmm, hard feelings between the two? And yup, Routzhan was proactive alright. And pushy. "Perhaps the connection between your student's death and her English assignment is merely coincidental." He spoke to soothe them, but he had his doubts. "I thought you should know. It is not, however, something we want getting into the news outlets."

"No, of course not." The president turned to her PR expert. "I'm counting on you to keep a lid on this, Maria. And stay in close contact with the detective, so we continue to find out things like this and deal with them expeditiously."

Maria gave her a brisk nod.

"There is one other thing I need," Raleigh said. "A list of the students in Heather Hillcrest's American Literature class."

"Are you sure that's necessary?" Maria blurted. "It will be very hard to contain the situation once students are involved."

"It can't be helped. But I assure you that my partner, Detective Maroni, and I will be very tactful during the interviews. If you'd just email me the list at your earliest convenience," he said as he handed Maria one of his business cards. "And we'll be sure to explain to the students the need for discretion."

The president's expression had turned worried. "Is there anything else you need or that I should know?"

"Nothing of which I'm currently aware. Thank you for your time, ma'am."

Routzhan pulled a business card out of her suit jacket pocket and wrote something on the back. "Here's my contact information, lieutenant, including my cell number. I expect we'll be talking frequently."

"I'll add you to my list." Or if he was lucky, palm her off on his PR guy.

His next words included both women. "But all you really know at this point is what's been reported in the media. Stick to that. When there's more to share, you'll hear from me."

⋅　　⋅　　⋅　　⋅　　⋅

Heading up the stairs to the second floor of Hamilton Hall, he shifted his focus to the next task—interviewing Meg. But his cop thoughts were crowded out by his personal ones. Yes, he was attracted to her. She was a fine-looking woman, intelligent and compassionate. But the timing sucked. He had to put his feelings on hold, be professional. Get his game face on.

He slowed as he approached her open door and heard music. "Beethoven?" he murmured as a smile twitched his lips. Taking a deep breath, he squared his shoulders under the tan corduroy jacket to settle his shoulder holster in place. Standing in her doorway, he stopped and studied her domain.

The office was almost a perfect ten-foot square, with large windows lining the wall that faced the faculty parking lot. Instead of a series of diplomas, the items on the walls highlighted its occupant's interests. He noted the framed photographs of smiling people in exotic locations: Meg standing at the base of an Aztec ruin; a parka-clad Meg amongst a group of people in front of a colorful, onion-domed cathedral...likely Russia. He particularly liked the one of Meg cracking up as she stood beside her friend, the much taller black woman who scowled at the camera, both wearing orange Mae West life vests. For some mandatory lifeboat drill, maybe? Rounding out the photographs was a faded one of a white-muzzled chocolate lab looking adoringly at a young, pigtailed Meg. Beside the photo hung a worn leather dog collar with a brass nameplate: Buddy. The other walls were covered in posters of national parks—Yellowstone, Canyon de Chelly, the Great Smoky Mountains—and what looked like student projects, handsomely framed.

And then there was Meg herself, eyes closed, apparently napping. But he was in no hurry to change the situation. In fact, having the opportunity to study her suited him fine. She sat pushed back from her desk, facing the open door, her eyes closed. One elbow rested on the arm of the chair, the heel of that hand supporting her head. The other hand lay in her lap, palm up, near the intriguing line where red sweater met black pants. Her face was calm but pale, accentuating the dark circles under her eyes. That she hadn't slept well didn't surprise him. How worried that made him, did.

Her breath was slow and rhythmic, with a little puff of air escaping her lips at the beginning of each outbreath. A soft smile built on his face, but he remained silent. After a minute or so, he cleared his expression and knocked on the metal doorframe.

In a flash, she sat up straight, then blinked several times. "Oh, Lieutenant Raleigh." She fumbled to turn off the music and stood hastily. "Please come in."

"Thank you, ma'am." He stepped across the threshold and waited, hands clasped in front of him. "Is this a convenient time?"

"Yes, of course." She glanced at Raleigh's hands. "I don't have class until 11:00."

"I'll try not to take too much of that time." He nodded his head toward the stack of student papers. "I can see that you're busy."

"Oh, those...an occupational hazard. English faculty often drown in these things." She waved a hand at the pile but kept her eyes on him. "We get more than anybody else."

He just stood there, unsure of how to respond. Wondered if the double entendre was intentional or a Freudian slip. "I imagine so," he said, his tone as neutral as his face.

"Yes, well," Meg said nervously. "Won't you have a seat?"

"Thank you." He stood until she sat back down. Then he sat in the visitor chair across from her desk, settled his palms atop his brown slacks, and waited for her to get comfortable.

She pulled her chair closer to the desk.

"I trust you're feeling better this morning?" he said.

"Oh...yes. Thank you. I had a little trouble sleeping, though."

"That's not unexpected. The news was quite shocking."

She looked puzzled like she'd been expecting something else.

"Professor Adams, I—"

Raising an eyebrow, she interrupted him, her tone a little sharp. "It's 'Meg,' remember?"

"Meg." He nodded. "I made some notes from what you said last evening. I'd like to review them for accuracy. If that's alright?"

"Of course. I'm astonished that I said anything coherent last night. I might've misspoken. And probably left things out.

"Let's find out, shall we?" He fished a pen and a small spiral-bound notepad out of the inner breast pocket of his comfortably rumpled jacket.

Flipping open the notepad, Raleigh began reciting from his notes and ended with, "In short, your relationship with the deceased was somewhat social as well as academic." He looked up. "Is that correct?"

"Sort of." Meg flushed slightly. "I mean, yes, I've had her as a student for three semesters. And she drops by the office some. But it's not unprofessional to have coffee with a student."

"I didn't mean to suggest otherwise. But by your own admission, she made an appointment with you to discuss something this morning about which she was either..." He checked his notes and then looked directly at Meg again. "'Excited or agitated.'"

She gave a quick nod.

"Plus she was in your 2 o'clock class yesterday, which must have ended between 3:15 and 3:30. And that's just a few hours before she was murdered."

Meg's eyes moistened.

He noticed but didn't comfort her. Couldn't get personal. "You might have valuable information about her activities and state of mind that day. All I'm trying to do right now is ascertain how insightful your observations might be, how well you knew the girl."

As she sighed, her features lost some of their sharpness. "Oh, I see. I'm sorry for getting defensive, but this is even harder than I thought it would be. I've never known anyone who was murdered. Never been interviewed by the police. It's unnerving."

Raleigh's manner thawed for a moment, his gray eyes warmer. "I'm very sorry for your loss." He paused, uncertain of how much to share. "This isn't easy for any of us who knew her."

Meg, seldom at a loss for words, didn't respond. In the silence, each respected the other's grief.

Then he veered away from the personal. "Anything that you can add will help me see the big picture."

"Of course." She smiled weakly and nodded. "What do you want to know?"

"You could start by telling me about Heather the last time you saw her. What she said. How she was feeling. What she planned on doing."

"Right. Well, yesterday I was running a little late to class, and she was standing outside the classroom, waiting for me as it turned out, but also finishing a phone call."

"Do you know what the call was about? Who she was speaking to?"

"No, not a clue. I do remember her saying something like, 'Wow, really? I'll call you later. Gotta go.'" She shrugged. "It sounded like generic 18-year-old speak."

"And this was right before class. Say about 2 o'clock?"

"Oh! You'll check her phone records. It might have been the killer setting up the meeting at the museum, right?"

He didn't reply.

Meg smiled uncertainly before continuing. "After that, she turned to me and said, 'I really need to talk to you. When's a good time?'"

The detective held up a hand. "Can you recall her tone of voice? Both on the phone and when she began talking to you?"

"The phone call didn't seem to faze her. Just run of the mill, I think—if I had to guess." Meg leaned back in her chair. "When she first started talking to me directly, her tone was earnest at first then got excited, or maybe even agitated near the end."

"What did she say? As close to her exact wording as possible."

"Well, she said 'I *really* need to talk.' Then something like,'I don't have time to stay after class today because something's come up. But I need your advice.' I think that's nearly exactly what she said. I told her that I had a faculty meeting at 3:30 anyway and class at the Academy after that at 5:00, so I wouldn't be available until the next day."

"Did she say anything else?"

"Um, she said she'd come by during my office hours and fill me in on what was happening. It was then that she sounded either excited or agitated because she added that by the next day she'd 'really, *really*' need my advice. Then we both walked into class."

When he finished taking notes and looked up at Meg, her face was drawn. But she was holding up pretty well. The woman had some grit to her.

Meg's voice trembled when she said, "I should really be talking to Heather now, not you."

He drew in a breath and let it out slowly. "I know this is hard, Meg. But it's really important." His smile was serious but encouraging. "And you're doing a great job."

"Thanks," she said after a ragged exhale.

"So that's what happened before class," he said, businesslike again. "Was there anything else that involved Heather during class itself, or afterward?"

"Near the end of class Heather shared a lot of information she had collected about Edgar Allan Poe. It was a big deal for her because she's so introverted. She hardly ever talks in class unless I call on her...sorry, 'talked.'" Meg stopped her story abruptly, correcting herself again. "She hardly ever talked."

Meg kept quiet for so long that Raleigh looked at her questioningly.

"Is that how you knew her?" she asked. "As quiet and shy?"

At first, he wasn't going to answer. But what could it hurt? Give a little to get a little. A classic interrogation technique. "My daughter's too young to drive yet. Most of the time I spent with Heather these past four years was usually in the car, taking the two of them different places. And no, they weren't quiet."

He wondered what it would be like to go places with Meg...chatting away, laughing. After a few quiet moments, he caught her questioning look and cleared his throat. "Is there any more you'd like to add to your statement about that last interaction?"

After a brief hesitation, she admitted that one of Heather's classmates, Jon Sellers, had been unnecessarily rude to her.

He hastily dropped his gaze to the notepad and tightened his fingers around the pen. "Can you describe this Sellers character?"

"A bright, attractive kid, but his sarcasm ruins it. At least for me. He's got longish black hair that falls below his ears but not past his collar; no facial hair; blue eyes behind round, steel-rimmed glasses..."

He tuned out most of her description once he figured out it was the Jon Sellers he already knew. But he was impressed at her accurate read of the kid's character, the specificity of her description and the fact that she didn't ramble like most witnesses. She sounded like a cop.

"And here's something else," she continued. "At the beginning of the faculty meeting, before your remarks, David told me that Jon and Heather used to be an item, but that it had ended badly. I really don't know those details. Heather never shared her social life with me."

Raleigh willed his face to stay placid, knowing he would follow up that lead. Personally.

He flipped back through his notebook. "Let's see if I've got this straight." After he summarized the last known hour of Heather's life, he looked at Meg again.

"Wow, that's very succinct," she said. "How would you like to visit my EN 101 classes sometime and teach the art of writing summary quotations?"

"Thanks, but I think I'd rather stick with investigating drug activity or larcenies and rousting bad guys. Less daunting."

She laughed. "And you surely have a higher likelihood of success."

Chapter 15

"Professor Adams?" said a muted voice from just beyond Meg's open office door.

Inwardly she groaned at Shaggy's interruption. "Good morning, Nate. Is it mail time already?"

"Yup." He sorted through the piles on his cart and picked up two rubber-banded bundles of mail; one internal, one external. "Here's your stuff." Ambling in, he leaned around the detective and set the mail on the corner of her desk.

The boy seemed unsettled that she had a visitor. But his need overrode his restraint.

"It's so creepy about Heather, isn't it?" He stared beyond her out the window as he continued. "I mean we were like, all there with her yesterday just a coupla hours before she got, um...dead. Everybody's talking about it."

The ensuing pause grew long. No one seemed to know how to break it. Then Nate's sad eyes sought out his professor's.

"Do you know anything?"

Meg caught the detective's cautioning glance. Nodding back at him, she addressed her student. "No, Nate. No more than you do."

He kept looking at her.

"I know it's upsetting, but the College is trying to help. I read an email on Communication Central this morning saying that the counseling staff is available to talk to students. Maybe you should go see somebody."

He shifted from one foot to the other, shook his head, and loped out the door.

"Sorry about that," Meg said to her guest. "Now—"

Before she could continue, Nate came back. "Sorry, Professor Adams. Those're the wrong ones." He replaced the first set of bundles with another and left with a subdued, "Have a good one."

"He's one of mine." Meg sighed. "A work-study student. Willing but not always able." Then she perked up. "If you want I could talk to him later, see what the students know?"

"No need. I've got my partner on it. He's not much older than they are. He'll blend in."

"Okay, sure." She hesitated. "It's just that I want to *do* something."

"You are doing something, giving me information."

She blundered on. "Heather might not have been in the museum if it hadn't been for my assignment."

"Meg, don't go there," he said firmly. "Your assignment didn't cause the girl's death. However, it does seem relevant. Heather was working on a project about the museum and then ends up murdered inside its walls. Since I don't believe in coincidences, I need to know what your project entails."

"Oh, okay. Well, they have to do research on one of six authors whose work is connected somehow to this geographic area. In addition to the internet research on the author and his work, they have to go visit the local site that's connected to the literature and write their impressions, tell how it makes them feel. The assignment involves both objective and subjective writing."

Raleigh looked thoughtful. "Have you given this assignment before?"

"Sure. Loads of times."

She looked up to catch him nodding to himself, a calculating expression in his eyes. She could almost see him making connections.

"Would you like a copy?"

"Yes, please. I need a copy on record."

She began to rummage on her desk. "I'll do whatever I can to help you catch this killer."

"You're already an asset." He shot her a quick smile. "You're the most informed contact I've located. As far as we know, you're the last person to've seen the victim alive, and you've given insight into her state of mind and intended movements. From your account, we've learned that Heather planned to meet someone after your class."

"And from there it's not a big leap to guess that the meeting place was the Barbara Fritchie Museum." She gave up on finding the paper on her desk and began looking for the file in her computer. "But it's an odd location for a murder. They could've met lots of other places more remote than that. I mean, it's just a block from the police station."

Because none of that was news to him, she didn't expect a response. Plus his smile was gone, so she knew he wasn't going to share his thoughts. It was like sitting in a stopped car while she waited for him to write her up for speeding. Cops were so uncommunicative. She found the right file and hit the print button.

"It's actually a retired colleague's assignment," she began, filling the silence. "But I admired it so much she gifted it to me."

She remembered when Anne first told her about the project and how it melded the intellectual and the emotional—thought and feeling. What resonated for her was how electrifying it had been to walk through Shakespeare's childhood home when she was sightseeing in Stratford. To see the signatures of famous people etched into the diamond-shaped window panes. Many of them were literary luminaries in their own right, like Charles Dickens and Sir Walter Scott. All of them going there to honor the Bard, just like her.

The printer finished humming at its task. She smiled self-consciously as she held out the page he needed.

He scanned the assignment. "Heather could've researched any one of these six men. But she chose John Greenleaf Whittier, author of the poem, 'Barbara Frietchie.' I'm familiar with the other names, but not this Whittier. Who's he?"

"Like Henry Wadsworth Longfellow, he was one of the Fireside Poets— 19th century New Englanders whose poems were so popular that they were read aloud to whole families gathered around their hearths." She chuckled at the perplexed look on his face. "Their version of a family video night."

"Gotcha." He pursed his lips while he read some more. "I did my due diligence on Fritchie. Got the Wikipedia lowdown on the museum and the woman for whom it was named. But it said that she probably wasn't the actual heroine. It would help if you filled in any gaps."

Of course she could improve on Wikipedia's blurb. Not that her students imagined they'd need to do so. She let out the long-suffering sigh of educators everywhere.

"In the poem, General Stonewall Jackson marches his troops past her house on their way to what will become known as the Battle of Antietam."

"*That* I've heard about. A pivotal battle that ended as a tactical draw. But since the Confederate troops were the ones to withdraw, militarily it was a Union victory."

"You're right on the money." Very knowledgeable, in fact. Maybe he was a history major in college. Or did he even go to college? "But the poem takes liberties with the history. Like adding conversations and motivations which can't be substantiated. For instance, having Jackson order his troops to shoot down the Union flag flying in the old woman's upstairs window. In the poem, they shatter the window and manage to break the flag's staff, but Dame Fritchie snatches it up and continues to wave it. To quote her famous line from the poem: 'Shoot, if you must, this old gray head / but spare your country's flag' she said.'"

Meg looked to Raleigh for a comment, but none was forthcoming. "Then the poet imagines Stonewall's reaction."

Looking the detective square in the eye, she recited that section of the ballad:

A shade of sadness, a blush of shame
Over the face of the leader came;

The nobler nature within him stirred
To life at that woman's deed and word:

'Who touches a hair of yon gray head
Dies like a dog! March on!' he said.

Having finished her recitation, Meg went silent, determined to remain so until he reacted.

Raleigh's face looked troubled. "It's dramatic. But it's fiction, right?"

"Yes and no." She wondered how this Southern boy felt about the legendary Stonewall. "The poet crafted the language to convey his own point of view. Factually speaking, we don't know what the general said, much less what he felt, and he didn't actually ride with the troops as they marched down Patrick Street. And while there's evidence that some version of the event occurred, various details are in dispute. But I'll bring you up to speed and give you the unvarnished facts first, okay?"

"I appreciate it," he said, running a hand through his hair. "I really need an accurate overview of things."

'Overviews R Us," she said with pride. "So here goes. There's no question that Stonewall Jackson passed through Frederick on his way Antietam, twenty-five miles to the west of here."

She recounted how Whittier had received a letter from a novelist friend of his in Washington D.C, a Mrs. E.D.E.N. Southworth, which included an account of the Barbara Fritichie story and a suggestion that it might be material for a rousing poem. Based on her info, he'd written 'Barbara Frietchie,' using the German spelling of her last name.

She waited a moment, giving him time to process the information. "We also know that Whittier was a staunch abolitionist, a Quaker. When published, his poem became a rallying point for the Union cause."

She paused again, watching the detective as he gazed out the window behind her and tapped the pen lightly against his lips. After a few minutes, she found him looking at her again. *Busted.*

When he spoke, his tone was casual, but he watched her closely. "Did Heather ever mention a letter she found in an old diary?"

Frowning, she wondered at this shift in questioning. "The one that appears to have been written by Fritchie herself? Yeah, sure."

"You've seen it?"

"No, not the letter itself. She told me about it, though." Meg's eyes lit up. "And she gave me a xerox of the first page."

"Really," he said quietly. "Do you still have it?"

"Sure. It's here somewhere." She shuffled through the first pile on her desk. "This could take a while," she confessed. "The xerox might even be at home. Is it important?"

"Somewhat."

The lieutenant leaned forward as if his proximity would produce the desired results.

"Okay, I'll keep an eye out for it."

"I'd appreciate your making it a priority." He blew out a breath. "Not right this minute, but sometime today."

"Sure, but why is a copy so important? Heather had the original." Sudden understanding flooded her face. "It's missing, isn't it? The letter is missing, and that's why she was killed."

His features became notably neutral, gray eyes keen but cool, very much the investigating officer. "This is an on-going investigation. I can neither confirm nor deny your suppositions."

She wanted to start in on him for being such a hard-ass, but he spoke again before she could get it together.

"Meg, I can't tell you anything. You have no need to know."

Her face flushed at the reproach and she looked down abruptly.

Raleigh exhaled a long breath. "I'm sorry about this," he said, voice subdued. "But you don't want to know everything that I know."

Her stomach tightened as she imagined what that *everything* meant. Probably icky, grisly crime-scene things. "You're right. I'm sorry. I have to remind myself that I'm not in charge. Occupational hazard."

"I can understand that you want answers. And given your connection to the girl, you want to help, too. It's just that answers frequently come later than we'd like."

In the ensuing quiet, the phone conversation of a neighboring professor became faintly audible.

The detective shifted in his chair. The tension around his gray eyes remained, but the eyes themselves had lost their chill.

"I don't mean to be rude, Meg. But I really can't discuss the case. It's not personal. It's just procedure."

Her desk phone began to ring, and she was glad for the reprieve. But one glance at the caller ID was enough to have her blood pressure elevating. Damn that Al.

As the phone continued to ring, the detective looked at her with concern. "Do you need to get that? I can step out."

"No, not necessary. My phone's been ringing off the hook all morning. A couple of calls were from concerned parents, but most were from reporters. Not just the local ones, either. It seems that Frederick is never newsworthy unless it's something whackadoodle or scandalous. I don't have time for any of that nonsense."

Raleigh's face took on a sly, almost gleeful expression. "You could always forward those calls to your PR director, couldn't you?"

"That's genius. Maria will have a cow."

Then her cell phone started chirping, and she bristled at the sound of its ring tone. She tried to pick it up before Al's face flashed on the screen, but she knew that Raleigh saw it.

"Sorry, I have to get this. But it'll be brief."

He rose to leave, but she waved him back down.

Chapter 16

She tried to keep her tone civil as she answered her ex-husband's call. "Yes, what do you want?"

"Well hello to you, too," Al said in a light-hearted tone. "Hey, I have some great news."

"It's not a good time, Al."

"This can't wait. We just found out we're pregnant. I'm gonna be a father. Isn't that wild? And Julie's super-excited. She wants to talk to you herself."

Meg felt gut-punched, but she had to say something. "Wow. That is big news."

The detective had dropped his head and was studying his notes, and for that, she was grateful. She needed some time to get herself under control.

"But can we do this later? I'm on office hours, and I have someone here. Thanks. Bye."

The detective looked back up before she was totally back together.

"That was my ex." Come on Meg. Say something sensible. "He was calling about our last joint tax return." She willed her voice to stay firm. "Okay, where were we?"

"You were explaining the inaccuracies in the Barbara Fritchie story pursuant to Heather's letter."

"Okay. Sure. Just give me a minute to rewind." Get a grip, girl. Be professional here.

She sorted through what he needed to know and gave him the highlights. That everyone agreed that Confederate troops had been hassled, taunted by flag wavers. But there was some controversy over who'd done the actual waving immortalized in the poem. Even the official signage at the museum acknowledged that fact.

Raleigh's one raised eyebrow indicated his continuing interest and understanding.

"Even though Whittier conferred literary fame on Barbara," Meg continued, "she probably wasn't the person who deserved it. There are at least two other possibilities. First, there's Mary Quantrell, a middle-aged woman who lived nearby. Then there's someone with a lesser claim to fame—a seventeen-year-old Nannie Crouse from Middletown, a dozen miles away. Sort of halfway between here and Antietam. Heather believed that this letter, written three days after the incident itself, weighed in on one side of that dispute."

Raleigh nodded and made some notes. "I read those signs at the museum last night, the ones indicating that Mary Quantrell had the stronger claim. But what bearing does this controversy have on the letter's significance?"

She exhaled a long breath. "A lot actually. The controversy began almost immediately. Not long after the poem's publication in *The Atlantic Monthly,* a year after the event supposedly took place, Whittier received letters protesting the story's accuracy and asserting Mary Quantrell's claim. And one of those letters was from Quantrell herself."

It was included in Whittier's papers at Swarthmore College. Meg had seen it when she was doing research there. And the woman had added another name below her signature—"Barbara," in quotes—a little twist of the knife.

Meg fiddled with her pencil. "But at that point, Stonewall Jackson had already died from an unsuccessful amputation. Dame Fritchie had been dead for a year, so she couldn't give any input. And since the poem had already gained popularity and political momentum, Whittier declined to amend it. Making Mary quite contrary, I imagine."

She waited for Raleigh to chuckle, but he kept on making notes.

"Now all these years later," she continued, "Heather became involved. A couple of weeks ago she was cleaning out her great-aunt's attic and found a variety of Civil War artifacts. Including an old, leather-bound book with a letter folded inside. But here's the important part. The letter appears to have been written by Barbara Fritchie—at least the signature's in that name. And in it, the author referenced the flag event, expressing her admiration for the woman who'd confronted Stonewall Jackson. That brave, venerable young woman—Nannie Crouse."

At that, Raleigh glanced up. "Crouse? The woman with the weaker claim, right. That's quite a turnaround. That would really heat things up, wouldn't it?" He paused. "What would be the value of finding such a letter? Do you know who might want it, and why?"

Considering, Meg rolled the pencil between her thumb and index finger. "Well, there's a huge market for Civil War memorabilia. Any letters from that era which referenced specific historical battles or incidents would excite interest from collectors. And anything in Fritchie's handwriting would be an extraordinary find and be worth big bucks."

As her thoughts deepened, the pencil lay still. "But if it turned out to be an authentic letter written by Barbara Fritchie which confirmed Crouse's claim to be the actual heroine of the poem, it could start a bidding war among collectors. Museums would be interested too."

Raleigh's gaze turned speculative. "Major ones, like the Smithsonian?"

"I'd say so."

Meg followed his train of thought. Everyone knew that money meant motive. She decided to press the point. He might not tell her anything, but he couldn't stop her from thinking.

"Speaking in purely hypothetical terms," she said, "if the letter is missing it might be a motive for murder. Someone might have killed Heather to try and sell it themselves. Or maybe she died during a transaction gone bad, like haggling over the price, or something."

He didn't seem to hear her, just tapped his pen on the notepad. "Besides collectors or museums, who else would be interested in such a letter?"

Meg sighed. He was one hard nut to crack. "Civil war experts would be interested. Historians or people in academia. Someone whose research is looking for more proof that Nannie Crouse is the real heroine of Whittier's poem would ki—" Meg stopped herself, the color draining from her face.

He didn't comment.

"It's not just a figure of speech this time, is it?"

"No."

Meg shuddered. "And it's not hyperbole, either."

The pause grew long as the gravity of that statement dominated their thoughts. Raleigh steered them back on track.

"Tell me this, what would a Civil War expert or an academic gain by this letter's coming to light?"

"Aside from the money? Somebody who burst on the scene with evidence proving Crouse's claim could write his or her own ticket in the academic world." Rolling the pencil aside, she continued. "After the letter's publication, anyone could write about its significance, so the big winner would be the person who broke the story." Her voice dropped. "In which case, Heather would just be in the way."

"That's one theory," he said grudgingly. "What other scenarios are there? Who else might gain and why?"

Meg sighed and leaned back in her chair, shoulders sagging with fatigue. "I guess an expert or an academic might kill to get access to the letter and suppress its publication—or destroy it altogether—to maintain the *status quo*. For example, someone invested in maintaining the assertion that Mary Quantrell was the actual heroine of the poem wouldn't want any evidence to the contrary. And surely not from someone as notable as Barbara Fritchie."

"Hmm," said Raleigh, head down, scribbling notes. "Anyone else?"

"A crazy collector might." Meg rubbed her tired eyes. "Some people avidly collect artifacts, even black market ones. Not to study or display them—especially if acquiring them involved murder—but for the exclusivity of it all. An authentic letter from Barbara Fritchie would be a one-of-a-kind item. And the world has no lack of crazies."

"And if the letter can't be authenticated or turns out to be a hoax? What then?"

"Well, a Crouse scholar would be mighty frustrated." She unsuccessfully tried to stifle a yawn. "I can just imagine it. After coming so close to vindication after all these years, only to have the 'proof' be proven worthless, I'd be pissed. And someone might very well act on that anger."

He nodded but didn't say anything.

"On the other hand, a Quantrell-friendly scholar would be relieved, exuberant even. Without the letter, the reigning contender is still on top. The *status* remains *quo*. And if it turned out to be a hoax?" Meg shrugged. "I dunno what would happen in the collecting world. The letter itself might be worth something just because of the ruckus it raised. But a potential buyer thinking he had access to the real deal would be hopping mad, wouldn't he."

Raleigh was looking out the window again, brow furrowed. "I reckon so."

She smiled to herself. When he was deep in thought, his voice went back to his Southern roots. She wondered if the phrase was a regionalism or a Raleigh family catchphrase.

He refocused his attention on her. "So, while Mary Quantrell had the guts, Barbara Fritchie was handed the glory because the poet got bad intel. But this letter, if genuine, negates that view and transfers everything to young Nannie Crouse. Is that pretty much the bottom line?"

Meg's lack of sleep was telling on her. Snappy patter was beyond her. "That's it in a nut shell." She rubbed her eyes and tried not to yawn again.

Raleigh went back to looking out the window, which allowed Meg to get back to watching him think. She enjoyed it.

Returning from his reverie, his interest was fierce.

"Can you think of anyone else who would know about this letter that Heather found? To your knowledge, had Heather made any attempt to have it authenticated?"

Meg blinked away fatigue. "Her family knows...the great-aunt, her mother. Here at school, I know Heather talked to both me and her history professor, Robert Brunner. She xeroxed the same page for both of us."

In the hallway outside her door, students were beginning to stream past, chatting together, or talking on their cell phones.

"We're almost done here, Meg. While I really want to see that xerox, you'll need to be getting off to class soon. Just get it to me later today, please. Right now, I'd like to hear more about this history professor. He's the same guy who introduced me at the meeting yesterday, right?"

"Right. As for Robert's involvement, I was able to tell Heather about the literary significance of such a find, but she had questions I couldn't answer. So I referred her to him because he would know more."

Raleigh's inquisitive look formed his unasked question.

"I thought he might know how she could go about authenticating the letter," she continued. "And if it were authentic, how valuable it would be. He could tell her what its publication would mean to the field of Civil War scholarship. But I don't think she'd gone beyond Robert and contacted anyone officially. Not this soon."

His eyes narrowed in thought. "It's clear why Heather would tell you about the letter. You were her mentor. And talking to a history professor makes sense. What else can you tell me about him? Personally. Professionally."

"Robert? He's very much old-school. Lecture oriented, scholarly, ultra-traditional. More like a conventional four-year university professor. He keeps applying for those types of positions. I think he'd be happier in that environment."

"So why does he stay here?"

"Those positions don't open up very often. He's probably waiting for someone to retire from Duke or the University of Virginia or someplace like that. Plus he has strong family connections here. The Brunners are one of the founding families of Frederick. They built Schifferstadt here in Frederick before the Declaration of Independence was even written."

The lieutenant nodded—an investigator considering how a man balanced complacency and ambition.

"Besides," Meg continued, "he's a Civil War scholar. He wants to live and work in an area with that kind of history. When I settled in Frederick, I was amazed at how saturated the town is with all that. Frederick fairly reeks of the Civil War because it's so close to Gettysburg, Antietam and Harpers Ferry. All big names in the War Between the States. TCC's even hosting a conference about it this weekend—Frederick, Maryland: A Civil War Crossroads. It's a big, big deal for us, for Robert especially."

"And the conference would bring a lot of scholars to Frederick?"

"Yup. Some are already here. Our academic dean has a sister who's one of them. I know for a fact that she—the esteemed Dr. Charlotte Slattery—is in town already because Dean Plunkard's been parading her all over campus. They even wandered into my classroom yesterday. During Heather's class, as a matter of fact. Plus Robert introduced Slattery in the faculty meeting yesterday after you left." She yawned, trying to make it as unobtrusive and feminine as possible. "And she's the reigning expert on Civil War poetry. She'd be a contender for wanting to get her hands on Heather's letter."

"I see. And this Robert Brunner is a Civil War scholar. What's his area of expertise?"

Meg looked as uncomfortable as she felt. "The long and short of it? Nannie Crouse."

Chapter 17

"Oh Meggy-Meg. I'll be there in a second," Joan sang out from down the hall on her way back from class. "How did you make out with that detective who's got you all in a lather?"

Meg's face flushed from lack-of-sleep pale to shut-up-Joan crimson in half a breath, but she couldn't take her eyes off the man sitting in front of her. And where his features had previously registered professional interest, a new-found amusement flitted across his face.

Meg popped out of her chair. But before she could say anything, Joan did.

"Or didn't you get as far as 'making out,' you little slow starter, you?"

On the first "you," Joan was still out of sight. By the second "you" her slim leg and Ferragamo-clad foot had appeared in the open doorway. By the last "you" she was crossing the threshold.

Meg looked ready to commit murder.

Catching sight of the lieutenant, Joan brazened it out by gliding up to him and extending her right hand. "Hello. Good to see you again. And so soon."

Raleigh stood and shook her hand. "Yes, hello." His pleasant baritone was slowed by that slight Southern drawl. "I recall meeting you the other day, but Meg forgot to introduce us. I'm Lieutenant Raleigh, a detective with the Frederick City Police."

On one level, Meg knew she should try to get control of the situation, should be the one making the introductions. But she couldn't help herself. While his attention was diverted, she had to check him out: broad shoulders, self-assured movements, confident carriage. A lion surveying the veldt, one wearing a fine-looking corduroy jacket over a chambray shirt.

When the pause grew long, Joan stepped into the conversational void.

"And I'm Professor Glotfelty," she said, her voice almost a purr. "TCC's preeminent speech communications teacher. A useful specialty since some feline's got Meg's tongue."

Instead of joining the lagging conversation, Meg's gaze dropped lower.

Eyebrow raised, Joan stage-whispered, "Earth to Meg."

Snapping her eyes up and shaking her head, Meg rejoined them. "Oh. Sorry. Joan, this is Lieutenant Ra—"

Joan interrupted, smiling impishly at the detective. "We had our meet-and-greet while you were off in la-la land." She swung her smile toward Meg. "Staring into the 'middle distance...or some such place.'"

Caught out, Meg swallowed almost audibly then blinked like a great horned owl.

"I've got to be going," Raleigh said smoothly as he bent to gather his things. "Meg's been very helpful, but she has to get off to class. And I have a coupla more stops here on campus." As he straightened, he looked directly at Meg. "By the way, I enjoyed the *Eroica.*"

Her brow wrinkled in dismay. He couldn't have said what she thought she heard—the erotica? Flustered, she searched for a different topic. "Oh, wait. Your windbreaker." She turned quickly and pulled it off the back of her chair. As she came around the desk to hand it to him, she snagged her toe on a wayward book bag and stumbled once again into his bracing arms.

Joan snorted in glee.

After he'd settled her back on her feet, she was relieved to see that his face remained neutral. But his eyes hinted at something more.

"Steady there, Meg," he said, his tone playful. "And I was referring to Beethoven's 3rd Symphony, the *Eroica.* The one you were listening to when I arrived?"

Blushing yet again Meg managed a reply. "Yes, of course. The 3rd. That *Eroica.*"

He smiled broadly. "And you won't forget to get me a copy of that document we discussed, will you? The sooner, the better. You can take it downstairs to Security, and I'll have someone pick it up."

"I'll remind her, Lieutenant," Joan piped up, grinning. "I don't know what's gotten into her. She's usually so reliable."

Meg gave Joan the evil eye. Smoothing her features, she turned to the lieutenant. "You may count on me to deliver it there as soon as possible."

"Great. And thank you for the overview, Meg." His gray eyes grew warm and friendly. To Joan, he added, "Always nice to see you." He looked at Meg one more time, smiled, and left.

Hands on her hips, Meg whirled to face her friend. "How *could* you?"

Joan chuckled.

So did Lieutenant Raleigh as he walked down the hall.

. . . . .

Jogging back downstairs, he got busy on his cell phone while he stood in line for coffee at the college's modest version of Starbucks. One call was to Maroni, asking him to talk to the vet tech, and checking to see if he'd met with Heather's great-aunt, Edna Stouter, on the whereabouts of that letter. He also told him that Mrs. Hillcrest had given permission for him to search Heather's room and look for the letter. His instincts told him it was the motive, and he expected it to be missing. He was almost certain that Heather had died because of it.

After finally buying two coffees and stirring a fair amount of cream and a lot of sugar into one, Raleigh made his way over to his friend's office.

Hearing approaching footsteps, David looked up from his paper grading, his pleasant, jowly face lit with affection. "Ty Raleigh, my old compadre. Right on schedule. Have a seat and hand over that spare cup of joe. And it better be black."

Ty complied with both directives. "Nice to see you, too, Calloway."

Whereas Meg's office was very personal, this one was plain, but not stark. The desk faced the window on the right-hand wall, leaving a lot of room behind the seated occupant for bookcases and file cabinets, all of which were tidy. Shoulder patches from scores of police departments—from Togiak, Alaska to Lviv, Urkaine—were affixed to a large bulletin board running along one wall. The desk itself was uncluttered, with only a single batch of student papers visible. The office included two comfortable, well-worn armchairs which looked like hand-me-downs from home, chairs that welcomed the streams of students who visited their professor for advice and encouragement.

Ty savored his first sip. "Well, I've been walking the hallowed halls of academia all morning, and that's been an education in itself. You have a no-nonsense president who is bird-dogged by one seriously proactive PR person."

"Oh, you mean Routzhan? She's all about spin, always takes the party line. She's usually pretty uptight, but the extra work of this conference really has her knickers in a twist. And the president...well, that's just politics, innit. We've had worse. Run into Dean Plunkard yet?"

"No. I figured two high-level management types were plenty enough for one morning."

"You're right. Gotta pace yourself. Plunkard's a piece of work, an ass-kisser from way back. That's how she got into administration. Now that she's made the transition she's not faculty friendly. We're too unpredictable. Might do something out of the ordinary and make a problem for her. Like our friend Meg. There's no love lost between those two."

"Because..."

"Because Meg speaks her mind when the rest of 'em play ostrich and stick their heads in the sand. I can't make trouble because I don't have tenure yet. Nobody likes Plunkard's directives, but only Meg has the cajones to challenge her."

Ty chuckled. "Who knew education was so much like law enforcement. I thought cream was supposed to rise to the top, not curdle when it got there."

"The workplace is the same everywhere, my friend. At least we don't have to take down drug dealers and dodge bullets." David crossed one khaki-clad leg over the other. "But enough chitchat. You've got bigger fish to fry. From what you told me last night, sounds like you got saddled with one nasty murder. And it's personal."

"Damn right it's personal." His coffee lapped at its cap as he settled into the shabby wing chair. "Whoever did it is little better than an animal. Worse, actually. Animals don't kill their most promising young."

The professor smoothed his tie over his tattersall dress shirt and watched as the younger man stared at his cup.

When Raleigh lifted his eyes, they held storm clouds.

"How could that child have been a threat to anyone?"

"There are monsters among us, son. You already knew that. It's why I got out. That kind of work takes a heavy toll." David tested the coffee, took a sip. "You knew the victim. How're you holding up?"

The anger in his eyes smoldered. "I'm raring to go on this one."

"And I have no doubt that you'll hunt him down and haul him in." David's gaze turned sympathetic. "Meg allowed as how your daughter found the body. That's really rough. How's she doing?"

He looked down for a long moment. "I'm really worried what this could stir up for her. It's only been five years since her mom's murder."

"And she's done just fine. New school in a new town, new friends. I imagine there've been some rough patches, and there'll likely be more ahead. But she'll come out on top."

"Hope so." A look of dad-pride filled his eyes. "You're right about one thing. She's resilient."

"But you didn't come here to talk about Lindsay. The case, maybe. Or could it be about the someone who was just in here this morning asking about you?"

Ty abandoned his next sip of coffee. "Meg Adams?"

"None other."

He took a long, thoughtful drink. "What did you tell her?"

"Next to nothing," David said. "Only that you weren't currently married, in those exact words, nothing else. Told her it was her job to find out."

"Appreciate it."

For a moment or two, Ty lightly tapped the half-empty cardboard cup on his knee. "Anything you'd be willing to tell me about her?"

"Nope. What's good for the gander is good for the goose. I'll tell you the same thing I told her. She's not currently married."

Ty shifted in the chair, hiked one foot to rest on the opposite knee. "Yeah, I sorted out that she was divorced. The ex called her half an hour ago while I was over there interviewing her. It kinda shook her up. Something about taxes." But he wasn't buying it. She looked ready to cry, but they hadn't been tears of frustration.

Clearing his throat, David's face became stern, and his voice turned crisp. "And just so you know...that Meg Adams is one quality woman. A real class act."

"Thought she might be," he replied in measured tones.

Calloway leaned forward, his look almost challenging. "You interested?"

He returned the look, his gaze unwavering. "I'm interested in finding out if I'm interested."

Both remained silent and wary, each circling the other's connection to Meg, overlapping in conflicting viewpoints. When David responded, his tone was neutral, but his posture remained stiff.

"I can see why. If I were your age, in your shoes, I would be, too."

Ty lowered his cup to the scarred leather armrest and said nothing.

The professor rolled his desk chair a fraction closer. "Just one thing." He paused. "I like you, Raleigh. You're a good man. After your life turned to shit, you soldiered on, worked to turn it around. I respect that." His eyes narrowed. "But that Meg is somethin' real special."

The younger man remained composed and silent. Calloway gazed at his friend with a mixture of compassion, misgiving, and concern before he continued. "It's high time you got back in the game, but she's still mighty brittle. Wouldn't take much to break her."

While they regarded each other—dark green eyes locked on gray ones, both pairs resolute—the heat clicked on, circulating the air in the room.

"I hear you, *Dad*," Ty said with care. "I intend to be a gentleman."

"Thought so," David muttered. "Just making sure."

Ground rules established, the two men drank their coffee companionably, each thinking different thoughts about the same woman.

"Have you meet Joan yet," David said, changing the subject.

"Tall, attractive black woman? We've crossed paths. She stepped into the office just as I was about to leave and in thirty seconds minutes flat managed to embarrass Meg half to death."

David smiled wide. "Yup, that Joan's a trip. Funny as all get-out, smart as a whip and often just as cutting. She and Meg go way back. Same hometown, I think. And when Joan was changing careers, Meg told her about the opening here. Probably coached her so she'd get the job." He chuckled and shook his head. "Are your ears burning yet? I bet those two are talking up a storm right now."

"They can talk all they want, but that's as far as things can go right now. I have a mighty full plate. This investigation. Lindsay. It's not the time to begin anything else."

"No, you're right. You need to keep your focus on catching this whack job. There'll be plenty of time after that."

Ty gulped down the rest of his tepid coffee. "You and I know that, but who knows what it will seem like to her." He threw the empty cup in the trash. "I was pretty pulled back this morning when I interviewed her—had to be. Not rude, just very professional. But that's not how it went yesterday evening." He stopped talking and dropped his eyes. No, that wasn't how it went down at all.

Calloway didn't prompt or question him, just waited it out.

Ty looked up, face troubled. "I noticed her during the first class, a couple of weeks back. Ran into her leaving a restaurant once after that. And even though yesterday was the first time we'd actually had a real conversation, she and I were starting to click, ya know?" He slid the fingertips of one hand back-and-forth over the surface of the worn, leather-padded arm of the chair. "Then we heard about Heather, and all hell broke loose."

Its job done, the heat shut off with a discreet click.

"She was thunderstruck by the news, and I needed to bolt, but not before I put her back together as best I could. Made sure Groves kept an eye on her until he handed her over to you. But this morning I was all business, had to stay on track." His hand stilled its wanderings.

David said nothing.

"She's probably confused." His expression was earnest as he searched Calloway's face. "But I don't want her, or you, to think I'm playing head games."

"I see where you're coming from. And as for Meg," he smiled affectionately, "she was already confused when I saw her at 7 a.m. That girl overthinks everything. But she was sure interested in finding out about you." Chuckling, he leaned back and laced his fingers across his middle-aged belly. "I don't imagine you did anything this morning to blunt that curiosity."

"But you won't say anything, will you?"

"About this conversation?" David tapped his thumbs together several times. "Your history? Not a word." He drew in a deep breath. "I might reinforce the idea that you're focused on solving this murder. That it wouldn't be appropriate for an investigator to get involved with anyone right now, especially someone who's close to the case." More thumb tapping. "Might even indicate that she should cut you a little slack. That's it."

Some tension eased from Raleigh's face. "Thanks."

"There is something you're gonna hafta sort out." He hesitated. "As you likely figured out from the faculty meeting, guns are an issue for her."

"Mine comes with the job." He fell silent, his expression bland, his body taut. What else was there to say? It would be a problem, or it wouldn't. Nothing he could do.

Raleigh looked out the window. He'd never yet had to take a life in the line of duty, had worked every other option to see that it didn't come down to that. But it was always a possibility.

However, he wasn't sure what would happen if he were to be the one to find the man who'd murdered his wife. Some nights he dreamed about that man's blood.

Calloway cleared his throat to catch his friend's attention. "That's all I have to say about the whole shebang. I'm not a meddler. The way I see it, if something's meant to be, it'll find a way to happen. If it's not...you can't push a rope, can ya."

The younger man didn't respond. The two men simply sat and looked at each other.

David seemed to like what he saw, sincerity perhaps, or perhaps an expression that was more common on a younger face. Whatever he saw prompted him to smile knowingly.

"But the woman who left here this morning was kinda tied up in knots."

Raleigh looked down briefly, a shy smile on his lips.

"Seems to me she'll keep hanging on," David added.

Ty's hopeful expression slipped away as he looked at his friend again. "Here's another concern. The more I dig into this, the more Meg seems involved, y'know? She knew the victim, knows about the letter. The murderer might also know about those connections. If he does, she could be in danger."

"I hear you. But it can't be helped. It is what it is."

"I know. She's the most reliable, most informed contact available. And still..."

"You're worried."

"Yeah. That."

"Well, I can keep an eye on her here."

"Thanks. And it wouldn't hurt to alert Security, either. But I don't know those guys well enough to know who's sharp and who's not."

"Leave that to me. I know who to talk to on what shift. She'll be safe here on campus. Her house is another matter. It's really remote." David looked thoughtful. "Maybe I can convince her to stay with Joan here in town. Dunno though. She's really independent and not easily spooked."

"Give it your best shot, okay? I'm afraid if I say something she'll overreact."

"Not to worry. I'm on it."

David's cell phone chimed out a tone. He rolled his eyes. "A reminder. Got a meeting with Dean Plunkard in ten." He grinned. "But I can be a little late. After all, I'm talking with the lead investigator of our student's murder. The old harpy will just have to suck it up."

"I don't need much more of your time. While I'm on campus, I want to talk to that history professor, Brunner. I assume Meg told you about the letter that Heather found, the one maybe written by Barbara Fritchie."

"That letter. Oh yeah." David snorted. "Both she and Brunner have been jabbering about it nonstop. Does it figure into the case?"

"Somehow or another, I reckon. Lindsay knew about it, and Mrs. Hillcrest said something about it last night when I asked her if anything out of the ordinary was going on with Heather. Right now, I'm collecting background information about it. I got Meg's take, but now I need to know what Brunner knows. What he told the victim."

"And if he ran his mouth to anyone else."

"That too."

"Well, it's hardly a secret around here. But you're in luck. Robert's office hours are the same as mine on Wednesdays. His office is five doors down." Calloway's bland face contrasted his sarcastic tone. "Corner office, facing the mountains."

"He was in charge of the meeting yesterday. A big shot, huh?"

"Middling-size fish in a small pond. Head of the department. Chairperson of the Faculty Association. Bet it doesn't take five minutes for him to show his ass." He stood up. "Let's go. We'll get this show on the road."

"Calloway, I don't need your help," Ty said firmly. "Can't use it. Don't want it."

"Come on, Raleigh. Let me back in the game. Education can be mighty tame."

"You just said you weren't a meddler."

"That was about matchmaking stuff," he huffed. "I was a parole officer for over twenty-five years. Makes me a professional buttinsky."

"Sucks being you, then, doesn't it?" Ty drawled.

Chapter 18

When both of them were standing in Brunner's doorway, David cleared his throat. "Hey, Robert, got a minute? There's someone here who wants a word with you."

The office was immaculate, with windows that displayed the late fall foliage of the Catoctin Mountains. The walls were filled with diplomas, framed documents bearing official seals and embossed letterheads, plus prints of Civil War personalities and sundry battles. Two items drew the eye. One was an etching, a reproduction, of Stonewall Jackson lying on an iron-framed bed, arm amputated, waiting to die. The other was a black-and-white poster of Elvis in three-quarter profile, an early one from his hound-dog days, smile crooked and eyes smoldering.

The florid fifty-year-old seated behind the expansive mahogany desk didn't look up from what he was reading. When he spoke, his voice was patrician and nasal.

"Customarily, visitors make an appointment, Calloway. I'm very busy here. There are a lot of details about the conference that need my attention. So unless it is important..."

"I'm afraid it is, sir," Ty said, walking into the room. "It's about murder."

Brunner's head jerked up, and a wary expression troubled his small eyes. "Murder?" Undoing a single button on his upscale wool jacket, the professor sat straighter. "I recognize you. You were here yesterday talking about campus security. But you're a detective?"

David stepped in to stand beside his friend. "Lieutenant Raleigh is a former colleague of mine. We worked together some when I was still with Parole and Probation. Ty was with the State Police battling drug lords, political corruption, and a serial killer. Right now he's heading up the investigation into last night's murder in the Barbara Fritchie Museum."

"It's a pleasure to see you again, Professor Brunner." Raleigh extended his hand. "I wish the circumstances were more agreeable."

Reluctantly rising from his chair and revealing himself to be a full head and shoulders shorter than the detective, Brunner complied with the unavoidable handshake. Then he resumed his seat, leaving his guest standing.

David shot Ty an apologetic look. "I'll just leave you two to your business."

The remaining men evaluated each other in silence.

"I am sorry for your loss," Ty said to his host as he seated himself.

"*My* loss?"

He raised an eyebrow. "One of your students was murdered last night. Heather Hillcrest was your student, wasn't she?"

"Oh yes. A terrible misfortune." He checked the positioning of his striped silk tie. "It's always so tragic when a young person dies."

"I'm on campus this morning gathering information about her. Finding out who she talked to, her movements, things like that. Since you're one of her current professors, I'd like to ask you a few questions."

"I'm extremely busy preparing for a conference I'm hosting here at the College. I will, of course, assist the investigation but I hope this doesn't take too long."

"Thank you. I'll bear that in mind. What can you tell me about her?"

"That she was a very average student. Well-mannered and pleasant looking, but not academically talented. Bright enough by Frederick County public school standards, I'd say."

Ty was perplexed by the professor's mean-spirited impressions and filed that tidbit away. He masked his growing distaste for the man, saying simply, "Thank you for your insights. And when did you last have contact with Heather?"

Robert ran a hand over his thinning blonde hair. "I believe it was yesterday. No, no. It was the day before that. Monday. She attended my Western Civilization class at 9:30."

"Did she say anything noteworthy? Did anything unusual or untoward occur?"

"No. She never spoke in class. Few do."

Little wonder, Ty thought. Not a warm fuzzy kind of guy. Probably lectured most of the time then groused because there was no discussion. "Did she ever contact you outside of class?" She must've. Both Meg and David confirmed that he received a copy of some part of that letter.

Brunner looked away momentarily and hesitated. "Yes, once. She made an appointment with me through the department secretary. Subsequent to that, Miss Hillcrest came here during my office hours that same afternoon, wanting to discuss some Civil War era artifacts she had recently discovered."

"I understand that you are a Civil War scholar." Ty nodded at the office wall, opting not to comment on the king of rock n'roll.

"I have garnered a certain stature in that field, yes."

"So it follows that the deceased came to you with questions about her recent discoveries...about their potential value, how to go about authenticating them, perhaps. What could you tell her?"

"Only what I know from personal experience. She showed me photographs of a sword. But they were poorly shot cell phone pictures that didn't reveal its true character, so my expertise wasn't all that useful. I did explain that a typical sword in good condition like one I bought would be worth $200-300. The market varies. As for authenticating items, I suggested she start by contacting the officials at the National Museum of Civil War Medicine here in town. Or the Gettysburg Museum of History. I find it best to start local and make personal connections."

"What was her mood at that time?"

"Her mood? I'm not in the habit of registering the emotional wellbeing of students." He touched a finger to his reddish-blonde moustache. "I suppose you could say she was excited."

"Thank you. That's very insightful," Ty said dryly. "Did she mention other artifacts?"

"None that I recall." He took a sip of water from the bottle near his desk phone.

The detective gazed out the window and stayed quiet.

Allowing his suspect to stew in the manufactured silence, Ty contemplated the mountains in the distance. Mountains that had sheltered the native Indian tribes—Tuscarora, Seneca, Shawnee—before they had been the battleground for the white settlers against their own European fathers. The same hills and valleys that later became the battlefield for brother against brother, North against South. Mountains that had seen so much displacement and death.

He turned back to Brunner. "You're sure there isn't anything else?"

The professor's face flushed and for several long moments he sat very still. "Well, she did have me review a single page from a copy of a letter. One which she thought was valuable."

"What did you think?"

He shrugged. "There's no way to know at present. The syntax, vocabulary, and sentence structure, as well as the penmanship, were all consistent with 19th-century correspondence. However, all she shared with me was a xerox copy of the first page. The original needs to be examined by an expert. The age of the paper and ink should be verified as well."

"What about the letter's content?"

"What about it?"

Ty pinned him with a cool stare, a tiger eyeing his prey. "Cops don't like coy answers, professor. It makes us think the person has something to hide. But perhaps I didn't make myself clear. Let me reframe the question. An object's value may have little to do with its physical attributes and more about what it represents. The parchment on which the Constitution is written is valuable, but the ideas conveyed by the document are more so. So again I ask you, what was the substance of Heather's letter?"

The professor didn't look chastened, but he did reposition himself in his chair.

"It could help right an egregious wrong," he said finally, his voice becoming passionate. "Are you familiar with John Greenleaf Whittier's ballad, 'Barbara Frietchie'?"

"I have become somewhat familiar after last night." But it might be more useful to play dumb...to see what that teased out. "In essence, a gutsy old woman shamed a Confederate general by waving a Union flag in his face."

"If one believes in that enduring misunderstanding, yes."

"I take it, you don't."

"Certainly not."

Raleigh listened while the professor tore into Whittier for not bothering to fact check. Claiming that the poet was spoon-fed his information from a fellow writer, a woman who wrote popular novels. It was clear that he viewed them as substandard. He thought Whittier should have relied on newspaper articles of the day that cited a number of women whose actions drew wrathful Confederate attention. There were numerous episodes of civil disobedience when opposing troops marched through a town, very often flag waving.

"However, such actions were carried out almost exclusively by women and children, as they wouldn't be imprisoned or run through by a bayonet. That was a more genteel era," Brunner said with a sigh. "Today, women would share the same risks as men. Yet another benefit of the ERA mindset."

Although he was surprised by the man's attitude, Ty didn't comment on it. But he did wonder if Brunner and the feisty Joan had ever locked horns. Seemed likely.

The professor continued his lecture, his face pinking with eagerness. "The poem's subject matter is also flawed because historians have categorically established that General Jackson did not ride down Fritchie's street on his way through Frederick, nor did he travel with the troops. And there is ample evidence to prove that the ninety-five-year-old Dame Barbara could not have waved a flag that day."

Ty looked attentive but didn't comment.

"Here," he said with some urgency, "here's proof. I've written an article on this very subject that references the diary of Fritchie's neighbor." He pulled open a desk drawer, selected a folder, and withdrew a few stapled sheets of paper, offering them to the detective. "You can read this to help you sort out the facts of the situation."

Noting the professor's eagerness, Ty took the papers. That's the key to his guy. He's all about being right, always protecting his ego. Time to shift gears, step up the game. Time for a little baiting. "So you're one of those 'spoilsport historians' mentioned on the sign attached to the museum. One of those who challenges the Barbara Fritchie mystique."

"I don't think of myself as a spoilsport, lieutenant," he said in a tight voice. "I am an academic historian."

"I mean no offense, I assure you." Ty made his face bland and his tone soothing. "I was merely repeating the language used on the sign I read last night during my initial investigation at the crime scene. It says that experts believe Mary Quantrell was the more likely heroine. In fact, Whittier may have conflated the two women or mistakenly picked the wrong one."

"Whittier was assuredly mistaken. The account he penned never happened. If he'd wanted a real heroine, he should have written about Nannie Crouse of Middletown."

He dove into his desk drawer again and drew out another stapled set of papers. "Here is my monograph on Nannie Crouse. Read that, and you'll be up to speed on the disservice done to a courageous young woman." He leaned forward in his chair and placed his hands on the leather edged desk blotter. "In fact, I am working to help her descendant bring that information to public prominence."

Ty pasted an admiring expression on his face. "Well, I'll be eager to see how that plays out. But how would my victim's letter rectify the dishonor done to Nannie Crouse?"

"According to Miss Hillcrest, Barbara Fritchie's letter—if she was indeed the author—was written to Nannie's aunt, Elisabeth Crouse. In it, Dame Barbara asked the aunt to congratulate the girl who had, and I quote, 'bested the rebel horde and their overlord.' Dame Fritchie goes on to say she wishes she had been in a position to do something similar."

"Yes, I see. That would change things, wouldn't it?"

"If it could be authenticated, yes," he said, eyes alight with fervor. "It would have an incalculable impact. But not in the hands of a naïve, overly-enthusiastic student."

Brunner stopped short, coughing mildly as if clearing his throat, then took another sip of water.

"And you would be a better steward? Is that what you mean?"

"I said no such thing."

"Well, the letter has direct bearing on your personal crusade to vindicate Nannie Crouse. You would stand to substantially bolster your academic reputation. *If* you had it in your possession."

"How dare you?" His voice lowered with menace and disbelief. "You're investigating me."

"I'm investigating the case. A student is dead, and the letter likely has some bearing on her death. And because you're an expert on the subject, she shared it with you. And now it turns out that it would be very valuable to your pet cause. That's a lot of coincidence."

"You already knew I'd seen the letter, didn't you. Who briefed you?"

"I'm more interested in your belief that Heather was ill-prepared to be a proper guardian of the letter. What were you prepared to do about that?"

His face darkened, but Brunner ignored the question. "Your source is likely that intellectual lightweight, Meg Adams," he fumed. "Her and her MFA in creative writing. Probably from some lackluster state school, as well."

Ty registered the fact that Brunner had ignored his direct question. But he'd come back to that. Right now, he wanted to see what would happen if he pushed a button or two. Angry men made mistakes.

"Well, Professor Brunner, as far as academic credentials go, an MFA is the highest degree in creative writing, equal to your Ph.D. And Professor Adams went to Columbia University." He fixed the professor with an austere, unwavering gaze. "Is Bucknell, your alma mater, also an Ivy League school?"

Brunner's belligerent stare had no impact on his antagonist.

"It isn't, is it," Ty said innocently. "Unlike some of your students, I do my homework. All it took was a smartphone and a long wait in the coffee line."

"You go too far, 'lieutenant.' I will not bear these insults. You have no business interrogating me. I've done nothing wrong. You are doing your unsavory job in a deplorable manner. I have a mind to—"

"This is still just a conversation," Ty interrupted harshly. "You'll know it's an interrogation when I read you your Miranda Rights."

"You, sir, have crossed the line." His face reddened quickly, and his words came faster. "I will be speaking to your superior officer—and the mayor—about your flagrant lack of respect as well as your sarcastic tone and groundless insinuations."

The detective shrugged. "As you wish."

"And I trust you are investigating Ms. Adams, as well. She and that girl were probably in cahoots. I know for a fact that Meghan also received a page of that letter, maybe more. Isn't she just as suspect as I?"

"I've already spoken to Professor Adams, who is cooperating fully." He paused, then dangled the next sliver of bait. "And she has an alibi."

"Alibis can be manufactured. Or broken."

"I am confident about this one. At the time of the murder, she was in attendance at the Civilian Police Academy, as was I. Her whereabouts are amply accounted for."

Brunner looked at the ceiling and tipped up his bottle of water for a long drink.

"But where were you yesterday evening between 5:30 and 6:00 p.m.?"

He brought the bottle down with a thump. "I won't dignify that with a response. I am finished speaking to you."

"But I still have questions, Professor. And may have more, later."

The flush in the academic's face deepened a shade or two. "I am not saying anything further until I talk to my lawyer. Send your questions to me by e-mail, and I will respond in kind."

"I fully understand you're wanting to consult counsel. It is your Constitutional right." When he continued, his equitable tone became brisk with authority. "But law enforcement has rights, too, and one of them is to question—face to face—anyone who might have information about the commission of a crime, in this case, murder. We can talk politely here in your office, or you can call your lawyer while I escort you downtown. Then the three of us can hash it out in an interrogation room." He paused. "Now, where were you yesterday evening?"

Brunner sat stiffly in his chair and settled one pudgy hand atop the desk. His eyes met the detective's in challenge.

"After the faculty meeting, over which I presided, I escorted a visiting scholar—Dr. Christine Slattery—to the president's office. That would be President Delores Collins since I doubt you would be acquainted with her. We chatted there for a bit. The three of us and one of my most talented students, Jon Sellers. The group broke up around 5:00. Then I went home to ready myself to attend a reception that evening given in honor of Dr. Slattery at 7:30 in the president's home.

"Can anyone corroborate your movements after you left the college?"

"No. No, my word is above reproach."

Raleigh shot him the most skeptical look in his arsenal. "Again, do you have any confirmation?

"No. My wife is out of town, consulting on an interior design commission in Chicago."

And it was the maid's night off, Ty thought to himself. But he wanted to go back to the letter. It was the key.

"Did you mention the letter to anyone else?"

"I may have. I do not have total recall of all of my discourse."

Ty imagined that the little prick would want to conceal the letter from his academic rivals. No need to give them a whiff of it until it was safely his. But he'd ask...ratchet up the tension.

"First coyness, professor, now sarcasm? Please, just be as specific as possible about your conversations regarding the letter."

"I chatted about it with a few people here. Your friend, David, among them."

Ty imagined that Calloway was going to suffer for that. Oh well. He was a big boy.

"And I discussed the letter with Maria Routzhan, the public-relations person for the College. She often assists me with publishing my own work as she's very interested in and knowledgeable about local Civil War matters. We had once thought that she was related to Nannie Crouse, but after considerable investigation, it turned out she's not. Very disappointing, especially since that knowledge came on the heels of her mother's health woes. So I've been supporting her aspirations to publish on her own. It will be an uphill battle since her credentialing is in human resources, not history. Still, Maria's professional position here makes her well placed to publicize upcoming articles and scope out publication opportunities for me if and when the opportunity arises."

"Oh, so you're already imagining this letter as an opportunity to further your research. Which brings us back to my earlier question. Since you thought the deceased was too inexperienced to be the guardian of the letter, what were you prepared to do about it?"

"Nothing criminal, I assure you." He hesitated, and his small eyes darted toward the door and back again in a single breath. "I told her that it needed to be safely secured until it could be assessed for authenticity."

"And did you offer to keep it safe for her? Or perhaps you offered to buy it outright and relieve her of the burden of such an important find?"

Brunner's face grew crimson. "Yes, I mentioned that I would be interested in acquiring the letter before it was assessed." The professor leaned forward as if trying to transmit his good will. "Selling it at that point would have been to her benefit. After all, it could turn out to be a worthless fake."

"Very charitable, I'm sure. How much did you offer her?"

Rebuffed, he sat back "That is no concern of yours. It isn't a crime to buy personal property. However, she wasn't interested in selling it." He pouted. "She couldn't, in fact, because it belonged to some elderly relative."

"Do you know of anyone who might want to harm Miss Hillcrest or who might benefit from stealing her letter?" He gave Brunner a hard look. "Or arranging to have it stolen?"

"That's enough. How dare you insinuate I could be involved in something that sordid."

"I'm not sure you appreciate the gravity of this situation. I am conducting a murder investigation to secure an arrest that will lead to a trial and a conviction. A conviction which could result in life imprisonment without the possibility of parole, depending on the case built by the prosecuting attorney."

"I know how the law works, 'officer.' And we are done here."

"It's *lieutenant*, and you don't call the shots. A young woman has been murdered, perhaps over a letter, a letter whose contents she shared with you. And you have not been candid. I gave you three opportunities to admit you knew about the letter's existence, and you were only forthcoming the third time. Your lack of cooperation concerns me. I'm sure you can appreciate the urgency of the situation. The longer we wait, the more likely it is that your student's killer will get away. And none of us wants that, do we?" He rose to leave. "Good day, professor."

"Well, I never..." sputtered Brunner to Ty's retreating back.

He was only just out the door when he heard Brunner's voice snapping out a question.

"What took you so long? I've called Maintenance three times and told them that the air is not circulating properly in here."

A dark-haired man in a blue TCC work shirt had to edge past Ty to enter the office. They made brief eye contact, and the other man shrugged as he walked into Brunner's office.

"Good luck with that," Ty muttered to himself.

Chapter 19

Walking into David's homey office again, the detective plopped in the leather chair and closed his eyes. "That went well."

Calloway looked up from the papers he'd been grading. "I can just imagine. Got on his high horse, did he?"

"A frickin' Clydesdale."

"Told ja!" He waited. "And that's no mean feat 'cause he's such a short little fella."

The detective opened his eyes to see his friend holding an outstretched hand about four feet off the floor. They both gave in to laughter.

"And what about that Elvis poster?" Ty ventured.

"It doesn't track, does it? The boring, buttoned-down, ultra-conservative educator and Elvis the Pelvis—gyrating and making the girls' panties wet—sharing an office."

Raleigh laid his hands on the armrests of the chair and shook his head in disbelief.

"And get this," David added with a smirk. "His dog's named Presley."

"There's just no accountin' for people, is there. But how do you work with a guy like that? He's such a pompous piece of work."

He shrugged. "We work around him."

Ty looked down at his own hands, scarred and sturdy. "I almost let him get to me once."

"You? 'Rottweiler' Raleigh? Wow."

"I haven't brought out the big dog yet, but his superior attitude was pissing me off. And why is he so down on Meg?"

"She's a woman who doesn't know her place, isn't she? Plus, Meg doesn't drink the administration's Kool-Aid. But Bobby-boy mixes it up and hands it to Plunkard, so she fills the Dixie cups. And Routzhan hands them to rest of us. Toadies, all of them."

"Every workplace has 'em," Ty agreed. "Brunner was dissing Meg's degree, implying it was 'soft,' like she couldn't have hacked it at any rigorous college." Ty relaxed deeper into the chair. "But I knew he was no Ivy Leaguer...blindsided him with that."

"Ah. Coming to the aid of the fair maiden, are we?"

"Knock it off, Calloway," Ty rumbled softly.

"Okay. But did you parry with your degrees from *the* Johns Hopkins University?"

"No. Why would I?"

"Because that's how the game is played in academia. My college is bigger than yours. Let's pull 'em out and compare."

"If I'd had to pull out my, ah...sheepskin to prove my masculinity, I wouldn't be much of a man, would I?"

At Calloway's snort of laughter, Ty felt the last hour's tension begin to slip away.

"I don't usually let suspects rankle me like that. But then again, I'm usually not dealing with the upper intellectual, social strata, either."

"I feel your pain. But just so you know, he's gonna push back. He's just that kind."

"He's already made the threat. Went on about making phone calls to my superiors. So I might have to suffer through a tongue lashing from the Commander. Worth it, though. Had to get as much out of him as I could up before he lawyered up. You know...innuendo, insinuations, veiled threats."

David's expression had a cunning edge to it. "Did Brunner have an alibi?"

The lieutenant sighed audibly, tired of his friend's attempts to horn in. "Calloway, you don't have any official status anymore."

"I'll take that as a 'no.' If he did, you'd've just come out and told me."

"That's an unwarranted assumption, my friend."

"Well, it's what I would have done."

"Just one of the many ways we differ. But do you think Brunner is capable of murder?"

"I thought you didn't want to include a civilian in the loop?"

"I'm asking, not sharing."

"I already know what you're thinking."

"Oh?" said Ty, sitting up and getting ready to leave. "Do tell."

"That Brunner likely wouldn't bloody his hands with an actual murder. He hasn't got the stones for it." David leaned forward. "But if the stakes were high enough, he might not be above hiring someone to do his dirty work."

"Yeah, there's that."

· · · · ·

Murder on his mind, Ty left Calloway's office and returned to Hamilton Hall, heading toward the college's security office again before leaving campus. He passed back through the now noisy cafeteria, its students chatting in groups, checking Facebook on their laptops, or texting their friends. Often all at the same time. A lucky few had scored one of the coveted booths or cushy chairs and were sprawled in repose, perhaps even studying. Others simply stood around, trying to see who else was there and preening to be seen. Walking through the open space, he scanned the crowd, a habit honed over the years.

He noticed the scraggly boy from Meg's office. Nate, was it? The mail carrier. Then he focused on another face, and his own went on alert.

Jon Sellers, Heather's ex, was slouching against a pillar near the stairs, two of his buddies flanking him. All of them wore the garb of the disdainful: ripped, low-slung jeans, tee shirts emblazoned with the tour logo of obscure bands or some youth-culture manifesto, and the ubiquitous hoodie.

The detective picked up his pace but didn't speak. He was about five strides away when the suspect noticed him.

"Jon Sellers. I'd like a word with you."

Sellers executed a fast 180 and hustled out the double doors toward the parking lot. Instead of following him, Ty hooked a quick right into the service corridor that served the book store and led to the loading dock. He sped to the end of the hallway, dashed out the crash doors, turned left, and stopped sharply just before the corner of the building to await his quarry. Hearing Sellers approach, Ty stepped out directly into the youth's path, forcing him to either stop or shoulder his way through. The student halted just one step short of running into Raleigh.

"I guess you didn't hear me call out to you, Jon," he said evenly.

Sellers narrowed his eyes and rammed his hands in his pockets. "Guess not."

"I need to talk with you."

Jon pushed his shaggy hair off his face and adjusted his glasses. But he said nothing.

"About Heather Hillcrest," Ty continued quietly.

The boy shrugged and shook his head. "I've got nothing to say about her." The lank hair fell back in his face. "She's nothing to me."

"Perhaps. But that wasn't always the case. And now she's dead." Muscles tense, he readied himself for a quick response. "We need to talk."

Sellers stood still and looked away.

"If not now, someplace here on campus, then later, down at the station."

The boy tightened his grip on his slack-bellied backpack and stared impassively at a point just beyond his adversary, avoiding direct eye contact.

"Or, I'll just drop by one of your classes—or work—and walk you out. Is that what you want?"

He slid his gaze to meet Raleigh's, twisted his lip into a sneer, and his "whatever" stare turned truculent. "You would, wouldn't you?"

"I can, and I will," he said flatly. "You aren't giving me much choice."

Students crisscrossing the sidewalk on their way to or from classes had to step around the immobile pair, but the two men remained fixed on one another.

Sellers shifted the slight weight of his backpack with the shrug of a shoulder. "I'm on my way to work, and if I'm late again, I'm fired."

"I'd be willing to keep this friendly and private. I'll drop by your place after work. Ok?"

Jon took his time but finally nodded.

"Good answer," Ty said. "What time?"

"6:00," he mumbled.

Taking a photocopy out of his pocket, Ty looked it over. "Jon Dexter Sellers, owner of a 1993 Honda." He shook his head. "Not an organ donor, I see." Looking back up, his expression hardened. "The Burke Street address on your driver's license is the current one?"

When the boy didn't respond, Raleigh snapped the paper loudly between his fingers. "I will not play hide and seek with you, Mister Sellers."

"It's the right one, 'Lieutenant' Raleigh."

Ty nodded, back in neutral. "Then you may expect me at 6:00 p.m."

Hoisting his backpack up a little higher, Sellers shot off a, "Fine," and stomped away.

• • • • •

Instead of going to the cafeteria for lunch, Lindsay snugged herself into the tattered, overstuffed armchair in the prop room. The drama teacher often let her chill there. Mrs. Thornton was cool that way. This room, crowded with costumes and weird-ass props—gaudy lamps with beaded dangles, lopsided gumboots, transistor radios that didn't work—was the best place to lose yourself.

And Lindsay wanted just that.

She'd spent the morning feeling curious eyes on her, fending off rude questions. *Assholes.* Her eyes closed, and she tried to relax. Drooping her hand over the armrest and idly reaching out, she made contact with something kinda fuzzy, like long strands of coarse hair. Peeping between half-opened lids, she smiled. The Cowardly Lion's costume from the upcoming show. Twirling the strands between her fingers, she closed her eyes again, resting, hoping to drop into sleep. Instead, memories of yesterday played behind her eyelids: a crumpled body, a hand wet with blood, blonde hair spattered with... She bolted upright, heart beating fast.

Reaching down, she slid the composition book from her backpack.

Wednesday: October 29th

This day fucking sucks! I wish Dad had let me stay home. But noooo. There's no one to "supervise" me. Like I need supervision. What an overprotective jerk! He doesn't know half of what I do. But he thinks I need the routine, that I should show up here and act like everything's normal.

Things'll never be normal again.

Susan's been avoiding me all morning, and everybody else keeps staring at me. Even people I don't like, some I don't even know. It's like I'm some kind of celebrity: the girl whose best friend is a corpse.

Most of them had never even talked to Heather.

And Dad says to keep quiet about the murder. Well, duh! Why would I talk about that? I'm not clueless. If the word gets around, Dad's worried that the killer will figure out that I was Heather's BFF, that I might know something about that stupid letter. He's scared that something bad will happen to me.

So am I.

Chapter 20

Rolling his shoulders to relieve the morning's buildup of tension, Raleigh sat at his desk and read over Maroni's report: "After searching the house, no sign was found of the letter or a leather-bound book that might have contained same. The homeowner—aka mother of the deceased—was distraught and broke down several times. This officer suggested she ask her doctor for some tranquilizers."

Hmm, that was good advice. Ty knew that Matteo was still pretty green, hadn't had to deal with many victims of grief on his own. But it sounded like the lad was on top of things.

He went back to scanning the report. The burner phone had no prints on it. Heather's was loaded with hers. The museum owner stated that a full-length, linsey-woolsey cape was missing, and in addition to himself, two others had keys. A tour guide who said it was still in her possession. And the head of the museum's advisory board: Professor Robert Brunner, who had not returned a call about its whereabouts.

Imagine that. The good professor hadn't mentioned that he had a key to the crime scene when they'd had their little heart-to-heart. Too bad he hadn't known to confront him about it then. No matter. They'd keep pressing him on it and see what popped.

And the vet tech, Lescalleet, corroborated Routzhan's story. He hadn't seen or heard anything odd at the museum when they'd left the vet's office together yesterday.

"Well, we can check that off the list," he murmured.

And it seemed that Heather's great-aunt, Mrs. Stouter, didn't have much to add about the Civil War items that Heather unearthed. Or what the girl had done with them.

What had that child been up to? He'd known her pretty well, or so he thought, for over four years. He'd included her in a lot of outings with Lindsay...movies, concerts, kayaking, even a vacation at the beach. She'd always been a sweet-tempered girl. Well, not a girl. She'd blossomed into the sort of eye-catching teen that made dads worry. Plus she was a little too trusting and sort of young for her years, whereas Lindsay was wary and more seasoned than he'd like her to be. He guessed they met somewhere in the middle. But unlike Lindsay, Heather wasn't a natural risk taker. Someone had exploited her enthusiasm and naiveté. And that bastard was gonna pay.

He picked up the next pile of papers, the treasure trove Brunner had foisted on him. Probably dry as dust. To keep himself on task, Ty opened his top desk drawer and pulled a candy bar out of his cache. Scanning the documents and munching on his treat, he had to admit that the first article made it pretty clear that Barbara Fritchie wasn't likely to've been waving any flags that day. Her neighbor, Jacob Engelbrecht, had kept a diary for nearly sixty years. And while his entries cited info about who died and how, various trials and executions, and the passage of a few Osage Indians through town, he made no mention of the Fritchie incident. In fact, he said that the old woman had been too ill to attend church three days earlier.

But the article about Nannie Crouse piqued his interest. It maintained that this seventeen-year-old girl had wielded a Union flag to taunt the passing Confederates, calling them traitors. When they'd attempted to snatch it from her, she ran inside and wrapped herself in it. So they put a gun to her head, took the flag from her, ripped it, and tied it around a horse's tail. But—and this was the kicker— someone had subsequently found the flag on the Antietam battlefield and returned to her.

"Dunno if it's true." He chuckled. "But I'm pulling for you, Nannie Crouse."

His desk phone rang. In its display window, he could see it was from his commander's secretary. Shit. That couldn't be good.

•   •   •   •   •

Ty turned the door handle to the outer office of the Criminal Investigation Division, walked in and nodded to the secretary. "Good morning, Sharon. Is he available?"

She looked up, her expression sympathetic. "Afraid so. He said to send you right in."

"Not to worry," he replied, walking to the door with the polished brass nameplate. It wasn't the first time he'd been called on the carpet. Not likely to be the last. He knocked and waited.

"Come," rumbled the voice from within.

Ty entered and closed the door behind him. "You wanted to see me, Commander?"

"No. And I wouldn't have to if you hadn't fucked up."

"I'm sorry to've disappointed, sir."

João stared him down. "Sorry, my ass. We've got a situation here. You never told me that you knew the victim."

God, it was hard to be deferential to this prick, especially in this circumstance. He probably should have fessed up earlier. "It makes me that more motivated, sir."

"I've got more than half a mind to pull you off the case. All it would take is an objection from the prosecutor's office. Homicide's always an attention-grabbing crime, but this one's become real high profile real quick, what with a sympathetic victim and all."

Ty only half listened to the rest of the tirade. About how it involved the college and lots of impressive people who were gathered for that Civil War conference. How his police force was taking a beating in the media. The fear of opening up the department for possible lawsuits. When he tuned back in, João was still blustering on.

"Added to that is your ham-handed investigative technique. You're no rookie, Raleigh. I expected better of you. Robert Brunner is a prominent citizen from a prestigious local family. You've been here long enough to know that."

"I treated him with respect, but he wasn't forthcoming. The situation required some—"

"Some damn tact! He not only bellyached to me, but he also complained to the mayor. And who do you think called me?"

And since shit rolls downhill, Ty was catching it. "I regret that you were impacted, sir."

João's lip curled. "Not likely. But be that as it may, you watch yourself on this one. It's a news-worthy case, and the suspects aren't lowlifes. I expect you to be courteous, up to and including the point of ass-kissing. Get yourself down to PR to get some pointers. Bernie's expecting you. You need to close this case fast. Fast and tight. Dismissed."

Feeling sufficiently chewed out, Ty closed the door to the commander's office and found Hannon in the outer office, a look of sympathy on his unremarkable face.

"I'd have come in if Himself had gotten any louder," he confided.

Ty blew out a breath. "Thanks."

Hannon cocked his head at Raleigh. "What did you ever do to get that far on his bad side anyway? Sleep with his wife? Or just shit in his dog dish?"

Rearranging some papers on her desk, Sharon stifled a laugh.

Ty hung his head and shook it a couple of times, mumbling, "I have not a clue." Then he looked up, his gray eyes lit with irreverence. "But I must have done it really, really well, huh."

Hannon chuckled, "Hang tough, big dawg."

•　　•　　•　　•　　•

Knowing it wouldn't be a cakewalk, either; Ty dutifully reported to the department's PR guy.

"Hey, Bernie," he said.

"Hey, yourself," said the pudgy, slick-suited older man as he closed a slim folder on his desk. He ran a hand across the back of his balding head.

Sitting in the visitor's chair he was offered, Ty wondered why PR people were always such pains in the ass. Guess it came from guarding the company's back, selling their snake oil.

Bernie's face lit with a professional smile. "I know this is a big case for you. For all of us, really. Frederick doesn't get many murders, so this will generate a lot of coverage. We have to be careful, don't we?" He steepled his fingers over his belly and sighed a professional sigh. "Such a shame it had to happen to a nice girl from a respectable family. And she was going to college, too. Such a shame," he repeated, working up steam "But it seems like you've ruffled a few feathers, my friend. Important feathers."

Ty nodded as if he agreed to the rest of Bernie's bullshit, all the while wondering why the higher-ups didn't just grow a pair and back their people. But he had a game face. Easy enough to slip it on, get out of here and back on the job. "I hear what you're saying, Bernie. You can count on me from here on out." Yeah, count on him to do what needed to be done to crack this case and bollocks to Brunner.

"So we're finished here, right?" Ty said. "Don't want this high-profile case cooling off, do we?"

Bernie's lips had the same little smile pasted on them as before. "Yes, we're done, lieutenant. For now. But at some point, we may need to have a press conference. I'm fiddling with the idea of telling the *News-Post* about your previous experience at solving murders before you left the Maryland State Police and came here. The details of how Lieutenant Stephen T.

Raleigh caught the SDS serial killer who terrorized Baltimore's Inner Harbor. That Stalk, Drug, Strangle case would make good copy."

It would make his job hell. "I don't think that's such a good idea, Bernie. The cases aren't at all related. It's old news, and it would be a huge distraction. Plus it takes the attention off the victim by putting it on the detective. A nineteen-year-old girl was murdered. She's my focus."

"Just a thought," he said, eyebrows lifted over calculating eyes. "But it's my call. Mine and the Chief's. Unless some enterprising reporter here in town gets digging." He shrugged. "At present, just shoot me your reports, and I'll keep the media informed."

Fine, he thought. Let this asshole spend the time. His was too precious to waste.

"Oh," Bernie added as the detective rose, "good luck working with Maria Routzhan." His chubby face broke into a rub-it-in grin. "She's quite...erratic. Helpful as all get out sometimes, even a bit pesky. Then she'll leave you high and dry the next time by not following through."

He made no comment, but Bernie's grin had more to say.

"And she's obsessed with the Civil War. She's always going on the about the Battle of Middletown, or Professor Brunner said this, and down with Barbara Fritchie that. She keeps trying to cozy up to the local Civil War heavy hitters. But she probably won't be bothering you much, seeing as how you're a Southern boy."

Ty could hear him chuckling as he left.

Chapter 21

On the drive over to the Sellers address, Maroni filled Raleigh in on his interview of Heather's classmates, those he'd been able to contact so far. Only one of them—a criminal justice major, T.J. Evans—had had anything useful to say.

"The kid seems like a straight shooter, Lieutenant. Since he's looking to be a cop, he wanted to give me all he could. Long story short, Jon and Heather were hot and heavy for a few months. Then she saw he'd posted photos of her on his Facebook page. Really personal ones, graphic even."

"Such as?" He smiled to himself when Matteo blushed.

"It's reported—in a whole lot of X-rated detail—that one was of Heather, nearly naked, posing on a bed and looking like...like she really wanted it."

The older man's eyes darkened. The dad in him had his stomach tightening.

"Yeah, I know," Maroni said with a sigh. "But it gets worse. Apparently, another photo was a close-up of her face, looking 'hot and bothered.' His words, Lieutenant, not mine," Maroni added softly. "And it showed a man's gloved hand at her throat. A black leather glove. Kinda like *Fifty Shades of Gray*."

"Goddammit! I knew that little bastard was bad news."

"Yeah, Evans called him 'a douchebagging motherfucker.' When Heather found out about the photos, she went ballistic. Made him take 'em down." He shook his head. "Like that'll help. They're all over the planet by now."

Ty pushed out a long breath. "What did Heather ever see in that little shit?"

"Young people just make mistakes." Maroni shrugged. "Made a few myself."

Ty ran a hand through his hair. "Okay. Just so you know, I had...ah, an interaction with Sellers." He paused, wondering how much to reveal. Decided on full disclosure. "I was over at the Hillcrests' house earlier this fall to pick up Lindsay, and Sellers was there on the porch browbeating Heather—yelling at her, swearing, jabbing his finger in her face. She was angry, crying. And Lindsay was as antsy and yappy as a Jack Russell terrier. So I, ah...intervened."

"Intervened?"

"Yup, flew up the steps, grabbed him by the arm, and pulled him back." His hands tightened at the memory. "When he tried to shake me off, I stepped in front of him and pushed him in the chest, two-handed."

"Hard?"

"Hard enough. Then I just stood there, anticipating his next move." And really hoping the little sonovabitch would make one, he admitted to himself. "Might've been that he could see my gun. Don't really know what my jacket covered at the time."

Maroni shot him a crooked smile. "It's hard to keep track of those things sometimes, innit?"

"Yeah, well...but it's the only time recently that Lindsay looked like she approved of my skill sets. After the dirtbag skulked off, she fist bumped me."

"She's a smart girl."

"She can be," he muttered.

At 5:45 they arrived at the Sellers address—a house amidst a warren of streets in a long-established neighborhood, one of the original 1940s tract housing developments in Frederick, built to welcome home the returning, family-minded WWII veterans.

After sitting for a bit, they observed a middle-aged, mid-sized woman leave the house, a small, nondescript rancher—half brick and half faded green aluminum siding. It squatted on shaggy grass. The woman entered an unremarkable Chevy parked out front and drove off.

Maroni began to run the Chevy's license plate. "Whaddya think? Landlady or mother." He nodded toward the departing driver. "A fistful of speeding tickets and some points toward a suspended license, courtesy of DWIs? Or squeaky clean, model citizen?"

Ty shook his head at Maroni's cavalier attitude. He turned to look at the house. "Either way, it isn't a very cheerful place."

"I'm gonna guess ne'er-do-well mom."

"It's an option." But it just showed that his kids were still really young, that they hadn't disappointed or embarrassed him in a big way yet. "I'll bet you a cup of coffee that parents aren't always to blame. That a bad apple can fall from a fruitful tree." Maroni's unconvinced look needled him a little.

"You know...viruses, pests, unseasonable weather. And the next year it's all good."

"You're on."

The dashboard console flashed its incoming information.

Ty lifted his chin. "Enlighten me."

"The vehicle is registered to a Cynthia Gordon Sellers, this address."

"Likely the mother, then. And her driving record?"

Maroni hesitated. "Clean." He scowled at Ty's amused look. "But I'm only going to spring for regular coffee. Not some fancy cappuccino or whatnot."

A few minutes later an older model silver Honda Civic pulled up. Sellers exited, pulled open the rear door and took out his backpack. After a surreptitious glance at the detectives' sedan, he entered the house.

Maroni started getting out of the car, but his partner stopped him.

"Wait here,"

"Why?"

Raleigh exhaled through pursed lips before he continued. "Interviewing him on his home turf could be advantageous. He'll feel more in control, relaxed, might even let something slip. An advantage which vanishes if he feels ganged up on."

Maroni nodded at the explanation, but he still seemed puzzled. "So why am I even tagging along?"

"He'll know you're out here. Like an insurance policy."

"From all accounts, he sounds like a right nasty piece of work," Maroni said, his face grim. "Think he'll turn on you?"

Ty shook his head once, decisively.

"And you're sure because..."

"I've done this kind of work for a lot of years. I just don't get that kind of vibe from him." But he knew that anything was possible. He'd already seen more of the unpredictable than he sometimes cared to remember.

"But you might turn on him, is that it?"

"I'm not planning on it."

"But you're gonna press him hard, right?" His next words were full of eager curiosity. "Is it Rottweiler time?"

"That particular interview technique can be very effective in the controlled situation of an interrogation room. Out here in the field...not such a good plan. Too many variables."

The rookie detective watched as his partner turned to stare out the window.

"It's already messy between Sellers and me." Ty felt his shoulders tighten and the space between them itch. "For this kind of face to face with a hostile interviewee, you really only get one time at bat. They usually clam up after that or stick to their script." He looked at his partner again. "I just want a lot of swinging room when I step up to the plate."

Maroni didn't look satisfied, but he didn't say anything, either.

Tapping two fingers on the dashboard while he thought, Ty finally spoke. "Why don't you move the car and park in front of him in case he tries to bolt."

He complied, then shut off the engine. "Now what?"

Ty cracked open the car door and started to lean out. "Give me forty-five minutes. If I'm not out by then, come a'knocking."

"I don't like this." Maroni frowned. "You might need backup."

Settling back in and shutting the door, his gray eyes darkened as he spoke. "And if I do, you're, what? Fifty feet away?"

The younger man stared out the windshield in silence.

"Maroni..." He dropped his head briefly and blew out a breath. "You're my partner, Matteo, the man I trust to have my back. If I need you, you'll be inside within minutes as opposed to my waiting ten or fifteen for someone from headquarters." He paused. "But what I need for you to do right now is keep an eye out in case he tries to rabbit."

Maroni started to say something more then stopped himself. But he still looked worried.

Recognizing the young man's distress, Ty gave him a tight-lipped smile. "Appreciate your concern, really. I also know that you're chafing at the bit to crack this case. We all are."

He weighed his next words to cut their sting. "But here's where I'm uneasy. This kid is a sarcastic little shit who loves to push people's buttons. I've done this work for over fifteen years, and I'm worried about keeping my act together. So I don't want to split my focus by having to be worried about you, too. See what I mean?"

"Yeah," Maroni said, eyes averted.

Ty waited until his partner looked up again. "And if things turn ugly...if he pushes me too far and you're there? Well, we're partners, but we're not married. You'd be obligated to testify against me if he brought charges."

"Obligated?"

"Yes, obligated. Law bound, even." His eyes flashed, and his voice rumbled. "I don't buy into that Blue Wall crap...cops covering for other cops."

The young detective looked his question at his mentor but didn't voice it.

Instead of thawing, Ty's manner grew colder and harsher. "If I saw you do something criminal—take a bribe or use excessive force, participate in racial profiling—I'd turn you in. I expect you to do likewise. Because if we make exceptions for our own kind, there's no integrity in what we do, is there?"

Neither man spoke for several moments. After a bit, Maroni nodded, and the older man relaxed.

He opened the car door again. "Okay, I'm going in. You know what to do?"

"Stay with the car and sit on my thumbs, play lookout for forty-five minutes, then knock if you haven't already turned up. What's not to get?"

. . . . .

The lieutenant rapped on the windowless front door. Presently, Sellers opened it and stood there with one hand on the doorknob and the other on the frame. Waiting to be invited in, Ty turned slightly to offer a wider view of the street, allowing the boy to see the other detective get out and lean against the sedan's rear quarter panel.

Jerking his hand off the doorknob, Sellers retreated into the house, leaving the lieutenant to close the door and follow him.

Ty shook his head, thinking it wasn't his day to get invited in.

Once inside, Sellers led the way down a hall that smelled musty underneath the efforts of a cheap floral air freshener.

Near the end of the hall, Jon stopped and opened a door. Without looking to see if the detective was following, he flipped on a light switch and pounded down the stairs into the clammy basement apartment. At the bottom of the stairs, they were standing in what passed for a living room/sleeping area, messy and cluttered. The space was concrete block, framed out, with two sets of shop lights for illumination, one of which winked unreliably for a bit before it steadied. A washer and dryer occupied the far end of the box-strewn, linoleum-floored rectangle. Drywall had been hung on one long wall, but the rest was unfinished. It didn't look like there were plans to continue.

"Let's get this done," Jon snarled.

"As you wish." He intended to keep his conduct formal and civil, but he didn't know if he could trust it to last. Or that he should. Flexibility was crucial. "Shall we sit?"

"Whatever."

Jon uprighted the futon to its couch position. As he sat, he pushed the bedclothes aside, picked up the book that had just tumbled to the floor and set it beside him.

Raleigh eyed the much stained, burnt-orange corduroy recliner, then dragged over a hardback chair and sat. Adopting his most professional persona, he began. "Let me set the stage. This is an interview to gain baseline information in a homicide investigation. You haven't been charged with anything. Are we clear?"

"Crystal." Sellers glowered in contempt. "I've already taken criminal law classes."

"Good. Let's begin." He took out a notebook and pen. "We can skip ahead a bit. I don't need to ask if you knew the deceased."

"Yeah, I knew her," Jon said with a sneer. "Biblically."

He didn't take the bait. "How long did you date?"

"It wasn't exactly dating. We bumped uglies for a few months."

"Which months, exactly?"

Sellers shrugged. "Midsummer through the first part of the semester."

"When did it end?"

"You know exactly when it ended. You were there."

"Yes I was." He wrote something down and looked back up again, his eyes granite gray. "Three weeks ago, then."

Jon leaned back into the couch, resting one ankle on the opposite knee. "If you say so."

"I just did."

Each glared at the other. Nothing escalated, but Jon looked away first.

"Let's move on to new business." Time to throw him a curve. "What can you tell me about the antique letter Heather found?"

"What letter? I don't know anything about any letter." He scowled. "She and I don't exactly share info anymore." The scowl turned into a leer. "Used to be we shared a lot."

Ty's jaw muscle tightened. "Can you account for your actions Tuesday after your English class?"

"Yes."

He waited a beat. "Please do."

Sellers pushed back his hair. "I escorted Dr. Slattery, our visiting scholar, to the faculty meeting and was invited to stay until it ended at 4:30. Afterward Dr. Brunner and I walked her to Dean Plunkard's office. They're sisters, you know. Then the four of us talked for quite some time." He laid one arm along the back of the futon and smiled. "About the upcoming conference, issues on campus. I even made a few suggestions about how to force the college's Jurassic Park faculty to infuse more technology into the classroom."

"Essentially, you followed Brunner around like a lap dog and sniffed at the VIPs?"

"I don't like your sarcasm!"

"Nor I yours."

The two men locked eyes, faces bloodless in the glare of the fluorescent light.

Ty made an "after you" gesture. "Please, continue."

He sulked a bit before he went on. "I left around 5:00. Drove home and changed clothes to attend Dr. Slattery's reception at the president's house at 7:30."

"It takes you two hours to shit, shave, shower and shampoo?" He shook his head and gave Jon a disbelieving look. "That's a mighty long time to primp, son."

The trap snapped shut.

"I am *not* your son!"

"Clearly," Ty said, his voice low and threatening. "No son of mine would be such a dick with women."

"Don't fuck with me. You grabbed my arm and pushed me that day. I could press charges for assault...police brutality, even."

"And your witnesses?" he asked archly. "My daughter?...Heather?"

"Go to hell!"

"Tsk, tsk." The detective smiled. "Same quick temper and lack of self-control as I remember."

Sellers struggled to remain silent.

Ty pressed his point. "Same sort of reactive behavior as you exhibited in your English class yesterday, just hours before Heather was murdered."

"Who told you about that?" he said, anger changing to stunned surprise.

"I heard she really put you in your place. Had the class laughing at you."

"It wasn't like that at all. I got the last word in."

"That's not what my sources say."

"So what? Who gives a shit?"

"I do." But if this kid was the murderer, maybe the letter wasn't important here. Maybe it was just an argument gone south...a crime of passion. Or was he working for someone else?

Tension built as Jon's hand tightened and loosened around the book at his side.

"Having the last word seems very important to you. Is that why you lured her into the museum, argued with her, brutally attacked her, and left her for dead?"

"You don't know what you're talking about."

"Or did you just happen to spy her walking alone in that deserted spot and follow her to hurl a few last insults, get bested again, and explode into rage?"

"No!"

"Did you bring the weapon with you or just grab the first thing that came to hand?"

"I didn't kill her."

"She dumped you, publically humiliated you, so you had to even the score, didn't you?"

Sellers leapt up. "I couldn't care less about that little twat."

In the brittle silence, the fluorescent light's muffled hum crackled like a lightning strike.

The detective stood when his suspect did, fluidly but not hurriedly. The air between them was charged: Sellers breathing hard and hands balled; Ty merely watchful.

At a sudden noise, Sellers flinched and looked for its source—the book that had fallen from the couch.

The detective barely suppressed his smile.

Jon narrowed his eyes. "Get out. I'm not talking to you anymore."

"That's unfortunate because there are still things I need to know. Of course, I'll leave if you wish. But then we'll continue this later, downtown." He shifted his stance, readying himself for any possibility. "I'm sure some of your friends can give you directions. Billy Simms, perhaps. Or Rob Neff." He paused. "What'll it be? Now, or later? Here, or there?"

Muttering, Sellers sat back down on the futon.

"Smart decision." Raleigh resettled himself in the hard chair—alert, silent, waiting.

"You're just trying to rattle me, old man. It won't work." Jon's face and neck went blotchy red, one hand squeezed the armrest.

Ty shrugged and tapped his pen on the waiting page of the notebook. "Let's get back to yesterday. How long did you grace the reception with your presence?"

"As I just said, it started at 7:30, so—"

"And I'm sure you were the first one there."

Sellers glared. "I stayed until about 9:30. Then I went home."

"Can anyone verify your timeline before you arrived at the reception?"

"No. I live by myself." His full lips curled into a snide smile. "The better to entertain the ladies."

"You live in your mother's unfinished basement. The ladies are 'entertained' by all this?" He waved his pen to highlight the room and its contents. "Or is it just your natural charm?"

"My mojo's working just fine." His smile became broader, his tone snarky. "I popped Heather's cherry, didn't I?

Ty felt the adrenaline whoosh through his body. "You might've been her first." His voice deepened and slowed with self-control. "But surely not her best."

Sellers brushed his unkempt hair back with one hand, then stretched that arm across the back of the futon and shifted his smirk into a smarmy smile. "I had her squirming."

"They'll do that when they want it to end."

"Personal experience, huh?"

The fluorescent bulb sputtered, then burned steadily again.

Ty's hand tightened around the pen, but his words were cool and precise. "I've worked with a lot of rape victims. Listened to lots of very, *very* personal stories."

Wisely, Sellers didn't offer a rejoinder.

After a long blink and a small smile, Ty nodded, savoring his next move: liar's bluff. "But I sure got Heather's take on you. She and my daughter were best friends, as I imagine you remember from that afternoon on Heather's porch." He waited, banking the tension. "I chauffeured them lots of places. They chattered endlessly, and it's amazing what one can overhear while fiddling with the radio, pretending to listen to NPR."

Sellers shrugged. "Like I care."

"You should. It might improve your game." The next pause played like a long drag on a cigarette in film noir. "The way I heard it," he said calmly, loading each word. "Heather got more satisfaction from the guy whose cherry she popped than she ever got from you."

"That little slut." He kicked at the book that had fallen from the couch, sending it skidding toward the officer.

Raleigh stopped it with his shoe.

"Fuck off!" Jon stood abruptly, bristling with rage. "We're done here."

"For now," Ty agreed, rising nonchalantly.

"This is harassment! You don't have anything on me."

"You're right. I don't."

Sellers smiled with wolfish satisfaction.

"I don't know if there is anything I can have on you." He raised an eyebrow. "Yet."

Shoving his hands in his pockets, Jon shifted from one foot to the other.

"But I'm looking, and I'm good. If there's anything, I'll find it." And then, my little friend, he promised himself, the gloves come off.

"Good luck with that."

As Ty started to leave, he picked up the book beside his foot and scanned the cover: Friedrich Nietzsche's *Thus Spoke Zarathustra*, the philosophical novel outlining the author's ideas of man and Superman.

He tossed it to Sellers as he strode to the stairway. "I wouldn't test that luck by leaving town..." At the foot of the steps, he called back over his shoulder, "Übermensch."

• • • • •

Raleigh emerged from the house with more than ten minutes to spare. The neighborhood had wound down for the day, the street now crowded with parked cars that had jockeyed for the closest spaces to their owners' homes. The street lights slanted their comfort and safety down through the raggedy-leafed trees. On his way to the sidewalk out front, Ty paused to let a jogger pass. When he got in, his partner didn't start the engine right away.

Maroni seemed full of questions but asked only one. "He didn't cave, did he?"

"No."

"Did you unleash the Rottweiler?"

"Only after he brought out his pit bull."

Maroni frowned. "Metaphor, right?"

Ty nodded. "Lots of growling. One or two barks. No biting."

"Wow. So what did Sellers say?"

"Too much about too little."

Maroni might have been disappointed, but he wasn't bold enough to push for more.

Noting his partner's dissatisfaction, Ty relented. "I'll fill you in tomorrow. It's been a long day." And a strange one, he realized. From Meg to Brunner to Sellers.

The younger man started the car but didn't pull away from the curb.

Ty adjusted his shoulders against the seat back. "I need a shower. That apartment's almost as nasty as he is."

After checking his mirrors, Maroni drove off slowly.

Raleigh felt exhausted and dejected, crashing after the adrenaline spike of the confrontation. And while his partner's desire for details filled the car, he didn't have the psychic energy to talk it all out. Leaning back against the headrest, he closed his eyes and made the effort to share a little. "Sellers doesn't have an alibi between 5:00 and 7:30."

"That's good, innit? It's just circumstantial, but it makes him a person of interest, right?"

"And he said he didn't know about the letter. But I reckon he's a fine, fine little liar."

"That's all?" Maroni said, disappointed.

Eyes still closed, he nodded. "The highlights, yes." He ran a hand through his hair. "As for nuances...it's something you had to be there for, like a play."

"One you wouldn't let me watch."

After a three-intake yawn and a long, audible exhale, he opened his eyes and looked over at Maroni. "Okay. Next time, front row seat." He looked out the windshield. "For all the venom and mockery the suspect can spew."

Maroni stopped at the intersection and waited for the jogger to pass in front of them, her ponytail dipping and rising. He gave his mentor a puzzled look. "Shakespeare?"

Shaking his head several times in long, deliberate movements, Raleigh stared out the passenger window at the homes they were passing, the light from the interspersed street lamps glinting off mute windows.

"Nope." Ty put his elbow on the window ledge and leaned his head on his closed fist. "Just some worn-out old cop."

Chapter 22

Raleigh strode into his second-floor office early the next morning to begin planning the day, a Starbucks latté in hand. A venti. He'd had some coffee at home, but this case called for espresso. As he sat in his chair, he thought of Lindsay as he'd found her there two nights ago. Not a turbulent teen all full of herself and disdainful of him. The horror had stripped away all that bravado and given him back his sweet, sensitive daughter. For a little while.

A ringing phone in the next office brought him back to himself. After a sigh and a long sip of revitalizing coffee, he called Maroni.

"Hey, I've got a job for you. Need you to go out and get cozy with the Security folks at TCC. Nose around a little. Didn't you work with some of them before you made detective?"

"Yeah, sure. We crossed paths when I was still working a beat and hauling bad guys out to the county jail. A few of the corrections officers out there do some moonlighting at TCC."

"Great. The college has already reported a spate of thefts over the past coupla weeks...computers, photography equipment, some of it high-end. Ask around, quiet-like, to see if there are any suspicious types they have in mind."

"I gotcha. Gut feelings they can't put in their reports."

"The college wouldn't hire drug felons, but it has a reputation for giving out chances to hard-luck cases. And like-minded folk tend to find each other. Could be we're looking at a murder for hire. Could be that the...ah, 'collector' talked to some 3rd shift janitor with a few misdemeanors who knows a more accomplished criminal. Someone who could be hired to steal a letter. If we find him and put on the pressure, we'd track it back to the collector himself."

"I follow you. Start looking for the kinda guy who could roust a defenseless girl. It's an angle. I'll check it out and get back to you."

"And one more thing. Ask Brunner about his key. Don't get in his face about it. Don't want to overplay our hand. Play it straight. For now."

"Sure thing," he said and ended the connection.

It all just ate up time. Time he felt slipping away, but it had to be done. And then there was the financial aspect. Because if Brunner was involved in this, he'd've paid somebody else to steal the letter. And then that somebody had gotten scared or sloppy or overzealous and murdered the mark. Maybe. Maybe that's how it'd gone down.

He picked up his cup again and leaned back in his chair, thinking, making connections, seeing possibilities. The same personal gain motive and murder-for-hire scenario applied to the visiting scholar, Slattery. But he didn't know her or her whereabouts at the time of the murder. Yet.

He'd follow the money. If either of them had hired someone, that someone needed payment. Sorting that out meant a talk with the prosecuting attorney to see if he had enough probable cause to check the academics' financial records.

Snapping the chair up straight, he got on the phone. A few calls later, he'd gotten the PA caught up with the case and an okay to start the research into the money once a judge signed off.

Since Maroni was out in the field, Ty got busy with the background check on Brunner and Slattery in the Maryland Judicial Case Search database. Hmm...several DWIs for him, but not in the last six years. However, there were also arrests for disorderly conduct and assault. Both were dropped. Well, well, well. Charlotte Slattery, however, was clean.

He'd confront Brunner on that, but he had more pressing matters. A call to the coroner, not his favorite part of the job. "Mort, what can you tell me about the Hillcrest girl? I'll take anything you've got."

"Check your email. I just sent you some preliminary notes. The first strike was face to face. Like the killer could've known her, might've wanted to see her reaction."

Or he just liked to see the lights go out, Ty mused, remembering other killers he'd put away. Other outcasts and bent minds. Sipping on his venti, he opened the file and scanned the cold facts. For the last two hits, she was on the floor. Serious bleeding on the brain, swelling, was cause of death. Poor girl never had a chance.

The coroner broke into his thoughts. "The murderer was average height, but above average strength. Right-handed. That's it so far."

"Yeah, I figured. Cold bastard, wasn't he?" He swiveled in his chair—rotating it on its axis in little quarter-moon twists—meditating on the fact that such a callous murderer hadn't delivered a killing blow. And that was odd.

"Ok. Thanks, Mort. You're quicker than the forensics folk. From them, I've got nada."

"And Raleigh...I heard your daughter found the dying girl. Tough break."

"Yeah, but she's holding up okay, thanks." He brushed aside the concern. It was just a reminder of her vulnerability. "Things to do, friend. Gotta go. Thanks for the quick turnaround."

He tapped the cardboard cup on the desk. One girl dead and another still in pain. He went to take a sip, only to find the cup empty. Damn, this was a shitty day.

Just as he picked up his cell to call the college's PR person and see about getting in contact with Charlotte Slattery, he noticed the time. Damn it. He'd have to hoof it to make his meeting at City Hall. A shitty day just got shittier.

·   ·   ·   ·   ·

When Ty entered the mayor's office, Bennett Lamond had his back to the door as if studying the row of portraits that lined the rear wall. He turned around and waited for Ty to close the door before he let loose.

"Ah, Lieutenant Raleigh, there you are." He ran a forefinger over his graying moustache. "I was told that you were a highly successful detective with the State Police before you came to Frederick. Decorated for valor, even. And that you have an impressive closure rate, both there and here. So why am I having to take flak about the slow pace of this investigation?"

Ty was used to interacting with politicians. It came with the territory. But it never sat well when they got in his face. And it never made the job easier. But he hid his irritation and delivered his spiel about how slow-seeming investigations were actually systematic examinations into meticulous lines of inquiry—interviews, background checks and the like.

"The case has been open for less than 24 hours, sir. I believe we've made significant progress."

"Oh? I'll be sure to tell that to President Collins when she calls again, complaining about frightened students and cantankerous parents." He half-turned to the wall behind him, pointing to the portraits. "You see these? These are the famous Fredericktonians."

Ty was puzzled but looked anyway. It postponed the berating he knew was coming.

The collection of a dozen or so mahogany-framed portraits greeted any visitor who entered the office. Some were black and white photographs, some color, and a few were old-timey photos. Barbara Fritchie was included, of course, but his attention was drawn to a blow-up of *Life Magazine*'s iconic V-J photo, taken that day in Times Square, of a Navy sailor enthusiastically kissing a white-uniformed nurse.

Noting the direction of Ty's gaze, the mayor broke into his thoughts, "Surprised, eh? The woman is Greta Zimmer Friedman. She went on to marry a scientific researcher for the Army who got a job at Fort Detrick and moved them to Frederick. She later graduated from our prestigious Hood College, worked there for ten years or so."

Ty looked appropriately impressed but wondered where this conversation was going.

Lamond pointed to one of the color portraits. It featured two sandy-haired, middle-aged men. "These gentlemen are stars in their own right. The Voltaggio brothers, chefs who competed on that reality show, *Top Chef.* Michael won and moved out west, but Bryan owns a few restaurants here in town."

Before Ty could formulate a reply, suitable or otherwise, the mayor indicated another color photo, a woman this time. "And if you're into mystery novels you'll recognize Barbara Mertz aka Elizabeth Peters and Barbara Michaels."

He turned to face the detective, became more businesslike. "And then there's our *most* famous Fredericktonian. Mystery writers and celebrity chefs come and go, but the heroic Barbara Fritchie is part of Civil War culture."

Ah...here it comes.

"I've had a call from a friend of mine." Lamond confided, his tone snake-smooth. "A certain history professor of your recent acquaintance. He tells me that your unsolved murder investigation involves a letter that concerns both Dame Barbara and another contender for her fame." He glanced at his phone as it began to ring, raising his voice in competition. "My friend tells me that your investigation may change the *status quo.* That's unfortunate, but it can't be helped. Personally, I'd rather see things stay the way they are. It's better for the city's tourism."

Ty was more than ready for this to end. Best just to agree and move on. "I reckon so."

The mayor let the phone ring on. "However, the town could probably weather an assault on Fritchie's legend. They're not likely to take Whittier's poem out of the literature books. And her photograph hangs in the Smithsonian's National Portrait Gallery. But this unsolved murder makes

Frederick look bad, like we're too bush league to get the job done." His expression grew stony, his voice strident. "The whole episode makes *me* look bad. It may be the responsibility of my police force to solve this murder, but it's *your* damn job. See that you do it. Quickly."

Lamond picked up the phone and waved Ty out of his office.

As he closed the door, Ty caught the mayor's parting words. "And lay off Brunner!"

·   ·   ·   ·   ·

In his own office once more, the lieutenant was itching to get back to real work. He needed to get contact information on TCC's visiting scholar. As an expert on Civil War poetry, Slattery had as much reason to want that letter as Brunner did. Maybe more.

He was just about to call the college's PR director when his phone rang. Caller ID, Maria Routzhan. Maybe his luck was changing.

"Yes, hello."

"Lieutenant, tell me there's new information to help resolve this unpleasantness? I do hope so because the College took such an undeserved beating in today's newspaper. Between this matter and the conference, I'm up to my armpits in alligators."

Ty suffered through the woe-is-me crap but didn't get a word in before she started up again.

"And the story was even picked up by the Baltimore and Washington news stations. The only time they cover Frederick is when it's either something horrific or embarrassingly bucolic."

He'd caught some of the coverage. But when contacted by the outlets he'd shunted their calls over to Bernie, per procedure at this point of the investigation. That resulted in his being labeled as "unavailable for comment" and even "elusive." João would probably give him some shit about that.

"I'm sorry, Ms. Routzhan, but there haven't been any significant developments. We're just following the usual leads," he said, giving the standard responses he'd give if he were a PR flack.

He smiled at the irony, but before he could ask about the visiting scholar, Routzhan started talking again.

"It's bad enough that the College is getting a black eye, but the press is beating the Barbara Fritchie tom-tom, too."

"Well, that's to be expected."

"Yes, but that loathsome harridan doesn't deserve any more newsprint than she's already gotten. It has very much upset Robert."

"Understandable, since Brunner's looking to bolster Nannie Crouse's reputation. And did I understand him to say that you have an interest in that?"

"Had. I *had* an interest in Nannie Crouse's story."

"Oh, why's that?"

"Well, I'd thought that I was related to her. My mother told me that we were descended from Nannie Crouse...mother to daughter through four generations. She told me when I was in elementary school, trying to help me with my self-esteem. But it turns out that she was wrong."

"I'm sorry to hear that." *Shit.* He'd walked right into this monologue. But Brunner said he was working with a descendant of Crouse, and that Maria was out of the running. So who was it?

"Robert's research proved that I *was* descended from one of Nannie's children, but that daughter turned out to be a foster child. One of the many orphans created by the Civil War. So Nannie was a good woman, just not any relation to me. It was very disappointing."

"It sounds like it must have been." Lordy, these Civil War people were intense.

"From your Southern accent, I imagine you might have Confederate ancestors. Haven't you researched your roots?"

"No, ma'am," he replied. "I'm rooted right here in the present. Being a cop and a father is enough identity for me."

"Maybe that's for the best. The disappointment can be cruel."

Enough of that, time to get back on track. But something still niggled at him, a thread left hanging. "Um...Dr. Brunner indicated that he was working with Nannie's descendant to fortify his claim that the teenager was the real heroine. Do you know who it is?"

"No," she said after a pause. "He's never mentioned it to me. What he thinks is proof is probably just another will-o'-the-wisp. He's always coming up with little snippets of information that he hopes will lead to his big break." She exhaled a long breath. "Faculty are such glory hounds."

An interesting observation. "Well, Ms. Routzhan, this conversation has been pleasant, but I'm trying to rustle up a break in this case. And you can help. I need contact information for one of the scholars who's in town for your conference. A Dr. Charlotte Slattery."

"I'd like to comply," she said, her voice nuanced with well-practiced regret, "but I'm torn between aiding the investigation and protecting the privacy of faculty under my aegis. Added to that, Dr. Slattery is a highly distinguished academician and a guest of the College. Could you tell me why you need to speak to her?"

Used to dealing with nervous-nelly types, he kept it simple. "All I can tell you is that it's in connection to the murder." He just needed the damn number.

There was some chatter on her end that he couldn't quite make out, so he waited for a response as patiently as he could and toyed with the idea of threatening her with obstruction of justice.

"Well, Lieutenant," Routzhan began, "Dr. Slattery just passed through the office here, and she says it's fine if I give you her number. However, she asked that you please wait until after lunch to call since she's meeting with Dr. Brunner this morning about the conference."

"Sure, no problem," he said, scribbling down the number. Afterward he thought about the opposing views of the two academics and wished he were a fly on that wall.

He leaned back in his chair and scrubbed his hands over his face. The morning was gone, and he had nothing to show for it. He couldn't wait to get back in the field with Maroni.

Chapter 23

The detectives savored the pale, midday warmth of late October as they walked toward the museum. Two nights ago they'd viewed everything in the cold, fluorescent glare of crime scene lights. Daylight didn't show the Barbara Fritchie house to any better advantage. The building was in decent repair, but it wasn't a showpiece.

Maroni had found out one of the maintenance guys at the college—Doug Dahlrymple, new to the crew—hadn't come back from lunch on the day of the murder, gave no explanation, either. And the crew chief said he seemed a little sketchy.

"Apparently he keeps to himself and always leaves campus at lunch. Not much to go on, but I ran him, and the guy has a record, a variety of misdemeanors, mostly in his late teens and twenties. Disorderly conduct, petty theft, possession of marijuana, and an assault. There's one felony...involuntary manslaughter. That's quite a little history." He pulled up the man's college ID picture on his phone.

Scanning the photo Ty's eyebrows lifted. "That's the guy I saw going into Brunner's office yesterday morning."

Something tugged at his memory. Assaults, maybe? He took out his notebook and checked his info on Brunner's background. The arrest dates matched. Sketchy Doug and Brunner had both been arrested for assault and disorderly conduct here in Frederick on the same day back in 1985. However, only one youth had had the charges dropped.

"'And thereby hangs a tale,'" he murmured and thought of Meg. He wondered if she'd be impressed that he knew his Shakespeare.

He returned his attention to Maroni and apprised him of the matching arrest dates, adding, "We need to talk to this Dahlrymple."

"I'll keep digging there. And I asked Brunner about his key to the museum. He opened his desk drawer to show it to me and found it missing. Got all flustery and pissed off. Might've been acting, though."

Ty was about to comment when he heard a low conversation headed their way. Both men turned their attention to the footpath beside the museum. Ty recognized one voice immediately.

"...such a shame," said Maria Routzhan, but her tone lacked conviction.

"Yes, that this historic building has been allowed to deteriorate is a travesty to history," replied a stylishly dressed woman in her 50s, trim, and well-coiffed. "The museum may be a tourism ploy, but it keeps Frederick on the map as a town where the Civil War still resonates."

"Hello, ladies," Ty called out as they came around the corner.

"Oh, Lieutenant Raleigh," Maria said, her hand flying to her throat in surprise. "I didn't expect to see you here."

"Nor I, you. But here we both are." He indicated the other man. "This is my partner, Detective Maroni." Putting on his best Southern-bred manners, he added, "And who is your companion?"

"This is the person you were asking about earlier." Battling with her over-sized shoulder bag, she gestured to her left. "May I present Dr. Charlotte Slattery."

Well, well, Ty thought. Quite a coincidence. And coincidences made him twitchy. "I can't believe my luck," he lied without so much as a prick of conscience. "I am very pleased to make your acquaintance, ma'am," he drawled. Over the years, he'd found that a Southern-boy facade could be a useful ploy. Folks expected less of him.

Slattery tossed her expertly-colored blonde head and lifted an eyebrow. "Oh, Lieutenant." Slowly lowering her designer sunglasses, she looked him over. "The pleasure is all mine."

She was obviously checking him out, but as a man or an adversary, he couldn't tell. That women found him attractive was not news. For him, it was just another tool in his toolbox. One he employed if it seemed useful.

Maroni seemed puzzled, as if he were wondering where all this was going.

Looking a little put off at Slattery's coy behavior, Maria glanced at the lieutenant and changed the subject. "You're here on the case, of course. Have you made any progress?" She stole a surreptitious look at the door. "Are you going back inside?"

Ty made a point of dragging his eyes from the blonde before he spoke to Routzhan again. "Although it sounds like a cliché, it's often useful to go back to the crime scene a time or two. But that can wait a spell." He looked back to Slattery. "I've run into just the woman I needed to see," he said, his thoughts still on how to handle things with the scholar.

She moved away from Maria to stand closer to the two men. "Well, I'm delighted at the way things turned out. Otherwise, it could have been hours until we met," she said in a sultry voice. "Ever since my sister Joyce deputized Maria to squire me around this week, the little dickens has been keeping me quite busy on campus."

"Joyce Plunkard, our academic dean, and Dr. Slattery are sisters," Routzahn clarified.

Ty brightened his face in interest. "It's fortunate that you can combine business with pleasure. It's often difficult to make time for family. Have you been here visiting very long?"

Her smile was wide and white. "I flew in last Saturday, and I'll be staying for ten days. Maybe longer." She paused and looked him straight in the eye. "I like to keep my plans...flexible."

Smiling boyishly, Ty agreed. "Flexibility is a very desirable trait."

The two forgotten people in the foursome, Maroni and Maria, glanced at each other in discomfort and then looked away.

Slattery tapped her folded sunglasses on her bottom lip. "I came to the museum because I needed a change of pace after my frustrating morning meeting. Robert was in such a peevish mood once he found that his key was missing from his very own desk drawer. It's always been hard for him to let go of something and move on."

"Oh, so you already know Dr. Brunner." And pretty well, it seemed.

"Goodness, yes. For ages and ages. We went to graduate school together, were quite...chummy for a bit."

That changed things. He assumed they'd be rivals, caught up in their own causes. But lovers, too?

She nodded her head toward Maria. "Mommy here was so intent on trying to soothe him that I practically had to browbeat her to drive me down here."

Maria shot her an angry look.

Charlotte's voice dropped low with suppressed excitement. "Here to the scene of the crime." She tapped her sunglasses on the lieutenant's shoulder. "And look how wonderfully it's turned out. I'd wanted to visit the museum again even before it was made more interesting by the murder of that poor student. But now I'm rubbing elbows with the lead investigator."

"Detective Maroni and I share the case, ma'am." More *interesting*?

Maria's watery blue eyes and Maroni's serious brown ones flew wide at Slattery's behavior. To disguise a snort of disgust, the rookie detective cleared his throat.

The scholar turned her sharp eyes to the younger man and gave him an appraising look, but she continued to speak to Ty. "Is there any chance of getting inside? I've never visited a live crime scene before. It would be fascinating."

Now that's a bizarre request, he thought. Just morbid curiosity or something more? Reliving a thrill-kill, or taunting the cops? "Sorry, ma'am. No possibility at all. The scene is still sealed. Only police personnel are allowed in." He became conversational again. "But did I understand you to say you've been here before. How's that?"

"Since I'm an expert in Civil War poetry, the Barbara Fritchie poem is of great interest to me. So naturally, I've toured the museum." She shrugged one silk-clad shoulder. "Several times, in fact. To soak up the ambiance, study the artifacts. They have a quite lovely portrait of the poet himself, John Greenleaf Whittier, and a German-language Bible that belonged to Fritchie's father. It is one of the first non-English books published in the United States...so valuable that it has been restored by the Library of Congress. And as Maria was just remarking as we walked up, it would be a great pity if we lost historical artifacts due to the museum's going downhill."

"I'm not sure I paid the poet or that Bible any mind last night. It was my first time here, and I was kinda busy."

Lightly touching Ty's arm, she murmured, "I remember my first time...here."

The already agitated PR woman blushed quickly and hitched her bag higher on her shoulder before addressing her charge. "Dr. Slattery, don't you think we'd better be getting you back to your sister's for that reception?"

"I'll be fine, dear," she said, looking from Ty to Maroni before looking at Maria again. "You just run along. I'll chat with these two gentlemen, and afterward I'll skedaddle back to Joyce's townhouse. It isn't far."

And with that, Charlotte Slattery, Ph.D., dismissed Maria Routzhan like a Southern belle would have dismissed a maid.

"Of course," Maria said with a curt nod, clearly used to taking orders, or perhaps just relieved to be going. "I have a million details to attend to before the conference. Good day, gentlemen."

Ty watched Maria depart, but he was thinking about Slattery. Despite her stylish dress and elegant air, she was no genteel Southern lady. No magnolias or sweet tea on the veranda for Charlotte Slattery. She was a carpetbagger. Where a Southern woman would wheedle with charm, this woman did exactly what she wanted and dared others to object. Was the missing letter something she'd wanted? He very much needed the answer to that question, but the circumstances weren't optimal. Best save motive for later and just go for the basics—alibi and acquaintance with the victim.

"I'm sorry, professor," he said, "but since you're an expert on Barbara Fritchie and were also in town during the time that the murder was committed, I need to ask you a few questions."

"Oh, am I a suspect? How flattering."

Ty put on a charming smile. "Not a suspect, no. I'm just getting a sense of things. Did you know Heather Hillcrest or have any contact with her, either spoken or electronic?"

"No. She didn't even exist for me until the TV news broke the story yesterday morning."

He nodded in reassurance. "It was a long shot. But even so, I need to ask you where you were on Tuesday evening between 5:30 and 6:00?"

She laughed out loud. "No foreplay? You're just going to get right down to it."

"Yes, ma'am."

"I was out having dinner with my sister. We left around 5:00."

"That's a little early for dinner, isn't it?"

"Not if you have to drive to Gettysburg, it isn't." She ran a slim hand through her blonde hair. "And we had to be back by 7:30 for that tedious reception that Delores hosted."

"Which restaurant in Gettysburg?"

"So with you, it's guilty until proven innocent?" she pouted.

"No, not at all. Just being thorough."

"Garryowen, an Irish pub. We had reservations. I ordered the Gaelic scallops, and they were delicious. Joyce paid with her credit card. Do you want the receipt?" she joked.

When two suspects alibied each other, it was time to get digging. He'd have Maroni check it out.

Ty chuckled. "No, that won't be necessary."

To Maroni, he sent their private signal. *Just hang back some. I need a little maneuvering room.*

The younger man raised his eyebrows in acknowledgement. "I thought I saw something over by that window last night. I'm gonna check it out." He moved closer to the museum but not quite out of earshot.

Once they were alone, Slattery sidled up to Ty and began a conversation before he could direct it to his own ends.

"Lieutenant Raleigh, did you know that the logo on your police cars represents the 'clustered spires' referred to in Whittier's poem? Are you familiar with it?"

"A bit," he replied and went on to recite the first lines.

> Up from the meadows rich with corn,
> Clear in the cool September morn,
> The clustered spires of Frederick stand
> Green-walled by the hills of Maryland.

"Impressive," she chuckled. "Does the department quiz you about that in orientation? Give you a crib sheet to use on the mean streets of Frederick to dispel riots and such?"

"No, ma'am. Just naturally curious, I suppose."

"Sort of *de rigueur* for a detective."

He shrugged modestly. "For the successful ones, at least."

"Here's something I bet you don't know," she teased. "That you and Winston Churchill have something in common."

"Other than the fact that we both have mothers who were born in America?"

"True but boring. This is much more interesting. History-making, even."

He laughed out loud. "No, I can't imagine what that might be."

At his partner's outburst, Maroni glanced toward the pair but went right back to studying the foundation of the building.

"Then I'll just tell you. During WWII, Churchill came to the States and then-President Franklin Roosevelt whisked him away to Camp David, known as Shangri-La in those days. Passing through Frederick on their way back, the Prime Minister asked to stop at the Barbara Fritchie House. Once he was outside on the sidewalk, he recited the ballad from memory. All sixty lines."

"Impressive," Ty said, stealing her line. "And he's clearly a better man than I am. It was touch-and-go to see if I could recite those first four lines."

"Oh, I don't know," she cooed. "You seem like a very fine man to me. A man of action and refinement. I was quite taken with your 'performance.'"

"That's my entire poetry repertoire." The woman was shameless. Time to take back the reins. "And I'm better with questions than couplets." He sent her a lingering look. "I may have a few more for you. Later, perhaps?"

"I'm so glad. But please don't give poetry the brush off. There's so much more we could share. About Barbara Fritchie and Whittier. That, and more." She glanced toward Maroni and back before she spoke in a hushed voice. "But not here, not now. Perhaps someplace more private."

"I'd be delighted to accommodate your request, ma'am."

She shuddered. "Please let's dispense with that word. Call me Charlotte."

"And you may call me Stephen."

"Give me an address, Stephen, and suggest a time."

"Just so you know, I have a reputation as a very, ah...hard-hitting investigator." Then he lowered his voice, murmuring, "I have your number, Charlotte. I'll be in touch."

"I trust those are more than metaphors, lieutenant. Ta, ta."

Once she sashayed off, Maroni walked back to Ty and looked at him in astonishment. "I could almost book her for solicitation."

"Nothing gets past you, Maroni."

"And you were flirting right back."

Ty didn't respond, enjoying his partner's indignation.

Maroni stared at him. "She's old enough to be—"

"Your mother, not mine," he interrupted with a grin.

"She's gotta be pushing 55!"

"Twice your age means twice your experience, too," he taunted.

"I thought you were sweet on that other professor lady, the one from the Academy?"

"'Sweet on?' Sounds like something my mother would've said."

"It's just that I thought I noticed some kinda spark between you two."

"Spark?" he repeated, uncomfortable with where this was going.

In the face of his mentor's uncharacteristic sarcasm, the young man fell silent.

Ty knew he'd hurt the lad's feelings. "You're a good detective, Maroni. Always trust your instincts. Don't let someone's defensiveness throw you off track. Even mine. Got that?"

He looked uncertain. "Yes sir."

"So then, if both of your suppositions are accurate—my 'spark' and my flirtatiousness with Dr. Slattery—and you believe you have a solid read on my character, what conclusion would account for all three?"

"Uh...that Slattery is playing you, but you're also playing her?"

"Good read. I need to determine if she's just 'lonely' or working her own angle. I found out that she was in town on the day of the murder and several days before that. Plenty of time to find out about the letter. Maybe even from her old grad school chum, Brunner. I'm already trying to get a look at her finances."

"At the very least she's trying to distract you."

"Have you ever known me to be distractible?"

"Not so far, sir.

Chapter 24

Meg pulled into a parking space in Frederick's Shab Row for a late afternoon caffeinated pick-me-up. The small log cabin specialty shops had originally been built for wheelwrights and other artisans who had served the stagecoaches on The Old National Pike. Over a century later, an entrepreneur had rehabbed the moldering buildings and some adjoining properties, including an old gas station. The latter was now the Frederick Coffee Connection, and Meg's destination. The eatery excelled as both a lunch place and a nighttime hotspot for live music and poetry readings—an alternative to the bar scene. But at 4 o'clock in the afternoon, it was quiet.

She turned off her truck but had to wait while Rocinante snorted, bucked, and finally laid himself to rest. The Miata had gone to Al in the divorce. The rat-bastard. She slumped back in her seat, agitating her dangling earrings. But their chiming didn't help her feel less downcast. Her afternoon classes hadn't gone well. The students were glum, and she was off her stride. Plus her meeting with Raleigh had been really strange. She couldn't get a read on him. Maybe she should give up even the pretense of dating, bring home a clowder of cats from the animal shelter and surrender to death by allergy. Hooking up with that detective was a pipe dream, one with way more minuses than pluses.

Meg collected her sweater and purse and patted Rocinante goodbye. Inside the small café, she walked past the cannily mismatched tables and chairs toward the old-fashioned wooden counter. A much tattooed and pierced young man, with a hand-knitted Rastafarian tam, was finishing up someone's cappuccino. She managed not to shudder when she noticed his Aztec earplugs.

"Good afternoon, ma'am," said the rasta-barista when it was her turn. "I hope your day is going well. How may I serve you?"

"I'll need a minute, thanks," she said, chastened by his graciousness. "Haven't decided what I want yet." She studied the blackboard that listed the specials of the day.

· · · · · ·

Lieutenant Raleigh opened the door of the café, surveyed the room out of habit, and walked up behind the woman at the counter.

He smiled to himself and speculated about the nature of coincidence. "Hello, Meg. It's nice to see you again."

She spun around and looked up at him. "Yes. Yes, it's nice..." Her face registered stunned surprise. "...to be seen."

"Well, yes it is, isn't it?" His initial amused expression broadened into a warm smile. "Now that we've established the niceties, may I buy you a coffee?" No harm in that. This was just a chance meeting of acquaintances, nothing more.

"That would be 'nice,'" she parried. "But I really had my heart set on a latté."

"Me too."

"Two lattés," said the barista. "Anything else?"

"I can recommend the chicken salad, Meg. All white meat, light mayo, dried cherries, a few walnuts, and some kind of special seasoning whose ingredients the owner won't reveal, even to law enforcement. Whaddya say?"

"No, really. A latté is plenty."

He put a hand over his grumbling stomach. "Please, won't you reconsider? Lunch never happened for me today." He'd spent it in the mayor's office, enduring yet another tongue lashing. "I'm too hungry to wait until you leave. And it would be 'nice' to sit and talk a spell, wouldn't it?"

The barista followed their banter like he had something to learn.

"If we're being candid, I'm famished, too."

He nodded to the young man behind the counter. "Make it so."

"Their chicken salad is the best around. Thank you." Then she leaned forward and whispered, "But the names here are so lame. Like our Church Street Clucker. Really?"

"Agreed," he said, matching her low tone. "My daughter loves their veggie burger, but she refuses to call it a Patrick Street Pattie."

"They could do better, don't you think?" Her eyes crinkled with mischief. "Instead of using local street names for the sandwiches, maybe they should try authors or literary characters."

"You have one in mind?"

"How about the Sylvia Plath? A vegan delight featuring a complex combination of unusual flavors to die for."

"Or the Hemingway," he riffed. "A tuna fish sandwich that's gone before you know it."

They laughed at each other's cleverness while Raleigh handed some bills to the cashier.

He studied Meg while he put his change away. Her eyes were an uncommon shade of brown...soulful and intelligent. And not all gunked up with cosmetics.

Stuffing a few bills in the tip jar, he gestured Meg to a comfortably shabby oak table in the corner. It looked out the plate glass window that had survived from the café's gas station days. He pulled out a chair for her. "Will this do?"

"Absolutely."

"Great. Because I kinda need the wall at my back."

"O...kay," she said, looking baffled.

He waited until she sat down, then he followed. Meg spent some time hitching her purse and bulky sweater over the back of the chair.

"The corner is a cop thing. It means you're less vulnerable to unpleasant surprises." And that was the end of any cop talk, he promised himself. Even though he'd offered to discuss his views about guns on campus over a coffee, no way was he gonna go there right now and screw this up. "Just so you know, the corner thing causes my daughter to roll her eyes. But she's a teenager, so her dad annoys her nonstop."

"How's she doing? I can't imagine how awful it would be to find a friend brutally attacked and dying."

"I think she's doing okay, but she has an appointment with a therapist this week." He ran a hand through his hair. "Kids get pretty close-mouthed at fifteen. It's kinda hard to tell what's going on. But I don't like to leave her alone right now." He checked the clock on the wall beside the sandwich board. "Maroni's wife is picking her up, running errands and then dropping her off when I get home." He shrugged. "Just somethin' else for her to roll her eyes about. A lack of autonomy."

The tattooed barista set down the lattés with a courteous, "Here you are. Enjoy."

"Thanks. Exceptional service, as always." After the kid left, Raleigh looked at Meg. "You work with students that age. What's up with those earplugs?"

"I was just thinking the same thing before you snuck up behind me." She shot him a coquettish look. "Are you stalking me, Lieutenant Raleigh? Or am I a suspect?"

"Neither, Professor Adams. I'm just hungry. But I did see your truck as I drove in. It's a hard buggy to miss."

"Don't cast aspirations on my truck. Rocinante is very sensitive."

"Come again? Rocinante? That name sort of rings a bell from the dim past."

"It's the name of Don Quixote's noble steed."

"Oh yeah, right. So, if that's Rocinante," he waved a hand toward her vehicle, visible through the window, "that would make you Don Quixote?" No way. Not with that sweet face and that sexy, curly hair. "Or more likely, the regal Dulcinea."

Meg's face was a study in astonishment. "You do know that she wasn't a princess, just a peasant girl in his home town, right?"

"I do."

Those words hummed in the air. Raleigh broke the silence.

"But *he* believes her to be the most beautiful woman of his acquaintance."

"You know a lot about the novel. Were you an English major?"

"Good god, no," he laughed. "I do read a lot, but my mom was death on musicals. One time she and a lady friend had tickets to see *Man of La Mancha*, but at the last minute, Miss Barbara canceled. My dad and older brother both found important excuses, and my sister Lisa was too young, only seven. That left me. The dutiful eleven-year-old son."

"No way."

"Way," he said sheepishly. "So no, not an English major. I majored in psychology."

He took in the surprise on her face. She was probably wondering how he got from there to being a cop. It baffled him some days.

"Oh," she said as her brows lifted. "Where did you go?"

"Johns Hopkins. But I could only afford it because I got an athletic scholarship."

She made an outrageously obvious point of checking him out from top to bottom.

"Not football, I'm guessing—not beefy enough. But not basketball, either—not freakishly tall. Baseball?"

"That game is toooo slow. No, I played lacrosse."

"Ah, a manly, Native American sport. Lots of running."

"Yup." Okay, she seemed interested. Time to switch it up. Probe her a little. "You were an English major, obviously. But where'd you go to college?"

He'd already checked, but he didn't want to tip his hand or appear too eager. Besides, she'd expect the return volley.

"Columbia University, for my graduate degree in creative writing. But my undergraduate school was about an hour from here. McDaniel College, in Westminster. It's a small liberal arts school."

A Megadeth tee-shirted server appeared with their sandwiches. "Here you go."

"Great timing," Raleigh said, leaning back to make room for his plate. "I've no doubt that my guest needs nourishment. She just listened to my whole life story in a single sitting."

Meg looked like she wanted to contradict him. But he'd already tucked into his meal. In less than fifteen minutes, he'd chugged his latté, cleaned his plate, and was wiping his mouth with an unbleached paper napkin. She had only taken a few ladylike bites, chewing each thoroughly.

Now crumb free, he asked, "Will you excuse me a moment?"

She nodded. After he walked to the counter, she wolfed down the rest of the first half of her sandwich. When he returned, she was nibbling on a chip.

"Thought you might like some dessert." Knowing her weakness, he passed her a bag of peanut M&Ms and enjoyed her smile as she popped one in her mouth. He was finishing up a Skor, the candy bar that had it all—crunch, toffee, and chocolate.

"Thank you kindly for the treats, Lieutenant."

He frowned a bit as he sat back down. That "lieutenant" thing needed to get straightened out. He looked at Meg thoughtfully. "The other night at the Police Academy you asked me to call you by your first name, but I didn't make the same offer." He chose his next words with caution. "It didn't seem right, given the, ah...unfortunate circumstances."

Meg stopped rooting for another M&M and waited for him to continue.

This was his next logical step, but once he took it, things would change. It would be more prudent to wait.

At the long pause, her face clouded with uncertainty.

Taking a breath, he fixed her with an earnest look and plunged in. "But now it seems sort of odd for you to keep calling me 'Lieutenant Raleigh.'" But he couldn't move too fast either, should keep things in check. "It's likely that we'll continue to run into each other for the next few days, what with the funeral and all. So we shouldn't have to be so formal." Tired of second-guessing himself, he went for it. It was just a name, for chrissake. "My given name is Stephen, but I only use that for work. My friends use my middle name—Tyler. Or even Ty, if you like."

They shared a look across the table.

"I like 'Ty' just fine."

That prompted smiles. His was Mona Lisa-like, enigmatic emotion in the eyes and an almost indiscernible shift in the lips. Hers began as a reasonably self-contained grin but was threating to unleash itself in full-bodied, Golden Retriever ecstasy.

"Well okay, then...Ty. It seems that we're on equal footing now."

He resettled himself in his chair and cleared his throat, a troubled look growing in his eyes.

Her face fell at the change in him.

"Not quite equal," he said. The timing seemed right, but he didn't relish telling her. Wondered how it might color things. "You've been very gracious not to press me on this point. But as we're anteing up, it seems only fair. You haven't asked me why I'm a single dad."

Meg ducked her head for a moment. "Well, given my upbringing, it would be prying." She shrugged. "Guess I figured you were divorced, like me."

He held her gaze, eyes worried. "It's a logical assumption, but no. I'm not divorced."

The server wandered back to check on things but slid on by when he caught their vibe.

"My wife and I met at Hopkins. And when we married, we stayed on in Baltimore because we'd both gotten jobs there." He took a deep breath. "As you probably know, it has a reputation as a dangerous city. Lots of murders."

Meg's face paled.

"One night, our home was targeted by a burglar, and she was killed during the home invasion." He looked away for a moment. "After that, Lindsay and I moved to Frederick. It's been just us for the past five years."

"Ty, that's awful," she whispered, her eyes brimming. "I'm so sorry."

"It was awful. Something you never imagine happening to you." He looked beyond Meg briefly, memories surfacing like a series of black and white photographs. But no pain in them. Not anymore. "However, Lindsay still needed a dad." He shrugged. "You do what you have to do."

Meg held his gaze. "And I'm sure you're doing a great job."

"Time will tell." At that, he brought up his hands and landed them atop the table. "Lately, it hasn't been as easy a job as it once was, that's for sure.

And speaking of time... He looked up at the clock. "She'll be getting home soon. I'm sorry, Meg, but I've gotta go."

"No worries. Really. I have to get home to my grading. Thanks for the study break."

He pushed back his chair and stood up. She rose to her feet, removed her purse from the back of the chair, and placed it on the table. The barista hurried over with a cardboard to-go box for her unfinished sandwich.

She lifted her sweater from the chair—a beige, buttonless, ribbed cardigan with a floppy crocheted collar—and looked up at him as she shrugged it on.

He walked around the table toward her. "This has been 'nice.' Maybe we could—"

"Ouch!" Meg whimpered, her head tilted sharply to one side.

"What's wrong?"

Her hands were busy at her neck. "My sweater's caught in this darned earring." She kept fooling with it to escalating sounds of distress. "Ouch, ouch, ohhh..."

Ty looked on, deciding on a course of action. "Want me to help?"

"No, no...I've almost got it," she insisted. "Ow wow wow!"

"Here. Let me see."

He moved to stand at her shoulder, leaned over and scooped aside her unruly dark hair to get a better look. She fidgeted away.

"Stand still," he said gently. "I haven't done anything yet."

Then he did.

The one hand on her shoulder didn't provoke any response. But when he brought his other hand behind the errant earring, the backs of his fingers inadvertently brushed her neck. The innocent touch produced less than innocent results, a sensation of electric warmth suffusing both of them at the point of contact.

They remained linked, rooted by the spreading heat. She closed her eyes and shivered as his touch feathered along her neck, resulting in the earring's coming free of its entanglement and the slow withdrawal of his hand. In the loud silence, each took notice of the other's breathing. They turned to face each other, both flushed.

Ty cleared his throat. "Well...that's sorted out."

"Ye-, yes," stammered Meg. "Thank you."

She started to say something else but stopped when he began to speak. "Meg, I...ouch!"

He jolted forward a little but then turned around and started talking to someone behind him.

"Lindsay, that hurt!" he scolded. "You can't go around punching people like that."

Meg moved to one side to watch events unfold.

He was rubbing his upper arm. And his daughter—garbed in artfully mismatched items and sporting spikey black hair—was grinning at him.

"Hey, you!" Lindsay sang out. "Shoulder's sore again, huh? Must be gonna rain soon."

He dropped his hand and shook his head. "What're you doing here? You didn't walk, did you?" he asked, worry tinting his voice.

She rolled her eyes at him. "I'm stopping by for dinner, duh. What else would I be doing here? And no, I didn't walk. Mrs. Maroni and I were finishing errands, and I saw your SUV here, so she dropped me off."

Meg stepped back from the fray. "It was *nice* bumping into you, Lieutenant Raleigh."

He turned toward her. "Yes, it was." He wanted to say more, but the moment had passed. He kept it light. "I'll probably see you around." His daughter was not ready for him to spring anything like this on her. And he didn't yet know what 'this' was. But he knew what he wanted it to be. "G'bye, Meg."

"Goodbye."

•　　•　　•　　•　　•

After Meg slid into the truck and gingerly shut its contrary door, she looked back into the café. Father and daughter stood at the counter, probably ordering her some dinner. Meg didn't start the truck right away, just sat and looked through the plate-glass window. And looked some more. Then, as if aware he was being watched, Ty turned partway around, one hand still on the counter. He scanned the room, then beyond, until finally, his eyes met hers. He smiled.

Knowing he was still looking at her, Meg turned the key and let the truck rumble to life.

So...he went to Johns Hopkins University? As a psych major no less. And now he's a cop? How did that happen? But he had to be really, really smart...and an athlete, too. The whole Greek ideal of *fortitudo* and *sapientia*—strength and wisdom. Oy! He was soooo far out of her league. Oh well, in for a penny, in for a pound.

Her truck threatened to stall, so she goosed the gas a little.

And what about his choice of candy, that Skor. A subliminal message about his end game? Maybe. But then again, sometimes a Skor was just a candy bar.

"Onward, faithful companion," she said to Rocinante. "Grading awaits."

Chapter 25

"Come *on*, Lindsay." Ty tapped on his daughter's closed bedroom door again. "The thing at the funeral home started at 7:00, and we're already twenty minutes past that."

"Almost ready," came the muffled reply.

He laid his hand on her closed door, imagining how hard this must be for her. He'd told her she didn't have to show up. That everyone would understand. But she was determined to go.

Patting the door lightly, he turned and jogged downstairs to the living room and sat in his lounge chair. Putting his feet on the ottoman, he closed his eyes and gave in to his worry. About her mood swings, the atypical spates of silence. About the dark circles under her eyes each morning. Had her nightmares returned? The ones about loss and helplessness. She hadn't had any of those since they'd moved to Frederick.

Then there were his own fears. What if the murderer had been hanging around long enough to see Lindsay going into the museum? He tried to tamp down his anxiety, but he'd learned a long time ago to consider all the possibilities, including the unlikely ones. Because the unexpected could take the biggest bite out of your ass.

Like being bowled over by Meg. He sure hadn't been expecting that. Didn't quite know what to do about it, either.

He'd picked up the unread morning paper and was unfolding it when his cell phone rang. Reading the display—Morningside Asstd Living—he pushed himself upright, muttering, "Hell's bells! Has he wandered off again?"

His tone turned the greeting into a question. "Yes, hello?"

As he listened, his features relaxed a bit. "Oh...Dad. Hi. Is everything okay?" He settled back in the lounger and picked up the paper. "Just checking in again, huh?"

On the front page, he noticed two photos—one of Professor Brunner; the other, Heather—and the headline: "Civil War Conference Honors Slain Student." He'd lay odds that Maria Routzhan had orchestrated that spin.

"Yes, Lindsay's going to the viewing with me, just like you called it. She's upstairs getting ready right now." Wrestling one-handed with the paper, he turned to an inside page to skim the rest of the story as he half-listened.

"Right...right." He tossed the paper to the floor, leaned the chair farther back and closed his eyes again. "Yup, I remember. I'm supposed to follow her lead, let her grief unfold naturally. You told me that last time." And the two times before that. He pinched the outer corners of his eyes between finger and thumb.

The music coming from Lindsay's room floated downstairs. Something sad, slow, and yearning.

"Yes. I know. It's all about her timeline. So you've said."

Lines of tension formed around his eyes and creased his forehead. "Sorry, Dad. I didn't mean to sound snappish." He sat up and brought his feet to the floor. "Been putting in a lot of overtime. I'm just tired. You know I value your opinion. After all, you're the expert in clinical psychology." Knowledge the old man had used with his clients. His own children, not so much.

Abruptly Lindsay's music stopped. He glanced up the stairs, left the living room, and walked to the back of the house into the kitchen.

"No, I don't have a handle on that yet. If her nightmares have come back, she isn't telling me." He leaned one hip against the edge of the kitchen table. "I wish I could set her on my lap like when she was four and snuggle her against my chest."

As he listened, his gray eyes grew cool. "You're right," he said, voice tinged with sarcasm, "they can't stay babies forever. But still, I've been keeping pretty close tabs on her since this all began."

He leaned toward the bowl of fruit on the table and started to pick up a banana. Then his expression tightened. "Oh come on! I'm not being controlling." When he stood abruptly, the table scooted back a bit, honking its agitation. "I will *not* take stupid chances where her life is concerned. What if the murderer already knows about Lindsay? Maybe he'll attend the viewing tonight hoping she'll show up so he can find out who she is? What if he assumes she knows where the letter is? What then? I'm doing this for her own safety, for chrissake!"

He clapped the phone against his shoulder while he got himself together. He ran his other hand roughly over the back of his head then slid it down to his neck and tried to squeeze away the tension. As his heart rate slowed, he put the phone to his ear again. Walking over to the back door, he raised his arm to lean against the frame and looked out the window, resting his forehead against the cool glass. Some movement in the alley caught his attention. Oh, just old Mrs. Simms walking her cocker spaniel. His mom had had one, too. Polly... He smiled at the memory. Good ol' Polly-dog. She'd spent every night on mom's hospice bed that Thanksgiving. He'd come home early from Hopkins and, six days later when the bed was empty, Polly'd returned with him.

He tuned in again. "I'm sorry, Dad. I know you don't like it when I swear." He's just an old man, Ty reminded himself. Failing more and becoming less, season by season.

He listened for a while longer, but his patience was spent. "Hey, Dad... Dad. Lindsay's finally coming downstairs. I have to get off the phone now, okay?" When had he started lying to his father? "Yes, it's been good talking. We should do this more often."

He tried to remember the last conversation he'd had with his mom...couldn't recall it.

"Sure, sure. When things slack off, I'll come down for a visit." He blew out a breath. "Yup, I'll bring Lindsay, sure thing...love you, too, Dad. Bye."

He broke the connection, tossed the cell phone on the table and watched as it clinked against the bowl and launched a thin cloud of fruit flies. While they settled, he looked up at the kitchen clock. Palming his phone, he strode to the bottom of the stairs, put one hand on the oak newel post and looked upstairs. Lindsay's door was open now, but he didn't call out right away. He stood quietly for a moment, wishing she didn't have to do this hard, hard thing. Again.

"Lindsay? The longer we wait, the more people there are to deal with, y'know."

At that, an unexpected version of his daughter descended the stairs, looking at him the whole way. She stopped on the bottom step and waited for his reaction.

She was clad in a black, short-sleeved, A-line dress with a square neckline. It was cut a couple of inches above the knee. She wore no jewelry except dainty pink zirconium earrings. To accessorize the outfit, she had donned black lace gloves—fingerless and opera-length. For shoes, she wore a pair of ankle boots from Doc Martens featuring a Victorian rose print on a black background. Her makeup was a trifle more subdued than usual.

Ty blinked in surprise, then beamed. "Well, that was worth waiting for."

She gave him a small smile. "Thanks." Then she frowned. "You really think it's okay?"

"More than okay, perfect even. It's you." God, she was amazing. She'd found a way to carry on.

The girl's delicate features were pinched with sadness as she stood there, immobile. He reached out his right hand, index finger extended, and she reciprocated until their fingertips touched. It had become their version of a hug ever since she had entered her teens.

"And Heather would love how you look."

"Yeah she would," Lindsay said, tearing up just a little. "She helped me pick out these boots last week. FedEx dropped them off this afternoon." She gazed at her father, a puzzled expression gathering on her face. "And look at you. You're wearing your good gray suit."

It was an understated and well-tailored slate-gray suit partnered with a pale gray dress shirt. The neutral tones were interrupted by a lavender tie in unpatterned silk with a dull sheen.

He glanced down at what he had on. "It's alright, isn't it? It fits okay?"

She stepped off the stairs and touched him on the sleeve. "Very alright. You used to wear it to concerts and plays and stuff all the time. Just haven't seen you in it since Mom's funeral."

Looking down, he fiddled with his cuffs and didn't respond.

"But the tie's new, isn't it? At least I don't remember it."

He was pleased and a little surprised that she'd noticed. "I wanted to wear something special for Heather. Not the same old suit and tie I put on for court all the time. The salesperson kept badgering me to get a pink one. If I'd known about your shoes, we could've matched."

Lindsay winced. "Eww. Not *pink* pink. You're not some goofy Weather Channel guy. You'd look better in ashes of roses. It's duskier, more dignified. But that one is just right. Makes your eyes look more friendly, not so much Detecto-Dad." Her smile was a subdued version of her usual impish grin. "Now if you'd just get that one ear pierced..."

Ty raised an eyebrow and wagged a playful finger. "Not gonna happen, missy. Come on. We gotta get going. You need a sweater or something? It's late October."

He took it as a good sign that she rolled her eyes at him before heading out the door. Once at the car, he unlocked it and held the door for her, provoking a huffy sigh.

After he got in, she spoke. "Did you hold the door for Mom when you were dating?"

He nodded gravely. "I did."

Her face was full of curiosity. "And she unlocked your door from her side?"

A small smile tugged at his lips at the memory. "She did not."

"Because she was totally beautiful and came from a really wealthy family."

"Yes. And all that was very intimidating for me, a lad from Tennessee. She was way, way out of my league." He was puzzled at this line of questioning but played along, grateful that her mood was lifting. "I wondered why she even gave me a chance."

"Probably felt sorry for you." Her tone was teasing, not mean-spirited. "All those old-fashioned manners." Then she lightly mocked his accent. "And that 'Soth-urn draaawl.'"

He didn't laugh at her imitation, but he did turn his head to smile at her.

"One time when Heather and I were talking," she murmured, serious now, "she said you were handsome. And I laughed at her." Lindsay hesitated. "But she was almost always right."

"Oh...huh." Not knowing what to say, he became quiet, touched by her admission.

Nodding slowly, she sniffled. "She really liked you, you know."

"I do know. I liked her too. A lot. She was smart and sweet and funny."

Lindsay's next words were almost a whisper. "I miss her."

"Of course you do...of course."

Neither spoke as they sat in the dark, replaying their own memories, asking their own unanswerable questions.

She inhaled a shuddery breath. "I miss both of them."

Ty took her hand and squeezed it. When he continued to hold it, she didn't pull away.

•   •   •   •   •

The funeral home was located in the heart of downtown Frederick, on Church Street, nestled among some of the clustered spires immortalized in Whittier's poem. Originally built in 1852 as a mansion, complete with classic Italianate architecture, it had changed hands many times. The building was a commanding, three-story brick structure with lots of ornate, white-framed windows and a variety of porticos. Anybody who was anybody was laid out there.

Its parking lot was packed when they got there and the parlor even more so. The crowd was a mix of ages and styles—somber suits and dresses vying with graphic tee shirts and jeans. The dead girl's friends and her mother's. Members of their work, church, and school community.

Ty walked in and took two prayer cards, a soft-focus photograph of a seagull soaring over breaking waves, and handed one to Lindsay. She looked lost, poor kid, like she didn't have a clue what to do, so he nudged her forward. "Why don't you sign the book for both of us?"

She did, then stood stiffly and looked around.

At the head of the room, in front of a malachite-green marble fireplace, Mrs. Hillcrest stood beside an off-white skirted table. It bore a bouquet of baby's breath and tightly furled pink roses which rested between a framed copy of Heather's senior picture and a square mahogany box.

When his daughter didn't move, Ty placed his palm in the small of her back and steered her toward the left-hand wall, to the display of photographs. They joined the line of people studying the snapshots: a diapered baby, nose-to-nose with a white long-haired cat; Heather in a slinky, bronze-y brown, floor-length gown, her hair swept atop her head arm in arm with her date at the prom; at graduation, her cap dripping off the back of her head. Scores of others portrayed her at different ages and in different situations. Sorrow and anger wrestled inside him, reminding him there'd be no more pictures.

Lindsay stopped in front of a photo near the end which featured her and Heather on the boardwalk at the ocean, both in tie-dye shirts and short shorts, hands diving into a mammoth cardboard tub of Thrasher's French fries. Next to it was a large, sepia-toned photograph of them dressed in Wild West saloon girl outfits with massive taffeta-ruffled skirts and fluffy ostrich feathers in their hair. Ty stood between them dressed as a riverboat gambler, one cowboy-booted foot crossed over the other, an arm around each of them. All three were trying not to smile and failing in different degrees, Ty most of all.

He gestured to include the whole display. "That's a nice tribute." When his daughter didn't reply, he put his arm around her.

After a while, she leaned away from him and gazed closely at the beach photo. She ran a finger down its edge, slowly, and paused when she reached the bottom corner. Then she dropped her hand to her side.

He touched her elbow. "You want to go over and say something to Heather's mom?"

Not answering, she scanned the crowd to her right and spotted a knot of other teens. "I'm gonna hang out with some of my friends, okay?"

"Sure. Come find me when you're ready to leave."

As she turned to go, she nodded to the man standing beside and slightly behind her father, also in a suit, with his hands clasped in front of him. Her smile was small and shy. "Hi, Mr. Maroni. Thanks for coming." Without waiting for a reply, she turned and left.

"She seems to be doing okay," the younger man observed. "Sad but not depressed."

"Yeah. That worries me a little, though. Can't tell if she's really okay or if she's just keeping a lid on it all. If that's the case, when she blows, it's gonna be ugly."

Maroni nodded. "Well, let me fill you in on my afternoon." He dropped his voice. "I went back to the college and pinned down that sketchy HVAC guy, Doug Dahlrymple. He says he had a bad sinus headache the day of the murder and that's why he didn't go back to the college after lunch. He lives alone, so there's no one to corroborate his story. And get this. When I caught up with him at work, he was wrenching on some massive pipes. They were old and sorta rusty, but they didn't give him any problem. He's strong enough to have smashed a skull."

"And I saw him being summoned into Brunner's office the day after the murder. They might be working together." He looked around to make sure they couldn't be overheard. "The forensic report's in, but it wasn't useful. Not surprising since our crime scene is a museum. Too many prints."

At a sudden squall of laughter, both men turned to find its source. It was coming from the group of students Lindsay had joined. Kids dispelling their nervous energy. Only Lindsay remained quiet, a fact both men acknowledged silently when their eyes met again.

"I need to pay my respects to the family," Ty said. "How 'bout you?"

"Already did. Figured you'd be tied up with Lindsay for a while, so I got here early to study the crowd. Like you've told me...a lot of perps like to watch their handiwork play out.'"

"Good plan. What did I miss while Lindsay was getting gussied up?"

"Not much. I mean, folks are mostly behaving like they do at these things. Religious types hang out together, kids hang with kids, adults with adults. But there was almost a set-to when Heather's deadbeat dad showed up."

Ty ran the backs of his fingers along his jawline. "Hmm. Anything else of significance?"

"Just some commotion when several people complained to the funeral director guy that a photographer was out front on Church Street taking pictures as people walked in."

"Like paparazzi? Here in Frederick?"

"Yeah. Crazy, huh? Plus there was a reporter out there asking about people's memories of the dead girl and trying to get'em talking about the murder itself."

"What?"

Maroni nodded. "The funeral director went outside to try and talk some sense into the pair of them. But the reporter took the standard media line. Said that the murder was news and people were curious, had a right to know."

"They do deserve the facts. But the family also deserves its privacy."

"He claims our department spokesman is giving him the brushoff."

Way to go, Bernie. "Which reporter was it? Skip?" He sighed at Maroni's nod. "I'll call him later. Try to give him enough scoop so he'll back off."

"Well, it was the PR woman from TCC who got everything under control."

"Oh...how's that?"

"The mother got wind of it all while she was talking to that lady president and Routzhan. Mrs. Hillcrest got real upset, and the PR woman gave her boss a look, said she'd take care of it and went outside to talk to the reporter and his camera guy."

"Well, that was handy."

"And dragged me along like I was her sidekick," he grumbled.

Ty grinned. "Oh, the joys of working for the public."

The younger man mumbled something and shrugged.

"I'm not surprised that Routzhan stepped up. She's actually really good at her job, not that I'd want it. This murder is a train wreck for the college, for the conference, too. But that's what PR people do, take care of things. Usually in one of three ways: schmooze, deflect, or protect. A little effort up front beats all hell out of doing damage control down the line."

"Whatever," Maroni said, sounding only slightly older than Lindsay. "Not my kind of person. Insincere...and kind of pushy. At least she was with me."

"It's just the job," he shrugged, relieved that he wasn't the only one she annoyed.

"Routzhan told the reporter she'd collect some 'personal insights' from the teachers. And that she had her camera in the car and would stay after to take some pictures of the table with the bouquet and the big photo, and some from the display of candid shots...if that was alright with Mrs. Hillcrest. After the mom agreed, the reporter went away happy."

"Gotta hand it to ol' Maria, that was quick thinking. Anything else I should know?"

Maroni reported that most of the suspects had turned up—except for Dahlrymple and Sellers—and that the college types were keeping to themselves in the overflow room.

"Brunner has himself stuck up the president's skirts. The dean and that sister of hers are holding court with anyone who'll listen. And when that Slattery woman spied me, she made a big deal outta asking about you."

His eyes sparkled at Maroni's weak attempt to restrain his dislike. "Did she now?"

"She did. And that got your English teacher's attention."

Ty felt a flash of discomfort at that revelation. "Oh." He paused but decided not to react to that *your* or press for details. "Well, I would have expected Meg to be here."

"Speaking of which," Maroni said with mock innocence, "I notice that Lindsay isn't the only one who got gussied up. A purple tie? For real?"

He put on a bland face. "I think it's time I paid my respects to the family."

•   •   •   •   •

Mrs. Hillcrest, face pale under her make-up, was shaking hands and receiving hugs as people filed past her, some pausing longer than others. Her black suit was unadorned except for a 2-inch photo button with her daughter's picture on it, pinned to her shoulder. She invited each mourner to take one from a woven basket that rested beside the bouquet. She didn't seem to recognize the tall man in the gray suit, finally focusing on him as he spoke.

He'd dreaded this moment. Of seeing Heather's mom here, a hostage to ritual, knowing how devastating it was to lose your own heart.

"How're you holding up, Betty?"

She looked up at him with eyes glassy from tranquilizers. "Do you know anything yet?"

"We're doing everything possible." And still, it wasn't enough, he knew. Not enough for a dead child's mother. So he shifted the focus. "Lindsay's here. She hasn't worked herself up to come see you yet, but I expect she'll be along directly. If not, I hope you'll understand."

"Of course I do. This has been a horrible ordeal for that child. It might be too much for her right now. If she wants to back out of reading something at the service, I'll understand." She dipped her head to hide the few tears leaking down her cheek.

Taking her hand, Ty squeezed it briefly. He stepped away and looked around the parlor for his daughter and saw her in a corner with a few friends. He tried to catch her eye, but she wouldn't look his way. Deciding to respect her process, he walked toward the overflow room where the TCC people had congregated.

Chapter 26

Positioned apart from the others, Joan and Meg were standing along the wall that separated this room from the main one but several feet down from the archway that connected the two. Both were wearing demure black dresses and subtle jewelry. Meg had also pinned Heather's photo button on the left shoulder of her dress.

"I cannot stay here much longer," Joan said. "I don't know what is more nauseating. The cloying scent of those stargazer lilies in the College's ostentatious bouquet or the staged sympathy of our 'esteemed' administration and those self-important Civil War conventioneers." She clucked her tongue. "As if any of them gives a Fig Newton about that poor dead child."

"Joan, hush up! Robert might be close enough to hear you."

She cut her eyes at Meg but also lowered her voice. "He could well be her killer." She stared at him for a moment, eyes narrowed. "Or paid to have it done."

"I know. It's all so creepy. We're standing amidst a passel of murder suspects."

Joan toyed with her necklace while she sneaked a peek over at the other TCC folk. "Just look at that Slattery woman. She's ambition personified. Once she saw the photographer outside, she sidled right over. That hussy's not here for the deceased. She's here for the exposure." Joan abandoned her necklace play. "A quality her outfit has a little too much of. That neck of hers has too much crepe for so deep a décolletage."

Meg arched a brow in agreement. "She reminds me of Lady Macbeth, intent on being the queen. Murdering to protect her precious scholarly reputation."

"And our 'beloved' Dean Plunkard would have no problem murdering on her sister's behalf. Or covering it up if she knew. Stone-cold bitch."

The women stalled their conversation while a trio of students from Heather's American lit class walked past them on their way to the exit on the other side of the room. Meg acknowledged Nate's subdued wave with one of her own.

Once they were gone, she continued. "At least Jon Sellers hasn't turned up tonight. And he wasn't back in class today. If the gods are merciful, he's gone for good." Her look turned thoughtful. "Most of Heather's other teachers showed up. Di Salvia, the Spanish language adjunct and a couple of those nice math people."

"David made an appearance. And that curly-haired woman in counseling."

"All things considered, this administrative-heavy turnout lets Mrs. Hillcrest know that her daughter's passing has been noted at the highest level. As it deserves to be." She scowled at the larger TCC group. "I don't always see eye to eye with the higher-ups, but I...I, aye yi-yi!"

She stopped talking and stared beyond Joan, her mouth slightly agape. And while her coloring had been washed-out all evening, it was now reddening at an alarming rate.

Joan scrutinized her friend. "'You...you,' what?" Then she added in alarm, "Did you take both of those Ativan I gave you?"

"It's him!"

"Lieutenant 'Dreamboat' him?"

"Oh yeah," sighed Meg, embarrassed at her reaction but unable to stop herself.

"That's good, right? Now that he's here, we'll be able to go home soon. Or at least I will. I'll give it five minutes then I'm off."

Meg noticed that Joan was scoping him out, likely making her own assessment of the gray-suited man.

"That suit fits perfectly," Joan observed. "This occasion, his contours, and in your enchanted-bungalow, white-picket fence, 2.5 children fantasy." She looked around the room. "Speaking of which, where is the daughter? I'd like to actually meet her."

"Shut up, Glotfelty," she hissed. "You are so inappropriate." But she couldn't look away.

Charlotte Slattery floated over to Raleigh, took his arm and drew him into her group of power players: Collins, Plunkard, Brunner. And the ubiquitous Routzhan on the fringes. They stood in the middle of the room underneath the elaborate ceiling that would have been requisite in a large, 19th-century Italian estate. The two voyeurs quieted, straining to hear the conversation between the detective and the scholar.

"Good evening, Lieutenant," Charlotte crooned. "I didn't expect to see you again so soon."

Ty responded pleasantly. "Good evening, Charlotte."

"It's looking up now that you've arrived. Not only are you investigating a murder, but I just learned that you are spearheading the College's move to arm its security force."

Spearheading? Meg could feel Joan looking at her, but neither woman spoke, not wanting to lose their anonymity and eavesdropping advantage.

Charlotte squeezed the detective's arm. "Plus, you're famous. Maria got talking to your department's PR person, and he told her about how you'd caught that serial killer over in Baltimore."

"I'm just doin' my job."

She ran a fingertip along her exposed collarbone. "If I were the murderer of that Hillcrest girl, I'd feel incredibly threatened knowing that you were on the case."

"I'm tenacious and very motivated. I'll catch this killer, just like the other one."

"I imagine you will." She patted his gray-sleeved forearm. "Or, as they say, die trying."

Ty disentangled from her as he moved toward Brunner, aiming to mix business with ritual. Flattery would set the professor off balance, make him think he'd won the last round with his call to the mayor.

"I saw the write-up in today's paper. I'm sure you were behind the Conference's tribute to Heather. Nicely done. Very respectful. I'm sure her mother was deeply touched."

Brunner drew himself up as he accepted the compliment. "Well, it is gratifying to know that my gesture provided some comfort to Mrs. Hillcrest."

"How magnanimous of you, Robert," Charlotte chimed in. "And here I thought you only did it for the publicity." She cocked her head to one side like a malevolent sparrow. "Alluding to the girl's letter so you could natter on about history's shabby treatment of Nannie Crouse. However, without that document, literature still trumps history. And you still lose."

Uncomfortable with Slattery's jab, others in the group looked at various points in the room. But the detective's eyes sharpened with concentration.

Brunner responded in icy tones. "My intentions were entirely altruistic."

"Of course they were," Charlotte soothed. "The media attention was a mere crumb to feed your ego." Her tone remained syrupy as she continued, but her eyes grew chilly. "Because I should think the loss of this letter pushes your scholarship even deeper into the shadows than before. You can't feather your nest with a letter that's flown the coop, can you?"

Although Raleigh was closely following the conversation, a movement near the archway caught his attention: Meg and Joan shrinking back, trying to be wallflowers. But Brunner's response drew him in again.

The man's florid face was purpling with anger. "Your behavior, Charlotte, is egregiously and categorically unsuitable. We are here to honor the passing of a student, not besmirch reputations and spread calumny."

With that, he stalked off, leaving those assembled to stare after him.

Even the Dean appeared shocked. "Charlotte, how could you?"

Embarrassed, the group edged away from her and reformed in clumps, leaving the scholar alone with her sister.

President Collins broke off talking with her PR woman and was about to go after Brunner, but Maria leaned in for a whispered conversation and then hurried after him. All the while, Joan stared daggers at Slattery.

Plunkard turned as if to say something to Charlotte but stopped when she saw Ty observing them. Her expression became stony, and she held his gaze for some time before returning her attention to her sister.

That was odd, Meg thought. The dean was embarrassed by her sister's behavior, but that look telegraphed something else. Had it been a warning to Ty to back off from investigating Charlotte? Or a challenge from murderer to cop?

The detective kept his gaze on Plunkard, a considering expression on his face. Meg would give a penny for those thoughts. She looked away as Raleigh headed over toward her.

Squeezing her friend's hand, Joan spoke comfortingly. "Meggie, I am so sorry. Your poor student deserved better than all this drama."

Meg's eyes began to brim with tears. "Yes she does. I wish that horrible woman had never shown up. But don't say anything to her, please Joan."

Nodding toward the new arrival, Joan said, "If Lieutenant Raleigh weren't here to keep the peace, I'd give Charlotte the harlot a piece of my mind. But I won't sink to her nasty level."

"Thank you, ma'am." He smiled gravely at her. "Saves me the paperwork."

Joan enfolded her friend in a warm hug. "I should be leaving. Call me later if you want. Or stop by. Okay?"

Left alone with Ty, Meg sighed. "Why do people behave so badly at the worst times?"

Ty's handsome face clouded with concern. "I ask myself that all the time. Me, I'm trained to expect it, deal with it. But you're not."

Meg nodded as she looked through the archway into the main salon. "It's not just that awful woman. It's the whole thing. Seeing that square mahogany box leaves me shell-shocked."

"Unexpected deaths are often the most difficult, especially so if the deceased was young. Feeling numb is a normal response at this stage." He paused. "I'd be surprised if you'd had a different reaction."

"I'm sorry to be so maudlin." She inhaled a ragged breath, remembering his sad story. "But maybe you should've used that psych degree and gone into counseling. You're very good at this, you know."

"Either way I'd be talking to lots of bereaved people."

"Well, this bereaved person can't thank you enough."

"It's all part of our friendly service, ma'am," he said, eyes warm.

Meg's smile was tentative but genuine. Not wanting him to leave, she cast about for another topic of conversation. "Oh no, you don't have a photo button."

"They were running kind of low, so I thought I'd pass and give others a chance."

"The student government kids at school came up with the idea, so I can get my hands on lots more. Here, take this one."

She unpinned the button from her dress, taking care not to snag it in the knit material. Holding the button with one hand, she slid the other between the crisp dress shirt and his lapel. She concentrated on piercing the gray fabric with the pin; pushing firmly and feeling it sink into place. Once done, she patted the button and looked into his eyes. And found him looking at her.

"Thank you," he murmured.

Something in his eyes caught her. A tenderness perhaps, and the impression that he really saw her.

As she slid her hand away, she felt something hard under his jacket. A shoulder holster? He'd worn his gun to a memorial service? She abruptly dropped her hand to her side and stepped away.

His back was toward the cluster of TCC people and the archway to the main room, so he hadn't seen Lindsay finish talking with Mrs. Hillcrest and pass into the overflow room to look for her father.

But Meg had. She saw Lindsay's face cloud when her own hand left the detective's chest. Saw the light dawn as the girl recognized her from the coffee shop. Saw the confusion and wariness in her eyes as she drew near and called to her father.

"Dad?"

He turned toward her voice and took a step back. "Lindsay. There you are."

The detective looked relieved to know his daughter's whereabouts, but his normally composed expression seemed a bit unsettled, like an unfocused photo of itself. For her part, Meg stood quietly with her hands clasped in front of her, trying to master her face and her emotions.

"I've just been talking to one of Heather's teachers," he said. "Let me introduce you to the English professor who was her mentor, Meg Adams."

Lindsay's eyes snapped on the unfortunate professor.

"And Meg, this is my daughter, Lindsay."

The girl's brows drew together as she examined her dead friend's teacher. She crossed her arms, gloved hands on her elbows. "So you're Professor Adams?"

Meg tried for a light touch. "Guilty as charged." And instantly wished she hadn't.

"It was your assignment, right? The one that sent Heather to that museum?" Her blue eyes burned with glacial fire. "You might reconsider before assigning it again."

Before anyone could move or speak, Lindsay marched out of the room, through the crash doors and into the night.

Chapter 27

Ty stared at the door through which his daughter had fled, wondering what the fuck had just happened.

"I'm really sorry about that, Meg," he said, each word edged with embarrassment and anger. "Lindsay's under a lot of strain, but she had no call to go off on you like that. I'll get her back in here to apologize."

"No. Don't." Her cheeks burned, but no tears fell. "Neither of us needs that right now."

"Okay. I can see that." He wanted to say more, stay and sort things out. "But here's the thing. I have to catch up with Lindsay." He hated having to choose. "I'm worried the killer might've seen her at the museum and could go after her, too. I need to get her safely home." His eyes turned charcoal dark. "Where I can give her a piece of my mind."

Meg's face held neither understanding nor condemnation. "Go. Just go." She waved her hand toward the door. "Go after her."

Her guarded look and stiff posture felt like a gut punch. "I'll call you." She simply stared at him. Not good. "I'll understand if you don't want to pick up, but I *will* call."

"I'm sure you will." Her lack of inflection left it open to a variety of interpretations.

He didn't know what to say to that. As he walked away, another knot tightened his gut.

Outside on the porch, he saw Lindsay stomping across the parking lot toward their SUV. Before he could move to intercept her, he noticed Brunner and Routzhan standing out front on Church Street, talking. When another man crossed the street and joined them, Maria's posture stiffened, and she stalked off. It was Sketchy Doug.

Ty pulled out his cell. "Maroni, you inside or out?"

"Out."

"Good." He kept an eye on Lindsay as he talked. "Brunner and Dahlrymple just met up out front, and they're walking west on Church. Follow them, okay? I'm taking my daughter home."

"On it."

That done, he focused on Lindsay. She was about 100 feet away, walking briskly toward their vehicle.

"Lindsay, wait up."

Receiving no acknowledgement, he started to step off the porch and head in that direction when something else caught his attention. Sellers at the back of the parking lot. There, then gone.

Ty's anxious features harshened as he sped down the steps. "Lindsay Claire Raleigh, don't you walk away from me when I'm calling to you." When she didn't answer or pause, he dashed after her. "You just stop right there, young lady."

Lindsay had already passed their SUV. Her pace had slowed, and she was walking tentatively toward the unlighted back of the property line.

"Stop." Ty caught his daughter by the arm. "What the hell are you doing way out here?"

"I thought I saw that asshole, Sellers."

"If you did, he's gone now." He scanned the scene, hoping he was right. "Besides, being in the parking lot isn't illegal."

She twisted out of her father's grip. "He might have killed Heather. Do you get that?"

"I get it." He steered her to the car, unlocked and opened the door. "But the operative word is 'might.'"

"How can you be so neutral, so...so uncaring?" She was trembling, both angry and cold.

Trying not to let the words sting, he slipped off his jacket and settled it around her shivering frame. "This is how I catch the bad guys. Keeping my cool gives me the edge and lets me hear things, see things I might miss otherwise. Opens up opportunities for action rather than reaction."

"Yeah. And how's that working out for you?" she taunted as she slipped into her seat.

With a deep sigh, he got in the car and drove back toward home. Neither of them spoke.

After a few blocks, Ty chanced a look in her direction and broke the silence. "Lindsay, I know you're angry about Heather's death. But you're targeting the wrong people. We need to talk about—"

"Not now," she interrupted, voice brittle.

The detective held off, but he worried for the rest of the ride home. Once there, he unlocked the back door while she stood behind him on their leaf-strewn deck.

A gust of chilly air brought down more leaves, and he turned to see Lindsay cross her arms over her chest. With a quizzical look on her face, she reached into the breast pocket of his suit jacket and drew something out.

Her expression lit with excitement. "These are Mom's."

Perplexed, he turned toward her and examined what she put in his hand. A pair of dainty gold earrings...lover's knots.

"They are, aren't they?" He couldn't for the life of him remember how they'd gotten there. After rolling the trinkets in his hand for a bit, he lifted his eyes and studied his daughter. "What a perfect night for these to come back." He raised her hand up, placed them in her palm, and closed her fingers around them.

Blinking back tears, the girl looked from her fist to her father and back again. When he opened the door, she headed through the kitchen to the family room.

Ty followed quietly and watched as she sat on the well-worn leather sofa and opened her hand again.

●　　●　　●　　●　　●

Even though Joan had invited her over, Meg was going home. To bed. To sleep, but not to dream. She just wanted to forget the whole evening. Dead students. Snarky colleagues. Intriguing men. Outraged daughters. She didn't want to process any of it.

When her phone rang she eyed it warily. But it was Joan, not Ty. "What's up?"

"Meg, I need a favor."

"Name it," she sighed. Much as she wanted to beg off, she couldn't.

"I need you to come over and stay with Maya while I dash up to Hagerstown. Chloe and Douglass were in an accident coming home from his karate tournament."

"An accident? Oh no! Was anyone hurt?"

"No, thank god. But the car's totaled, and I've got to go get them."

When Meg knocked on the townhouse door, Joan rushed out and away, leaving Meg with Chloe's ten-year-old daughter.

"Hi-ya, Maya," she said after giving the girl a hug. "It's good to see you, but I'm sorry the circumstances are so upsetting. Are you okay?"

"Yeah."

Her brave little smile and moist eyes belied that, prompting Meg to give her another big hug.

When she pulled back, Maya added, "Mom said they're both fine."

"Okay, then. Shall we catch up over ice cream?"

"Sounds good to me," she said, taking Meg by the hand and leading her into the kitchen. The girl sat at the table while Meg went to the refrigerator.

"Maya, I loved that last short story you emailed me. The setting helps the reader see the world you've built. My favorite character is the dragonfly who was a scout sent by the priestess."

The girl beamed. "Thanks for looking over my story, Aunt Meg."

"I always enjoy reading good fiction."

And Maya's was. Not like some of the other stuff people asked her to read. Sure, she taught creative writing, but she got paid for that. She didn't mind David's asking her to proofread the articles he sent out for publication. They were friends.

Others nudged their way in. Like the office manager in the art department whose sentimental love poems exploded with similes. Or Maria's lackluster article on Middletown's role as a hospital in the Battle of Antietam. She should stick with press releases. Those kinds of people just wanted her to tell them how great their work was. But Maya, bless her, she had talent.

After Meg filled two bowls, she and the child sat beside each other on the padded bench in front of the butcher block kitchen table set in the three window bump-out. The adult in a modest black dress, the child in a flannel nightgown, printed with daisies.

Meg adored both Maya and Douglass. When Chloe and Joan had started dating, she'd been worried about how Joan would handle the whole step-mom thing. But the warmth that lay under her sarcastic wit had flowed easily, and Joan got on amazingly well with both of them. Just showed there was no accounting for logic where love was concerned, she mused.

"Aunt Meg, what's going on with that murder investigation? Mom won't let Joan talk about it in front of us. But I think it's important for kids to know stuff like that."

Uh-oh. Out of the fire into the frying pan. But the child was obviously worrying. "The police are asking different people lots of questions. They are running down leads. So they'll keep following the clues one after the other until the mystery is solved."

"But they'll catch that guy, won't they?"

Tough question. "They really want to, and they're trying very hard. I expect they will."

Maya played with her melting ice cream, one hand stabilizing the blue bowl.

Meg studied her. The girl's caramel complexion seemed a little pale. And she was so still, so subdued. "Are you feeling okay, honey?"

"Yeah."

"Does this investigation have you worried?"

"No. Not really."

"Then what is it? Something at school?"

She kept stirring her ice cream.

"You can tell me."

Maya raised her troubled brown eyes. "I'm a bad person. I made fun of the new girl today."

Wow, that was unexpected. Chloe's kids were well-behaved. "How come?"

"Because Madison and Hannah were teasing her, saying she had on K-Mart clothes and cheap sneakers. So I said she had a stupid Disney princess lunch box. But it was Alyssa who pushed her down and made her cry."

"How did that make you feel?"

"It made my stomach hurt."

"I'll bet. But you know what? That doesn't make you a bad person. You wouldn't feel so bad if you weren't good. I think you're a good person who had a bad day."

"Really?"

"Really. And I suspect that Alyssa girl must have a lot of bad days. That makes her kind of scary, doesn't it?" At the child's nod, Meg continued. "And you know what? People who act scary are often feeling that way themselves. They're insecure. Alyssa's probably mean to other people to scare them off so she won't get hurt. Does that make sense?"

"Kind of. I think so."

"Who are some of your other friends?"

"Kylie and Aaliyah."

"Did they tease the new girl, too?"

"No, they just watched. And they left when Alyssa got mean."

"Well, tomorrow you could hang out with the new girl. It sounds like she might be a nicer friend than those other three girls."

"Okay."

"And maybe next time you could stand up to Alyssa."

At Maya's dubious look, Meg changed the subject. She'd brief Joan and Chloe and let them sort that one out. "Okay, let's get you tucked into bed."

· · · · ·

When the rest of the family got home, it was late. Chloe and Douglass declined ice cream and went straight upstairs, leaving Meg and Joan to talk in the kitchen. The blue glass shades on the overhead light fixture created a glow that made the space intimate.

Joan took a dainty bite of a single scoop of ice cream. "What should have been a fender bender turned into a four-car pileup." The spoon clinked as she abandoned it in the bowl. "They had to call the police. Luckily, my babies were in car number four. No injuries just jangled nerves and a ream of paperwork."

"It sounds exhausting, but I'll bet you're relieved."

She nodded. "So what happened after I left the funeral home?"

"Remember you said you'd like to meet the daughter? Well, I did. It didn't go well."

"Uh-oh. How 'not well' did it go?"

"Pretty darn 'not well.' But Maya and I talked it out and decided that mean girls are just scared girls."

Joan's fixed gaze gave Meg an opening to elaborate, but she didn't need to anymore. Or the rest of her second helping of ice cream, she realized as she pushed the bowl away.

"Oh, there is something else, though. When I pinned a photo button on the detective's lapel, I felt a shoulder holster. He was packing heat."

Still in her funeral outfit, Joan shrugged a cashmere-clad shoulder, setting her silver chandelier earrings in motion.

"What did you expect? He's in the middle of a murder investigation, and that place was chockful of suspects. If something had gone down, he'd have needed more than a Cross pen."

Meg shook her head doubtfully and decided to change the topic. "I don't know what to expect anymore. Maybe Mercury is in retrograde, or something. But get this. I had a call yesterday from Al. He phoned to say that he and Julie are pregnant."

She saw Joan's stunned expression but kept on talking before her friend could reply. "Which will make me an aunt to the child of my ex-husband and my little sister."

"Jesus, Mary, and Josephine!"

Meg gave a little snort. "Yeah, the whole deal sounds like a cable TV trailer-trash special. But I'm too tired to get worked up over it." And it was a lot to process right now. If she got much more on her plate, she'd hit emotional overload. Better to let sleeping dogs lie. And slutty sisters.

"Don't play that game with me, girl."

"What game?"

"The it's-all-good game. That's a crock, and you know it. You might not want to talk about that Raleigh girl, and I'll cut you some slack on that, for now. But I'm not gonna let you slide on this Al and Julie thing. They're *pregnant*."

"So I'm supposed to do what? Get drunk? Pine away? Fall on my sword?"

"You can get as snippy as you like, but I'm not the one you're mad at."

"Mad? Damn right I'm mad. We were married for eight years. I put him through grad school. We had plans. To save for a vacation home at the beach. To travel overseas. To grow old together," she fumed.

"And to have a family. You went through all that testing, the fertility treatments."

Joan didn't know how deep that cut. She'd never told her about the miscarriage. "Yeah, we tried to have a family. It was part of the grand plan," she said, voice heavy with sarcasm.

"And what about Julie?"

"What about her?"

"About how you're mad at her, too."

"Mad doesn't begin to cover it. I was *mad* when I found out that Al had boffed his best man's date during our wedding reception. In the limo with the *Just Married* sign on the back."

"Dear God in Heaven! You never told me that," she sputtered. "If I'd known, the ink wouldn't have dried on that marriage license before I'd have driven you to the courthouse for an annulment."

"I didn't find out right away. And later it was too humiliating. The other dalliances—secretaries, barmaids...even clients—couldn't hold a candle to that one. Not until Julie."

Joan shook her head. "I thought I knew that girl. We all grew up together, same hometown, same schools."

"You were so much older. She was still in middle school when you started working in New York City. Then our parents died in that plane crash, and I had to fill in as mom." And that hadn't gone all that well. "People grow up, change."

"Hmmph. A woman starts sleeping with her sister's husband? That's not a change. That's a mutation. How could she do you like that? I remember how concerned she was when you were in the hospital a while back. She stayed with you for a week or so."

"Yeah. That's when the affair started." And she was surprised at how much it still hurt to think about it. "But you're right about her being supportive back then. I really needed her, at least at first." She held back the rest, just for a moment, unsure of how Joan would react. "Julie came because I had a miscarriage. A pretty bad one."

"Oh, honey. I'm so sorry." She clasped Meg's hands in hers. "Why didn't you tell me?"

"I'm sorry Joan. But I couldn't, just couldn't. You were in the middle of that custody battle for Chloe's kids, and I was too depressed. Al was messed up, too. Julie claims she was only trying to comfort him, that he turned it into a tryst. He says she came on to him, but he's a lying, manipulative son of a bitch. I don't care anymore. It's done. I'm over it...and them."

Joan gave her friend a searching look and squeezed her hands, but didn't push her on it.

"But Meg, now she's pregnant. How are you going to deal with that?"

"I don't have time for it right now. A dead student trumps a slutty sister." And it was enough to mourn Heather without revisiting the grief Julie's pregnancy had dredged up.

When Joan opened her mouth to jump in again, Meg took a preemptive strike. "I'll talk with my therapist about it, okay?" It wouldn't be the first time Julie was the topic du jour.

"Promise?"

Meg nodded. "It's not a hard promise to keep."

"Okay then. But there's one more thing I have to say. Don't let this whole Al episode screw things up for you with your lieutenant."

Meg's shoulders slumped. "Not likely, since the lieutenant and I don't have a 'thing.'"

"But you could," Joan said, cupping Meg's cheek. "And you should."

"I know." Meg's eyes teared. "And that's what scares me. I really want to, but..." She dropped her chin and pulled back from Joan.

"You're afraid. I know. But not all men are cheats and liars. Has this one given you any reason not to trust him?"

No. No, he really hadn't, she thought. He'd actually been upfront with the whole daughter thing. He'd been frustrated with the girl, but he wanted to protect her, too. And he was mindful of how her words had hurt Meg. He'd been surprisingly open and forthcoming about his feelings.

But her reply to Joan was, "It's too early to tell."

Joan raised an eyebrow. "So what are you going to do?"

Cut and run was her usual MO, but that was because the guys she'd been seeing were like Bad Date Brad. She shrugged. "Guess I'll just have to stick it out and see what develops."

The two women gazed at each other for a long moment, and Meg wondered what her friend was thinking. She was about to ask when Joan spoke.

"You know what? You seem more like yourself than you have in over a year. Stronger, less immobilized. I mean, there's a whole lot of drama going on, and you aren't overwhelmed."

"Thanks. You're right. I'm in a different place, and I owe a lot of that to you, you know."

Joan just tut-tutted in response and busied herself with rinsing the ice cream bowls and putting them in the dishwasher.

"You've been there many a time for me over the years, as well," she said, then pulled Meg up from the table. "What you need, m'dear, is a good night's sleep. It's late. Just stay over."

After bidding goodnight to her friend, Meg closed the door of the guest bedroom. The lavender and cream color scheme calmed her, as she was sure the interior designer had intended.

Meg was dog-tired after a day of unending surprises, both good and ugly, and couldn't wait to fall into bed. Someone had already laid out a nightie for her. She ran a finger over the pin tucking on the bodice of the ankle-length cotton gown. It was like something Jane Eyre would've worn.

She scanned the built-in bookcase to find something to read while she settled in for the night. She slipped her all-time favorite off the shelf—Anne Tyler's *Dinner at the Homesick Restaurant*—and into bed she slid.

Half an hour later, she hadn't turned three pages. Clicking off the light, she tried to relax. But she couldn't stop thinking about him, and that was confusing. He'd carried a gun to a viewing, for pity's sake! Added to that, he ran hot and cold with her. It'd really stung when he'd left her standing there. But then again, as a parent, he'd done the right thing. Lindsay was his only child, motherless and half scared out of her wits. Plus, she could be in actual danger.

Meg hadn't closed the pleated blinds before getting into bed, and now the moon was beginning to rise over the low mountains in the distance, seeming to reverse time as night turned back toward day. She traced the pin-tucked neckline of her nightgown with a restless finger, wondering if her Mr. Rochester was thinking about her.

The moon—lustrous and unconcerned—cleared the ridge.

She wondered if this, this...whatever-it-was with Raleigh was going to develop into something? Or was she going to end up like an Anne Tyler character? Memorable and quirky but ultimately unfulfilled.

Chapter 28

Ty stood in front of the leather sofa and studied his daughter, trying to gauge her mood. He saw her glance beyond him and knew she was studying the objects on the mantel above the cold hearth. Souvenirs that his wife had brought back from her overseas business trips. Among them, sets of nesting dolls from Russia. For Lindsay—Harry Potter and friends, all the way down to a tiny Hedwig. For him, the Beatles.

Lindsay took off her Doc Martens, eased into the corner of the couch and tucked her feet under her.

Ty watched the migration. Ordinarily, she'd go upstairs to her room, so he figured she must be feeling kinda low. "How about I fix us some tea and crank up the fireplace?"

When she nodded, he got busy building a two-log fire and then went to the kitchen to fix the tea. In the middle of that, his cell rang.

"Yeah, Maroni," he said quietly. "What's up?"

"I followed Brunner and Sketchy Doug. They went into Olde Town Tavern for a beer. When they left there, Dahlrymple let them into one of those old townhouses across the street. I checked, and that's his address. You want me to hang around?"

"No, go on home. But call the desk and ask them to assign someone to do surveillance. See who leaves when. It's high time you got back home to Jenna and the kids. I've got a feeling we'll need the overtime later."

"Roger that."

Ty finished making the tea, and when he returned to the family room, he found his daughter putting on the gold earrings.

He handed Lindsay some green tea in her favorite white porcelain mug, then sat at the other end of the couch with his Earl Gray. "Wanna talk?"

"Not really." She held the mug tightly but didn't drink.

The family room was nestled between the kitchen and the dining room. It was small and intimate, with a couch, coffee table and two comfy chairs crowded in. As the wood-paneled space began to grow warmer, the scent of burning applewood filled the air.

"I get it, y'know," he said.

The teen pulled her knees up and settled her bare feet on the edge of the coffee table. She held the mug atop her knees and warmed her hands. Occasionally she'd take a sip.

"After your mom was murdered..." He paused, seeing the memories play like a silent film in his mind's eye. "I was one pissed off man. Really angry."

Her face gilded by the firelight, Lindsay turned to look at her father, her blue eyes troubled. "I never saw you like that."

"Because I made sure you never did."

She dropped her head for a moment. "What was it like when you got angry?"

Ty delayed his reply with several swallows of warm, sweet tea.

"I mean," she probed, "what did you do?"

"Same as you. Got quiet. Pushed people away." He turned his gaze to the hearth, remembering the drinking, the reckless driving...the wreck that had totaled the car and left him sore, shaken and wiser. "Other times I'd snap at people for no good reason."

Lindsay's body language was tense with anxiety, but her face registered curiosity.

"I'm sorry, Dad. I didn't know how hard it was on you." She looked down at her mug. "I mean, I knew that it was sad for you but not how sad."

"You weren't supposed to know," he replied, his voice low and calm. "Sure, it was hard. She was my wife. The two of you were my life." And while he realized he was finally putting the past to rest, Lindsay hadn't. He'd need all his tact, all his ingenuity to help her get there.

"I saw your anger tonight." He looked at her, his gaze both understanding and serious. "But here's the thing about that. Anger is devious about how it sneaks out." He kicked off his shoes and put his stockinged feet on the coffee table. "You know, like when you get bad-tempered and mouthy with me when it's really about something that happened at school." He shrugged. "I'm the easy target. So I'm curious about what was underneath tonight's outburst."

The fire spread noisily as it touched off a pocket of resin.

Lindsay scooted back to her original position at the end of the couch, eyes averted, quiet. "I'm scared sometimes. I was supposed to be there, too. To meet Heather's mystery person."

"Oh my god, Lindsay!" He sat straight up and thumped his mug on the coffee table. "You're lucky to be alive."

"See, I knew you'd get all angry."

"You're damn right, I'm angry. Meeting with strangers is just plumb dumb. It's foolish and dangerous. You know better than that."

"Yeah." Her shoulders slumped. "But Heather kept asking me to go. For moral support."

Peer pressure. His daughter might have died because of peer pressure. Jesus H. Christ.

"If I weren't keeping you home for your own safety, your ass would be so grounded." Holding his mug tightly, he counted to ten. Then again. But he'd been down this road before. More was not better. "Okay. You were very, very lucky. Enough said."

He looked past Lindsay out the French doors that led to the side yard, half-seeing the fireplace flames play over the glass.

"So tell me the rest of the story. No more lies. Or half-truths, either."

She scooched around on the couch and sipped some more tea. "There's not much more. Heather was texting with somebody about the letter, and he suggested that they meet."

"He contacted her first?"

She nodded but didn't make eye contact.

Ty took a mental step backward, sorting out who might have known her number. Sellers, for sure. Professors would have access, so Brunner had it and could have told Dahlrymple. Plus, some staff members would also know, like counselors and office managers. Or a dean. Plunkard could easily get the number. To use herself, perhaps...or even give it to her sister.

He paused during a long pull on his tea and focused on a movement outside the French doors. Just a neighbor's cat, but he couldn't tell which one. At night, all cats were gray. Wasn't that a famous quote? But the speaker's name eluded him. He smiled to himself as he took another sip. Meg would know.

"Okay Lindsay, you're sure Heather didn't say who that was? Or even how they got connected?"

Lindsay nodded.

"Did the 'mystery person' know you were supposed to be there?"

"I don't think so."

"But you're not sure?"

"No, not really." Her face crumpled in dismay. "But I feel guilty, too. Susan glommed on to me after play practice, and I wasted time trying to ditch her. I was late getting to the museum. Too late to help."

"Or get hurt, either," Ty corrected, working to control his own reaction to these new revelations. "You know deep down that your being there wouldn't have saved Heather."

Lindsay looked up at him with a fierce expression. "But it might have. I could've helped her fight him off. Or maybe he wouldn't have tried anything if there were two of us there."

"No, Lindsay. It wouldn't have mattered. You wouldn't have been wading into some random cafeteria fight. This person is unhinged. Nobody knows better than you how brutal that attack was."

For a time, they both watched the flames writhe on the hearth.

"And back to the guilt and blaming. Just like you couldn't have stopped Heather's death...Professor Adams didn't play any part in causing it."

"But Heather was there because of her stupid assignment."

"Heather was there because of the letter. She'd discovered a letter that might be very valuable, and somebody found out that she had it. That person lured her there, then killed her."

He paused, searching for the right words. There was a lot riding on this explanation. "Had there been no assignment, Heather would've still met that person. Isn't that right?" he asked, using his interrogation room language. He hoped that steering clear of emotion was taking the right tack.

"Yeah. Probably."

"But you went off on that teacher anyway. That's not like you, Lindsay."

"I couldn't help it. Sometimes I feel like there's an engine inside my chest, and it just keeps racing...whirring and racing. I'd just finished talking to Heather's mom, and it was racing, so I went to find you. But you were with *her*, and the whirring got stronger, and I just exploded."

"Well, I can see why it happened, but it still wasn't right. You embarrassed her in front of people she works with."

Ty waited, but Lindsay didn't say anything.

"Your outburst embarrassed me, too. After you left, I tried to smooth things over, but I also needed to get to you. Make sure you'd stay safe." He paused. "So what do you think you should do?"

Lindsay made no response.

"It doesn't have to be tomorrow, but I think you owe her an apology, don't you?"

"I guess. But not right away, okay? I need to get past speaking at Heather's funeral."

"Okay. Maybe not right away. But soon, yes?"

"Yeah. Okay."

So far, so good, he thought. On to stage two. "But I'm still puzzled. You were really, really mean to her...so mean that it's hard for me to understand why. It's not just about that assignment, is it?"

Lindsay finished her tea in silence, but she didn't let the mug go.

"Is it because it seems like she's interested in me?" He paused, waiting for a reaction which didn't come. "Or is it because you think I might be returning that interest?"

That touched a nerve.

"It's been five years, and you haven't dated. Why now? Why her?"

"Whoa, there. I'm not dating anyone."

"But you want to, don't you? You're attracted to her."

"I'm interested in her, yes. At this point, I have no idea where it might go."

"But you'd like to find out? That's what you'll do when the case is solved."

"Yes."

"Don't I get a say in this? You always said I would."

"What I said was I would talk with you about it, keep you in the loop. Not that you'd have the final say. But dating anyone right now is out of the question. It would be inappropriate, a distraction. She's helping me with the case. Her insights are very valuable because she's so knowledgeable about TCC. She knew Heather, knew about the letter, and knows the suspects."

"What I saw in the funeral parlor wasn't just about the case. It looked like what I see in the halls at Frederick High every day." Lindsay glared at him. "She was touching you."

Shit, she saw that. He just couldn't catch a break. Not in the case, and not here. "She was only pinning on a button, Lindsay. It was no big deal." From her look, he knew she wasn't buying it. "I do sorta get the impression that she's pretty interested," he admitted, embarrassed. "But we're not dating. Nothing has happened."

"She might not want to take it slow like you are."

"But things can't go any faster than I'll allow." He picked up his mug again to buy himself some thinking time. "Meg's world and mine, and that includes you, are intersecting at the moment. She and I will likely keep running into each other. Like at the funeral. And we'll continue to talk while the case resolves. However, I can promise you this. Nothing will happen while this case is still active. Not until I catch Heather's killer." Taking in her scowl, he added, "I give you my word."

"Whatever." She went back to watching the fire. After a long pause, she looked back up. "There's something else."

Chapter 29

Trying not to look as keyed up as he felt at his daughter's admission, Ty leaned forward a little and set his mug back on the coffee table. Just in case she blindsided him again. "Okay. Shoot."

"Heather and Jon were having sex."

"I figured that might've been the case."

"It's mostly what caused the breakup. He kept pushing her to do things. Stuff she didn't like doing." She circled a fingertip around the mug's porcelain rim several times. "Nasty things."

He was about to push for details when Lindsay opened up.

"Like having creepy sex."

Ty stared at his daughter in alarm. "What do you know about creepy sex?"

Looking up from the mug, she rolled her eyes at her father. "You don't have to be having creepy sex to know about it, Dad. We live in modern America, you know." She continued in an off-hand manner. "There's *MTV, Law, and Order: SVU, Fifty Shades of Gray*. Loads of stuff."

"So you're not...?"

"Eww. No."

Thank god. But he'd have to start watching more TV with his daughter.

"First, let me say that I'm not just being nosey because my next question has bearing on the case. But can you give me an idea what kind of creepy sex was involved?"

Lindsay clucked her tongue. "Don't you know anything about teenagers?"

Ty shook his head sadly and mumbled, "Apparently not."

Both of them kept their gaze on the fire that was fading on the hearth.

"It's something they do to make it more intense."

He was on shaky ground here. "With drugs?"

Silence.

"No. With rope."

He managed to keep his tone somewhat neutral. "Bondage?"

Lindsay shook her head slowly. "Uh-uh. Around the neck."

"Garroting?" Stunned, he looked at her for confirmation.

The firelight cast her face in moving shades of light and shadow as she nodded.

His face hardened with anger. "He was doing that to her?"

Lindsay didn't respond right away, merely shifted on the couch cushion.

Ty struggled to keep his voice unemotional. "Or he wanted her to do that to him?"

"Both."

"That fucking bastard!"

Lindsay flinched as she brought her head up.

"I should've coldcocked him that day on Heather's porch," Ty growled. "Asshole, cockroach, sonovabitch. If I'd known this when I was at his apartment..."

His daughter looked at him in concern, like he was a dad she didn't know.

"That little shit has no respect for women." He thumped the arm of the couch before he went on, his voice loud in the small room. "Lindsay, if some boy even hints to you about participating in that kind of abuse just let me know, and he will flat out never bother you again."

She bobbed her head, eyes saucer round.

Becoming aware of how his reaction was impacting his daughter, he tried to moderate his outburst. "Sorry, let me reframe that." After several deep breaths, he went on. "Your mother and I made damn sure to raise you to have enough self-esteem that you wouldn't ever be victimized by some guy. Judging from your disgust with Sellers, I think we succeeded." He bit his lower lip as if to stop himself. "But, if you ever need any help with something like that, I'm here for you."

Lindsay nodded timidly and lowered her gaze to her lap.

The fire sizzled and flared in the tense silence while he got his emotions under control. "Well, at least Heather wasn't choked to death," he said. "There were no ligature marks."

"I know," she admitted. "I looked. You know, to see if I should untie something to help her breathe."

He couldn't think of a thing to say. He'd had no idea the girls were that close or would share those kinds of confidences. Lindsay was only fifteen, for chrissake.

"There are a couple of other things," she said, her voice trying to strengthen itself.

"Okay." But Jesus! How much more did he have to take?

"Jon said he'd hurt Heather if she talked about the...the garroting. And when he was angry once, he said if he couldn't have her, nobody could."

Ty nodded and pulled at his bottom lip before he responded. "You didn't write that in your statement."

"That was a witness report. Duh. I didn't witness any threats. This is hearsay."

He smiled to himself at how much she knew about police work. His work.

"But it points to motive." He paused, processing the information, its ramifications. "All this is why you unleashed on Meg tonight, isn't it?"

"Mostly. But I couldn't explain anything without talking about the creepy sex."

His tone invited confidentiality as he asked, "Is there anything else you haven't told me? Anything else I should know?"

Lindsay yawned and shook her head. "No, that's it."

"Alright, then," he agreed, business-like. "I'll write this up as an interview so we can get your information on record. All you'll have to do is sign it."

Putting her arms above her head, she stretched and yawned again. "I'm sorry, I didn't tell you sooner. I just didn't know how to talk about it." Lowering her arms, one hand floated to the gold earring, turning it around and around.

The room was nearly dark, their expressions almost hidden as they watched the fire extinguish itself.

"Do you still think about Mom?"

One ember popped, and shooting stars launched themselves up the chimney.

"Yes," he replied softly. "Sometimes more than others, but yes."

Silence.

"You go to the cemetery on her birthday."

"And I always invite you."

The silence deepened with expectation, but the teen stayed quiet.

"I also go on our wedding anniversary."

Lindsay was young enough to let the surprise show on her face but old enough to keep her thoughts to herself.

"And on the anniversary of her death, I call up Baltimore PD and talk to the cold case officer. He hasn't had any leads...says the trail is Ice Age cold."

Silence became a third companion in the room.

"But you'll never stop looking for the guy, will you."

"No," he said. "Never."

The quiet deepened.

"Because you loved her."

"Yes," he breathed. "And in some ways, I always will."

Wrapped in silence, Lindsay stilled...her waif-like features reflecting the turmoil of wanting her father to stop talking but knowing he wouldn't.

"But she's not coming back to us, Linny."

She ran one hand up and down the smooth material of her black dress.

Ty took a deep breath and let it out slowly before he spoke again, knowing that his relationship with his daughter teetered on the thin edge of a sharp blade. "And I'm beginning to feel like it's time to move on." He looked over at her, barely able to see her features in the dim firelight.

The girl sat motionless, awaiting her father's next words.

"And while I don't need your permission, and I'm not asking for your blessing, I do want something from you." He wouldn't plead, but he needed her to see how important this was to him. When he continued, his voice was low but earnest. "It would mean a lot if you wouldn't fight me on this." He waited. "If you gave me some space to find my own way."

She dropped her chin to her chest, hugged herself and shut her eyes.

"I'll try."

"That's all I'm asking."

•   •   •   •   •

Lindsay knocked on her dad's bedroom door and was invited in for their goodnight ritual, a habit she occasionally, intentionally broke. Happily, tonight wasn't one of those. He was lying atop the midnight blue duvet, still in his dress shirt and good trousers. Laying aside the magazine he'd been reading, he scooted over to make room for her to sit on the side of the king-sized bed. While he propped himself up with some pillows, she sat down— one flannel pajama-clad leg drawn up on the bed, the other still on the floor.

After a bit, he thumped her knee a couple of times. "How're you feelin'?"

"Just when I think I'm okay," she said in a small voice, "I start feeling not-so okay again."

Ty waited.

She looked at him and sighed. "At least the motor's not racing in my chest anymore."

"That's good." He gave her knee a shake. "Otherwise, it'd be hard to tell if I should take you to my mechanic or your Dr. Amy to get that sorted out." He studied her to see if there was more she needed to say, decided there wasn't. "Now off to bed with you."

They touched index fingers, and Lindsay padded out of the room, closing the door behind her.

He interlaced his fingers across his abdomen and looked over at the cell phone charging on the nightstand. He knew he was stalling. He should just call her.

When staring at the ceiling didn't spark any inspiration, he picked up the phone, pulled up her number, and stared at the blinking cursor in the text box. He hunkered back against the pillows and started typing.

"Meg, Lieutenant Raleigh here..."

His frown turned into a full-fledged scowl while he backspaced those words off the screen and tried again: "How're you doing? Tough evening, huh? Just wanted you to know I was thinking about you. Call me."

He didn't push "send" right away. Instead, he laid the phone on his chest and stared at the ceiling again.

"Shit." He lifted the cell, refreshed the screen, and studied the message. With a muttered, "Nothing ventured," he pushed the button that would launch the words. Then he replaced the cell on the night table and picked up his magazine again.

He'd been holding it open and staring at the same two pages for maybe ten minutes when the cell phone woke up, the ringtone indicating an incoming text. He picked it up: It was from her.

"Doing OK. New definition of tough day, though. Thanks for checking in. That helped."

His eyes sparkled while he pushed back to get higher up on the pillows. "Always glad to help. Probably won't see you tomorrow, lots to do. But you should get some sleep."

A response came quickly.

"Am just about to turn in. Get some rest yourself."

His small smile grew as he typed, "Will do." He paused and laid the cell on his belly. After a bit, he added, "Sweet dreams, Meg," and then pushed "send."

He held the phone and waited for a reply. When none appeared in short order, he plugged it back into its charger, walked to the closet and undressed.

Crossing back to the bed, he slid between the sheets, stretched out on his side and drew up the covers. Doing so made the forgotten magazine rustle in the stillness, so he reached around, found it and tossed it to the floor.

When the cell phone warbled again, he retrieved it and read the one-word message.

"Ditto."

Smiling, he put the little machine back in place, flipped his pillow over to find a cool spot, turned on his back, and looked out the bedroom window at the moon-bright night.

•   •   •   •   •

Fewer than five miles away, snuggled in her friends' cozy guest room, Meg stared at the ceiling fan and replayed selected scenes from her day: the lunch at the coffee shop and Ty's touch on her neck; her innocent gesture of affixing the photo button to his lapel that had become much more than that.

But she kept coming back to the moment when she first saw him step into the room at the funeral parlor in that terrific gray suit. There'd been no hint of a five o'clock shadow on his face, and his dark, wavy hair was begging for a tousling. And that tie. The color du jour, that I'm-confident-in-my-manhood lilac. A swath that began under his strong chin crawled down his obscenely broad chest and slithered southward. That lucky, lucky tie.

She tried to still her thoughts, but sleep wasn't in the cards just yet. First she'd have to get her smile under control.

•   •   •   •   •

Thursday: October 30th

Went to Heather's memorial tonight. Brutal. Finally told Dad about creepy sex. Almost as hard.

One nice thing happened, though. I found a pair of mom's earrings in dad's good suit. It was like a little hug from beyond.

But the worst part of a brutal day? Finding out Dad wants to date...not just date, but date Heather's teacher. It makes me sick inside to think about it.

If he can move past mom, will he pull away from me?

Chapter 30

A silver sedan, made ghostly by the moonlight, slips through the night. Its sole occupant is restless.

Things keep going wrong. The letter wasn't in the girl's car. And that house alarm...

The Watcher pops one CD out of the slot and glides in another, rejecting "Are You Lonesome Tonight" in favor of Nick Drake's "Black Eyed Dog."

"Poor ol'Nick." *Dead at twenty-six of an accidental overdose with only a few underappreciated albums to show for himself.*

The plaintive guitar riffs and the thin, melancholy voice of the doomed English singer/songwriter float into the air and intertwine with the cool, remote moonbeams.

The driving is aimless. There's no destination, merely an intention to keep the mountains on the right and the black dog at bay.

No self-destructive end for me. I have big plans.

Continuing on through the night, the car crosses the bridge that connects to Harpers Ferry. The moon glints off the Shenandoah River, its rapids silvered by the play of dark's light.

I'm already noteworthy. The dead girl's viewing proved that. It was so satisfying to see how far-reaching one's work can be. All those sad faces.

Slowing, the car crawls through the sleeping town. The one where abolitionist John Brown raided the arsenal. The raid that was a catalyst for the Civil War. Just as the "Barbara Frietchie" poem had been a rallying point. Small actions yielding seismic results.

The moon continues to rise, mute and aloof, while the silver car finally turns toward home.

Chapter 31

The next morning Meg decided to go into her office really early. She didn't want to run into anybody while collecting the papers she needed to grade for that night's class. She didn't have the time or inclination for pleasantries or idle chatter. Since it was well before eight, her chances of remaining incognito were good. Good enough that she snagged the best parking spot in the faculty lot. She patted Rocinante on the fender as she headed inside.

In all the flurry of getting ready for Heather's memorial last night, she hadn't picked up everything she needed. Proving once again that she wasn't on top of her game. Not even close. And those essays certainly weren't on her mind afterward. But it was high time to hunker down at home and grade, grade, grade. With all that was going on, she was even more behind than usual.

With any luck, she could just zip in and zip out.

At the top of the stairs, she peeked down both hallways and saw only closed doors and dark offices, except for the faculty workroom. Still in stealth mode, she listened at the open door and didn't hear anyone in there, just the friendly hum of the Xerox machine. So far, so good. She opened her office, shut the door behind her, and dug around on her desk for the errant papers. Then, noticing the message light blinking on her phone, she listened to all six calls, hoping one was from Ty. No such luck. Gathering her things, she headed out the door but stopped before pulling it shut.

Voices in the workroom. Damn. She scooted back inside and closed the door but for a crack, allowing her to see when the coast was clear. When she recognized one of the voices, she was damn glad she wasn't exposed in the hallway. Charlotte the harlot was on the loose.

However, Slattery wasn't alone. She was laughing like a fool—cruel laugher, mirthless—as she walked away with some other woman. One Meg didn't know. The conference was starting today, so maybe she was another participant. They were both carrying stacks of papers like they'd just finished making copies for their presentations.

The women were out of sight, but Meg waited a bit longer to make sure they were really gone. Still cautious, she stepped into the corridor and paused again. She did *not* want to run into that hussy. Hearing nothing, she grabbed her stuff, closed the door, and was walking toward the stairwell when someone bolted out of the workroom door ahead of her.

"Maria..." Meg began, puzzled.

But she didn't continue because Maria didn't respond, just rushed away. And the woman hadn't looked well, either. Face flushed, her breathing erratic.

What the hell! Why was Maria so agitated? Could it have had something to do with Charlotte and that other woman?

There was no way of telling without talking to either Maria or Charlotte, and neither was high on her let's-get-together list. Meg put it out of her mind and headed for home.

•   •   •   •   •

A little after 8 o'clock, the detectives were back at the sad little house on Burke Street, planning to interview Jon Sellers again. It was rather early in the day, but time enough for people to be getting ready for work. And early enough that Jon might still be at home.

Pulling to the curb in front of the house, Maroni said, "How'd it go with Lindsay last night? She give you a raft of shit after you got home?"

"No. We actually straightened out a few things. And she told me more about Jon and Heather." He caught Maroni up on Lindsay's revelations.

"Jesus, that's seriously messed up. And she's been sitting on that all this time?"

"Yeah, well. It took her a while to work up to telling me. Easy to see why, in retrospect. But that wasn't the only surprise of the night. I got a call a little after three a.m. from Putnam. He'd caught the call on a break-in at the Hillcrest home."

"Really? And you didn't call me in, too?"

"I didn't go over, didn't want to leave Lindsay alone. Putnam's capable and thorough. He said it looked like someone had broken the window on the back door, reached in, unlocked the door, and opened it. But the house alarm had gone off and the thief poofed. Putnam decided to check the cars, too. Heather's had been broken into."

"But not stolen? Someone's looking for something, then. That letter, probably."

"Seems likely. We'll just add that to the things we need to ask Johnny-boy about."

The men exited the car and walked to the door. Today it was decorated with cutouts of witches, ghosts and zombies. Huh. He'd forgotten that it was Halloween. Lindsay would want to hand out candy tonight. They'd have a battle royale over that when he got home.

"Jon's car isn't here," Maroni observed as Ty rang the doorbell.

"Yeah, but the Chevy is. Maybe the mom knows something." He pushed the little button again, and after the sound of the chime died away, he heard footsteps approach the door then stop.

This time he knocked. "Mrs. Sellers? I'm with the Frederick City Police. My partner and I would like to speak with you."

After some delay, the door cracked open, a brown eye visible behind the security chain. "Show me your ID."

He lifted his detective's shield and ID to the suspicious eye. "I'm Lieutenant Stephen T. Raleigh, and I'm here with Detective Matteo Maroni. May we come in?"

"Why? What's this about?"

"It's about your son, Jon. But it would be best if you let us in."

"Jon? Oh my god," she cried. The door shut and re-opened quickly. "Is he okay? Has something happened?" She ran a hand through her disheveled hair and stepped aside to let the officers enter. But she didn't invite them in any farther.

Ty's brow furrowed. "Why would you think something has happened?"

"He's been moody and snappish lately. I tried to get him to talk last night, but he brushed me off, said he had homework for his law class." She tugged at the belt of her oversized terrycloth robe. "He went downstairs to his room, but he didn't study. He was playing that trash rock music, and he doesn't do that if he's studying. When I got up this morning, he was gone. He's never up this early, and his car's gone. I called the police to report him missing, but they said I have to wait twenty-four hours. Has something happened? Just tell me. If it's bad, tell me quick."

"We have no reason to believe that anything has happened to your son, ma'am. We just want to ask him some questions."

Questions about his disregard for women and nasty sexual predilections, among other things. But now it seemed that the little shit had rabbited.

Mrs. Sellers rummaged in her pocket, came up with a tissue, and dabbed at her eyes. "Jon hasn't been himself since that girl died. He was depressed when he broke up with her, but boys'll get that way when girls break their hearts. He's gotten worse since she died."

Oh, so he told his mom *he* broke up with her. Interesting. "You mean Heather Hillcrest? The student who was found murdered in the Barbara Fritchie Museum."

She closed her eyes then nodded once. When she opened them, her eyes were teary.

Looking toward this partner, Ty gave a slight sideways nod toward the mother, urging Maroni to turn on the sympathy.

"We're very sorry to worry you, Mrs. Sellers. I know it can be upsetting when policemen show up at your door. Why don't you tell us a little more? Maybe we can help."

Ty looked beyond the woman into the living room. A small space made smaller by bulky, cheap, mannish furniture. Brown, imitation leather chairs disfigured with cigarette burns and little rips. A couch with dark purple pillows and a Baltimore Ravens throw.

When Mrs. Sellers didn't speak, Maroni tried again. "We actually came here to ask Jon some questions about this Heather. What can you tell us about their relationship?"

She twisted the tissue until it wanted to shred. "Heather seemed like such a good girl, the nicest girl he's dated. But it was all an act, he said. He caught her with another boy, a rough-and-ready motorcycle type. So he called it off. But he's been heartsick ever since." She worried the tissue some more.

Maroni flicked a glance at Ty. "Heartsick?"

A few tears tracked down her face. "He's always been a sensitive child. He was upset each time his dad was deployed and so happy when Dan mustered out. But things got bad pretty quick. And each time things happened, Jon would take off on his bike, sometimes all day. Some days I was afraid he'd never come back. Like his daddy." She paused. "That's what scares me now."

"What do you mean, ma'am?" Ty said. "What scares you?"

"Sometimes his moods get dark."

Well, fuck. That changed things. "When he went off riding his bike, back when he was a kid, did he go anyplace special?"

She shrugged. "He liked the outdoors, being in nature. He'd ride around Baker Park, maybe feed the ducks. But when he got older and could ride farther—and even now that he can drive—he'd go up to Gambrill Park. He likes to sit on that stone wall at the Middletown Overlook. He told me he'd sit there for hours. Thinking, just thinking."

Ty nodded to Maroni to finish things up.

"Mrs. Sellers, we're going to start looking for Jon right away. I know it's worrying, but try not to get too worked up. There might be a logical explanation. Maybe he spent the night at a friend's or something like that."

No response.

As the two men walked to the door, Ty paused and added, "I promise you that we'll call as soon as we know something. Okay?"

She pulled the lapels of the robe closer together, tucked her chin into the vee, and nodded.

Back in the car, Raleigh turned to his partner. "You're the local boy. I hope to Christ you know that overlook and can give me the particulars."

As Maroni rattled off the details, Ty tried to picture the space. A state park running along the top of a wooded ridge, elevation 2000 feet. The overlook itself a clearing where the lip of a rock formation jutted out of the mountain. It could hold maybe a dozen people. A mortared stone-on-stone wall ran around it, waist high, preventing sightseers from tumbling down a fifteen-foot cliff.

"The wall's finished off, so it's level on the top. And people do sit on it." Maroni paused. "There's been a suicide or two."

"Call it in. No wait, it's out of our jurisdiction. Call the Sheriff's Department."

But Maroni already was.

"Damn that kid," Ty muttered, half to himself, half to his partner. "He hasn't answered any of my calls, and he hasn't been going to classes, but this takes it to another level."

"They're sending some county mounties to check it out for us," Maroni reported. "If the car's not at the overlook, I'll alert all jurisdictions to initiate a BOLO."

Ty nodded, but his face was grim. "That boy sure has a talent for the unexpected. And for lying, seeing as how he has his mom snowed about who ditched whom. I don't think Lindsay's wrong, but you'd better check with Heather's other friends about the breakup. See if there was another boyfriend. Calloway has a line on a cousin, a Mackenzie. Tug on that. Use that list of friends Mrs. Hillcrest gave us. If you work it right, they might tell you what they didn't tell her."

"Got it. And I'm still running financials on all the suspects."

"And contact Doug Dahlrymple and have him come down to the station after his shift. Schedule it to begin after the press conference this afternoon."

"Better you than me. Those things are a pain in the ass."

His phone alerted. A text from Routzhan, asking for an update. Again. He'd get to it later.

"Let's move out. I've scheduled a couple of appointments at the college. A second poke at Brunner and my first with the dean, Plunkard."

Chapter 32

When they arrived at Professor Brunner's office, the door was open. But before Ty knocked, he waited to see his partner's reaction to the office itself. He watched Maroni survey the room and pause for several beats as he studied the incongruous Elvis poster. Their eyes met in a silent smirk.

Ty rapped on the metal door. "Dr. Brunner, it's good of you to meet with us again."

Brunner made no attempt to acknowledge the junior officer. "Lieutenant, I just want this unpleasantness to end. The sooner I answer your questions, the sooner I can be rid of you and get back to my conference."

Without waiting for the invitation that he knew wouldn't come, Raleigh sat, and Maroni followed suit.

"This won't take long," Ty said. "We're following up on the incident at the funeral home last night. Dr. Slattery made quite a point of embarrassing you about your research."

"She is an unthinkably crass and tactless person. Her comments were unwarranted and entirely inappropriate in any setting, let alone at a ritual honoring the dead."

"I agree completely. You were considerably more gracious to her than I might have been, and your colleagues seemed very supportive. Especially Maria Routzhan. When you left abruptly, she was quick to follow you out."

"Yes, Maria is a dear friend," he admitted. "We share many interests. The Civil War, of course, is principal among them. And we are both dog fanciers, Basset Hounds. Her Priscilla and my Presley are littermates."

Ty subdued a snort of laughter, and he didn't dare look at Maroni. "How interesting. I happened to be outside on the porch just after she followed you out of the building, and you two paused on Church Street, talking. You were joined by someone else, someone to whom Ms. Routzhan seemed to take exception."

Brunner's cheeks pinked. "I don't see where that is any business of yours."

"You'd be surprised where my business takes me. Murder always trumps good manners. Now, who was your third companion, and why did Routzhan stalk off?"

"I barely know the man." He leaned back in his chair, distancing himself from his questioner. "And I have no idea why Maria took offense."

"You barely know him?" He glanced over at his partner. "Maroni, did you hear that? Perhaps you can fill the professor in on where your business took you last night."

"I followed you, Dr. Brunner." He pulled a small notebook out of the breast pocket of his jacket and glanced through it before he addressed the professor. "You and your male companion left the funeral home and walked to the Olde Town Tavern where the two of you stayed for approximately thirty-five minutes and consumed one beer each. Then you went with him to his apartment across the street. At that point, I turned your surveillance over to another officer. He reports..."

Ty cleared his throat to get Maroni's attention, gave him the look that said, *don't spill all the beans.*

Maroni raised an eyebrow in acknowledgement. "He reports that you remained there until approximately 2 a.m., at which time your companion drove you back to your residence."

Brunner popped up out of the chair. "This is a gross invasion of privacy. I'll have the pair of you up on charges."

Ty's expression was grim. "Sit down, professor. We have a lot to discuss. You have a habit of withholding information until, like now, you're caught in a lie. Why is that?" He stared at the professor until the pudgy man sat. "I'll ask again: Who was your companion last night and why have you denied knowing him?"

Brunner folded his hands atop the desk. "His name is Doug Dahlrymple. He's a renowned Civil War re-enactor of my acquaintance. Our relationship is...awkward." He paused. "His social standing and mine are quite dissimilar."

"I hardly see why that matters, but be that as it may. Mr. Dahlrymple came to our attention in this investigation because he has a criminal background. Are you aware of that?"

"Yes, of course. But as you said, it hardly matters. All that transpired when he was a youth. He's a good man. I helped him obtain the job at TCC."

"That's very kind of you. But why did you make the effort? Are you friends?"

He shrugged. "We lost touch for many years. We've only just become reacquainted."

"But you did things together when you were both young, hung out at times?"

"We both went to the same high school, but as I said, we did and still do come from dissimilar worlds. Doug drank heavily and dabbled in drugs and other risky behavior."

"Hmm, that's odd. Because your worlds were similar enough to have you both arrested for disorderly conduct and assault on May 3rd, 1985."

He clenched his hands into fists. "We were only nineteen for pity's sake. A foolish age a lifetime ago. We were protesting animal rights. Things got a little out of hand. It has no bearing on current events."

"I disagree. The charges indicate that both of you are capable of violence. And Dahlrymple took it a step further. He actually committed battery."

"It was supposed to be a peaceful protest. A group of us were mobilized by Tom Regan's book, *The Case for Animal Rights*. Since Fort Detrick was right in our backyard and did, in fact, use animals in experiments, it presented the perfect target. One afternoon a group of us organized an impromptu...protest outside the main gate."

"It's easy to see how that could become disorderly. What about the assault?"

"We were just going to throw red paint on the gates, but when the military police came after us, we threw the cans as well. Some of them struck the MPs."

"Okay...but why were your charges dropped and not his?"

"I was the only one who was detained on site." Brunner paused, his face flushing with embarrassment. "The others ran faster than I. When the authorities interrogated me, they asked for more names. They knew there were four of us. If I gave them the other names, they'd cut me a break. So I named names. Doug was one of them."

"It appears you have a strong drive for self-preservation," Ty observed. "It's not a big stretch to imagine that you'd sacrifice Heather to further your own ends."

"That's patently absurd. Tossing a paint can that strikes someone is in no way analogous to murder."

"But you have a clear motive to do so—vindicating Nannie Crouse. Plus you possess a key to the museum and have no real alibi, indicating that you had the opportunity to commit the murder."

"I told you. Someone stole the key. I didn't murder that girl. All you have is circumstantial evidence."

Something of which Ty was keenly aware. None of what he had so far would convince a PA to charge such a prestigious citizen. And João would have a coronary. But there was another stone that he could overturn.

"Maybe your hands are clean. After all, you are an intellectual, a thinker, a planner. You could get someone else to carry out your plans. Dahlrymple, perhaps? He's already taken someone's life. And after all, he's been your patsy at least once before."

"That's insulting to both him and me." He glared at the detective. "And that death wasn't premeditated. It was a terrible accident."

"So *you* say. But you got him a position at TCC, didn't you? He's a felon, and that makes it hard to get jobs nowadays. Did your help come with strings attached?"

"Certainly not." His eyes went down to his desk and up again. "I may have felt a little guilty about turning him in all those years ago. It was a way to atone."

The man wasn't going to budge. Maybe he had no reason to do so. Time to regroup.

"Okay, maybe you were merely being generous. That still doesn't explain your conduct after the memorial service. And why you stayed so late at Dahlrymple's place."

His fleshy hands polished the smooth, wooden surface, then stilled. "He wanted to show me items from his collection of Civil War memorabilia and get my opinion on them. We discussed them over a few more beers. I also filled him in on one or two seminars from the conference, and the time ran away from us. I may have become a bit inebriated, what with the stress of the conference and Charlotte's horrible accusations. Doug saw me safely home, as a good friend would. Since you've obviously looked up my background, you're aware I've had some trouble with drinking and driving in the past."

Ty wasn't quite buying it. The man had caved too easily. In most circumstances, he'd push back before answering. And for a man who withheld information so routinely, a lie was a short step away. "I'd say that the time galloped away. It was after two when you got home. Wasn't your wife concerned?"

"As I mentioned before, my wife is in Chicago. On business. And in any event, a grown man may do as he pleases with his own time."

"Let's go back to an earlier question. Why did Ms. Routzhan depart so abruptly when Dahlrymple arrived?" He took a stab in the dark. "Was she jealous of him?"

"Are you suggesting that I'm gay?" he blustered. "That's absurd, lieutenant. I'm a happily married man."

Hmm. Well, if it wasn't that, it was something else. The man was overplaying his hand.

"No, professor, not at all," Raleigh placated. "Nothing of the kind. I'm just trying to understand the situation. You've yet to explain that scene to my satisfaction."

The man kept skirting the issue, so there was definitely something there. He'd push from a different direction. "I can simply ask Maria, you know. Why not just tell me why there is such animosity between those two?"

After a pause, Robert nodded once and folded his hands over his soft belly. "For some of us, the Civil War is an enduring fascination. That colorful past becomes more engaging than the quotidian present," he sighed. "Maria is one of those who finds her current lot in life unsatisfying and problematic. Her career is all-consuming but stalled, and her mother is ill. For years Maria has desperately wanted to be taken seriously in the Civil War arena. To become a player in local matters if not national ones. She had hoped that having proof of her relationship to Nannie Crouse would aid in that effort. With that dream vanquished, she wants to make her mark writing about Civil War subjects, especially how Middletown's churches and homes opened their doors as hospitals for the wounded on both sides during the battles of Antietam and South Mountain. Unfortunately, that subject is saturated, and the field is highly competitive, even for credentialed writers."

The professor stopped talking. Although the man didn't fidget, Ty could sense the turmoil within. He decided to wait it out.

Embarrassment colored his face as Brunner replied. "Knowing that they both wanted to publish, I had given them contact information for people I know in that field." His face got redder. "Both had submitted articles, but only Doug had had one accepted for publication. In the prestigious *America's Civil War Magazine*, where my articles often appear. Last night, Maria discovered that Doug was poised to publish."

"I see. That explains a lot."

"But not everything." He paused, looking relieved now that he was coming clean. "You know I am endeavoring to help Nannie's descendant supplant Barbara Fritchie's claim to fame."

Ty nodded as he saw where this was heading. "Who is it?"

The professor looked down at this folded hands and took his time answering. "Doug. Something else Maria found out about last night. I'm afraid Doug took to bragging."

"That adds another layer, doesn't it? She is jealous."

Brunner looked up, startled. "It is an unfortunate coincidence that Doug's fortune comes at Maria's expense. But the truth cannot be denied. She will simmer down after she thinks things through. Maria is a dear friend who has helped me chase down numerous leads." His features smoothed with that admission. "I've entrusted her with proxy rights to my computer so she can help edit my submissions as new information comes to light. More than anyone, she knows how unpredictable research can be."

And yet she'd clearly been upset, given how she'd stalked off. But jealous enough to murder? He couldn't quite see it. Nothing in her demeanor gave off that vibe, and her alibi was solid. And why would such a control freak balk at finishing off her victim? But he'd poke at that hornet's nest and see if it provoked Brunner into revealing anything else.

"An unexpected twist in your research is likely par for the course," Ty said. "But that sort of reversal, coupled with jealousy, could be a powerful motive for murder."

"Oh, come now," Brunner said. "That premise is manifestly illogical. Why would she kill a student of the college she cherishes and vigorously protects from bad press? Added to that, Maria only found out about Doug's good fortune last night, days after the murder."

No more hornets, but it was worth the shot. Time to switch things up. He raised an eyebrow at his partner, alerting him. They'd play their trump card and hit him with the information Maroni had withheld. "But it still leaves the question of why Charlotte Slattery visited you minutes after you arrived home."

Brunner's color paled from pink to white.

"Why would she be waiting outside your home at two in the morning? And why did she leave only ten minutes later? Not quite time for an assignation, is it?"

"Be careful, lieutenant," he said, sitting up straight in his chair and gripping the armrests.

"Dr. Slattery told me about the two of you in graduate school." Or at least what she intimated about them. "Do you mean to say she's lying?"

"None of this intrusion into my personal life has any bearing on that student's death." The professor rose. "We are finished here. If you need to talk to me again, I insist on having my attorney present." He walked to his office door and took hold of the doorknob, his knuckles turning white. "I must return to the conference. I'm moderating the next panel."

"Thank you for 'clearing things up,' Dr. Brunner," Ty drawled as he rose. "I think that's all for now."

Having been quiet for so long, Maroni was hardly out of earshot before he said, "Damn, that professor's a piece of work. He's hiding something, but...oh, wait a minute, incoming." He dug out his cell phone to read a text. "A buddy of mine from the Sheriff's Department. Says there's no sign of Sellers at the overlook. Ditto on the car."

"Activate that BOLO. Keep pushing the Sellers angle. Call his friends, find out where he hangs." He shook his head and ran a hand across the back of his neck. "You're right about Brunner. He's hiding something. Maybe it's just the affair with Slattery, or maybe he's up to something with Dahlrymple, but we need to find out. That's part of your task for the day, too. Keep digging on him and the others: Sketchy Doug, Slattery...maybe even do a pass on her sister, the dean. I'm going to interview her while you get started on all that."

"Gotcha."

They started walking again. "Since I'll likely be tied up with interviews and that press conference most of the afternoon, I need you to do one more thing for me. Call Meg Adams and remind her to find the xeroxed page of the letter that Heather gave her." Best to backpedal there a little bit. He'd gotten carried away last night, stepped over the line with that last text message.

"Me? Why not you?" He grinned. "You're the one she wants to hear from."

"Just do it."

•   •   •   •   •

By 11:00, she was tired of grading. It had to be done, but she couldn't keep at it like usual. She'd confined herself to her comfortably messy den, but the piles of essays seemed as if they had mated and multiplied. She was relieved when the phone rang. *Could it be Ty?*

She raced to the phone. When it turned out to be Maroni, she felt like a sappy teenager.

"Hello, Professor Adams. Have I caught you at a good time?"

"Yup, in fact, your timing's perfect." She sank into the lumpy green-plaid recliner she'd had since college and hoped her disappointment didn't show in her voice. "I'm just grading papers, and any excuse to stop is a welcome one. But I imagine you're doing exciting investigative things. Like background checks and poking into people's finances. Fun stuff like that." After all, she'd read her share of Louise Penny and Sue Grafton.

She didn't expect him to dish any info, but she could almost hear his struggle to find a suitable reply.

"Ah...well, the lieutenant's keeping me busy. And that's sorta why I'm calling. He's tied up with interviews and prepping for a press conference this afternoon. So he wanted me to ask you if you've found that letter yet. I mean, your xeroxed page of the letter in question."

"I'm afraid not. Not yet, anyway. But you can tell him I'll keep looking."

She hadn't forgotten about the letter. But neither had it surfaced, and she'd looked pretty thoroughly. After she'd the graded papers for tonight's class, she'd initiate a full-scale hunt.

Chapter 33

As Ty exited the elevator on the second floor of the administration building and turned toward the dean's office, Maria Routzhan popped out of hers.

"Lieutenant Raleigh," she called from her doorway.

Damn it, he'd hoped not to run into her. He hadn't returned her last two calls.

"I was wondering if I should try and contact you. Again," she added. "But finding you here outside my door seems like a sign." She looked up and down the hallway. "Could you step inside a minute? I need to speak with you privately."

The usually competent, brusque woman was gone, replaced by one with halting movements and restless eyes. As he shut the door behind him, Ty wondered what was up.

"I think there's something you should know." She bit her lip and frowned. "It's just hearsay. That's why I hesitated. But it might be important."

"Why don't you put it out there and let me judge its significance."

"Oh, okay...well, it's about Dr. Slattery."

She didn't sit, so he didn't move farther in. He waited while she fidgeted, one hand rubbing the wrist of the other, eyes downcast.

The pause grew so long he finally spoke, his voice kind. "You'll feel easier if you tell me."

She nodded. "Well, I was in the workroom over in Hamilton Hall this morning doing some last minute copying for the first session of the conference when I heard footsteps headed my way and a woman say that she needed to xerox some papers for her presentation."

Maria looked down and didn't go on, so he prompted her. "It was Dr. Slattery?"

She looked up briefly, then slid her focus to the wall behind him. "Yes, and another woman I didn't recognize. I didn't want to speak with them, so I hid behind the door."

Her posture was stiff, and she still avoided eye contact.

"The two of them were laughing and chatting as they entered, and in a very familiar way. I got the impression that they'd gone to graduate school together. The other woman asked how things were going with Brunner." Maria paused again, longer this time. "She asked if Charlotte was still...'hopping into his saddle' whenever she could."

At that phrase, the woman's face colored so quickly Ty was worried about her blood pressure. But afterward she could at least look at him.

"I wouldn't tell you all this, lieutenant, but it points to a certain long-term confidence sharing between the two that influences the rest of the conversation I overheard."

He nodded encouragingly.

"Charlotte snickered at her friend's question and said, yes, Robert was as good a 'mount' as ever."

She stumbled over that one word, but the rest of the account came out in a rush.

"The other woman went on to ask if she—Charlotte, I mean—if Charlotte remembered checking out and then 'losing' a key library book that Robert needed for an important research paper in a class that all three of them were taking. Because of that, he'd gotten a dismal grade on the paper, and the professor ended up recommending Charlotte instead of Robert for some big grant."

When she continued, tears filmed Maria's faded blue eyes. "That was a despicable trick. And maybe she's doing the same thing again. She could have stolen that letter so he can't advance in his career." Her voice dropped. "She could be the murderer."

Charlotte's 'confession' stepped things up a notch, motive-wise. Smiling at Maria, he gave her shoulder a brief squeeze. "As difficult as that was for you, I thank you for the information. It may prove valuable."

Maria drew in a quivery breath. "I don't want her to know I told you. There's no telling what she might do."

"I can keep this confidential for now. But if an arrest seems imminent, I'd need for you to make a formal statement. If the case goes to trial, you'd need to testify. Could you do that?"

When she hesitated, he pushed a little. "Could you do that for Robert?" Then a little more. "And to clear the College of any involvement."

She nodded slowly. "Yes. Yes, I'd have to, wouldn't I? It's only right."

"Thank you. But I'll keep this between us for the moment." He opened the door and moved into the hall.

She stopped him with a hand on his arm. "But why are you in my neck of the woods?"

"I have an appointment with Dean Plunkard."

And at that moment, a man in a bespoke suit walked out of the dean's office, passed them, and made his way to the elevator.

"Oh, my," Maria murmured. "Poor Joyce has just finished up a nerve-racking appointment with her husband's divorce lawyer, and now she has to talk with you."

Teasing, Ty said, "I promise not to use the thumbscrews."

"No, of course not."

Her laugh was thin, but at least she'd made the effort.

"I hope your meeting goes well, lieutenant. She's under a lot of stress. She doesn't need any difficulties with the police."

"I'm not intending to be difficult. This is just routine." He decided that being thorough necessitated corroborating Brunner's story. "And while I'm on that subject, there's just one more thing I have to ask you."

She looked nervous but nodded for him to go on.

"After Heather's viewing the other night, you had a set-to with someone outside on the sidewalk. What was that about?"

"Oh, that." She shrugged. "I was going out to soothe Robert's feathers when that...that mechanic walked up and bragged about getting published. And about being Nannie Crouse's direct descendant. Why do you ask?"

"Just checking my facts. And none of those things bothered you?"

"Of course, they bothered me. You must have seen how angrily I walked away. But those are small matters, aren't they? Not like having the cloud of murder hang over the college." She shuddered. "And that poor girl's killer is still on the loose."

"I reckon you're right."

Hearing a phone ringing inside her office, Maria paled. "I have to take that. It might be a call about my mother." She hurried inside and closed the door.

●   ●   ●   ●   ●

The dean's office didn't command the same sweeping view of the mountains as the president's, but it was one hell of a lot swankier than his. Two windows overlooked the quad with its commemorative garden, tidy and mulched for the winter. Her desk was genuine wood, not laminate like his. And the visitor chairs weren't lumpy or stained.

"Thank you for making time to talk with me," Ty began. "There's a lot going on, what with my investigation and your conference. You seem to have back-to-back meetings."

The dean didn't comment, just held his gaze. Her expression remained neutral, but her coloring was high.

"I just passed your last appointment in the hall. Do you need a moment to regroup?"

Her cheeks pinked a bit more. "I'm fine, thank you. Just very busy. How can I help you?"

Maria had sure called that one. The dean was stressed out. "Then I'll be direct so as to take less of your time. I'm verifying alibis for the time of the murder. Where were you between 5:30 and 6:00 pm this past Tuesday?"

She drew in a long breath. "It seems Maria's right. You are checking on everyone. At the time of the murder, I was driving my sister to Gettysburg. We had dinner there before the reception at the president's house."

"And you—" Ty didn't have time to finish his follow-up question before she pressed forward.

"I had the shepherd's pie. Charlotte ordered scallops."

"Well, that's good to know. But I was going to ask which restaurant. Glengarry, right?" Even though she'd just corroborated Charlotte's meal, he needed to be certain their stories matched, point by point. The dean didn't strike him as suspect material, but he'd play it out.

Joyce looked puzzled. "No. It was Garryowen."

"Oh, right. Sorry. I try to be thorough, but I'm not always right, am I?" He shot her a disarming look. "And since I'm checking into everyone, you won't be surprised to learn that I'm also looking into potential motives. I've had my ear to ground around campus, and you're seen as upwardly mobile. It occurs to me that a go-getting woman would see Heather's letter as an opportunity for some kind of advancement. Did you?"

Plunkard's chin trembled. "Of course not. What an unkind thing to say."

"I'm sorry, ma'am, truly. But to solve murders, I've got to ask hard questions. Like this one: Are you covering for your sister?"

Her hand flew to her throat, and she gasped. "No, of course not. And I wouldn't have to because she could never do anything so horrible."

"Maybe not," he agreed. "But what would you do to safeguard her professional reputation?"

"I love my sister, but I wouldn't kill for her. And this conversation is over. As you noted, I'm extremely busy, and it's time for my next appointment. Good day, Lieutenant."

Leaving, he assessed what he'd learned.

He knew that David and Meg didn't like the woman, didn't respect her. But he'd trust his gut on this one. That woman didn't have the steel to murder anyone. However, he could see why the faculty might not get along with her. She didn't seem all that bright, which would make it mighty hard to be an effective supervisor of intellectuals. And his quarry was really, really smart.

* * * * *

Meg dropped her pencil on top of the stack of graded papers, yawned extravagantly, stretched idly, and pushed away from her desk, satisfied. She always got more done at home.

"Lunch," she muttered. "I need fuel."

Even though she craved a tuna fish sandwich, she was too lazy to make it. Instead, she pulled a yogurt out of the refrigerator. Leaning one hip against the kitchen counter, she ripped the lid off the container and found her mind wandering. She picked up her cell.

"Joan," she said, twirling her spoon in the yogurt, "what if I went by Ty's house this evening after class, just for a look/see?"

Her best friend snorted. "What! Now you're stalking him?"

"No, no, no," she protested, laughing. "Nothing like that. Just a drive by, to see where he lives, the style of his house. Maybe stand on the sidewalk and peek in a few windows, see if he has bookcases...or whatever."

"I agree with you."

"You do?"

"I agree with your first statement, 'No, no, no!'"

"Come on, how can it hurt? It's Halloween. The streets will be full of strangers and—"

"—not one of them stranger than you."

"Oh, very witty."

Joan clucked her tongue. "Have you lost every shred of dignity you possess?"

"Yes. Yes, I have," Meg admitted. "But it's harmless. I'll be undetectable. It'll be getting dark, all sorts of kids will be out and about wearing costumes. I'm wearing one for class tonight anyway. I'll be another trick or treater. Nobody will be the wiser."

Meg pushed off the counter, and walked to the window, looked across the fields of corn stubble and out toward the low mountains. A few ducks paddled at the edge of the pond. In her ear, she heard Joan's long inhale as she readied her response.

"Let me get this straight, Meg. You are planning to be undetectable while scoping out a detective's home. Are you even listening to what you're saying? And how do you know where he lives?" Pause. "You didn't ask those cops at that Police Academy, did you? Say you didn't," she pleaded. "He'd never live it down. Humiliation is not a sound foundation for relationship."

"No. I didn't call Groves or Keefer, so I don't know where he lives." Yet. But she had a plan. However, she was beginning to regret calling her friend.

"What has gotten into you, child?" said Joan, her voice rising.

"It's what *hasn't* gotten into me, if you catch my drift. Not in months."

Watching a flock of geese approach the pond, she listened to Joan's agitated breathing. "So I take it you won't come with me?"

"Under no circumstances will I be party to this foolishness. You'd just best take your little mayfly-self right home tonight and grade some of those papers you are always putting off."

"Mayfly?"

"Yes, ma'am. Mayfly. They live for about four days, and all of that time is taken up with reproduction. Girl, what has happened to your self-respect?"

Her face clouded, and her throat tightened. "Al got it in the divorce."

"Meg," Joan said more kindly, "stop this. What if the detective sees you? Worse yet, what if his daughter sees you?"

The geese were descending toward the pond, but as shots rang out they changed course, skeining toward the maple-dappled mountains.

"Okay, okay. You're right. It's a really, really bad idea."

Joan sighed in relief. "I'm glad you've come to your senses."

"Thanks for the advice, girlfriend. Gotta dash. Talk to you later," she said, putting down the phone.

And it was good advice. But that didn't mean she had to take it.

Chapter 34

Damn that Bernie, and the commander, for calling this press conference. João had been particularly smug, knowing how frustrating it was to put an active investigation on hold. But it was a high profile case, and people were curious. And a little scared. Consequently, the venue was a public one, on the steps of the courthouse. The brick courtyard it shared with police headquarters featured a bronze statue of John Hanson, the Revolutionary War figure whose bold signature overshadowed all other names on the Declaration of Independence. The statue portrayed him—a prominent Frederick County patriot—with a quill in one hand and a document in the other. The impressive statue would make for a dramatic backdrop for the televised reports.

Ty stood on the courthouse steps along with Bernie, the commander, and the mayor, all of them facing more than a dozen members of the press and assorted looky-loos.

Since there were only a handful of reporters in Frederick, the sizable audience had to include journalists from all over, including Baltimore and Washington. Not unexpected, but still a pain in the ass.

"And now we'll hear from the lead investigator," João said in his booming voice. "Lieutenant Raleigh is a highly skilled and dedicated officer with a high success rate. We're fortunate to have him on the case. Some of you may remember he was the state trooper who tracked down and arrested the serial murderer stalking women in Baltimore's Inner Harbor."

Thanks, boss. But before anyone could follow up on that, he stepped forward and gave his customary spiel: the investigation was ongoing; that all possible leads were being followed; and no, he couldn't comment on specific details; and yes, this was an isolated incident. There was no cause for worry. He fielded the usual questions with the usual answers. Then someone threw him a curve. Not an out-of-towner, but the reporter who'd covered Heather's viewing.

"Lieutenant," Skip began, "my source indicates that you have pinpointed two professors as suspects in your investigation. Will you confirm this information?"

All heads swiveled to get a look at the *Frederick News-Post* correspondent.

Ty locked eyes with Skip. "Neither I nor this department has named any suspects."

"Then professors Brunner and Slattery are in the clear?"

Ty's face and voice turned stern and cold. "We've spoken to both of them. They're cooperating with the investigation." In varying degrees, and when forced to it.

"So you have no suspects at this time."

Eyes blazing, Ty let loose.

"What I have is the brutal murder of a young woman who had done nothing to deserve it. But let me make it clear that all of my efforts and those of the entire Frederick City Police Department are dedicated to solving this case. Heather Hillcrest deserves our full attention and I, for one, will not rest until her murderer is brought to justice."

With that he turned on his heel and strode back into police headquarters, leaving Bernie to finish up. And João had just better just back off, too.

He slammed his office door, plopped in his chair and picked up his phone.

"Skip," he snarled, "what the hell was that all about? Why the sneak attack? You could've given me a heads-up instead."

"Aw, come on, Raleigh. When else am I going to get to scoop those big city news personalities? And what about you, Mr. Tight Lips? Ready to start talking?"

"What I want to be doing is listening. Where did you get those names?"

"Nuh-uh, Raleigh. I name names, and I don't get any more anonymous tips. You know how the game is played. If you want to know something, I've gotta get something."

"Fat chance."

"It was worth a shot." His voice conveyed his grin. "I can't reveal the source because I don't know. The caller must've sucked down some helium before he dialed because he sounded just like Daffy Duck. You're dealing with one sly hombre here, Raleigh."

"Tell me about it."

He cut the connection and leaned back in his chair to think. Who had called Skip, and why had the caller given him those two names? Maybe there was a leak somewhere. But who? Not Meg, surely. The president's office was in the know, but Collins and Routzhan were seriously invested in keeping the story under wraps. But he wouldn't put it past either Brunner or Slattery to put in the call to further implicate the other. Or Sellers, just to stir the pot. But damned if he knew how the little shit would have found out. That kid was sly and slippery...and still MIA.

Looking at the ceiling, he interlaced his hands behind his head.

Or was Skip being used as a pawn to mess with him, throw him off stride? Well, it wouldn't take much, since he didn't feel like he'd ever hit his rhythm on this one.

But the disguised voice was interesting. Was the caller worried about being identified? Or was he just playing at being clever? Or simply unhinged. No way to know. He'd file it away as another puzzle piece. It would fit in somewhere, sometime.

He unthreaded his hands and sat up straight, agitated at the waste of time. He hoped this next interview would prove more productive. Sketchy Doug was due downstairs in interrogation at 4:00.

·　　·　　·　　·　　·

"Mr. Dahlrymple," Ty said as they shook hands. "Thank you for coming down today."

"Don't see as I had any choice."

"There's always a choice. You might've chosen to ignore my request and made me find you. Or you could've just skipped town. But here you are. I need to ask you a few questions."

"Fine."

"You know Professor Brunner, don't you? What can you tell me about him?"

"Robert? He's a standup kinda guy. A little prissy, but a good guy."

"Well, he's in a bit of hot water right now. What do you know about that?"

"You mean that dead girl and all? I only know what's in the papers."

"Hmm...you must know a little more than that. The rumor mill at the college must be working overtime. You can't tell me that you haven't caught the drift of all that."

"The murdered girl was one of his students. She had a letter that he could use to further his research. It's missing. So what?"

"What do you think he would do to get ahold of that letter? Would he try to buy it? Steal it? Would he kill for it?"

"No way. I told you. He's a standup kind of guy."

"Even standup guys get their backs up against a wall. He needs a boost to get himself noticed, to get himself a fancier job at a prestigious school. He sure isn't going anywhere here. Maybe he just snapped."

"Nope. Not Robert. He's too smart and too disciplined. Besides, like I said, he's way too prissy to get bloody. If he'd killed, it would be cleaner. Like poison."

Yeah, they were in agreement about that. "But maybe he had help. Maybe he got someone to do the deed for him. Someone like you, maybe."

"Hold on there. I'm no murderer."

"Technically, no. But you've already taken a life."

"It was involuntary manslaughter. A hunting accident."

"Maybe this was an accident, too. Maybe you were just supposed to rob Heather and things got out of hand."

"Uh-uh. No way. I've never robbed anyone. Robert never asked me to do anything."

"But he got you a job. It's not easy to find employment, especially something with benefits, when you're a felon. Why would he put himself on the line like that? Did you two strike a bargain? The letter for the job?"

"That's just wrong. You don't know dick. You're fishing."

"What about the Nannie Crouse thing? He's working to prove that you are related to her. It'd be a feather in your cap, you being big into Civil War re-enactment and all. But it would be a bigger feather if she were the real Barbara Fritchie. What would you do for that kind of fame?"

"Sure as shit not kill for it. I've already done time, and I'm not looking to do more. Besides, what would it get me? There's no money in that kind of fame. You're barking up the wrong tree, detective. If you are going to charge me, do it. If not, I'm outta here."

"You're free to go."

Chapter 35

By 4:00 pm, Meg was done grading her papers and getting ready to go back into school for her night class: EN 101 for the Frederick City police cadets.

"A Friday night class. How do I get myself into these things?" she grumbled. Not once since she'd become a full professor had she taught on Fridays. It was all David's fault. He'd scheduled the class to align with the other police science classes—giving English 101 the crappy time slot—and later sweet-talked her into teaching it, all the while admitting he owed her one.

But tonight wouldn't be all bad. Since it was Halloween, she'd get free food at school. During the evening break, the cafeteria gave away pizza and soda, plus a super-sized candy bar to people wearing costumes. Worth it. Plus, she didn't have to dress like an adult. Double worth it. To score the candy bar, she'd assembled the world's easiest costume during a stop at the local thrift shop: baggy pants, over-sized men's shoes, a scrody plaid shirt, and a disreputable tweed jacket. The perfect makings of a hobo.

After she'd dressed and added a mascara-smudged beard, she was putting papers in her book bag and organizing her desk when she found it. The one-page xerox of Barbara Fritichie's letter that Ty wanted. She looked at the clock. No time to drop it by the police station before class, but...

She picked up her cell phone and dialed David, chewing on her bottom lip while she waited for him to pick up. It went to voice mail. "David, hi. Um...here's the thing. I want to call in that favor you owe me. I need to know Ty's home address."

$$\bullet \quad \bullet \quad \bullet \quad \bullet \quad \bullet$$

Meg let her 5 o'clock class go on their break a little early. Why wait until the stroke of 6:15. After all, it was Halloween. And of course, she'd been the only one in the room wearing a costume. She should've figured the cadets were too straight-laced to play along. A smile touched her eyes as she wondered what Ty would've done in their place. He'd make a fine cowboy, like the title character in Owen Wister's *The Virginian*. A deep thinker, a wrong-righter...stalwart and Wild West manly.

She'd wolfed down her pizza and was fingering the free super-sized candy bar when she felt someone in the crowd jostle her.

"I wouldn't let my kid out of the house looking like that. It's disrespectful."

Turning to respond, she saw it was Bastian, one of the students in her cop class. His disgusted tone surprised her. He stood out from the others, maturity-wise. Not surprising since he was older than most, a career-changer in his upper thirties, and came from the West Indies.

"Looking like what?" she said, expecting an objection to some girl in a harem costume leaving too much cleavage and midriff exposed.

"Like that fool of a boy."

She followed his line of sight. "A clown," she laughed, spotting the Bozo-clad student.

Bastian frowned. "Not just any clown. Look at its mouth. The corners of that oversized red mouth turn up in sharp points. Real clowns use rounded corners so as not to scare kids."

Meg looked more carefully. He was right. It was kinda spooky.

Her student's frown deepened into a scowl. "And he's added a name tag, 'Pogo,' just in case nobody knows who he's imitating."

"Well, that would be me," Meg admitted.

"John Wayne Gacy, the serial killer."

Her eyes widened. "Really?" The little hairs on her arms stood up in alarm.

She'd heard the name, of course, but if she'd ever known the specifics, she'd forgotten them. On purpose. Even scary movies were too much for her. She'd never seen the first *Scream* or *Friday the 13th*, let alone the sequels. And certainly nothing based on a Stephen King book.

Well, not if she could avoid it. She'd once had a student in her Film as Lit class whose final project analyzed the adaptation of King's novel *It* into a 1990s mini-series. She'd endured the YouTube snippets of the supernatural, shape-shifting clown Pennywise as it slaughtered children by beheading, mutilating, and severing limbs. She'd narrowed her eyes and pretended to watch.

"Gacy was known as The Killer Clown," Bastian added. He proceeded to detail how, before he was finally arrested for raping, torturing and strangling thirty-three victims, Gacy had trademarked himself as Pogo the Clown and entertained at lots of events around Chicago. He even went into hospitals to entertain kids. "While he was on death row, he painted and sold pictures of himself as a clown. And that damn fool boy over there thinks it's okay to masquerade as that freak."

"I agree that it's in poor taste," Meg said. She knew some people were scared of clowns, but they weren't among her phobias. *Or hadn't been until now.* And she hoped that kid over there, whoever he was, never turned up in one of her classes.

"But there's nothing I can do," she added. "The student is just expressing himself."

Bastian shook his head and walked away, muttering, "Americans..."

Feeling like she was a poor cultural ambassador, and still a little unsettled, Meg surveyed the rest of her class. Everybody else was having a fine time snarfing down free pizza and soda.

Looking around the cafeteria, she spied Calloway, probably heading back to his office from the auditorium. The Civil War symposium was breaking up for the day, and he was standing in a small group of chatty attendees, all of whom had a slice of pizza. The freeloaders. Brunner and Slattery were on opposite ends of the crowd. She saw Charlotte cut him a look she wouldn't like to be the recipient of. The president and the dean seemed to be following the prevailing conversation, and Maria was taking lots of pictures of student revelers and conventioneers alike. Not that she looked too happy about it.

Nervous, Meg sidled up to her friend. "David, did you get my message?"

He eyed her costume. "Nice getup." Then he gave her a suspicious look. "Why?" He paused. "Why do you need Raleigh's address, and why should I give it to you?"

"I need it because I found the xerox of that letter he wants to see," she said quietly, "and I want to take it by his house after class. And you should give it to me because you owe me. Teaching writing to those police wannabes isn't all that fun. They're smart enough, most of them, but way too serious. Plus, you pulled a fast one with that 'he's not currently married' bit."

"Nope. I'm not giving you his address." David scowled at her. "If he'd wanted you to have it, you would. You need to hang back and let him do his job. Give the letter to the guys here in Security. They're in the loop. They'll get it to him. Or I can do it on my way home."

"Fine. Security it is," she snapped. But she wasn't done. She'd just see who was on duty over there. If it was her friend Josey, she'd ask her for the address. After all, Meg had written her son a letter of recommendation. Since her day job was with the city police, she'd likely know. But why was David acting all prickly?

She was so preoccupied with his bad mood that she didn't hear the summons.

"Meg...Meghan! Stand over here," Maria said, tone preemptory. "I need a few shots of faculty in costume to put on the website. Then maybe I can finally go home for the day. Just pose beside this other person."

Feeling put upon, Meg stood next to another costumed teacher, a math adjunct dressed as Einstein. "Sure, but this 'other person' has a name. Charles Maxwell, meet Maria Routzhan."

Maria clicked away at the two of them. "A derelict and a genius," she snickered. "Now, how about the two of you with some of those students over there?"

She looked at the students Maria was referencing. A few of them were from Heather's class. Meg did a double take when she saw Nate and Leti dressed as Shaggy and Daphne. Leti carried a stuffed Scooby Doo, and Nate waved its paw at her. When the student behind Nate turned around, Meg did another double take: Jon Sellers, dressed in a Confederate general's uniform. He seemed as uncomfortable to see her as she was to see him.

Turning to Maria she said, "I think I've had enough exposure. Why don't you try..."

She cast about for a different victim, but David gave her another scowl. Sliding her eyes past him, she watched Maria go up to Brunner and lay a hand lightly on his arm.

"Robert," she began, "I'd really like to wind up this photo shoot, and I need your help."

When he turned and saw who it was, his posture lost some of its characteristic stiffness. "Of course, my dear. What can I do for you?"

"You could help me out here by posing with some of these students, if it's no bother."

He touched her elbow and gave her a courtly nod. "Certainly. I'd be delighted."

"Ick!" Meg mumbled. Those two were awfully chummy.

In a low voice, Maria added, "Dr. Tremayne's session just ended. Were you able to mention my article to him?"

Brunner's face clouded. "Ah...no. No, not yet." He gestured Sellers over. "Now, where would you like us to stand?"

Lost in thought, Meg turned to leave and bumped into Charlotte Slattery. Literally.

The scholar had been glaring at Brunner and Maria, but her face darkened as she spoke to Meg. "Watch where you're going, you stupid girl."

She stepped back. "I'm...I'm sorry."

Scurrying away from the rebuke, Meg hustled toward Security and saw Josey just as she was coming out of the office to make her rounds. "Hey, friend, how's that son of yours doing at Rutgers? We're all so proud of him. It's not every student who goes from here to there."

"He's doin' really good. Thanks for asking."

"It was my pleasure, Sam's a great kid."

"Yeah he is." Noting the costume, she chuckled. "You didn't do the Confederate thing? Because of the conference, y'know."

Meg wrinkled her nose. "I'm not into all that stuff like a lot of people around here. For some of them, it's like the Civil War isn't over. This conference is right up their alley."

"I wish it were up Brunner's..." she paused before she added, "...alley. That damn event makes more work for the rest of us. They've doubled our patrols."

"I'm sorry to hear that." And she was; she'd bake her some brownies next week, socialize. It'd been a while. But she needed to get the info and slip back to class. "Say, Josey—"

"These conferences are a royal pain."

Okay, just a couple more minutes of commiserating. "Yeah, I just saw Maria Routzhan, and she was running ragged. Said she couldn't wait to get home."

"Yeah, she's dragging butt these days. Her mom's dealing with cancer. So she's been with her every minute she can. Looks like the end is near. And those two are really tight."

Cancer! Meg'd never considered Maria's life outside of work. She'd put the woman's current edginess down to dealing with both the conference and the murder investigation. *Shame on you, Meg.* She'd have to make a point of being kinder to the poor woman.

But she needed to get a move on. "Josey, I'd like to stay and chat, but I have to get back to class. Here's the thing. I need a favor. Do you happen to have Lieutenant Raleigh's home address?"

The woman turned her head to one side and looked at Meg with a question in her eyes.

Lordy, these cop types were suspicious. "I...um, I'm headed there after class to take him something he's been asking about. Something that pertains to his murder investigation. He lives over by Hood College, but I've only been there in the daytime." She hated lying to a friend. "Now that it's dark, I'm afraid I won't recognize it. Could you give me the street address?"

Her face smoothed. "Sure. My brother-in-law lives right across from him. It's 103 College Parkway. The only painted brick house on the street. You can't miss it."

"Gracias, friend." Meg went back to class in a much better mood, no thanks to David.

Chapter 36

It was always a pain in the neck to get on or off campus during the change of classes. Too much volume and parking was at a premium. Cars crawled along, hoping to inherit a newly vacated spot. Any kind of success involved a lot of sitting still and watching of tail lights. But traffic on Friday nights was usually much lighter. Not so tonight, though. This snarled up mess had to be a side effect of that benighted conference. *Thanks, Robert.*

Eventually, she was off campus and rolling down the ersatz Route 66 of TCC—Opossumtown Pike. On the left: a middle school, a church, middle-class housing, a strip mall with a grocery store and a fast food joint. On the right: Fort Detrick, an active Army medical research facility which had studied chemical warfare from WWII through the 1960s. They still stored anthrax there, but the weapons program had been dismantled years ago. Or so they said. After Detrick's long fence ended, a funeral parlor came into view. An ironic juxtaposition.

She made the drive feeling more nervous than excited. Too soon she was there, amid the tasteful brick homes on a tree-lined street in Ty's neighborhood. Pulling to the curb, she parked in an unobtrusive spot, a little annoyed when a silver sedan parked a few cars behind her. It made her feel too conspicuous, more nervous

Turning off the truck, she sat and watched a few kids in costume, little princesses and superheroes skipping ahead of long-suffering parents. By now it was a hair shy of 8 o'clock, and things were winding to a close.

As she was putting her hand on Rocinante's door handle, she caught sight of a jeans-and-sweatshirt-clad Ty dash out of his front door. She ducked down to spy while he got into the white SUV, turned on its headlights, and drove away.

As his taillights disappeared onto Motter Avenue, she reconsidered her plans. The daughter wasn't with him. And he wouldn't leave her alone, as she well knew. So he must be going to pick her up from somewhere. The round trip would take some time, allowing her to have a look-see at the yard and maybe even into the tasteful home with its windows glowing warmly in the night. When they got back, she'd pretend to have just arrived.

The streets formed a triangle around a small park that boasted rows of manicured flower beds, a few trees, and several wood-slatted benches. The old-fashioned, frosted globe streetlamps and gray stone archways added to the charm of the little neighborhood park that fronted homes populated by well-heeled old money. Not the kind of place she'd thought to find a cop's house.

Screwing up her courage she got out, intending to walk down Rockwell Terrace, the base leg of the triangle. Hearing another car door shut, she waited beside Rocinante for a bit.

Across the way, adults and children were laughing over someone's having tripped on an uneven patch of sidewalk. She locked the truck and looked behind her. A few costumed stragglers were going door-to-door—a scruffy, home-made pirate and an extravagant, pre-fab clown among them. She shuddered at the latter. *Damn that Bastian and his Gacy rant.*

However, this particular clown sort of irritated her because he seemed too tall to warrant the treat bag in his white-gloved hand. A high school kid, probably. Trolling for free candy.

Meg shook off her annoyance and started walking, her ill-fitting hobo shoes slapping on the concrete. Leaving the Rockwell Terrace leg of the triangle, she passed through the crosswalk and headed up the hypotenuse of College Parkway. She was actually on the street where he lived.

Number 103 was a Cape Cod affair with a covered porch. On either side of the front door stretched three long, thin panes of clear, leaded glass. Each of those was flanked by a pair of double-hung windows.

From the sidewalk, all she could see through the leaded glass panels was a stairway going up toward the second floor. The bigger windows had their wooden blinds drawn for the night. Considering her options, she decided not to stop out front. Too risky. But she did pause at the end of the street. Turning around to look back at his house, she was stunned to see a zombie and a Freddy Kruger standing in the open doorway of the Raleigh home. The light in the foyer illuminated Lindsay—wearing black tights and a baggy orange sweatshirt—as she distributed candy. The trick-or-treaters moved on, and the door closed.

"Damn, that was a close call," Meg murmured. She'd been sure the girl wasn't home. It was high time to scoot back toward her truck. Rocinante would protect her from prying eyes until Ty returned, and she could knock on his door and give him the letter.

Just short of his house, she stubbed her ill-shod toe on the edge of the cracked sidewalk. She stumbled, but before she could fall, a white-gloved hand reached out and steadied her.

Looking up, she intended to say "thank you," but her sixth sense kicked in. Something was terribly wrong. Then she felt a hard poke in the belly. She looked down. Holy mother of god—a gun!

"Oopsy, watch your step," advised the clown, his voice as out of place as the gun. It sounded synthesized, like a child's voice but distorted and metallic. She winced when he seized her upper arm in a too-tight grip.

It was like being in a car accident. Time slowed down. Details sharpened. Fear waited.

Not a Gacy clown. No, this one's mask had a really tall forehead. Tall and stark white. And the reddish hair hung down from the receding hairline like long strands of stale cotton candy. It wore a three-layered, ruffled collar around its neck; the gaudy blue-and-purple striped layer tucked between innocent white ones, with the same brash stripes repeated on the long sleeves. A short, black, buttonless vest flapped open to reveal a yellow jumpsuit, the yellow of hazard signs. Danger: flammable, corrosive, toxic. The three bloated pompoms, carroty in color, seemed to taunt her. But the teeth haunted her. Jagged, like a crocodile's, but yellowed and crusty.

Oh shit! The beheader. The mutilator. Pennywise the Dancing Clown.

Meg wanted to scream, yell for help, but no sound came. Terror cemented her to the spot.

He leaned in close and whispered, "You're going to do everything I say. Aren't you? Promptly and without argument. You understand?"

She nodded fiercely. His eerie voice—surreal, mechanical—left no room for doubt.

"Or I'll shoot and leave you to bleed out where you fall."

Her thoughts blanked, and her core went icy at the surety of his promise.

Wrenching her arm behind her back, he snugged the muzzle of his gun against her neck and prodded her along the brick walk and onto the porch. His polyester costume ssh-ed with every movement. He stopped her just shy of the front door. "Now, ring the bell."

It wasn't a matter of choice. She did as he commanded. When the door opened, he let go of her arm and thrust her into the foyer. Once inside, he slammed the door shut with one foot.

Tightening her hold on the trick or treat bowl full of candy, Lindsay glared at Meg. "You? What are you doing here?"

Words were forming in Meg's head. *Run. He's got a gun. Get help.* But they wouldn't come out. Couldn't come out. He hadn't willed it so.

Meg flinched and came back to herself when the gun dug hard into her kidneys. Shuffling to one side, she nodded toward the object in the clown's hand, hoping Lindsay would react sensibly. She didn't want either of them ending up as gun-violence statistics.

Lindsay looked from the gun to Meg in her makeshift costume, and finally focused on the clown. A worried frown built on her face. "What's up with you and Pennywise? Is this some kind of lame joke?"

"No. No, this is serious." She had to make the girl understand. "He grabbed me outside on the sidewalk and forced me to ring your doorbell. I don't know what's going on, but it's no joke."

"That's right," he said, positioning the gun on Meg's temple. "I'm deadly serious."

White-faced, Lindsay dropped the bowl, sending chocolate bars skittering across the hardwood floor.

He shoved Meg to stand beside the girl. "Ni-ce, very convenient," he said. "Two birds, one stone."

Feeling Lindsay trembling beside her, Meg took the girl's hand and squeezed it. But it was slack and cold.

The clown tilted its head, its red clumps of hair bobbing with the movement. It tapped a white-gloved finger on its white, white chin as if it were thinking. "Now...where's the letter?"

Meg stared at him, stupefied. Dread overwhelmed her. She couldn't give him what he wanted. Something horrible was going to happen.

"The letter the dead girl found and was shopping around." He jabbed the gun toward his captives. "You can either give it to me or join her."

"Heather," cried Lindsay as she stumbled forward a step. "You killed Heather?"

"Yup, no way around it." He shrugged. "You want to be next?"

Meg felt the hairs on her neck lift. Hearing Lindsay's whimper, she stepped in front of the girl. The clown made noises that might have been laughter. She stared at him, thinking fast and getting nowhere, scrambling to come up with a plan.

"Where's the letter?" he snarled. "Fritchie's letter."

Pulse pounding, Meg started backing up deeper into the foyer. She kept Lindsay behind her, forcing her backward, all the while looking for some weapon: golf clubs, a stout umbrella, a lamp, anything heavy. Anything she could use to get that awful gun pointed away from her.

"No one's coming to help you, you know. I watched the cop leave." The clown brought up his pistol and waved it from one captive to another. "Tell me! Where's that letter?"

"We don't have it," Meg whispered, legs trembling but still backing up.

"Liar. One of you does. Give it to me." The eerie voice got louder, angrier, a sullen child's tantrum gone amok. "Unless you think it's worth dying for."

Then Meg saw the two things she was looking for: a doorway and a weapon. She pushed Lindsay through the door, grabbed the can of Pledge from the hallway table and sprayed it in the face of her nemesis. While the clown pawed at his mask, Meg sped after Lindsay into the room and shut the door, locking it. She turned and bumped straight into Lindsay. *Damn it.* She'd locked them in a powder room, one with only a small, diamond-shaped window. No escape.

But Lindsay was already talking into her cell phone.

"Dad, dad. Come home *now.* Hurry! There's a crazy person in the house with a gun, and I'm locked in the powder room with Heather's teacher. Come quick. Please hurry, please."

The doorknob was jiggling angrily. When the clown started pounding on the door, Meg brought up the Pledge can and shouted, "The police are on their way. You'd better leave."

Through the door, they heard garbled words, felt the thuds as he kicked at the wood. Suddenly the jiggling, pounding, and yelling stopped.

Meg and Lindsay looked at each other, wondering what would happen next. The quiet was as unsettling as the noise had been. As minutes passed, the two of them strained to hear any sound, any clue to what was going on. They both jumped when the shouting and pounding resumed.

"Lindsay, are you in there? Are you alright?" yelled Ty.

"Dad," she cried and pushed past Meg to unlock and open the door. "Dad, I was so scared." She flew into her father's arms.

He hugged her and shut his eyes briefly, but the tension didn't leave his body. "Are you okay? Either of you hurt?"

"No, we're fine." Meg staggered into the foyer on wobbly legs. "Just scared."

Ty untangled himself from Lindsay to look her in the face—a fierce expression in his gray eyes. "What did the intruder look like?" When she didn't respond right away, he gripped her by the shoulders. "Lindsay, give me a description."

"A-a-about 5' 9", medium build. Wearing a Pennywise clown mask: white face, tall forehead, reddish hair at the sides. Ruffled collar at the neck, white gloves. A bright yellow, one-piece polyester suit with blue and purple stripes on long sleeves. And three orange pompoms down the front."

Meg stared at the girl in disbelief. She'd nailed it. Right down to the pompoms.

"The gun was a Glock, like yours."

Meg felt like Alice in Wonderland, as if she'd tumbled down the rabbit hole into a place where teenaged girls could identify guns.

Ty kissed his daughter on the forehead. "Good girl." He turned to face Meg. "I've called for backup." He gestured toward the powder room. "Go back in there and wait until an officer gives you the 'All clear.' Someone will stay here until I get back."

"Dad, don't go!"

But he was already running out the front door, slamming it behind him.

Chapter 37

Lindsay stood limp and listless, unable to follow her father's directions, so Meg shepherded her back into confinement. The girl sat on the toilet, hugged herself and rocked back and forth, shaking.

Meg's head jerked up when the blue and red flashing lights of a police cruiser began to strobe through the little diamond-shaped window. Lindsay didn't seem to notice.

Then it sounded like several officers darted through the front door and began searching the house. Several minutes later, a polite knock came on the powder room door. Cautiously, Meg opened it and saw a uniformed officer. She let out the breath she didn't know she was holding.

"It's all clear, ladies. You can come out now. After I leave, lock the front door and stay put. I'll be right outside on the porch."

Lindsay wasn't moving, so Meg took her by the arm, steered her into what looked like the living room and pressed her down on the suede couch facing the window. Looking for something she could use to warm the quaking girl, Meg caught a fleeting impression of expensive furnishings and tasteful décor—like a showroom's living room, high end. On a cops's salary? she wondered.

Then her eyes landed on something useful, a cashmere afghan draped over a bentwood rocking chair. She snatched it up and draped it around her charge whose blue eyes stared at nothing. She was rocking back and forth, hands in her lap.

"Well, shit," Meg mumbled.

Lindsay began to mouth some words. Her lips were moving, but no sound came out. That continued for several seconds, then she uttered low, low sounds. Not moans, not words, just wispy, raspy sounds.

Meg sat down and hugged the girl, rocked with her and hugged her until the sounds quieted. Smoothing the child's spikey hair, she murmured, "You're safe. It's over. He's gone." She repeated the mantra over and over, trying to believe it herself.

"No, no, no...not again...no," Lindsay whispered.

It tore at Meg's heart to hear such distress. No to what? And what was happening again?

"No, not again. No..."

"Lindsay, your dad is coming right back. He's chasing that maniac, but he'll be back soon."

It was as if Meg hadn't even spoken.

"Not again, not again. He'll get hurt, and it'll be my fault again."

"Lindsay, it'll be okay. Your dad will be back in a bit, you'll see."

"No...no..."

"It will be okay, I promise. It'll be okay."

Lindsay shifted out of Meg's embrace and seemed to see her for the first time. The teen's eyes were red-rimmed, watery. "You don't know that." Her gaze drifted away. "You don't know anything."

And she didn't. Meg had not a clue.

"It's just like with Mom...my fault again."

"I'm sure it wasn't your fault, sweetie." But what was the poor child reliving?

Weakly, Lindsay shook her head. "It was my fault, it was. Dad came to my room because I had a bad dream...a nightmare..."

Meg considered her options. Should she shake the girl and force her back to the present? Let her keep going? Shit, shit, shit. Why was she the only woman in North America who'd never watched Dr. Phil? She needed to be really, really smart here.

Lindsay looked down and continued, her voice so soft it was almost lost. "Dad turned on my music and rocked me back to sleep. We both fell asleep until the gun went off."

Oh, dear lord. *She's reliving the home invasion, her mother's murder. Ty didn't tell me Lindsay was in the house when it happened. That was, what? Five years ago? She'd been maybe ten.*

Lindsay began speaking again, in a stronger voice, but the words came slowly. "The Break-in Man shot Mom. It sounded so, so loud. Dad said, 'Stay here,' and ran out of the room. There was shouting and more shooting. Loud, loud shooting."

The girl moved her hands up toward her ears but let them drop back down. "Then it was all quiet and...and...and Dad was yelling to me to call 911, to just stay in my room and call 911. But I didn't, I wanted to see, had to go see..."

Meg tried not to shudder, not to interrupt. There was no way to make this better.

"There was all this blood, and Dad was trying to stop Mom from bleeding, pushing down where she was bleeding. Her face was white, and her nightgown was red, and he was bleeding, too, bleeding bad. Just so, so much blood.

Lindsay's breathing was ragged and shallow, but her voice became louder.

"And he kept yelling, 'Call 911,' so I did. But I went back and watched. He kept calling her name...'"

Lindsay started weeping, lightly at first, and Meg cried with her. Then the girl's words come out in a tearful rush.

"When the police got there, they were mean to him, like it was his fault like he did it. I kept trying to tell them, but they wouldn't listen to me. The ambulances came and took them away, took them both away. But they pulled the sheet up all the way over Mom, over her face. So I knew. Right then I knew. And it was all my fault."

She sagged back into the sofa cushions, dry-eyed and spent.

Meg wondered what she should do next. But what this child needed was her dad. Where was her father...where was Ty?

Lindsay began rousing and looked around, dazed. "Dad's not back?"

"No, not yet." Well, she's not panicking, and she's not belligerent, thank god. "He'll be back shortly. I don't think it's been much more than half an hour."

"Really?" Lindsay said through a long yawn. "It feels like this time tomorrow."

"I'm with you on that one."

Lindsay looked at Meg, her forehead wrinkled in confusion. "Just one thing." She cocked her head to one side. "I mean I'm glad you're here and everything. But why are you here?"

Crap. Of course, she'd ask that. It was a natural question. Meg scrambled for a plausible explanation. "I...I'd finished teaching and was on my way to a Halloween party down the street." She hoped the girl was too distracted to ask for specifics. "Then the clown stopped me on the sidewalk out front and forced me inside."

"Yeah," Lindsay said, "yeah, he must have seen Dad leave. Why else would he chance it?" She continued in a shivery voice. "Happy to see him leave, happy that you wandered by, happy to barge in and ask us stuff in that weird, creepy kid's voice."

With that remark, Meg figured she was off the hook. But then she saw Lindsay taking a long look at her. Oh crappity crap, crap. The scales were falling from her eyes.

"Your beard is sort of messed up. You might want to take a look at it."

"Oh, okay. Thanks." Meg went back to the powder room, wet some squares of toilet paper and rubbed at her cheeks. And rubbed. "Lindsay," she called, "do you have some makeup remover I can use?"

"Sure. Come on upstairs."

The teen led her rescuer to a bathroom halfway down the hall, opened the shiny white medicine cabinet, and pointed out her stash of makeup remover and skin care paraphernalia. Leaving Meg to her task, Lindsay walked into her bedroom and closed the door.

Meg scrubbed at her faux beard. It took some diligent scouring, but soon she was clean-faced again. As she left the bathroom, her eyes were drawn to a large, expensively framed photographic portrait on the wall beside the door to Lindsay's room. Intrigued, she went closer.

It featured two barefoot people in close-fitting black tee shirts and black jeans posed against a gray, cloth-draped backdrop. A tall man standing behind a petite, auburn-haired, very pregnant woman. A younger, thinner, darker-haired Ty and what had to be his wife. Her delicate hands were clasped around her big belly, her blue eyes luminous with joy. In that moment, her whole aspect took on the clichéd glow that graced pregnant women. But this was no cliché. Ty, all but aglow himself, rested his head against hers—ear to ear. He looked down at her fullness, his fingers intertwined with hers as they both cradled her belly.

Meg could not look away. As if she were gazing in a mirror, her hand rose to her own ear, touched her own untidy hair. She stared at the photograph, knowing that if she closed her eyes, she would still see it.

She stepped closer, fingertips touching the bottom edge of the silvery, deeply carved wood frame. The girl really took after her mother. Same slight build...same blue eyes. Even the same delicate facial features, resembling French or maybe Dutch women.

It came to her in a flash. The wife reminded her of an auburn-haired *Girl with a Pearl Earring*. Well, hell. She was living in the shadow of the dearly-departed, Vermeer-masterpiece, mother of his child.

Slipping her hands into the pockets of her tweed hobo jacket, she turned and walked downstairs to await whatever other surprises the night thrust upon her.

She was sitting stiffly on the suede couch when Lindsay eased back into the bentwood rocker. Neither spoke.

Meg knew she had to fill the time until Ty reappeared, but she was out of ideas. Although...

"Lindsay," she said tentatively. "I don't know about you, but when I get terrorized by a clown at gunpoint, I always get the munchies. Got any chocolate?"

Chapter 38

Lindsay bent to scoop candy bars back into the stainless steel bowl when some noise on the porch grabbed her attention. Alarmed, she straightened quickly and peered through the skinny panes of glass beside the door before yanking it open.

Ty left his key in the lock and dropped the plastic bag he was carrying as he returned his daughter's fierce hug. "Howdy, Squirt," he murmured, breathing her in.

He raised his head to look at Meg and was surprised when she flushed and looked away.

The teen stepped back. "Did you catch him?" she asked nervously.

"No, he was long gone," he admitted, reclaiming his keys and shutting the door. "No clues, either. No discarded mask or gloves to check for DNA, no footprint in a flower bed...nothing, nada." But neither did he leave a mark on you, he added to himself.

He cupped his daughter's cheek and ran his thumb lightly under one mascara-smudged eye. "Have you been crying?"

"Well, yeah. It was scary."

He pulled her to his side in a one-armed embrace. "I'll bet it was."

"Except I wasn't alone." She wiggled free and pulled him into the living room. "I had help, you know."

"Yes, so it seems. Thanks for being here, Meg." But that was an explanation he was right curious to hear.

"I'm glad I was able to make a difference." She didn't move off the couch, just sat, her back stiff, and her hands fidgeting in her lap.

Almost before Meg had finished speaking, Lindsay started to recap the night's events. "Dad, that crazy clown forced his way in and started asking what we'd done with the letter, and—"

"Whoa, Lindsay, whoa," he interjected. "You know the drill."

She huffed in exasperation. "Interrogate the witnesses separately to avoid contaminating their accounts."

"Right. It's getting late, so why don't you take a shower while I process tonight's events with Meg. Then I'll come up to get your version. Oh, and take your stuff up with you, too."

She looked like she might roll her eyes but instead said, "Sure, fine." As she headed up the stairs, she picked up the plastic grocery bag her dad had dropped when he came in the door.

That left the two adults alone in the living room. Meg sitting, eyes downcast; Ty standing, evaluating. He needed to question her, but she was so ill at ease.

"Meg, I need something to drink. Can I get you anything? Water? Some tea?"

"I am kind of thirsty. Some water would be good."

"Coming right up," he said and headed into the kitchen.

He returned with two bottles of water and handed her one before he walked across from her and settled in his black leather easy chair. He could tell that she was still shaken by the night's events, but she wasn't overwhelmed. That took resilience. "Thanks again for keeping Lindsay safe. She's so damn independent. For her to acknowledge she needed help is a big deal."

Finishing her first sip of water, Meg looked down, fingers gliding over the textured cashmere of the forgotten afghan on the cushion next to her. "Yeah, well...I don't deserve much credit. I mean, it seems like I'm the one who brought danger to her door."

"No," he said firmly. "Absolutely not. I put her in danger when I left her alone. What blame there is, is mine. I shouldn't have gone to the store."

"Then why did you?" she blurted.

He twisted off the bottle cap and puffed out a breath. "I had to get something for Lindsay." When Meg continued to look puzzled and reproachful, he told himself to get a grip and spit it out. "She needed tampons," he confessed. "I wanted to take her with me, or ask Maroni to make the run, but she called me 'way too overprotective' and insisted she wouldn't open the door to hand out candy. But I take it she reneged on that promise."

She nodded. "It's really tough being a single dad, huh?"

"Some days more than others." But this wasn't a chat between friends. He needed to address the elephant in the room, get the conversation back on track. "That explains my whereabouts, but what about you? How did you end up here?"

"Oh, right..." She glanced away for a moment, a sheepish look on her face. "I found that xerox you wanted. You were leaving as I was driving up, and I didn't want to just shove it through the mail slot." She ducked her head. "Plus I was curious to see where you lived."

His face assumed the cool look of a trained investigator. "You were stalking me?"

"No, no, please don't go there," she said hastily. "My intentions weren't sinister." Her shoulders slumped. "I just wanted to find out more about you."

There, it was out in the open. Good to know he hadn't screwed up his chances after Lindsay's outburst at the viewing. As he resumed the debriefing, he worked to keep his face neutral. "And how did you get my address?"

"I asked David, but he wouldn't tell me. He got all rude and huffy. So I asked Josey in Security. But don't get mad at her. She didn't give you up easily. I sort of lied."

Damn, she wasn't a bad investigator herself. "Could others have overheard when you asked Calloway for my address, indicated that you'd be coming here?"

"Well, there were other people around when I asked David. Students and faculty on break, as well as people from the conference." A frown of concentration crossed her face. "All the key players were nearby. Brunner, Slattery, and Sellers."

"Sellers!" He leaned forward suddenly. "Jon Sellers was at the college this evening?"

Meg looked puzzled. "Yes. We were both surprised to see each other, and a little uncomfortable, too. He hasn't been in class since...since that day. Why do you ask?"

He leaned back, stalling, weighing his words. "Maroni and I went looking for him, couldn't find him." But he wasn't about to tell her why, about Jon's erotic games with Heather. "It seemed like he'd dropped off the face of the earth. Good to know he's still in the area."

"Why? Is he a suspect?"

"Dunno yet. He's at least a person of interest." Ty paused. "I'm sorry. I interrupted you. Was anyone else around when you were asking David about my address? Sellers, the two scholars and..."

"Well, also the president, the dean, and the PR person. But David didn't tell me anything. And there wasn't anyone around when I actually got your address from Josey over in Security."

Ty took a couple of swallows of water, thinking. Someone must've followed her here. Even Sketchy Doug could've tailed her if he'd gotten a call from Brunner. So Meg was the primary target, not his daughter. But now the murderer knew where to find Lindsay. "Okay, so tell me everything that happened from the time you saw Calloway at the college until I found you in the bathroom."

He listened to her explain about the free pizza and picture taking. About the typical snarl of traffic getting off campus. She recounted her first sight of the clown and his eventual appearance out front. That he talked funny and wielded a gun.

At that detail, Ty's latched his full attention on her. He sat the water bottle on the floor beside him and leaned toward her, his actions tense and eager. "What did it look like, the gun?"

She shook her head. "I don't know guns, don't like them. It was some sort of handgun thing."

He let that pass. "Which hand was he holding it in?"

"Ahhhh, the one that wasn't holding a trick-or-treat bag? I don't remember."

"What did the bag look like?"

"It was actually one of those generic plastic buckets. An orange one."

"Did you recognize the voice? Was it male or female?"

"The voice was disguised, but nothing about it suggested the speaker's gender."

"Imitate it."

She shuddered again, hesitated.

"Come on, Meg. You need to talk about this, and I need to hear it. You and Lindsay are the only ones who have ever heard him speak." Heard him and lived to tell the tale.

Her face paled, and her breath became shallow. And still, he pressured her.

"It's hard to tell what one clue will break open a case. Something that seems inconsequential can be vital. That's why I need to know everything you know. What you saw. What you heard. Anything that sticks out."

"Okay, if it'll help." She picked at the label of the bottle before she continued. "Um...right before the clown appeared I tripped on your uneven sidewalk—you should have that fixed, you know—and the first thing I heard him say was something like, "You're going to do what I say. No arguing. You understand?"

Ty noticed her shivers as she recounted the event, but he didn't interrupt. "You said the voice was disguised. What did it sound like?"

At that question, her memory seemed to rebel. He had to coax out the details.

"It was kinda metallic," she said, her voice unsure. "Or even mechanical."

"Like a robot?"

"No. Not like a Hollywood robot. More like a regular voice somebody had messed with. But a child's voice."

"Okay. So some kind of voice disguiser worn under the clown mask, then. Like the ones you can buy at places like Party City."

"Yeah. That would make sense."

"What else can you tell me?"

She went on to recount the entire conversation, inside the house as well as outside, trying to recapture even the smallest details. Then she reported on the events that led her and Lindsay into and out of the powder room, both times. When she was finished, she leaned back into the couch cushions, drained.

"Just so you know," she sighed after taking a sip of water, "this isn't as easy as it looks on TV."

"Never is." He settled back in the chair, his elbows propped on the armrests, hands folded over his belly. "Reality is confusing and messy. But you did a good job. Your account was clear and detailed. Given your actions tonight, I'd say you're good at dealing with the unexpected."

Meg ran her hand over the sofa cushion. "Thanks for casting me in such a positive light. At least I helped get the two of us out of the mess I got us into."

"That clown was no match for the pair of you."

"The two of us and a well-aimed can of Pledge," she added with a shaky smile

"That was some great improv," he said, picking up his water bottle again. "The way you came out of the bathroom holding that spray can, I figured it was your weapon of choice. That, and the lemony-fresh scent still lingering in the foyer."

Their eyes held and they shared tentative, fleeting smiles.

His face grew serious again. "I alerted the emergency room to be on the lookout for that kind of eye injury, asked them to call me if any showed up." He glanced up the stairs as he heard doors closing and opening as Lindsay headed to the bathroom. "I don't imagine they'll call, though. The intruder acts like the quintessential lone wolf."

Meg shuddered.

"Don't worry. He's likely back in his den by now licking his wounds."

"I hope he stays there. But what happened here tonight is sort of good, isn't it? I mean, now we know that the letter is still out there somewhere. That's more than we knew before."

Ty didn't comment, wondering how much to reveal. She was a sharp cookie. Not a lot of people could be that analytical after such a harrowing experience. He could use that kind of help, but it was risky.

Meg worried the label on the water bottle some more and looked at him expectantly; when he didn't respond, she spoke again.

"We know that the murderer's not willing to let sleeping letters lie. What we don't know is his motivation."

"Here's what I know." His words came out low and rumbly. "He's forced his way into my home, threatened you and Lindsay." His eyes glinted like polished steel. "That bastard better hope there's a crowd of people around when I catch up to him."

"Be careful, Ty! That guy is obviously deranged, and your daughter needs you. She was really afraid, almost terrified, that you'd get hurt. Was upset it would be her fault...again."

His broke off in the middle of a long swallow of water. "She told you about that night? About her mom?"

"I don't think it had anything to do with me. If Vladimir Putin had been in the room, she'd have told him. The story sort of bubbled up and out."

Ty shook his head in disbelief. His daughter had never spoken to anyone about that night, not even him. "Well, Lindsay's therapist will be thrilled."

Meg looked like she wanted to ask a question.

Her actions tonight and something in her expression persuaded him she'd earned an explanation. "Dr. Hilke's been waiting for Linny to talk about it for...well, for forever. Said it would come out when she was ready."

"I guess tonight's home invasion triggered something." Her voice turned quiet. "It must have been awful...for both of you."

Looking down, he pushed out a long breath. "She still has nightmares sometimes."

His eyes, when he raised them to Meg, held a trace of his own past struggles.

"And even though she's obnoxious to me a lot of the time nowadays, Dr. Hilke thinks she worries that something bad will happen to me and she'll end up alone."

"Of course she worries. Of course she does. And being obnoxious is probably one of the ways the worry comes out."

"I reckon so." At least that was his dad's take. He finished his water and twisted the cap back on. "But here's what's most intriguing. She opened up to you. Not me, not her therapist." And when Lindsay had needed someone, Meg had stepped up to bat.

She blushed. "I'm glad I did something right, and that everything turned out okay."

"Speaking of that." His brow furrowed with indecision. If he followed through with the plan he was beginning to consider, he'd be putting her in danger. "It isn't procedure, but I think you deserve the big picture." He hated what he was about to do. But he couldn't see how else to flush out the killer. "You deserve a full disclosure because I might have to ask for your help. So you need to know what you'd be in for if you did." What she'd be in for if he used her as bait. But right now it was still an *if.*

She looked him in the eye and nodded solemnly. "I want to know. I want to help."

Chapter 39

Ty hesitated, deciding where to start. Better bring her up to speed. "Your information about the orange bucket was right on target. It was in the street out front. We bagged it, but it's highly unlikely to yield any useful information. Now, about the gun. I found one in the yard, just beyond the porch steps. The intruder must have dropped it on the run."

"You found his gun? You didn't tell us that when you came back in. And Lindsay even asked if you'd found anything."

"Sorry. That's the first rule of investigation: Ask, don't tell. Lindsay's heard me say it enough times, she'll understand. And investigators typically keep some details secret and use them to tease out or trip up suspects."

"But I'm not a suspect." Her tone bordered on petulance. "So what else don't I know? Or aren't you going to tell me?"

"I've just started telling you," he said patiently. "The gun itself? It's just a toy, an airsoft gun." When she looked confused, he tried again. "Sort of like a paintball gun."

"Well, it looked real enough."

"That's what he was counting on. Those airsoft guns are very realistic, but they're required to have orange paint on the muzzle's tip to distinguish them from real ones. The intruder put black paint over the orange." He paused long enough to register the fact that the upstairs shower was now running. "However, he used it to threaten both of you, and that makes it an assault. Plus he forced his way into the house so we could've charged him with unlawful entry. If we'd caught him, those two things would've been enough to hold him and start our interrogation."

Meg sipped more water and unbraided some afghan fringe that she'd just braided. "Go on."

Ty frowned. "I need to make you accept the fact that he's after you. Or she, if it's Professor Slattery or her sister."

"I don't like that fact."

"Hence, my need to convince you." He sat up and leaned forward, closing the distance between them. "By your own account, you saw the clown soon after you got out of your truck, yes?" After she nodded, he spoke his next words very deliberately. "He was stalking you."

Her posture stiffened, and she went very still, but she didn't say anything.

"The *News-Post* reported that a Frederick High student had found the body, but because Lindsay's a minor, they couldn't release her name. And an anonymous student would be impossible to track down. So he wasn't here trying to get to her tonight. You were the target. Lindsay was just a bonus." His eyes darkened with concern. "Imagine if you'd gone straight home? It's much better that you ended up here."

One hand flew to her throat, and her breathing quickened.

"And the disguised voice?" He watched her closely. "That's because you know him. You'd recognize his regular speaking voice."

She finished her water, put the bottle on the end table, and pulled the afghan into her lap. "Okay, maybe I don't really want to know all this."

"That's kinda why you have to hear it. The intruder must have been really psyched that you led him to Lindsay. Since he was probably at the funeral home, he most likely noticed Lindsay there when she was, ah... 'talking' to you. Overhearing her outburst, he put two and two together and figured out that she's the anonymous Frederick High student. Or if it was Sellers, he knew Lindsay and Heather were tight, and he would've assumed she knew something." He smiled grimly. "And having you both together here, the murderer thought he could compare your stories about the missing letter. He assumed one of you had it. Probably still does."

"But we told him that we didn't," she protested sharply.

He shook his head at her naiveté. "This guy's a twisted whack job who lured a young woman to her death and would've thought nothing about offing you and Lindsay. Why would he believe you?" He slowed his words for emphasis. "Honest people can be duped into believing lies. Dishonest people have trouble swallowing the truth."

Meg looked uncomfortable with this new idea.

"He knows that if he had the letter, he'd use it to his advantage, so he believes the same of others." Ty gave her a searching look before he continued. "But in the murderer's mind, you're the key."

"Me? Why me?"

"He might imagine that Heather would've given the letter to the teacher whose assignment started the whole ball rolling—you know, for safekeeping—or shared its location with her." He shrugged. "It's a logical assumption."

"But it didn't happen like that," she insisted. "She only gave me one measly xeroxed page, the same one she gave Robert."

"We can't assume the murderer knows that, even if it's Brunner. He might not believe what he's heard. Plus the murderer is focused on you because he's already ruled out some other places the letter could have been."

"Other places?"

"He tossed Heather's car looking for it and tried to get into her mom's house for the same reason. Or so we assume. But he tripped the security alarm and bolted."

Meg started to speak, but he anticipated her question. "That's one of those details we've managed to keep out of the papers. And now we know for sure that he didn't find anything, or he wouldn't be stalking you."

"Holy crap. I'm in a world of trouble, aren't I?"

"I'm afraid so. However, we have enough evidence to warrant some protection for you."

"I've got no complaints about that," she said with conviction. "But hey, I just thought of something. Robert has a xerox copy of that same page. Has he been stalked, too?"

He shook his head. "I figure if he'd been hassled, he'd have been in touch right quick."

"But doesn't that point the finger at him?"

"It might." He shrugged. "At the moment, the focus is on you. Clowny's merely guessing, using his own misguided thinking. He might've assumed that you were here at the house playing your own angle, trying to get information out of Lindsay, perhaps. Or even that you and she are in on some plot together."

"What? That's just crazy. Heather was my student. She and Lindsay were friends."

"As I've been trying to tell you, he likely *is* crazy. Maybe a sociopath. He doesn't understand friendship or loyalty. Either that or the letter's so important to him that he'll use any method to get it. Finding the two of you here together was a huge stroke of luck for him." He paused, reluctant to proceed. But the information would serve as a warning, make her more careful. "If you hadn't outwitted him, Clowny would've likely taken the pair of you to his lair to, ah...extort the information out of you." His throat tightened as he imagined returning to an empty house.

She stared at him. "That's creepy. How do you even come up with stuff like that? Did you read nothing but H.P. Lovecraft and Stephen King as a child?"

"I've been trained to think like a creep. If it makes you more comfortable, think of it as creative writing." He saw her grimace. "This is how investigation works, Meg, by getting inside the bad guy's head. But we also have to think outside the box. It's still possible that there's someone out there we haven't considered. But the rest of what we've surmised would remain true. Someone's been following you, wants to kidnap you and see what you know."

"Thanks," she mumbled. "That makes me feel much better."

"As for motive...if it's Sellers, he might have stolen the letter to sell or to try and make a name for himself somehow. Or it could be that he killed Heather in a fit of rage that has nothing to do with the letter. But both Brunner and Slattery have strong motives, similar motives. Both of their reputations are impacted by the existence of the letter, and both are ambitious."

Hearing the shower cut off, he knew Lindsay would be ready to tell her version soon. "And now we consider other factors, like body style and opportunity. Sellers could've been your clown, but not the other two. Brunner doesn't match the body type. Too short, too stout. Slattery's the right size, but I noticed her at the store when I was picking up those tampons." He thanked God that she hadn't seen him. He'd have been that much longer getting to Lindsay and Meg. "And while neither is the intruder, either of them could have an accomplice."

"Yeah," Meg nodded. "Yeah, Sellers sucks up to Brunner like some big ol'Dyson, and the dean might try to protect her sister."

He didn't contradict Meg, but Plunkard just didn't play for him anymore. However, his gut feeling could be wrong, and it didn't pay to be complacent.

"Yeah, I hear what you're saying," was his only comment.

But Meg didn't have the whole picture, either. If he intended to keep her safe, she needed one more piece of information. He dug out his cell phone, pulled up a photo, and showed it to her.

"Take a good look at this guy. He could also be involved."

"I've seen him. He works at the College, doesn't he? Some kind of maintenance guy?"

"Yup. And he has a connection to Brunner. If he approaches you, get yourself somewhere with lots of other people right away and call me immediately."

"Don't worry about that. I have you on speed dial."

He gave her a little smile. "Since someone out there is a threat to you, the department will grant you protection. It'll be unobtrusive. You won't even know it's happening."

"Thanks, I'm all for protection. But what about Lindsay? Whack Job is after her, too."

"Since Heather's murder, I haven't left my daughter alone. At least not until tonight," he amended and vowed not to let her play him again. "I drop her off at school and I, or a designee, pick her up, bring her home and stay with her. She's sort of been on house arrest without the ankle bracelet. And after the funeral, I'm shipping her off to her aunt's in Chevy Chase."

"Good plan. How's she handling all this, though?"

He sighed and leaned back in the chair. "Since she doesn't fight it—much—I figure it makes her feel safe."

"And why wouldn't she? From what I've seen tonight, you're a really good dad. Protective, concerned, and physically affectionate. And a lot more open with your emotions than most."

He usually brushed off compliments, but he worked hard at being a father. "When your kid needs you, wants you around, it feels great," he admitted. "The best narcotic ever."

"She's an amazing kid. In lots of ways," she added, with only a hint of sarcasm. "But how was she able to give you such a detailed description of the clown? Does she have a photographic memory or something?"

He stretched to get more comfortable in his chair, settled back a little more, and pushed up the sleeves of his JHU sweatshirt while he thought about how to reply, how much to reveal.

Looking at Meg again, he noticed that she was staring at him, her color rising. Then she blinked the stare away. What was that about?

"Yes, Lindsay is...amazing." He smiled. "But her memory isn't exceptional. It's just a thing we did when she was little." He clasped his hands behind his head and looked up at the ceiling, remembering. Remembering what fun it was and how they'd had to stop because his wife had disapproved. "If we were in the mall or grocery store or anyplace with a line of people, she and I would play a game we called 'Peeping at the Perp.'"

"And this game entailed...?"

He rubbed his head briskly, dropped his hands to the arms of the chair, and smiled at Meg. If she was interested in stuff like this, maybe they might actually click as a couple. If he could get the timing right. "We'd be standing near a cashier's counter, and I'd say something like, 'On the count of three, turn and look at the second person in the line. Then you'll have ten seconds to figure out the person's age, height and weight, memorize what he or she is wearing, and report back. Okay? Ready, set, go.'"

"That explains it, then."

"Explains what?"

"How she was able to rattle off the specifics of the intruder's costume, down to the three orange pompoms. It was uncannily accurate but a little surreal. I felt really inadequate."

Ty tilted his head regarding her. "With a little practice, I think you'd be just as good. Maybe even better."

She blushed, and he saw something stir in her eyes. Those warm, sable-brown eyes.

Oh boy. It looked like the time had come to address the elephant in the room. He cleared his throat and leaned forward.

"Meg, I can't afford a private life right now. I need to solve this case." He glanced up the stairs, aware that the shower had stopped running. "And then there's my daughter. She needs some time to get adjusted to the whole notion of me having a social life. Because I haven't done much of that." Be honest, he told himself. Don't start out with half-truths you have to amend later. "Actually, I haven't dated at all since Tisha's death. You're the first woman who's, ah...caught my fancy."

He didn't think it possible, but her blush deepened. However, he was a little worried that she hadn't said anything yet. For a chatty woman, she was being awful quiet.

"Wow," she whispered.

A door opened upstairs, and Lindsay sang softly as she moved from bathroom to bedroom. Another door shut.

"Again, wow. I'm thrilled. And flattered. You've also, ah...caught my fancy."

An upstairs door clicked open again. "Hey Dad, you finished processing yet?"

"No," he said with a rueful smile. "We're not done here." Not by a long shot, he hoped.

"I'm gonna journal then. Come up when you're finished." Her door shut quietly.

The two adults sat in silence for several heartbeats.

Ty straightened in his chair and cleared his throat. "I'm afraid that's all for now, Meg. I have to get Lindsay's version of tonight's events. And it's been a grueling few hours for you. After the adrenaline rush of dealing with the intruder wears off, you're gonna crash big time."

Meg yawned. "You're likely right about that. I'm beginning to feel it."

"Just a couple more things. I need for you to stay mum about what happened here tonight. The details of the forced entry, I mean. You can't tell anyone about that, okay?" He needed to stress that point, make that distinction because surely she'd be talking with Joan about the personal stuff. Guaranteed. "We can use some of those specifics to trip up a suspect."

"Okay. Sure thing."

"And promise me you'll stay with a friend until we catch this killer."

She blinked at him sleepily, seeming not to understand.

"You can't go back to your place alone. It's too isolated."

"Um, okay. I guess I can stay with Joan and Chloe. Their guest room is practically my home away from home anyway."

"The department doesn't have a safe house. We're too small for that. But I'll have people watching you from here on out. In fact, there's a police cruiser out front waiting to escort you wherever you need to go tonight. Just keep a low profile and stay inside as much as you can. You'll be going to the funeral tomorrow, of course, and there'll be lots of law enforcement on site. But beyond that, let me know when you're going out and where. There are too many suspects for us to tail, so we'll keep tabs on you instead." And he actually hoped that the murderer would attempt another contact. One where he'd be around to intervene. "You have my cell number. Call me anytime."

·　　·　　·　　·　　·

Once safely tucked inside her truck—and watched over by a cop in a cruiser—Meg replayed the night's events, marveling at everything she'd need to tell Joan. Not everything, of course. She didn't want to hamper the investigation. She'd confess that she'd dropped by Ty's house to hand over the xerox. That wasn't a secret. Both she and David would know she'd wanted to go by his house. But nothing else. Joan would have to wait to hear about the creepy clown and Lindsay's confession. Hmm, she could probably mention the portrait, though. But mostly she wanted to talk about Ty.

She couldn't decide if she'd mention the tony Rockwell Terrace neighborhood where he lived. Or the fact that she was pretty sure the black leather chair he'd been sitting in was one of those ultra-pricey Eames chairs. Knowing Joan, she'd want to start sniffing around for a corruption scandal. But surely there was a very innocent explanation. She hoped.

And there was other stuff she'd keep to herself, to be sure. Like how she could hardly hold herself in check when he'd pushed up the sleeves of that sweatshirt and revealed those toned, tanned forearms and nicely corded veins. And those hands...mon dieu. She just bet those hands were clever. And unhurried.

Oooh, and how about his admission that he hadn't dated in five whole years? That was some dry spell...and herculean willpower. Women must've been throwing themselves at him daily if Charlotte the harlot was any indication. But she, Meg Adams, was the one who'd caught his fancy. And—if she could manage not to get abducted, tortured, and killed—she'd work on keeping it.

She turned the ignition key. "Giddy up, Rocinante. Enough of this windmill tilting for one evening."

·   ·   ·   ·   ·

Friday: October 31st

What a fucked up night! The murderer knows who I am. Shit! Guess Dad wasn't just being uptight. Still, it pisses me off. That asshole was right in my house, and he got away.

And then there's all the Mom stuff. Why did I blab it all out to that woman—that Meg Adams? She got Heather killed, wants to jump my dad's bones, and then I dump my biggest secrets on her!

Weird.

Chapter 40

The silver sedan lurches into its driveway and comes to rest.

"Shit, piss, fuck and damn!"

The driver, wearing a long black raincoat over a clown suit, makes sure the coast is clear then exits. A bit unsteady, the figure stands a moment between door and frame, unlocks the door and storms inside.

"That bitch tried to blind me."

Hands trembling with rage, the creepy clown pulls off white gloves, yanks away the mask and voice-disguising device, and stuffs it all into a shopping bag.

"She'll pay for that."

Slamming the door, the Watcher dabs at eyes that stream with tears.

"They'll all pay. Man, woman, and child."

Chapter 41

Saturday morning began as a perfect fall day. Blue skies and crisp air. Still in his suede moccasins, sweatpants, and the ratty waffle-weave robe he'd had since college, Ty walked out his front door and picked up the paper. The neighbors were engaged in their weekend morning chores. Walking dogs, raking leaves, bringing in bags of groceries.

Normal people had normal Saturdays, he brooded as he brought the paper into the house. They're not thinking about motives for murder and suspects' movements, or having to ship their kids off to relatives for safe keeping. Nor were they crafting scenarios to flush out a murderer, ones that involved endangering a friend. More than a friend, he hoped.

Tossing the paper on the kitchen table, he sat down with his third cup of coffee. He unfolded the paper, and the headline had him plunking down his cup so hard that coffee sloshed over the rim.

"Fuck!"

The headline read: "No Arrest in Sight." It rode over a line of pictures: Heather's senior portrait and his headshot from the department website. Between them was the black silhouette of a man's head superimposed on a gray-tone rectangle.

That was a cheap shot. Luckily, he knew that reporters didn't get to write their own headlines or choose the images that accompanied their copy. Otherwise, he'd kick Skip Lawrence's ass from here to Kansas.

He snapped open the paper and started reading. Unlike the headline and photos, the story was accurate and fair. It *was* day four of the investigation. No arrests had been made. The full resources and manpower of the Frederick City Police were devoted to solving the murder.

But damn it all to hell, this was the day of Heather's funeral. Her mother would see that front page. He didn't care about his professional reputation taking a hit. Careers did that over time. However, he was pissed at seeing the family of the deceased being additionally traumatized by the press. Plus he was frustrated that he hadn't found any answers for the Hillcrests or justice for Heather. And, if he was honest with himself, he worried what Meg would think.

He pushed up from the table and threw the paper in the trash before Lindsay could see it. She didn't need that kind of shock, either.

Frowning, he went back for his coffee, cleaned up the mess, and poured the cold remains down the sink. Putting both hands on the counter, he stared out the window. He hadn't slept well, which wasn't all that uncommon in the middle of a big case. But his usual routines weren't producing the usual results. Mindless activities typically freed up his thinking and expedited problem-solving. He'd folded and put away his laundry. Polished his dress shoes for the funeral that afternoon. The dishwasher was emptied, and he'd made a list of what they needed from the store, and still, he hadn't come up with any brainstorms.

Going upstairs, he tossed his robe on the bed, pulled on a sweatshirt, and laced up his running shoes. He was grateful that Maroni's wife had offered to take Lindsay shopping for whatever the hell it was she needed for the funeral. Pantyhose, hair mousse, some damn thing. He needed a good long run. Get those neurons firing.

An hour later he'd broken a decent sweat and was in the zone, but no new ideas had popped to the surface. He'd been over and over it, but he knew there was no other way. After the funeral, he'd have to ask Meg if she would knowingly put herself in harm's way to lure out the murderer. And he was betting she would. Not a comforting thought, but time was running away from him, and he felt like he was standing still.

Almost home again, he was passing the tennis courts in Baker Park, scanning the players, when he noticed an ill-matched foursome. A closer look revealed them to be the women from the college: Dean Joyce Plunkard and her sister Charlotte Slattery vs. President Delores Collins and Maria Routzhan. He slowed and trotted up to the chain link fence to watch. Three of the women were wearing sensible shorts and tee shirts. Only Slattery wore a fancy white outfit that would have been appropriate for Wimbledon. Figured.

Each team had a weaker member, but Plunkard seriously sucked. Aim-wise she wasn't that bad, but she didn't have any power. Her successful volleys were predictably placed and easy to return, and a few times they didn't even limp over the net. The PR woman could actually generate some spin. Both Charlotte and Delores were competent players but seemed to be in it just for the exercise. Presently, Plunkard faulted again, and her sister laughed. Maria looked disgruntled, and the president smiled stoically.

Turning her head, Charlotte noticed him, called a time out and sashayed over to the fence.

"Good morning, Lieutenant. Just passing through, or do you have time to lob a few balls with me?"

"Good morning, Charlotte," he chuckled. "No, tennis isn't my game. I'm more of a jogger. But I'm glad I happened to see you. We need to schedule the rest of our talk."

The other women congregated near the net and chatted, but kept an eye on the duo.

Charlotte tucked a lock of stray hair behind her ear. "Well, we're all going to that girl's funeral at 2:00, but after that, I'm free until about 7:00. I've been looking forward to our 'talk.' It's been years and years, and you haven't called."

"You've been on my mind. Just hadn't found the right time."

"Hey, Charlotte," her sister called out. "We've decided to call it a day, thank god. But we're going for coffee. Do you want to join us?"

Ty raised an eyebrow. "Seems like you're free now."

"Now? We're all sweaty."

"I have a few more pesky questions. We can get them out of the way now, then around 5-ish, maybe we can..."

"Meet for cocktails?" She raised an eyebrow for emphasis.

"Something like that," he smiled.

Charlotte waved a hand toward her sister. "You girls go on without me. I'm going to play with my new friend."

Joyce rolled her eyes, Delores smiled pleasantly, and Maria's face grew pink.

Charlotte propped her racket against the chain link for her sister to retrieve and joined Ty on his side of the fence. He walked them to a nearby green-painted bench under a nearly leafless maple tree, sitting down once his suspect had.

"Hello again," she said.

"We need to talk about your relationship with Robert Brunner."

"Why? He's a vexing little man. So proper, so pompous. He used to be quite fun back in the day, but it's not unusual for people to become more conservative as they age. Or so they say." She smoothed back some uncooperative strands of blonde hair. "I rather enjoyed ruffling his feathers the other night."

"You certainly got under his skin. But why bother?"

"Because he's so eager to challenge me. To find support for his pathetic theory and supplant me. Capture the limelight for himself."

"And what would you be willing to do to keep the limelight for yourself?"

"I have an alibi for the time of the murder."

"Yes, you do. However, if you didn't actually strike the blows, you might have paid someone."

She stretched out her arms along the back of the bench. "And where would I find a murderer?" One hand began to lightly caress his shoulder. "Academic research is my bailiwick, not murder for hire."

He moved enough so her hand fell away. "You are a very resourceful, well-connected woman. I don't doubt you could find a way."

"Possibly," she said, looking thoughtful. "But first, I would've had to have known about that letter. And since I didn't, you can't prove that I did."

He said nothing because that's one of the things that'd stopped him up 'til now.

"If I read you right, lieutenant, you'd have looked into my finances. I'm sure that murder for hire costs a pretty penny. My biggest payment recently has been a rather sizable amount to the Fifth Avenue Saks last month, when I was in New York. There's certainly nothing in Frederick worth buying."

And that was another fly in the ointment. They hadn't found any big withdrawals.

He raised an eyebrow at her. "There are other methods of payment."

"Indeed, there are. Rather enjoyable ones, too. But as you've proven, one can't always bend other people to one's will."

He smiled mildly. "And where were you last night about 8:00 p.m.?"

"In a hot fantasy with you."

"Answer the question."

"I was with my sister."

"Where?"

"You are so bothersome."

"What I am, is persistent. Again, 8 o'clock?"

"We went to the Safeway to pick up a few things. Joyce used her debit card, so you can check that, too. And I saw you there." She sulked again. "But you were on the phone and scampered away before I could say hello."

Huh, he had been spotted. However, that grocery store run cleared both of them as the creepy clown. And while the clown had confessed that he was the murderer, he could have easily lied to protect his employer. It didn't take much imagination to see Charlotte setting up that kind of ploy. She was undoubtedly a backstabber and a self-promoter. But even though she had plenty of moxie, there was no proof against her. What about the sister? *Nah.* Plunkard had such wimpy serves, no way she could've smashed Heather's skull. She just didn't ring for him, not even as an accomplice. But he wasn't ready to rule Charlotte out yet. Not entirely. Her sister couldn't be her accomplice, but someone else could. Even Sellers, for that matter. Or someone who hadn't even come to light yet. There was too much he didn't know.

Charlotte wrinkled her brow. "What happened last night?"

"An unlawful entry."

"Related to the murder?" Her eyes sparkled with curiosity. "Well, that's obvious, or you wouldn't be asking me about it. What happened?"

He shook his head.

She pouted. "You never tell me the good stuff.

"And you're candid with me? I get the feeling that there's more behind your harsh words to Brunner. You really went after him. It seemed like too much squeeze for not enough juice."

"I told you. He vexes me."

"Is that why you went to his house at 2 o'clock that morning? For more 'vexing?'"

She smiled. "I wonder who you were following. Him or me? No matter. Yes, I went to his house. But I'm sure you know I was there too short a time for anything fun."

"Then why go?"

"You're right about one thing. Robert and I have been...'vexing' each other for years."

"So I've heard. It seems that you scuttled his research when you were both in grad school. You got the big grant by denying him access to information he needed."

"My, my, my. You are thorough. That was decades ago. But what of it?"

"Are you still trying to ruin his chances for advancement?"

"By stealing that dead girl's letter, you mean? It's an intriguing thought, in the abstract, but I never knew about the letter. So neither of us will ever know how ambitious I am, will we?"

It kept coming back to that. She didn't know about the letter, but he still had one thread to tie off. "So why were you at Brunner's house at 2 a.m.?"

"I went to have it out with him. We're both career-oriented professionals with similar interests. We go to a lot of the same conferences. His wife is an exceptionally boring, emotionally stunted woman. And frigid, or so he says.

Therefore, when the opportunity arises, we warm each other up. For such an unremarkable little man he's remarkably invigorating."

"But not that night."

"No. He'd told me earlier that it was over. And that's not how I roll. I'm always the one who calls things off. I went over to clarify that for him." Her face lost its ferocity. "Is that what you wanted to know? That I was there reclaiming my pride. Happy now, are we?"

"No. It's not a happy story." He held her eyes for a moment. "But you can do better than Brunner."

She chuckled. "And I will."

"Of that, I have little doubt. Thank you for your time." Rising, he held out a hand to help her off the bench. "I'll let you get back to your day."

She took his hand to rise but didn't let go. "My day is wide open. Would you like to help me fill it? Give me a leg up on 'doing better?'"

"No." He took his hand back. "I'm sorry, but no."

"Well, I'm sorry, too." She searched his face. "But you are attracted to me. I'm not wrong about that."

"You have much to offer a man," he murmured, sparing her feelings.

"Thank heavens. When a woman loses her radar, it's time to consider retiring from the field. And I'm not the retiring kind."

"No, not remotely," he laughed.

"But you were tempted."

Ty didn't break eye contact, but he didn't respond, either.

"It's just some unencumbered fun. Why make it difficult, when it's actually so easy." She raised an eyebrow at him, but his expression didn't change. "I'd've had more fun having coffee with the girls."

He smiled. "I'd be pleased to buy you a cup of coffee. There's a Starbucks with a few outside tables two blocks over."

"That'll have to do," she sighed. "I can feast my eyes on your youthful vigor and imagine what might have been, while I dream of better days to come. But if you change your mind..."

She placed a finger just below his Adam's apple and drew a line down his damp tee shirt. "All you have to do is whistle. You do remember how to whistle, don't you?"

Chapter 42

By 1:30 that afternoon, scores of people had gathered at the Methodist church in Middletown, including the suspects from the college. All except Sellers. Mrs. Hillcrest and Auntie Ed were already inside. Others were reluctant to go in. Lindsay among them.

"Stephen, chill out," she snapped at her dad. "They're saving us seats in the second row."

Ty didn't bother to respond. Absently, he ran a hand down the buttons of his dress uniform. He wore it out of respect for the dead, but it was also a directive from his commander. A show of police presence to placate the masses, he supposed. Whatever.

Maroni, also in his dress blues, addressed Lindsay. "You look really nice."

She was wearing a long, unadorned dove-gray dress along with her new Doc Martens and her mother's earrings. But she was fidgety, and her mood was somber.

"Thanks, Mr. Maroni," she said, voice muted. "Only I don't know what to do with my hands. This dress doesn't have pockets."

"Got just the thing." He drew out a white handkerchief and gave it to her. "You can play with this. Scrunch it up, or whatever. No big."

Her face softened. "Thanks."

Ty scanned the parking lot until he saw what he was looking for. A battered truck pulling in next to a red Prius. When he felt Lindsay following his gaze, he quickly looked away. Then he caught Maroni's eye, and the young detective drifted over toward the newcomers.

"Good afternoon, Professor Adams, Professor Glotfelty," Maroni said, nodding to each in turn before he focused on Joan. "We sort of met the other day at the Barbara Fritchie Restaurant, but I didn't introduce myself. I'm Detective Matteo Maroni, Lieutenant Raleigh's partner." He smiled soberly. "Professor Adams, the lieutenant said to tell you that he can't talk to you right now, but he'll call later."

Although Meg was pale, she returned the detective's small smile with one of her own. "Lindsay's being prickly, you mean."

"I think he used a different word, but yes. She's nerved up, poor kid."

"And she has every reason to be," Joan said curtly. She gave a toss of her head, challenging the center of gravity on her plum-colored hat. The crown was domed, but the front brim rose up on one side into a single column that tapered to a point. Both of its edges were studded with Swarovski crystals. Her sedate dress was a shade darker than the hat, and she'd added a necklace of crystal beads. "That girl has been through hell and back."

"Yes ma'am," he agreed. "But I'd best not spend too much time with you two, or she won't be speaking to me either." Turning to go, he added, "It was nice to meet you."

Joan glared at his back as he walked away. "Humph, it won't be so nice if he ever calls me 'ma'am' again."

Meg tugged at the waistline of her one black dress, thinking that it was getting a lot of wear. "Get over yourself. He's a decent guy." She looked up at Joan with a puzzled frown. "You need to find a mirror. That last head toss unsettled your boater."

"Don't give me any sass about this hat. Chloe already said I look like a mutant unicorn. As if. She has excellent taste in women but absolutely no fashion sense." She dropped her voice to confide, "My milliner was inspired by the genius who crafted Aretha's chapeau for the Obama inauguration. But I take your meaning. Let's find the ladies' room. A hat this stunning needs to be anchored just right."

A few minutes later, Meg left Joan to obsess over her hat and went back into the churchyard to calm her own nerves. She breathed in the aroma of the new mulch on the flower beds that had been put to rest for the season and listened to the pine trees shush as breezes blew through them.

But today, nature failed to soothe her. Her thoughts wouldn't still. Poor Mrs. Hillcrest had been so tentative when approaching her to speak today, sounding like she might be asking too much. In the face of that, it was impossible to refuse. But she still felt uneasy about being a participant in the funeral service. Speaking in public was no biggie, but she'd never had to worry about the likelihood of a murderer being in the audience, somebody who'd tried to kidnap her and might've even killed her. And could try again. She'd faced down agitated, irate students and fractious parents, but nothing like this. Not once in her entire life had she imagined such a scenario. But today wasn't about her.

Funerals were held to honor the dead and ease the pain of the mourners, Meg reminded herself as she walked into the vestibule. It was a lovely church, an A-frame with a contemporary feel. It didn't have stained glass, and the honey-toned wood floors were bamboo, not oak. The wood trim framing the clear glass windows was a shade darker than the floors. In keeping with tradition, the walls were light colored, but not white. Something warmer, like a pale peach. And the sanctuary was bursting with flowers. Not the overly sweet smells of spring. No hyacinths or daffodils. Instead, chrysanthemums in bronze and burgundy, with their sharp, strong scents and variety of shapes—pots of cushion mums, ones with spoon-like petals, arrangements of tiny pompoms accented with asters. And of course, roses. The flower of love.

Joan came up beside her, quiet for once, and they both went in. Since Mrs. Hillcrest had asked Meg to speak, she and Joan were seated in the third row, right behind the Raleighs. As she sat, she noted Ty in his uniform and the daughter, looking like a Goth version of Emily Dickinson and trying her best to hold it together. That was tough to watch.

Meg wasn't particularly religious, but she was very respectful of rituals. However, this one was just plain hard. She stood when she should, joined in the choral responses, and sang when everyone else did, but her attention kept wandering. Lines from poetry came unbidden, and she found them both unsettling and spot on—athletes dying young, elegies for girls thrown from horses.

Steeped in her musings, she was surprised at how soon the minister introduced Lindsay. He then sat down in one of the heavy, wooden ceremonial chairs that flanked the altar.

Stiff-shouldered and clutching a handkerchief in both hands, the teen walked up to the pulpit, her long gray dress made silvery by the afternoon sunlight slanting through the roman arched windows, each one framing a tableau of the surrounding harvested fields and rolling hills.

Once at the lectern, she gripped its bottom corners and stood silently for a moment, her delicate face ashen. Looking out on the congregation, she whispered, "Oh my god!" But it was audible enough that the microphone picked it up and shared it with everyone. She blushed furiously and spun around to the minister. "I'm so sorry, really."

He smiled kindly and gestured for her to continue.

Twisting the handkerchief, she turned back to the congregants. "I'm really, really sorry about that." Face blotchy pink, she added, "There are just so many of you."

The sanctuary was silent. Everyone was waiting; some may have been waiting for her to break down, others for her to mess up again. Meg was silently cheering her on.

Lindsay closed her eyes, took a deep breath, looked at a point above the heads of the people in the last row, and spoke a few lines that sounded rehearsed. "I'm here today to say goodbye to my friend. I want to honor her memory by sharing one of her favorite poems, one by Robert Frost. It's ca-called..."

Meg took Joan's hand and squeezed hard.

After a few blinks, the teen began again. "It's called 'Nothing Gold Can Stay.'" She closed her eyes to recite the poem. Her balance was wobbly at first, but she reached out and caught the podium. Gaining confidence, she spoke the lines with clarity and feeling. Once done, she opened her eyes.

The congregation breathed again, expecting her to step down and rejoin them. Meg let go of Joan's hand. But Lindsay just stood there. And stood there. And stayed there until polite coughs and murmurs elbowed at the hush. People nearest the front observed the glistening of tears forming in her eyes. The minister started to rise from his seat behind her, and the murmuring grew. Lindsay glanced at her father, and in his expression, she seemed to find what she needed.

"I practiced that poem all morning, and I can't get that word 'gold' out of my mind." She looked down at the hanky hanging loosely from her hand and bunched it up to fit in one palm. "You know how it is sometimes—how things get stuck in your brain, like some song that keeps replaying itself?" She paused again. "Well, right now the song in my head is that corny summer-camp song about friends. You know..." Then she sang: "'Make new friends, but keep the o-old. One is silver and the other gold.'"

Lindsay's lips turned up slightly into a melancholy, wistful smile. "Heather was a golden friend, and I'm here today only because she can't be."

As she raised one hand and briefly touched her earring, her expression became somber. She exhaled a shivery sigh and clasped the lectern again before going on. "Now she'll never have a chance to finish college, land an awesome job doing historical research, write a novel, get married, or ever be a mom. And that's so not fair. She'd have been great at all of that." One hand skated around the edge of the polished wooden surface. "But that's the way it is. Life without Heather has to become our new normal. Like Frost said, nothing lasts."

Meg blinked back tears.

After waiting a few beats, Lindsay continued. "And that puts a lot of pressure on the rest of us, pressure to really live our lives. To do our best and work our hardest, try to reach our full potential because Heather can't." She leaned forward and clutched the podium tightly. "But not because she didn't want to try. Heather never meant to leave us. She can't because someone took away her choices."

"A-*men*, sister!" Joan affirmed loudly, shocking Meg and everybody else.

Once the neck craning died down, people returned their attention to the small figure at the pulpit. Swaying slightly, Lindsay smiled at the outspoken black woman in the elegant hat without seeming to see the woman sitting beside her, then stepped down from the podium to make her way back to her father's side.

As she returned to the congregation, the minister padded up to the microphone to speak again. "And now we'll hear from..."

"Dear God in heaven," Meg murmured to herself. The girl's father was already worried about her safety, but now she'd spit in the killer's eye. Because there was a good chance, he was in this very room. That girl had a lot of chutzpah. Well, Meg already knew that, first hand.

She felt a poke her in the ribs, forcing her to come back to her surroundings. She turned her head to face Joan, who nodded none too subtly toward the front of the sanctuary. Following that hint, Meg saw the minister beckoning to her. She stood. But, afraid that everyone was staring at her—and some were—she kept her eyes averted as she inched sideways out of the pew and into the aisle. As she passed the Raleighs, she slid her gaze Ty-ward just in time to see him take his daughter's hand.

Once she ascended the dais, the minister reseated himself as Meg took the lectern. Squaring herself to face the congregation, she felt in her pocket and took out a piece of paper. As she smoothed it on the wooden surface in front of her, its crinkling caught the mic's attention, drawing even more notice toward her.

And that's why nobody else saw someone slip into the sanctuary and sit in the last pew. A young man with steel-rimmed glasses and an enigmatic expression on his face: Jon Sellers.

Meg drew in a deep, calming breath. "As Reverend Payne mentioned, I was one of Heather's professors at TCC." She stopped, suddenly self-conscious in this unaccustomed role. "She was my student three different times. The first time was last spring when she was still a high school senior taking freshman composition for college credit." Settling into the familiar rhythm of the lecture, Meg relaxed. "Only in her papers did I come to know her that semester, because she was so shy, so reluctant to speak in class. Later she told me that she was afraid she'd embarrass herself because she wasn't sure she belonged in college, didn't think she knew enough, couldn't compete." She smiled and shook her head at the memory. "But as you've already heard, she was great at everything she did. And if she'd been able to go on with her education, we would be reading articles and books by her in the years to come."

The audience reacted with quiet pleasure, enjoying the fact that one of their own was the subject of such high praise.

"Her writing was that good—insightful, exuberant. Her style boasted first-rate vocabulary and unexpected turns of phrases." She felt in her pocket and drew out a folded sheet of paper. "Just this semester, when I graded papers in Heather's American lit class, I always put hers on the bottom. That way, I knew there was something I'd enjoy. Plus a weak paper looked even weaker if it followed one of hers."

Outside, a cloud passed over the sun, dulling the room momentarily. Meg glanced out the window at the fallow fields and huddled trees clinging to their last leaves.

"But I mentioned that she had taken classes from me three times, and it's the middle one that's the most revealing. During this past summer session, she was enrolled in a creative writing class. It took a lot of wheedling and cajoling before she signed up, but she did. And again she was a quiet success. I'm going to read one of her poems, so you can see for yourselves. It came out of an assignment where the class had to imitate a poem by Billy Collins, a recent poet laureate. It's entitled 'Today,' and in summary his poem declares if ever there were a perfect spring day, today's the one."

She waited for the audience to absorb the information.

"The assignment called for the poem to begin with the word 'if.' And the word 'today' had to appear in the last line. Plus, in keeping with the structure of the original, the poem had to be a run-on sentence."

An undercurrent of laughter whispered through the room.

"You're amazed that a teacher would require a run-on sentence, right? Well, just listen and hear how cleverly Heather uses that sentence, and listen for her rich imagery and far-flung imaginings. But most especially, listen for its message. It will remind you of what her friend Lindsay just told you. About how we should conduct our lives now that Heather has left us."

Meg unfolded the paper, smoothed it out and started reading:

Today   by Heather Hillcrest

If only once you realized your inner strength
and saw self-doubt float away like dandelion fluff,

or like a maple leaf drifting along on a stony brook's
rippling surface, moseying through meadows,

fields and town, unconcerned about status and destiny;
you would rewrite *Wuthering Heights* until Catherine,

although dog bitten, limps away from Thrushcross Grange
and runs off with Heathcliff to sleep under a caravan

on moon-lit nights, bears his dark-aspect gypsy babies,
grows old with him and shares their grave with naught

but moor flowers and birds—grouse, curlew, plover—then
you would fling yourself skyward until fingers became feathers

skimming the soft currents of air, unbuffeted
by pulse-chilling fear or breath-catching indecision

until the soap bubble prison you'd blown around yourself
popped its filmy skin, and your unmurmured dreams

sighed their long sought-for freedom in cloudless relief
because today, today you gave them your blessing.

She looked up from the paper spread in front of her, rolled it up
diploma-like, and leaned slightly closer to the microphone. "Amen."

As one the congregation responded. "Amen."

Meg descended the dais, her egress slowed by the room's thick hush. She
kept her eyes on the wide plank floor as she returned to her seat. Almost
there, she looked up quickly when she heard a ragged inhalation: Lindsay's.
Although now silent, the girl's lips were parted, her eyes were downcast and
thin tears streamed toward her chin. Without a thought, Meg leaned over

and urged the poem into the girl's small, clasped hands. Her offering was accepted but went unacknowledged. She chanced a glimpse at Ty and read the thank you in his quiet, gray eyes.

She barely remembered slipping back into the pew beside Joan.

Chapter 43

Ty had been to many funerals, too many it seemed—his older brother, his mom...then Tisha—but this one had been plenty hard in its own way. Untimely deaths always were. When he'd worked homicides in the State Police, he'd always gone to funerals connected to the cases he investigated. It was respectful. But he never went to the gatherings afterward. It seemed like he'd be an intrusive reminder of the family's loss. Today he'd stayed. No way around it.

The church ladies had laid out quite a spread in the fellowship hall, and Mrs. Hillcrest had made a point of steering Lindsay inside and connecting her with Heather's friends. He kept an eye on his daughter while he filled his own plate. She'd hit the salads, of course, but he was glad to see she'd snagged a couple of deviled eggs before she went to sit with other young people. Leafy greens were great, but bodies needed protein. To that end he'd piled on the country ham, beef brisket, and chicken salad, making sure not to skip either the mac n' cheese or the potato salad. Couldn't snub the church ladies' hard work.

He spotted Meg sitting with Joan and David, and although there was room at their table, he didn't join her. They'd made eye contact a couple of times throughout the afternoon, but she seemed to understand why he stayed away. He took a seat next to Maroni.

The College crew was hanging out together, as usual. He'd seen the female foursome—Collins, Routzhan, Plunkard, and Slattery—sharing a single pew during the service. Afterward, the PR woman had aimed for him like a heat-seeking missile. Angling for an update, he assumed. He'd dodged her by engaging Betty Hillcrest in a lengthy conversation. He'd also noted that both Brunner and Dahlrymple had attended but hadn't sat together. And now at the grub up, Dahlrymple was nowhere to be seen.

Ty was cleaning his plate and eyeing the dessert table when Lindsay appeared again.

"Dad, can we go now, please."

"Sure thing." He said his goodbyes to Mrs. Hillcrest and looked around to give a final nod to Meg, but she wasn't there.

Once outside, he shepherded Lindsay into the car and shut the door. He was walking around to the other side when his cell phone rang.

"Yes, hello."

"Ty..."

He heard Meg's breath quicken after she spoke. His senses heightened at the sound of alarm in her voice. "What's wrong?"

"Ty, you said I could call anytime, and I haven't, but now I am. There's something on my windshield. It's a picture of a clown, and on the bottom it says: 'This isn't over. Not by a long shot.'"

Fuck. He hadn't seen that coming.

"Don't get in your truck, Meg. Don't even open the door." His tone was commanding. "Drop the picture back on the windshield. Don't touch it any more than you already have. Then go to Joan's car and get inside. Lock the doors and have her honk the horn. Tell her to tap it twice at ten-second intervals. Maroni will be there quick as he can. Do what he says."

Before he broke the connection, he heard her unasked question in the stunned silence: *Why Maroni: Why not you?*

Leaning over, Lindsay opened his door a crack. "Come on, Dad. I want to get home."

He scanned the parking lot while he dialed his partner. "You need to find and secure Meg. The murderer's left a threatening note on her windshield." His words came out low and tense. "I told her to get into Joan's car and start honking the horn so you can locate them. Put Meg in your car, forcibly if you have to, and drive her to Joan's house. Tell her to get inside and stay there. Not to leave for any reason. I'll be sending two plainclothes officers to cover the doors, front and back. Then get that picture to the lab and have them check for prints. There won't be any, but have 'em check anyway. Clear?"

"Crystal."

·   ·   ·   ·   ·

It was almost nightfall before he could carve out time to call her. The way he'd left things, he was worried she might not even answer.

"Hello, Meg?"

"Yes."

Such a small word tossed out in an offhand manner. He couldn't decode the tone.

"How are you holding up? You alright?"

"Yes. Yes, I'm fine. The shakes have worn off. Well, Joan gave me something to help with that. But I'm okay."

His breath came a little easier.

"Good. There are officers positioned front and back, so you should feel safe."

"Yup, safe as houses," she agreed with a mild chuckle.

She sounded a little off. Not goofy, just a little distracted. He wondered what kind of "something" Joan had on hand. "I'm sorry I couldn't call sooner."

"It's okay. I get it. You had to make sure that Lindsay was tucked away."

He didn't respond. She sounded sincere, but...

"Hey, I get it. Really," she continued. "Having a kid is a huge responsibility. It's great that you take it so seriously, too many parents don't. I really admire that kind of commitment. That loyalty."

Ah, a reaction to the philandering ex. But the pause grew long like she wanted to say more.

"If I ever get the chance..." She hesitated. "Well, I hope I'd be as good a mom as you are a dad."

"I bet you'll be great."

His statement just hung there. And while he didn't know what else to say, it was giving him a lot to think about.

"I did spend time with Lindsay," he added quickly. "After she started speaking to me again. Things eased up after the funeral. But let's get back to you. How're you feeling?"

"About like you'd expect. Kinda down, but I'm coping. Joan and Chloe are going all out to keep me nourished and entertained. I persuaded them to have their kids stay with friends while this whole thing resolves. Good thing, too, because I've played enough *Star Wars* Monopoly to last the year. Right now, I'm actually hibernating in the guest bedroom. I needed some Meg time, some privacy."

"I hear that. And I'll be getting some soon myself. I'm taking Lindsay down to her aunt's tomorrow. Right now she's upstairs packing. That'll take the rest of the night."

With the mention of night, both of them grew quiet.

"Meg, your eulogy was eloquent. I'm sure it was hard to stay composed, but you hit every right note."

"Thanks. But I think Lindsay's words will be remembered the longest. She's quite something, you know."

"Yeah. Yeah, I do." He waited a moment before he went on. "But she's not unique in that regard."

"Oh. Um, well, it's been an emotional day. I tried to nap, but that wasn't working. So I think I'm gonna turn in early."

"Good plan. Ah...Meg? There's something I have to ask before you go." But he wished he didn't.

"O...kay."

He noted the tone of her voice reacting to the change in his. She might not be quite up to speed, but she was still sharp. He had to ask. Now. Delay wasn't an option.

"I need to ask if you'd be willing to participate in a sting to draw out the killer." He listened for any sounds of objection. When none came, he bulled ahead. "It would all happen remotely. You'd never face the murderer, but we'd need to use your email to set the trap. If you're willing, we can discuss the details tomorrow. But if you're not, I absolutely understand."

Silence.

"While we set it up, we'll continue to monitor you 24/7. As for the sting, I'll arrange for additional means of protection once it's in play. That would just be a precaution because—as I've said—you'll never come face to face with the murderer." He paused, reluctant to go this route. And that was unprecedented.

He'd always approached these kinds of ops in a straightforward fashion. Devised a plan, prepped his team, and coached any civilians who might need to be included. And while he'd always spent time anticipating pitfalls, experience had taught him he'd probably end up having to shoot from the hip. But if Meg didn't agree to help, he lost the offensive. And defense was not his game.

The silence had grown as tangled as his thoughts while he waited for her answer. Damn it, why didn't she say something? He'd been a cop the whole of his married life, and he hadn't felt this conflicted. But then again, Tisha had never been in the crosshairs.

"Can I think about it tonight and give you my decision in the morning?"

"Of course. Of course, you can. In fact, I insist on it."

Silence.

"But I probably will."

"I know."

More silence.

"G'night, Ty."
"G'night, Meg."

•　　•　　•　　•　　•

Saturday: November 1ˢᵗ

Heather's funeral was today. It was really hard. Almost harder than Mom's. I was only ten that time, so it almost wasn't real. This one was too real. But I did okay.

So did that Meg lady. She read one of Heather's poems, the one about having the courage to follow your dreams.

Dunno how I'm gonna do that. My thoughts are really mixed up right now. Dreams don't seem all that important...the future's kinda bogus.

And I don't feel very brave.

Chapter 44

Ty didn't have to wait long for Meg's answer. It came at 7:00 a.m. He was surprised that she'd waited that long. Of course, it was possible she hadn't even slept. He hadn't gotten much rest either, what with worrying about her safety and his boss's reaction. When he'd explained the sting to João last night—making it clear that it was contingent on Meg's agreement—he'd gotten the green light. And an admonition: "Don't fuck this up, hot shot, or there'll be hell to pay. And I'm not talking about any pussy installment plan, either."

Typical João...leadership through intimidation. Like Ty needed the added pressure. He'd be off the hook if Meg said no. Off the hook and out of ideas. But of course, she said yes. Neither of them were quitters.

By 9:00 a.m., he had his team assembled in the briefing room at headquarters. It was a soulless, utilitarian space—scuffed, off-white walls and hyper-polished linoleum flooring—but the smells of coffee, sausage, bacon, and sweetened yeast invigorated the bland environment.

Maroni—outfitted in shabby, civilian sweats—came up to the front, munching on one breakfast sandwich and balancing another, a cup of coffee and a couple of doughnuts on his plate. "Man, lieutenant, you really put on a spread. These croissant things sure aren't from Mickey D's. The coffee's killer and this is my second éclair. Thanks."

"It doesn't come free. Good eats mean hard work. Better find a seat and get ready."

He always started an op this way. They'd have to be on alert for long hours, waiting for action that was unpredictable and often dangerous. An unexpected treat like this was a team building event. And he had the coin to spare.

Walking to the front of the room, he looked them over, pleased at his selection. All five of them were seasoned plainclothes officers who'd seen action and who knew how to hold and maintain, not shoot at will.

"Eat fast and get ready to listen closely. We have a lot to go over," he said.

Cramming the rest of a doughnut in his mouth, Maroni went to the table behind Ty, picked up the folders there and started handing them out.

"I brought you in to close the case of that murdered college girl," Ty began. "Take a close look at the pictures in your packet: a student, a maintenance guy, and two professors. One of them is our perp."

He gave them time to look over the photos, begin committing them to memory.

"The victim was in possession of a valuable letter that the murderer hoped to steal. It remains missing. Since that's what the perp wants, that's our lure. To coax him out, we've engaged the help of a college professor who was close to the victim. Hers is the last photo: Meg Adams. She's someone to whom the victim could've conceivably given the letter."

"So this lady professor is the bait."

"No. She's not the bait, but her role is vital." He looked at Meg's picture and saw only a civilian attached to the mission. Nothing more. Not now. "As a civilian, Professor Adams is ill-prepared to take such an active role. And it's not needed. The letter is the bait. But it must be put out there in a way that is believable. We will use her email account to send a message to all the suspects. It will give an invitation to the murderer to exchange the letter for the professor's safety. Heretofore he has threatened her welfare. The message indicates that she will not pursue the matter and will not involve the police, as long as she is left in peace."

"Why not just have her blackmail the murderer? Offer to exchange the letter for cash."

"I considered it." And João had lobbied for it. Ty'd had to do some fast talking to get that off the table. "Her previous interactions with the murderer do not establish her as that kind of player. When she's been contacted, the murderer has worn a costume and disguised his voice. Since then, contact has been initiated by written means. All those pieces indicate that he knows her. And knowing her, he won't see her as some ballsy blackmailer. If we offer cash, I think the murderer will smell a trap."

"Even though we set up a convincing sting, he might not play along," Maroni ventured. "Or he could outwait us. Try for Professor Adams again later. He's plenty smart."

One of the old-timers spoke up. "Yeah, but we gotta do something, kid. The longer we wait, the colder the case gets. We're coming up on a week since the murder, right?"

"Not quite. Today makes day five. But I take your point, Connors. And not all of the suspects are local, and one of them is in the wind. We need to act."

Connors gave one definitive nod. "Let's do it then."

Ty divided those assembled into two teams. Beginning tomorrow, Team A—under Maroni's supervision—would be stationed in Hamilton Building, the one that housed Meg's office. Two officers in plainclothes would rotate locations. From lounging in the cafeteria, keeping tabs on both those entrances, front, and rear; to hanging out in the game room on the other end of the building, covering the third point of exit and entry. He only needed one shift a day because they'd only be there while Meg was.

President Collins didn't want a big police presence on campus, so he was keeping it to two men. But he and Maroni would also be on campus. No way was he hanging back.

Team B would cover the dropsite once it was established. It would be a post office of the murderer's choosing, open from 8 to 4. Again, only one shift was necessary, but he was assigning three men. One inside, with the postal workers, two outside in unmarked cars. They would be the takedown team. He'd leave Team A in place until the murderer was in custody. He was taking no chances with Meg's safety. None.

Even with those plans in place, he felt unsettled. It seemed that the murderer might be escalating. And change was always destabilizing. Not that the bastard wasn't crazy enough already. Crazy like a fox.

•　　•　　•　　•　　•

His Sunday afternoon was spent taking Lindsay down to Chevy Chase to stay with her Aunt Caroline for the duration. It was only an hour's drive, but it felt much longer.

He stopped at the gated entryway into Caroline's neighborhood and punched in the code. His daughter turned in her seat to give him a frosty stare. One he'd been well acquainted with for well over fifteen years. "It's only for a few days, Lindsay."

"You so don't get it, do you? It's not about how long. It's about how overprotective you are. I have a life back in Frederick. Friends, plans, a Spanish test this week."

"You're wrong, I do get it. But you don't *get* me. The one time I leave you alone, the murderer gains access to the house and holds you at gunpoint. Wasn't that scary enough?"

Lindsay glared at him but didn't answer. When he stopped the car at her aunt's front door, the teen hopped out and rang the bell, leaving him to collect her suitcase. Why she needed it was beyond him. She had plenty of clothes here. More than at home.

He joined her on the stoop. "What kind of a father would I be if I didn't do everything I could to protect you?"

The door was opened by a woman with close-cropped gray hair, clad in beige silk trousers and a seafoam green angora sweater. The cool tones and soft lines of her outfit did not match her expression.

"I don't know, Tyler," Caroline said. "What kind of father are you?"

Hello to you, too, he thought to himself. She'd never liked him. He hadn't been good enough for her little sister. Not enough breeding or money.

He was about to respond when Lindsay cut him a look and took over the conversation.

"Be nice, Aunt Caroline. He's trying his best."

Ty set the suitcase down while the two women hugged. A brief, A-frame embrace.

"Thanks, Dad." Lindsay picked up her suitcase. "I'm just going to run this upstairs."

That left the two adults alone in the marble-tiled foyer.

"Hello, Caroline," he said.

"You aren't staying long, are you?"

The inflection indicated that it was a question, but he knew it was a statement—the polite sarcasm of the well-bred. "No, not long. Just until Lindsay comes back down and we say our goodbyes."

"I've been following your current gruesome case on the news, and they've managed to keep Lindsay's name out of it. What I don't understand is why you didn't bring her to me immediately. What were you thinking, leaving that child alone for even an instant! It just underscores the reasons why I should have been the one to have custody of her."

"Well, you certainly tried." And she had the money to do it. "But when the judge asked Lindsay, she picked me."

Caroline smoothed a lock of hair behind her ear. A gesture so like her sister's that it made his heart stumble.

"At least you are better at protecting your daughter than you were your wife."

She might have said more, or Ty might have replied, but Lindsay bounded down the stairs.

"Thanks for the ride, Dad. Keep me posted, okay? Let me know when you take that clown down."

"Will do, Squirt," he said, reaching out his forefinger to touch hers.

She reciprocated, but then pulled him in for a quick hug. He felt that ache in his chest again.

"Be careful, okay?" she whispered in his ear.

"Yeah. That's the plan."

She stood in the doorway as he got back into his SUV.

The hour's ride back to Frederick was just another chore. With Lindsay off his mind, he should have felt relieved, better able to focus on the upcoming sting. But his thoughts were heavy. He worried about Meg, about keeping her safe. He stewed about how to proceed if the murderer didn't take the bait. Because the investigation was at a stalemate. Fuck it all to hell and back, he'd never had such shitty luck.

Chapter 45

That evening, Ty and Maroni got out of his SUV, walked through the chilly drizzle toward Joan and Chloe's townhouse. Usually, if there were any civilians involved in the operation, he'd've had them transported to headquarters and included them in the briefing. But Ty didn't want to take any chance of the murderer seeing Meg at HQ and figuring out that something was in the works. He couldn't afford to tip his hand.

He was about to knock when Meg suddenly opened the door. Her movements were quick and sharp—her face pale, pinched, and anxious.

Ty tried not to look as exasperated as he felt. "Meg. We discussed this. You shouldn't be the one to open the door."

"You are not the boss of me," she snapped. "I'm not some fifteen-year-old girl. And there isn't any clear and present danger. I saw the pair of you coming up the walk."

Maroni glanced from one angry face to the other. "How about we go inside and get out of this rain? It looks like our Indian summer is over."

Joan slipped up behind Meg and put a hand on her shoulder. "Detective Maroni is the only one making any sense here. Everybody's nerves are on edge. It's got Chloe so antsy that she's taken off to check on Maya and Douglass. Now get yourselves inside, detectives."

"Fine," Meg said as she stepped back to allow the men to enter.

Ty shut the door firmly behind him and watched Meg's stiff back as she headed into the living room. Well, she could just be that way. He wasn't going to apologize. She needed the reminder to follow directions and to take this situation seriously.

"Chloe made cookies before she left," Joan said as she waved them further inside, "but I'm not serving anything until you two hotheads settle down."

They gathered in the living room for the strategy meeting. Everyone was in weekend wear—jeans and sweaters—but the typical Sunday night, end-of-the-weekend solemnity was replaced by something deeper, more brooding. The women sat on the floral sofa, and the two detectives perched on pastel colored, small scale wing chairs. Women's chairs in a feminine room. The effect would have been comic if the circumstances hadn't been so dire.

"Here's the plan," Ty said, brushing past anyone's need for small talk. "Meg, you'll send an email from your TCC account to each of the suspects—Brunner, Dahlrymple, Sellers, and Slattery—telling them you want to negotiate. The letter for your safety."

Joan raised an eyebrow and stared at him, incredulous. "That's your plan?"

"I don't have that frickin' letter, do I," Meg said, arms crossed and eyes flinty. "Never even seen it. How's that gonna work?"

Ty didn't react to either rebuke. "He's banking that you do. Everything he's done points to that. Stalking you; accosting you and Lindsay; putting that note on your windshield. If we dangle the letter in front of him, it'll draw him out. Traps succeed when you use the right bait, and that letter's his."

He took a folded piece of paper out of his pocket and opened it. "Trust me Meg, this will work. I've done it before. It's how we caught that serial killer in Baltimore." He held it out to her. "Just look it over, okay?"

She frowned at him as she snatched up the paper. Both women leaned forward to read it.

You're scaring me! That has to stop; so let's make a deal. One that doesn't involve the cops. I will give you Barbara Fritchie's letter, and then you will leave me alone, forever. I don't know who you are, and I don't want to know. I don't want any compensation, either. I just want you to cease and desist. To that end, I'm sending this letter to all the suspects. But only one of you will be able to seal the deal by answering these two questions:

1. What were you wearing when we met unexpectedly last Friday night?
2. What weapon did I use against you?

Send your answers to me through the dropbox in TCC's campus mail. That'll keep it anonymous. Also include in your response the location of a post office of your choice and a PO box number where I can mail the Fritchie letter to you. That way, you have the control.
All I want is to be left in peace.

"Ooh, very clever," Joan said. "And you got one thing right. Nobody else does know the answer to those questions. Not even me." She turned a reproachful eye on Meg. "You hussy."

"He told me not to tell."

Seeing Joan about to retort, Ty broke in. "We sequester certain details to employ in occasions like this. Clowny's response will be evidence we can use in our case against him."

Meg looked up from re-reading the email, her expression fretful. "One of these phrases doesn't match the tone of an email I would send."

He narrowed his eyes. Seriously? She wanted to edit the damn email?

"That one phrase—cease and desist—sounds too much like cop-speak. I'd never use it."

Maroni nodded. "I can see your point. What would sound more like you?"

"How about...'I just want you out of my life.'"

Ty had reached his limit. "Oh. Good idea. Let's bring attention to the fact that he likely wants you out of his life *permanently*. 'Cease and desist' is a phrase in common use. It shouldn't cause any problem for someone who just a minute ago insisted that she didn't see any 'clear and present danger.' Because that's Supreme Court speak."

"It's also the title of a novel by Tom Clancy," she retorted. "But wording always matters. The email needs to strike the right tone, or he's not going to take the bait. Surely you know that."

He'd opened his mouth to respond when Joan smacked her hand down on the coffee table.

"That's enough, you two," she said. "Maroni and I are headed into the kitchen to make a pot of nice, soothing chamomile tea. While we're gone, the pair of you are going to iron out your differences. I'm the communications expert, so pay attention to what I'm going to say." She looked from one to the other. "When you talk to each other, use 'I' statements. None of this 'you never follow directions' or 'you're not the boss of me.' The way you two squabble, anybody would think you were already married."

Both of them bristled at that observation, but neither spoke.

"When I come back with tea and cookies, I want to see happy faces. *Capisce?*"

She rose and looked to Maroni. "You're with me."

Once the others were in the kitchen, Meg sighed. "I'm sorry about the knee jerk reaction. But you're not acting like yourself, either. Ever since you've gotten here, your attitude has been so...so paternal. Patronizing, even. Joan's right, though. The tension is getting to me, to all of us."

He wasn't backing down. "I'm sorry that you felt disrespected, but I can't apologize for my actions. It's what I'd do to safeguard any civilian under my protection. Assess current conditions. Be dispassionate. Take charge. Worrying about people's feelings is a wasted step in this kind of situation."

Her guarded eyes held questions, but the tone of her voice conveyed simple curiosity. "Are you like this a lot?"

He paused, recalling Lindsay's earlier words, wondering if he was a control freak. "I'm like this when I need to be."

From the kitchen came a burst of laughter, and although the tension in the living room didn't dissipate, it lessened.

She cocked her head and considered him. "Okay, maybe so. Don't expect me to like it, but I can live with it. For now, at least."

You may live because of it, he thought. Aloud he said, "Truce?"

A ghost of a smile flitted across her face. "Détente."

"I can live with that." He returned her slight smile.

Maroni carried in a tray with tea things and set it on the coffee table. Joan passed around a plate of plump molasses cookies.

"That's better," she said, assessing both faces. "Another couple of days and you'll be able to kiss and make up...with compound interest." She settled herself on the couch as she took in their disconcerted expressions. "Continue, lieutenant," she said with the wave of a hand.

He took out the iPad he'd brought along. "Meg, I'm sending you the email addresses of all the suspects, plus an attachment with the message itself...the amended message." He started typing. "All you have to do is log into your TCC account, open this communique, then cut and paste the information into a new email and send it to everyone." He launched the transmission and handed the device to her.

In his own mind, he'd pretty much ruled out Slattery and Brunner as the actual murderer. But either of them could be pulling the strings behind the scene. And in a murder-for-hire scenario, the puppeteer would keep dictating the action, withholding payment until the letter was delivered. The gofer would get the instructions and end up at the post office. Once arrested, they'd turn up the heat until he rolled on his big boss. Or that's how he hoped it would pan out. Unless it was Sellers acting on his own. And man, would that be sweet.

Meg got busy on the keyboard. Once finished she studied the little screen, bit her bottom lip, and pushed *Send.* "Now what?"

"Now, we wait."

Meg closed her eyes for a moment and pulled in a breath. "How long? I mean if it's Sellers, he's on the run." Her face fell. "Oh, I meant to tell you this, but in all the drama I forgot. Jon was at the funeral. I saw him sneak into the back of the church when I started to speak and sneak out again right before I finished."

Ty nodded slowly, wishing she'd remembered sooner but knowing that it likely wouldn't have mattered. "Well, at least we know he's still in the area."

"Swell. But how do we know he's even checking his email?"

Maroni cleared his throat. "He's a millennial, like me. None of us can last a whole day without technology. He's been smart enough to keep his cell phone switched off so we can't locate him, but you can bet he's still in the loop. I expect he's reading everything he can get his hands on...emails, Facebook, even the newspapers."

Ty nodded. "He'll be anxious for information simply because he's isolated himself."

"But it might not even be him," she argued. "I mean, you're gonna stake out that post office, right. But it could take a long time. The murderer might smell a trap and never show up."

He felt Maroni's gaze on him, but Ty answered Meg's worries with a shrug. "If we have to wait, we wait. He'll show. To use the murderer's own words, 'this isn't over.' He's cocky because he's still at large. Plus he's obsessed about that letter. One or both of those things will trip him up." And sooner rather than later, he hoped.

Ty shot her a smile, the one he used to reassure others. "It's just a matter of time before that clown's in custody."

She nodded, adding a thin smile; Maroni looked down; Joan searched each face, concern etched on her own.

"And remember I said I had some ideas about additional security for you?" Ty continued. "We've doubled your plain clothes protection, but let's step things up. I'd like you to wear a wire. That way we can hear what's going on at all times, and if you get a feeling that something isn't right, you can alert us without having to do more than say something innocuous, like 'uh-oh,' or something like that."

Noting her silence and furrowed brow, he figured he'd lost that round.

She sighed. "Okay, I guess that makes sense. I can do that."

"Great. That'll close any gaps in coverage. Indoors you're pretty much secure. This house is closely watched, and the College is probably the safest setting because it's so public. Too much activity, too many eyes to see things. You're most vulnerable going from one place to another."

The plan was coming together as well as could be expected. He wasn't sure if Meg was complying because she was being practical or was just plain scared. Either one worked for him.

He turned to his partner. "Why don't you familiarize her with the technology?"

Maroni pulled the apparatus out of his pocket. Pointing to the little mic, he said, "You're gonna want to clip that under your clothes." Deadpan he added, "Like on your bra or something."

She arched an eyebrow, a ploy that was known to make uppity students straighten up and fly right. "Fine. Give it here, little man." She practiced clipping it on and off the neck opening of her sweater.

"Yup, that's the way. Now, that matchbox-looking thing at the other end of the wire is the battery pack. You'll have to tuck that somewhere else. When you toggle the button on the battery to the ON position, the device will broadcast from sixteen to twenty-four hours. So activate it when you head out in the morning and turn it off after you get home." He grinned. "That's it. You're all set."

She sat up straighter and slipped the battery inside the waistband of her jeans, then experimented with the ON/OFF button. "I feel silly," she said, sinking back into the sofa cushions. "Like an actress in a low budget action/adventure movie."

"I, for one, feel relieved," Joan said. "Thank you, gentlemen."

Ty nodded. "You'll drive yourself to school tomorrow, Meg. Things have to go as normally as possible. But I'll stay on your tail as you head in and wait around until you're inside."

"Gotcha."

"Joan, since you don't have class until noon on Mondays, you need to stay here until then. Keep to your regular schedule." Knowing that Meg's best friend was strong-willed and impetuous, he waited for some backtalk, was surprised when she didn't offer any.

"Okay people, we're ready to do this," he said, sounding like his old lacrosse coach. "To review. Only the people in this room know that she's wired. Keep it that way. We control the situation by controlling the information." He let out a tense breath, more troubled than he let on.

He looked straight at Meg this time. "It'd be best if you pretty much stayed at your desk unless you're teaching a class. Since Routzhan informs me that President Collins doesn't want a large police presence on campus, TCC's security is in charge of monitoring you while you're inside. They'll make periodic passes by your office and any classroom you're teaching in. And I also have two men in the building. All you have to do from here on out is maintain your routine activities."

"Sure. I can do that."

He studied her. "That goofy kid brings the mail by your office around 10:00 a.m., doesn't he."

"Shaggy," she smiled. "Usually. But it can be different students sometimes, and the time can vary. But it's typically in the morning."

"Fine. Since Clowny has to craft a reply and rent a PO box, it's improbable that his return letter will hit campus mail early enough to be delivered to you by tomorrow morning. But he'd still expect you to check your mail before you left for the day. Which would be...?"

"Probably a little before 4:00. I'd want to beat the Fort Detrick traffic."

He nodded. "We'll have eyes on you when you make the mailroom run and then all the way back home."

"Okay."

Ty paused, thinking. "The murderer knows my face, and he might be too cautious if I'm skulking around. So while I'm on campus, I'll be hanging out in Calloway's office."

Meg brightened. "David's an old hand at law enforcement. He could be useful."

"So he keeps reminding me," Ty muttered. "The disadvantage of that location is the proximity to Brunner's office. But he surely won't be the one to make the drop. And Security has people keeping a discrete eye on Sketchy Doug." He held up a single earbud. "I'll be monitoring your body mic with this audio receiver. While I'm stationary, Maroni will be moving around campus, checking on our plainclothes guys and staying in constant contact with me by radio." A faint, reassuring smile touched his lips. "We've got you covered."

She nodded again, a small, taut shift of the chin.

"Staying vigilant is a smart move, Meg, but worrying isn't. It saps your energy. Besides, this sting is gonna work," he said firmly.

"Okay, got it."

"I want you to summarize it for me. In your own words. Just to make sure. Alright?"

"Park where I usually do," she began, looking out the window as if she could see the gated parking lot on campus. "Then go sit in my office and pretend not to be scared, teach my classes, and wait."

Meg turned her head to look at each of them. When she spoke again, her voice was firm and steady. "The plan sounds pretty solid. And I'm oh-so-ready to have the last laugh on that clown."

"That's the spirit, professor." He figured he'd struck the right note when she gave him a brief, brave smile.

Once back in the SUV, Maroni turned to his partner. "That ended up okay, but there were a couple of times I wasn't so sure. She can be kinda feisty. I didn't see that coming."

Ty shrugged. "It's not hard to figure. She's an intellectual, and she's used to being in charge of her own classroom. No problem challenging the administration, either, from what I understand."

Maroni gave him a shrewd look. "That's a lot of woman to handle."

"Yeah, well. I don't seem to be drawn to the docile type," he drawled.

"Me either." Maroni grinned. "Keeps things lively."

•   •   •   •   •

Sunday: November 2nd

Aunt Caroline is trying hard to keep my mind off things. A matinée at the Kennedy Center, dinner at the Mayflower Hotel with friends of hers. And Mom's. Boring, rich, totally white people. Tight asses.

I wonder what's happening at home? Since Dad wouldn't tell me anything, it must be some sort of covert op. Every time he got a call last night, or this morning, he left the room. Yup, something big is going down.

But I'm kinda glad I'm not there. I mean, I'm safer here and all, but it's not just that.

Even after he catches Clowny, I'm gonna hang here at Aunt Caroline's for a little while longer. I promised Dad I'd give him space to find his way. Well, I need space, too. I just don't want to watch things start. That touch in the funeral home was too much. Something that wasn't meant for me to see. Something I don't want to watch.

At least not yet. Not now.

Chapter 46

The next morning Meg drove through intermittent showers to the College, cantered Rocinante into the parking lot and left him in their favorite spot—under a honey-locust tree, now bare—one that she could see from her office window. She patted him on the fender. "See you later, noble steed." And even though she knew Ty wouldn't make himself visible, she couldn't help but look.

It was then that she noticed the unusual number of people milling about this early in the day, especially considering the sputtering drizzle. She walked through the crowd of students, some of whom were passing out placards and picket signs, both pro- and anti-gun control.

Oh, boy. She'd certainly lost track of things. The forum about arming security was set for Wednesday night in Everett Hall. That was two days away, but it seemed that some students were jumping the gun.

However, some looked like they couldn't decide whether to go or stay given the uncertain weather. Others had the set jaws and resolute expressions of people who were not to be deterred. And who surely wouldn't back down if the other side didn't.

She returned the fist bumps of a few of her students, the pro- ones, and nodded to the anti- ones who'd made eye contact. But she didn't have the time or energy for anything extra today. That she hadn't known this rally was in the works showed how out of touch she was, how caught up she'd become in the murder investigation.

· · · · ·

After watching Meg get out of her truck and enter the building, Ty parked and crossed the parking lot, zigzagging through the crowd of damp, agitated students holding limp picket signs. Ignoring them, he set out for David's office. Until Meg got a reply in her campus mail, all he could do was wait. A miserable pastime. So he'd busy himself for the time being making sure she was safe here on campus. Or so he imagined until Maria caught sight of him.

"You? What are you doing here?" she demanded.

"My job." His run of shitty luck hadn't ended. That woman was like a bad penny.

"Well, of course. I'd expect you would be. But why here? Your presence here today could escalate things." She looked toward the picketers. "Especially if you're armed. Are you?"

He nodded once. "I'm about to check in with Security. That's your protocol, isn't it? I haven't been informed of any change."

"No, there's been no change. Yet. But I don't want things to get out of hand."

"If they do, it won't be because of me. I don't intend to incite an incident. I've always been successful in de-escalating problematic situations. No shots fired. On my part or anyone else's."

She gave him a long look. "Oh. Well. That's good to know. But I'm glad I ran into you. President Collins asked me to set up a brief meeting. She needs to discuss something with you. Are you going to be here awhile? I'll access her schedule and call you when she's free, shall I?"

"Sure. Fine. Whatever." *Civilians.*

.   .   .   .   .

Inside her office, Meg hung up her raincoat on the hook behind the door. Walking behind her desk, she ran a hand over the sweater on the back of the chair, her slender fingers playing with the floppy edges of the crocheted collar.

Once seated, she dragged some papers out of her book bag and plopped them on the desk. Then she looked through her CDs, pulled out one, and slid it into her disk drive. Soon she was listening to the first four notes of perhaps the most famous of all classical music compositions: da-da-da-dah.

She knew about the myth that the notes signified fate knocking at the door and about the people who vehemently debunked that myth. She also knew that during WWII, the Brits had adopted it as their musical mascot and turned its Roman numeral into the famous "V" hand sign.

But for her, Beethoven's 5th was Ty. In turn energetic and tender. Forthright then intuitive. It was both complex and comforting, exactly what she needed. Plus at the symphony's conclusion, audiences stood up and cheered. That's the kind of ending she wanted to this sting.

So she listened to it and played at grading papers. The symphony was drawing to an end when someone knocked on her door.

"Professor Adams," said the lanky, bespectacled Sellers as he pushed back the hood from his head.

Meg breathed out an "uh-oh," imagining Ty's heart rate rising and muscles filling with oxygenated blood, preparing for action.

"Yes, Mr. Sellers," she said, dipping her head toward the mic. "What can I do for you?"

·   ·   ·   ·   ·

Ty was sitting in David's office, both of them drinking coffee, when he heard Meg's, "uh oh." He pulled out his radio as he leapt up and ran out the door.

"Maroni! Sellers is in Meg's office. Get your team in there."

·   ·   ·   ·   ·

Jon walked deeper into the room and placed a hand in his hoodie's pouch. "Well," he began, "I have something to give you."

Meg gripped the armrests of the chair. "Oh?"

In her mind's eye, she saw Ty and Maroni racing to her rescue.

Sellers drew out a small, green leatherette diary studded with dull silver stars. He held it out to her. "It's one of Heather's journals. Poems, mostly. I thought her mom might want it back. Could you get it to her?"

"Certainly, Jon," she murmured, taking the book and placing it on her desk. "Thank you. I'm certain it will mean a lot to Mrs. Hillcrest. It was very considerate of you."

Sellers dropped his eyes and pushed his damp hair from his forehead. "I know people are looking at me as a murderer, and that's why I got your email."

She glanced into the hallway outside her door, hoping to see reinforcements.

"But I don't know the answers to those two questions." He looked out the rain-steaked window. "And I couldn't've hurt her. I loved her." He shrugged, turned, and left.

·   ·   ·   ·   ·

Hearing Jon's last words, Ty halted his charge toward Meg's office and contacted Maroni again. "Hold up. Give me your position."

"I'm over by the student rec room."

"Sellers is not, I repeat, *not* the murderer and is no threat to Meg. Have your men resume their positions. I'll bring you up to speed later. But we still need to talk to that kid. He left Meg's office, probably headed to student parking over behind the science building. See if you can round him up. Tag a couple of Security guys to help out, if you want."

"Will do. Glad the little fuck toad has finally surfaced. Kinda sad he's not our man."

"Me too."

He walked back into his friend's office and slumped in a chair.

"What the hell was that about?" David demanded.

"False alarm." Ty was beginning to explain when his cell phone rang. He raised a hand to forestall David's protest as he answered. "Yes, hello."

"Lieutenant Raleigh," he heard Maria say. "The President is between meetings and is available for the next fifteen minutes. Her schedule is tight today, but she's very anxious to talk to you."

"Fine. I'm on my way." He finished the last sip of cold coffee, threw his cup in the trash, and nodded to his old friend. "That was Routzhan. I've gotta go play nice with Dr. Collins." He was almost out the door before he called back, "I won't be long. But keep an eye out for Brunner. He's not in yet, and I want to keep track of his whereabouts."

"You got it."

•　　•　　•　　•　　•

Sellers had only just left, and Meg's heart rate had almost returned to normal when Nate appeared in her door, sans mail cart but carrying a clasp envelope.

Beyond him, someone passed by the office door, slowing slightly and talking on a cell phone.

"I'm sorry Professor Adams," Nate said, worry evident in every atom of his skinny frame. He held up the envelope. "This is from Heather...you know, dead Heather."

"What? I'm not following you. What're you talking about?"

The person in the hall finished talking then leaned against the opposite wall, waiting.

Maria? What was she doing here? Meg wondered. Probably going to accuse her of having incited the students to stage the gun control protest.

At his professor's scolding look, Nate hurried to explain. "Heather knew I worked in the mailroom and asked could I get this to you. Said it was important. She was in a wicked hurry to leave campus because she had some sort of big appointment or something—she didn't say what—but she didn't have time to get this to you herself."

Over Shaggy's shoulder, Meg watched the PR woman inch toward her office door, obviously eavesdropping now, the nosey parker.

Nate held the envelope with both hands like it contained the name of an Oscar winner. "Heather gave it to me an hour or so after class that day. And I put it in my backpack, so I wouldn't lay it down somewhere and lose track of it, you know. And I don't know how, but I lost the whole backpack. I've been looking everywhere for it, really freakin' out 'cause if I didn't get this to you, it was, like, breaking a promise to the dead. But then this morning I remembered to check the Lost and Found, and there it was. And the envelope isn't sealed, so I peeked inside. It's just some old letter." He passed the big tan envelope to Meg. "I shoulda got this to you last week, I know." His shoulders sagged, and his sigh begged her forgiveness. "But I messed up."

She seized the envelope and was about to lay into him when a quick movement behind the boy startled them both as Maria pushed Nate into the room.

Meg's head snapped up as she put it all together.

In a series of sudden actions, Maria stepped inside, yanked out a gun and struck Nate over the head. She aimed the weapon at Meg, her prominent blue eyes a little red-rimmed.

"You," Meg gasped. "You're not on the list. You didn't get the email."

"No. But I can answer the two questions: A clown suit and a can of Pledge." She smiled. "You see, Robert *did* get the email. It upset him so much that he called me, wondering if the College's lawyer could sue you for harassment. I said I'd be happy to look into it for him."

"But why? Why would you kill Heather?"

"It had to happen." She shrugged. "There'll be time for explanations later. Right now, we need to get a move on." With her gun hand, she gestured toward the envelope. "Open it. Make sure Fritchie's letter is in there. Something I should've done the first time."

Meg did, and it was, and she'd never been more scared in her life.

"Slide it back in the envelope and give it to me," Maria said. "I have plans for that letter."

She tugged Meg's raincoat off the door and tossed it to her captive. "Put it on. And you'd better cooperate. If you don't, I'll have to make sure this one dies." Maria toed the unconscious Nate, frowning a bit at his moan. "Just like little Heather. And even though there was no way around it, her death has weighed on me. You don't want his death to weigh on you, do you?"

Meg zipped up her coat, her thoughts flying. She'd attended countless freshman orientations on personal safety, enough to know that the odds of getting away from a kidnapper are better at the point of abduction than at a second location. But she couldn't risk it without putting Shaggy's life on the line.

"Get your purse, Meg. We're going for a ride."

She stumbled over her student's crumpled body as Routzhan pushed her out the door.

Chapter 47

The President's office was housed one building away on the north side of campus, but Ty's hurried stride ate up the distance. He didn't have time for this crap, he thought as he stepped off the elevator and into the executive suite.

"Lieutenant," the secretary said, looking up. "Oh my. Are you here to see Dr. Collins? I'm sorry but she isn't on campus this morning. May I help you?"

His eyes hardened as he listened to the conversation in his earbud and heard the murderer say: "No. But I can answer the two questions."

"Fuck." Ty spat out the word as he spun around and raced out of the office.

"Dear me," said the secretary.

Sprinting down the stairs on his way outside, he listened for something more from Meg's wire. But all he heard were muffled sounds. No words, nothing useful. She must have put on her coat.

"Goddamn, this rain!"

· · · · ·

With Maria's gun in her ribs, Meg was propelled out of her office through the hallway to the back stairwell, the one used only by college personnel who merited keys. They hurried down the stairs to the landing on the first floor.

Maria gestured to the big black umbrella leaning beside the door. "Pick it up."

Hands shaking, Meg did as she was told. Then she saw Maria pull the fire alarm and felt herself thrust outside into the rain. The cold droplets revived her somewhat. She knew that her chances of survival were dwindling with each passing second. Before she could formulate a plan, she was drawn to her captor's side, the gun jammed into her waist.

"Don't just stand there, you stupid cow," Maria hissed. "Get moving."

Meg opened the umbrella to cover them both as they walked side by side.

"Perfect," Maria gloated. "I've thought of everything, even the umbrella. We look like two girlfriends leaving campus for a coffee break."

Chaos reigned outside the building. As people streamed out and mingled with the picketers, the crowd was swelling. But Maria's quick getaway had already managed to have both of them picking their way through the nearly full parking lot just beyond the line of commotion.

The klaxon of the fire alarm throbbed in the air. To Meg, the sound seemed to set the raindrops vibrating. She was stumbling, clumsy with fear, and clammy from perspiration. But her thoughts flew. Should she make a break for it? Scream to get someone's attention?

She drew in a long breath and started to open her mouth.

"Don't even think about it," Maria warned. "If you try anything, I'll open fire on the protestors. And this time the gun's real. A genuine Colt six-shooter, manufactured in 1860." She chuckled. "There's no background check or waiting period to buy antiques. I bought it Saturday just for this. Just for you. But if you pull any stunts, you won't be the only one to die today. There'll be lots of grieving parents."

Even as Meg's confidence flatlined, she thought of Ty. Maybe, just maybe...

Maria leaned closer, whispering, "Hope is not a strategy, Meghan. And there's no such thing as luck. We create our own destinies. That's why I sent your lieutenant friend on a wild goose chase. He must be frantic by now. I've outsmarted him at every turn." She laughed. "And Robert. It wasn't hard to take the museum key from this desk drawer. Neither of them ever even suspected me. They don't have a clue about why it had to happen."

"Neither do I. Tell me. Don't I deserve to know?" Meg said, playing for time, aware that she was waiting for an opportunity that might never come.

"The girl's death couldn't be helped. It was a situation where the end justified the means. I had to get my hands on that letter."

"What—" She stopped herself just in time before she could protest that no end, no earthly reason could ever justify the death of a nineteen-year-old girl. Meg couldn't afford to agitate her captor, push her too far. Best to keep her talking. "What's so important about that letter?"

"It spoils everything. It glorifies that Middletown nobody, Nannie Crouse."

"So. Why do you care?"

"Because Robert wins and I lose."

Maria stopped them in back of a pickup truck and threw the umbrella on the ground. "It's time we got off campus."

Meg stared in disbelief. It was Rocinante.

"Unlock it and get in. And don't try anything. If so you much as twitch, you die here. Then later I'll take out that boy from your office. But it won't be quick. And he won't be the last, either."

When Meg hesitated, Routzhan brought up the weapon. "Do it. Do it now."

Her hands were clumsy with fear and cold. She fumbled getting the key out of her purse.

"Faster, you stupid bitch," Maria growled.

· · · · ·

Ty dashed around the corner of Hamilton Hall and surveyed the roiling crowd of rain-geared people. Hoods up and umbrellas everywhere. He stood motionless, scanning, searching.

"Just stayed focused," he murmured. "Stay focused, and be smart." He grabbed a tree branch and hoisted himself to the rim of a trash barrel, straining to catch sight of Meg or any signal she might send. "Come on, Meghan. Gimme something here."

He looked over at the leafless honey-locust tree, Rocinante's parking place, the last place he'd seen Meg this morning. An umbrella lowered and he spotted Meg and Maria. He jumped down and barked information to Maroni while he drew his own weapon and raced toward the truck. He saw Meg fumbling with her keys. Saw the gun in the other woman's hand. He stopped ten feet away and called out, "Maria. Maria Routzhan. This is the police. Put down your weapon."

She whirled around to face him, snaking one arm around her captive's waist and pulling the now struggling woman in front of her as cover. Maria held the gun against Meg's temple. "Stop squirming, bitch, or it ends now."

"Do as she says, Meg." He could sense her looking at him, but he couldn't spare her a glance, couldn't soothe or comfort. Had to keep all his attention on Routzhan.

"Stay back," Maria warned. "Or she dies. Right here. Right now."

"You don't want to do that, Maria. Let's talk."

"About what? Heather's murder? About how I'm facing life in prison?"

"There isn't any physical evidence against you. It's all circumstantial. With a good lawyer, you could get off."

"I answered the two questions. And your girlfriend just now gave me the letter. She knows who I am, what I did," Maria said, tightening her hold on Meg. "She has to die."

"If she dies, I can't help you." He nodded sideways toward the crowd near the building. "Look at all the witnesses."

"But she knows."

"It's her word against yours. And she doesn't know everything, does she? Neither do I." He was thinking fast, reaching for the right thing to say. "I don't know an awful lot. For starters, I don't know how it went down with Heather in the museum. Maybe she set up the meeting and tried to get money from you. That puts her in the wrong, that's extortion. Maybe she attacked you, and you just defended yourself."

"Stop talking. You're confusing me. You'd say anything to save your little girlfriend."

In his peripheral vision, he saw Maroni directing his team and Security to fan out and form a line to keep the crowd back, away from danger. Good job. *Now it's just me and her.*

"Nobody's going to die today, Maria." A shaky promise at best. Maria's anger was ebbing, and any sort of change threatened this fragile stalemate. She looked more distraught now, ready to cry. She was losing it.

"Just let Meg go, give yourself up, and we'll get you a lawyer. You'll have help."

"Lawyers can't help me. If the letter isn't destroyed, then Nannie Crouse becomes the real Barbara Fritchie. Robert's research is vindicated, and that damn Dahlrymple becomes famous."

"Dahlrymple?" Meg cried, scared and confused. "What's he got to do with all this?"

"Everything. You'd think he's a nobody, just some maintenance guy. But Robert is going to make him into a somebody." She had tears in her eyes. "I've always wanted to be special, not just some incredibly average, pop-eyed freak. My mother told me that I was unique, that I was descended from a Civil War heroine. But she can't even help me anymore because she's dying. She was wrong then, and she's leaving me now. Alone. I'm all alone. So I'm a nobody again."

Ty leaned forward, itching to do more. "That's not true, Maria. You're somebody. You have a prestigious job. People respect you."

"Liar! People don't even *like* me. I was bullied in school. The faculty here ignore me. My boss takes advantage of me, nearly works me to death. I'm overwhelmed and underappreciated."

Sensing movement to his right, he caught a glimpse of Brunner slipping through a gap in the security line. *What the fuck?*

"Maria!" Brunner called. "What's going on here? What are you doing with that gun?"

"Shut up, Robert. You're the crux of the problem. You started this." She began crying slow, thin tears. "You betrayed me. Over and over again. First, you betrayed my friendship. Wasn't I always there for you? Helping you with your publications, your research. I was trying to help you feel like a somebody. In return you were supposed to help *me* get famous, help *me* get published," she said, her voice growing shrill.

"Maria, you're overwrought," Brunner said. "Just put the gun down, and let Meghan go."

"When that Heather turned up with her letter, you tried to get your hands on it to prove that Crouse was the true heroine, the one who should've been memorialized in Whittier's poem. And Heather would be the one to help you get famous. Everyone would be talking about that fucking Nannie Crouse, and how some cute little co-ed brought her story into the limelight." She glared at him. "For all I know, you were screwing your student to get what you wanted from her."

Brunner stared, shell-shocked.

"Why not? You're nothing but a man-whore. When I found out about your tryst in the darkroom with that red-headed floozy of an adjunct, I was outraged. And you know what they say about a woman scorned. For years I've been your closest friend and confidant, your lover. But I wasn't special to you, was I? Seems like you'll sleep with anyone. Even that skanky Slattery," she said, eyes narrowing. "Now I can make *you* suffer. I'll burn the letter. You can see your dreams go up in smoke. Disappear into thin air like mine did."

Meg cried out softly as Maria tugged her closer. Ty willed himself not to react.

"Then there's the unkindest cut of all," she said, voice choked with tears. "That Doug person. You kept digging and digging into old records about Nannie Crouse's offspring. I read all your notes on that, or did you forget that I could proxy into your computer, both the files and the emails. I knew everything, sometimes before you did—like Doug's article being accepted for publication. He copied you on his email before he told you that night after the viewing. And what else did I find in your files? That you conclusively proved *he's* the direct descendant. I read that swell little piece of news before the damn letter ever surfaced. You robbed me of my destiny and gave it to him, a common laborer. A nobody."

Blinking her eyes to clear them, Routzhan backed up a pace, dragging her human shield with her. When Meg stumbled, Maria slid the gun down from her captive's temple to her ear.

Ty could hear sirens approaching, heard the rising noise of the crowd, noted that Maroni was inching closer and hoped it didn't escalate things. Because Routzhan was unraveling, fast.

Maria's tears fell harder. "Nothing has turned out right. I'm descended from some random orphan. I'll never get published. My mother is dying, and my lover betrayed me." She shifted her stance. "Know this, I'm *not* going to jail. Not going to be a nobody with a number."

Positioning the gun under her own chin, Maria shoved Meg away, hard.

"My god, Maria," Brunner gasped. "No!"

Time slowed as Ty watched Meg lurch into the tailgate, saw her try to steady herself. But her legs gave out, and she fell, whacking her head on the pavement. She lay still, inert.

He swiveled his focus back to Routzhan, moved a fraction closer. "You don't want to pull that trigger, Maria. Think of how upset your mother will be. And what about Dr. Collins? She'll have to deal with all the bad publicity for the College. Just put the gun down. Put it down, and we'll work things out."

Maria shook her head. "I can't." Her hand began to tremble. She looked at Brunner, swung the gun toward Ty and fired.

So did he.

As both slumped to the ground, onlookers screamed.

Maroni dashed forward, kicked Maria's weapon away and holstered his as he called out orders. "Call 911. Get some ambulances here, stat. And keep those civilians back."

He bent over the bodies lying crumpled on the wet blacktop. Maria first, motionless and opened eyed. He put two fingers to her carotid, then shook his head.

Next, he leaned over Meg and repeated the process. "She's got a pulse," he shouted.

Then he looked toward Ty and saw David bending down, heedless of the blood thinning in the rain.

Chapter 48

Before she opened her eyes, Meg heard voices.

"Who's gonna tell her?"

"Tell me what," she murmured, eyelids fluttering.

"Meggie..."

She opened her eyes to see Joan's worried face. Actually, she saw two of her.

"What's to tell?" Meg asked, blinking her way to wakefulness. She tried to sit up and was hit with a wave of nausea.

"Lie still baby-girl," Joan urged. "You've got a concussion. You're gonna be fine. You're in the hospital, but you're gonna be just fine."

Meg frowned, but that hurt so she stopped. "Hospital?"

"It's alright, honey. It's very common for trauma victims not to remember the incident."

"Trauma? Incident?" Then she remembered. "Maria. Maria knocked Shaggy over the head and stole Heather's letter and kidnapped me and kept poking me with a gun. I *hate* guns. She made me go outside in the rain and, and..." A shiver ran through her. "I was so scared."

Joan ran a calming hand down Meg's arm but didn't speak.

"So what else happened? Where's Maria?" White-faced and eyes brimming with fear, Meg whispered, "Am I safe?"

"Yes, sweetie. You're safe." Joan squeezed her friend's hand. "There was a shootout." She paused, then added in a hushed voice, "Maria's dead."

"A shootout? Wait. Ty was there. I remember him talking." Her core went cold with fear. "What about Ty? Where's Ty?"

"I'm right here," he said, shifting a little forward on the chair beside her bed.

Meg whipped her head around and gave herself some stabbing pain and more nausea. But it was worth it to see Ty sitting there, face pale and one shoulder whitened by bandages under a partially buttoned shirt. But he was smiling and reaching out his good hand to her. She wanted to cry in relief, but even the thought of doing that made her stomach wobble.

"Thank god," she breathed.

"She's already answered my prayers," Joan murmured.

"And mine," David said, patting Meg's blanketed knee.

The group became quiet, reflective.

Then David shuffled his feet and sent an uncomfortable look at Meg. "But that's not quite all that happened."

"What more could there possibly be?"

David took a deep breath. "Rocinante didn't make it, either."

At that, Meg pressed her face into her hands and would have sobbed if her head hadn't hurt so badly. Poor ol' Rocinante. She was sniffling and still getting herself together when a knock came on the door.

Maroni came in, trailed by a clutch of colorful balloons. "Hey, how're y'doing?"

Meg dabbed at her eyes. "Still a little rattled, but glad to be alive. You brought me balloons? That's so sweet."

He blushed. "They're not from me. They're from Lindsay."

She saw him hesitate.

"They're...um...for her dad. Sorry."

That figures. She kept her face neutral. "How'd she know he warranted balloons?"

"Her friends texted her. It's all over the local news. YouTube and everything." Then he pulled a pint-sized Care Bear and a card out of his pocket. "This is for you. From your student, Nate Fogle. His mom brought him by after they checked him out in the ER. We didn't let him in here, but he looked harmless, so we let him leave the gift."

"Dear little Shaggy," she sighed.

Joan gave an unladylike snort. "You'd better check the card first. See if he wants extra credit."

"That's cold, Joan," David laughed. "Even for you."

"Hmmph. Well, Meg, you slept through the doctor's assessment," she scolded. "You're doing fine, but he wants to keep you overnight. And you can't go back to work for a week."

Ty nodded. "That sounds about right."

Joan's look was a question in itself. "And what about you, Mister Man of Steel?"

"I'm cleared to leave. It's just a flesh wound, didn't hit any bones or organs."

Maroni cleared his throat and became very formal. "Commander João says to tell you that because you discharged your weapon in the apprehension of a suspect, you're on administrative leave." Then he cracked a smile. "And you get time off to get recover. Plus, when Lindsay got wind of all this, she tried to tag you and finally got me. Told me to tell you she'll call again tonight and says you'd better pick up. Long story short, she's glad you're both okay, but she's not coming home right away. Probably not until Sunday night. Something about a trip to Nassau to soothe her aunt's jittery nerves."

"Which means," Joan smirked, "you two have some unconducted business to conduct."

Meg blushed and even that hurt.

Ty let the comment slide, but his shy smile spoke for him.

"These two children look tired," Joan said to the others. "We'd best be rolling along."

After everyone left, Ty reached up and ran the backs of his fingers along Meg's cheek. He was about to speak when the door opened again, and Robert Brunner looked in.

Seeing just the two of them, he entered the room and set a bouquet of exotic flowers on Meg's tray table. "I came to pay my respects to both of you." He paused. "Meghan, I'm sorry that you had to suffer such an ordeal today."

Meg worked to hide her surprise. "Thank you for the flowers, Robert. They're lovely."

Brunner nodded, gave Ty a long look, then held out his hand. "I wish to thank you for your bravery, sir. You did everything you could."

Ty stood and shook the professor's hand. "I wish it could have ended differently."

"We all do," Meg added in a quiet voice.

Brunner looked down at the floor, and an awkward silence built. Meg and Ty exchanged glances, waiting for their guest to continue.

"I stayed away until the others left. I'm here to apologize." He looked at Meg briefly then kept his gaze on Ty. "I didn't know about her...um...psychological fragility."

"You bear no fault in this."

"Perhaps not. But neither does my behavior doesn't speak well of me. I am a professor of some note, a married man. I *have* been spending a good deal of time with Dahlrymple, time she clearly resented. In her mind, he had usurped her status as a descendant of a noteworthy Civil War figure, and I continually championed Doug over her. Therefore the fault was mine."

"In *her* mind," Ty said.

Brunner reached out and turned the flowers a bit, nodding. "After giving much thought to why Maria...snapped, shall we say, I see now what I should have understood all along. Her desperate search for identity. I know some of her story. We were...intimates. Maria never knew the name of her father, nor did her mother. It had always been only the two of them, and they were close."

Hanging her head, Meg thought about the woman who had tried to kill her and felt a twinge of melancholy. A troubled and lonely woman pushed beyond her capacity to cope. But when Meg's tears welled, they were for Heather. An innocent life sacrificed for delusions.

"There were other pressures," Ty pointed out. "You and Doug may have run roughshod over her dreams, but she'd maxed out in her career at the college, and the job was more taxing than satisfying."

Meg tried to come to grips with her conflicting feelings. Yes, Robert was a victim, sort of. But he wasn't entirely blameless, either. Cheaters never were.

"Added to all that," she said, "you were cavalier with her feelings. It was a thoughtless betrayal."

"It was. And one which shames me. But as to her scurrilous allegation about me and Heather, I assure you that I never attempted to seduce that girl. My considerable flaws do not include the sexual predation of my students."

"It was clearly a shot in the dark," Ty agreed. "One borne out of spite."

Brunner's sigh was long and heartfelt. "When Maria learned that her mother had cancer, she was devastated," he said. "Pancreatic cancer, one of the most vicious, and hers is very advanced. Mrs. Routzhan is currently in hospice with only weeks to live. I believe that was the tipping point—when Maria realized that the last piece of her identity, that of a daughter, was about to be wrested from her."

"And seeing no future for herself," Ty added, "Maria decided to seek revenge on the man she believed had deprived her of one. She stole the letter and killed Heather to punish you."

Averting his eyes, Brunner tapped the tray table several times, filling the silence.

Ty cleared his throat. "Well, it's clear now that Maria's needed help for some time." He paused. "But it seems your theory's been vindicated, Professor Brunner. That must feel good."

"In time, that may be pleasing, perhaps even exciting. But it will always be a bittersweet victory fraught with lasting ramifications—like the Civil War itself, I suppose."

"Like all wars."

Brunner turned back to Meg. "And I think you will be enjoying a victory, too."

"Me? How so?"

"Today's gunplay will likely tip the scale in your favor." Robert's lips slanted up in a wry smile. "President Collins was horrified by the possibility for injury and liability should our security staff be armed."

"Well that's a relief," Ty said.

Meg did a double take, surprise stamped on her face. "Say what?"

"There's too much risk. Most campuses can't afford to pay for the kind of training and insurance that's involved. And skimping would be disastrous."

"But I thought...in the faculty meeting, you—"

"I know what you thought, but I was just delivering the department's viewpoint. And for a while, I thought you were going to kill the messenger."

She looked at him, shaking her head in disbelief.

"One more thing," Brunner said to Ty. "Maria's mother is in no condition to take care of a dog. I shudder to think what will become of it under those circumstances. Is it possible..."

"These things have to go through channels, but I'll put in a good word for you."

"Thank you. I feel the need to do something on Maria's behalf. And little Priscilla shouldn't have to pay the price." He turned toward the door. "Well, then. I'll take my leave of you fine people. Good day to you."

The door had barely shut when Meg turned to Ty. "Now *that* was unexpected. I'm not sure how he and I will move forward from here."

He sat down and gingerly leaned against the chair back. "The relationship with evolve. Change is what the living do." Smiling at Meg, he stroked her hair. "And it's nice to end the day on an up note."

Savoring the touch, Meg sighed. "For a while, I thought I'd run out of notes. At least until I saw you. I mean, I was still scared, but I wasn't alone anymore. That was huge." She paused and looked away briefly. "And even though guns creep me out, I guess it's good you had one."

"I reckon so."

Silence.

"There's something you should know about me," Meg began. "About me and guns, I mean. I'm not some knee jerk liberal. My mom was a student at Kent State in 1970. During the National Guard shootings." Seeing the concern on his face, she almost stopped the story there. "It gets worse. She was walking back from class with one of the victims. Sandra Scheuer."

Ty closed his eyes briefly. "The one whose jugular was severed. The one who bled out on scene."

She nodded.

"Meg, I'm so, so sorry. For your mom, and for you. Things went horribly wrong that day. Stupid, unconscionable mistakes were made, even for those troubled times. They make us study that fiasco in the State Police Academy."

"They were sorority sisters," she whispered.

The room grew quiet and small, filled with things that both wanted to say, but neither was certain how to express. Meg broke down first.

"Have you ever...I mean, before today?"

"No." He looked away for a moment. "No, that was my first termination."

She searched his expression but wasn't sure what she saw. It wasn't his blank cop face, but she still couldn't read it. "How do you feel? About that, I mean."

He dropped his gaze to the floor and kept it there. "It's complicated."

Her face flushed. *Meg, you stupid, stupid girl. Could you be any more callous?*

"I'm sorry, Ty, really. I don't have any right to ask. It's too personal."

When he looked back up, his gray eyes were steady. "No, it's okay. We kinda have to talk about this, don't we? I mean, we work in very different worlds, come from different backgrounds. There's probably a lot of common ground, but this gun thing is going to keep coming up. Best to start talking about it now, find out if it's a deal breaker."

Meg blinked, surprised by his directness. But intrigued, too. This was no Al who sat beside her. "Okay, that makes sense."

Both of them fell quiet again. After a long exhale, Ty broke the silence.

"You wanted to know what I'm feeling about ending someone's life. So let's go with that."

Meg nodded slowly. Now that he was offering it up, she wasn't sure she wanted to know.

"Mostly I'm thankful that you're okay. As for her...well, I don't feel guilty."

Meg bunched up the hem of her blanket in one hand as she waited for him to continue.

"During training, our instructors spent considerable time making it clear that you only draw your weapon if circumstances clearly warrant it, knowing full well that you may have to use deadly force. And today...today, Maria orchestrated the circumstances." He stayed silent for a moment. "It feels like a failure on some level because I tried hard to talk her down. And that's always worked before."

She felt some of her resistance soften. Even Brunner had said Ty had done everything he could.

"And you know what else?" he added, looking at her with great intensity.

Meg studied him, marveling at his honesty. Seeing it for the gift it was and admiring the risk he was taking. How could she do less? She nodded for him to continue.

"I'm pissed at her," he admitted. "And that surprises me. But that bitch set me up."

Meg hazarded a small smile. "You want to know what I think."

His intensity vanished, and his expression softened. He really did want to know. "When I look at you, I see a good man who had to make a hard choice. A man I'd like to know better."

"Well..." He let out the breath he'd been holding. "We'll have to start working on that." His face turned serious again. "But I do have a confession. Involving an action I hope you won't hold against me."

She gave him a puzzled look.

"Rocinante's demise is my fault. Maria got off just the one shot, but I fired multiple times. That's what they train us to do. I'm really sorry, Meg because that truck had character."

"That truck had almost 300,000 miles on it," she said. "It was a mercy killing."

The two of them chuckled as Lindsay's balloons bumped happily against the window when the heat clicked on. Then Meg's laugh turned into a yawn.

"That's enough for now," Ty said. "You need rest."

"But I'd feel safer if you stayed a while." She blinked at him, groggy and exhausted. "Just 'til I go to sleep."

"I can do that."

●　　　●　　　●　　　●　　　●

Monday, November 3rd

Clowny's dead and I'm safe. It probably makes me a bad person, but I'm glad she's dead. Not that I'm gonna tell Dad that...maybe my therapist, though. I know that life isn't fair, that things don't come out even, but if Heather has to be dead then so should that bitch.

And here's something else that isn't fair. That Heather's teacher gets to put the moves on my dad. He could hook up with anybody, but just my luck he picks her.

I wish Heather were here so we could talk it out. She'd have some advice about how to handle things when your dad starts "dating" again. She always saw things I didn't. Wonder what she'd say now?

Lindsay put down her pen and looked out the airplane window. The clouds below were white and rumple-y, like meringue on top of a lemon pie.

She'd probably say something like, "Lindsay, stop being so snarky. It's not just about you. Look at the big picture for a change."

I guess she's right. It's not just about me. What about Dad? I mean, I know he's been lonely for a long time...and sad. He's a good guy, and he deserves to be happy again.

And that teacher lady. I kinda get that she isn't responsible for Heather's death, but it still pisses me off. She might be alright, though. I mean, she's smart and not all stuck up. She didn't pitch a fit or anything when I went off on her at the funeral parlor. Dad said I owe her an apology, and he's probably right. But it seems way too late for that. And I feel weird that I blabbed about the shooting to her...about Mom's murder and all. What do I say to her now?

I was right. Normal is over. Nothing is ever going to be the same again.

Pretty soon they'd be in Nassau, she thought as she glanced at her aunt's watch. Sitting on lounge chairs set up on the powdery, white sand. Swimming in the blue, blue surf instead of dealing with ass-freezing November rain.

But different isn't always worse, is it? It's just...different.

She shut her journal, put in her earbuds, and cued up Heather's favorite song—"Happy," by that weird hat guy, Pharrell. But after about thirty seconds she snapped it off, leaned back in her seat and stared out the window.

"We'll just have to see, won't we," she murmured and closed her eyes.

Chapter 49

The next afternoon was a busy one. Ty had filled the tea kettle and laid a fire in the hearth. Now he was picking up the newspapers and folding them so they'd fit in the wrought iron recycling bin beside the fireplace and putting books back on the shelf. Then he spied yesterday's orange juice glass on the coffee table. His, certainly, because Lindsay had already been at her aunt's house. And she'd be there through the weekend. Picking up the crusty glass, he took it into the kitchen.

He stopped in front of the sink, looked out the window, and shook his head at his own faint reflection. What was he doing? Back in college, he'd never fussed like this when a girl'd come over to his dorm room. Frowning, he slipped the glass into the dishwasher and shut the door. But this wasn't just some hookup over spring break. This was different. Meg was different.

He walked down the hall and into the living room where he could watch for her out the front windows, his mind busy. There was so much he didn't know about her. He'd planned for them to drink tea in front of the fire, but did he have a flavor she liked? Did she tend to be on time or run a little late? Early, even? She'd called and said she'd be over around three. He checked the anniversary clock on the bookcase. It was just ten 'til.

Plus she was recovering from a concussion. A mild one, admittedly. The overnight stay at the hospital was just a precaution. But it wasn't anything to sneeze at. Then again he wasn't in top form, either. He'd opted out of pain killers, but the bullet wound hurt more than he was willing to let on. Obviously, nothing was going to happen today. Added to that, his shoulder was weak. It wouldn't sustain his weight for long.

"Jesus, Ty," he muttered. They hadn't even kissed, and here he was strategizing about positions. What a jerk.

And yet he couldn't stop thinking about her, kept putting off leaving her last night even after she was asleep. He must have been too solicitous or something because the RNs kept giving him looks. And the charge nurse—a woman so mature that the other RNs called her "ma'am" to her face and

"Jesus's pediatrician" behind her back—had touched him on the arm and whispered that after twenty-four hours a mildly concussed person was "fully functional."

He couldn't remember the last time he'd blushed, and Ma'am was the only one who'd seen, but it surprised him that he was so easy to read.

•　•　•　•　•

Meg slid out of the taxi cab and paid the driver. Her friends were teaching today, so she was on her own. When the cab drove away, she stood on the sidewalk one door down from Ty's house and shivered in the cold November rain. She took a few hurried steps, stubbed her toe and steadied herself against a streetlamp.

That was the same damn broken piece of sidewalk she'd tripped on just before Maria had accosted her and forced her into Ty's home at gunpoint. How many days ago had that been? Two. Three, maybe. At least then she'd had Rocinante for emotional support.

Pulling her hand away from the rain-slick surface of the lamppost, the image of Gene Kelly popped into her mind. That fedora shielding his beaming face from the rain shower as he danced with the street lamp instead of the girl. She shivered again, deciding that his must have been a balmy spring rain. Rousing herself, she walked down the sidewalk and up the stairs toward the front porch.

Ty opened the door before she could knock, then stood aside to welcome her in. "Hi, Meg. How're you feeling today? Were you able to sleep?"

"Sort of. You know hospitals. They keep poking at you to see if you're alright. How about you?"

After closing the door, he rotated his shoulder cautiously. "Sore, but functional. I was about to put the kettle on for tea. Want some?"

"Sure. That would be..." She paused a bit before she added, "nice," wondering if he'd remember their first non-case related conversation in the coffee shop. His smile said he did.

"Very nice, in fact. Here, let me take your coat."

As she unzipped her rain slicker and stepped backward to shrug it off her shoulders, she slipped on the wet floor. Ty's quick hands caught her around the waist. Neither of them breathed.

Meg trembled. His hands were hotter than any hands had a right to be. Even after catching her balance, she imagined her knees might buckle. And then she knew. This was the man her mother had always warned her about as a teenager: The one in whose hands she would turn to putty.

He was staring at her, stunned.

Then she felt his fingers slide down the curve of her hip. He pulled her slightly forward; enough, so she had to tilt her head back to see his face. When she looked in his eyes, she wondered how anyone could call gray a neutral color.

They reminded her of a ring in her grandmother's jewelry box. The one she always picked when they'd played dress-up together. The one she'd inherited in her freshman year of college after the will was read. The one with the improbable name. A black pearl. It wasn't black at all, but a smoky gray. The depth of his eyes swirled with the same smoldering glow.

Then he stepped back, his fingers slipping away like the rain-lashed autumn leaves on the trees shivering outside. Her flesh missed his heat. She watched his empty hands sink toward his thighs then slide into his jeans' pockets.

Knowing that her mother would be appalled, but her grandmother wouldn't, Meg pulled him back to her. She slipped her arms around him for a full-torso hug, stretched up on her toes as he tilted his head down to hers. She relished in the delighted surprise building in his eyes and brushed his full lips with hers, barely touching at first. Then she closed her eyes and kissed him deeply, giving in to all the emotions she'd felt since that first night. The night he'd been so gentle with her after she'd first heard about the murder. There was gratitude for his having saved her life, of course, and relief that the killer could never hurt anyone again. But also the grief over losing Heather. The fear for her own safety. The dread that his daughter would never share him, and the nervousness when it seemed she might. But mostly she felt longing for what she sensed this man could offer.

Unconsciously, she channeled all of those emotions into that kiss, and the result was a whooshing rush of heat commandeering her body. It turned her hands and tongue restless, the muscles in her thighs and belly impatient. The velvety field of black behind her closed eyes was teeming with swirling colors: green, orange, red, and darting flames of searing white. Her lips felt wasp-stung—an endless, insistent tingling. And when the two of them finally broke contact, she swore there was a crackle of electricity.

"Wow," he said, his expression dazed as he opened his eyes and gazed at her.

"Oh my god," she panted, knees actually buckling. "I feel woozy."

Tightening his embrace to steady her, he whispered, "Me too."

They clung together until reality righted itself. Then as if the words were intuition made audible, Meg murmured, "I even thought I saw—or heard, or thought I heard—a spark."

"Yeah. Me too."

"Must've been static electricity."

He shook his head slowly. "Meg, it's raining buckets out there. You only get static electricity when the air is cold and dry. You know, low relative humidity?"

"Then..."

"I think that was us."

A gust of wind rattled the bamboo wind chimes outside the door and sliced across the porch, threatening to send some forgotten rattan furniture scurrying.

Ty pulled back and blinked himself into speech. "I...um...I can start the kettle simmering. D'you want some tea?"

She drew in a deep breath and whispered, "Maybe later." She touched his cheek, then dropped her hand to his chest and felt his heartbeat outstrip hers. "But maybe we could go upstairs."

He replied. That much was clear because his lips were moving; however, no sound came out. But one emotion after another passed across his face. Concern. Tenderness. Longing. Her furrowed brow and quizzical look prompted him to repeat himself.

"Are you sure?"

"Very."

Author's Note

Getting this book into your hands has been a long, strange trip, one taken in fits and starts. With more fits than starts.

During junior high, my reading tastes followed along behind my older sister, a mystery maven. We wolfed down Dorothy Sayers, Agatha Christie, and Margery Allingham, but my sister was especially taken with Arthur Conan Doyle. As a result, I'm pretty sure I was the only kid in seventh grade who knew that a gasogene was a Victorian device used to make carbonated water for beverages. And that Sherlock Holmes had one in his 221B Baker Street flat.

But that interest languished while I built a teaching career, one which I allowed to consume all my energy, creative and otherwise. One day, while advising a student to follow her passion instead of her parents' expectations, it hit me. What had happened to my youthful ambitions to be a harpist, a ballerina, or even an aviatrix? What of my love for mysteries?

I didn't sign up for flight school, but in-between marathon grading sessions as an English professor I stole visits with the novels by Louise Penny, Julia Spencer-Fleming, Laura Lippman and Dawn Lee McKenna. While keeping company with these delightful authors, a long-forgotten yearning resurfaced, like bubbles in a gasogene: I wanted to write...to be one of those women.

I also need to tell you that although this novel is a work of fiction, parts of it are very real, specifically the controversy over the Civil War era poem about Barbara Fritchie. In 1863, *The Atlantic Monthly* published a pro-Union, patriotic ballad by John Greenleaf Whittier entitled "Barbara Frietchie," using the German spelling of her name. It was based on historical events revolving around Stonewall Jackson's march through Frederick, Maryland toward what would become known as the Battle of Antietam.

Whittier's verse was enormously popular and rallied the Union troops. In the poem, a defiant ninety-year-old woman, Barbara Fritchie, flies a Union flag from her upstairs window as the Confederate troops pass her home. But two other Frederick County women—Mary Quantrell and Nannie Crouse—reportedly also flew flags as the troops passed, and their accounts are perhaps better substantiated.

However, these two contenders have had an uphill battle for fame: Legends die hard in these parts. There was a Broadway play based on Fritchie's life (83 performances in October 1899-January 1900), and her name was used to market canned goods back in the day. Not only that, the story prompted one of America's greatest illustrators, N.C. Wyeth, to paint the climactic flag-waving scene. And a Frederick-based motorcycle race— billed as the oldest running half-mile Dirt Track race in the US— is named after her, as well as the Barbara Fritchie Handicap at Laurel Park Race Course in Laurel, MD. This year's purse was $300,000. But best of all, the poem was lampooned in a 1962 cartoon with Bullwinkle (as Fritchie) and "Stonewall" Boris.

Until 2018, the city of Frederick boasted an actual Barbara Fritchie Museum. It was a replica of her home, as the original was severely damaged in a flood. It was painstakingly rebuilt several doors down from its original setting, and the items from her personal estate were replaced in it. And the improbable story about Winston Churchill recounted in this novel is irrefutably true. However, I regret to report that the building was recently sold and has become an Airbnb.

Additionally, the Barbara Fritchie Restaurant, the setting of the novel's first major scene, is one of our local treasures. Or, more accurately, it was. Between the writing of the novel and its publication, the restaurant has folded, despite its 107 years of service.

I am bereft, as I'd enjoyed many a meal there, some of which while writing this novel. Their pies were legendary. I'll especially miss the lemon meringue.

Barbara Frietchie by John Greenleaf Whittier

Up from the meadows rich with corn,
Clear in the cool September morn,

The clustered spires of Frederick stand
Green-walled by the hills of Maryland.

Round about them orchards sweep,
Apple- and peach-tree fruited deep,

Fair as a garden of the Lord
To the eyes of the famished rebel horde,

On that pleasant morn of the early fall
When Lee marched over the mountain wall,—

Over the mountains winding down,
Horse and foot, into Frederick town.

Forty flags with their silver stars,
Forty flags with their crimson bars,

Flapped in the morning wind: the sun
Of noon looked down, and saw not one.

Up rose old Barbara Frietchie then,
Bowed with her fourscore years and ten;

Bravest of all in Frederick town,
She took up the flag the men hauled down;

In her attic window the staff she set,
To show that one heart was loyal yet.

Up the street came the rebel tread,
Stonewall Jackson riding ahead.

Under his slouched hat left and right
He glanced: the old flag met his sight.

"Halt!"— the dust-brown ranks stood fast.
"Fire!"— out blazed the rifle-blast.

It shivered the window, pane and sash;
It rent the banner with seam and gash.

Quick, as it fell, from the broken staff
Dame Barbara snatched the silken scarf;

She leaned far out on the window-sill,
And shook it forth with a royal will.

"Shoot, if you must, this old gray head,
But spare your country's flag," she said.

A shade of sadness, a blush of shame,
Over the face of the leader came;

The nobler nature within him stirred
To life at that woman's deed and word:

"Who touches a hair of yon gray head
Dies like a dog! March on!" he said.

All day long through Frederick street
Sounded the tread of marching feet:

All day long that free flag tost
Over the heads of the rebel host.

Ever its torn folds rose and fell
On the loyal winds that loved it well;

And through the hill-gaps sunset light
Shone over it with a warm good-night.

Barbara Frietchie's work is o'er,
And the Rebel rides on his raids no more.

Honor to her! and let a tear
Fall, for her sake, on Stonewall's bier.

Over Barbara Frietchie's grave
Flag of Freedom and Union, wave!

Peace and order and beauty draw
Round thy symbol of light and law;

And ever the stars above look down
On thy stars below in Frederick town!

Note from the Author

Word-of-mouth is crucial for any author to succeed. If you enjoyed the book, please leave a review online—anywhere you are able. Even if it's just a sentence or two. It would make all the difference and would be very much appreciated.

Thanks!
Pam

About the Author

Pam Clark grew up on Maryland's Eastern Shore in a hometown of 300 people. She holds a Master of Arts in Writing from Johns Hopkins University. In 2016, she won the Book Doctors' Pitchapalooza contest, the American Idol for books, at UNM's Summer Writers' Conference. She is a member of *Mystery Writers of America, Romance Writers of America,* and *Sisters in Crime* and will be published in their San Diego chapter's upcoming anthology, *Crossing Borders.*

Thank you so much for reading one of our **Mystery** novels.

If you enjoyed our book, please check out our recommended title for your next great read!

K-Town Confidential by Brad Chisholm and Claire Kim

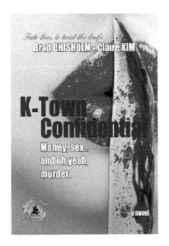

"An enjoyable zigzagging plot." –*KIRKUS REVIEWS*

"If you are a fan of crime stories and legal dramas that have a noir flavor, you won't be disappointed with *K-Town Confidential*." – *Authors Reading*

CPSIA information can be obtained
at www.ICGtesting.com
Printed in the USA
FFHW022302251019
55764677-61640FF